DARK PASSIONS

HOT BLOOD XIII

The Hot Blood Series

HOT BLOOD
HOTTER BLOOD
HOTTEST BLOOD
DEADLY AFTER DARK
SEEDS OF FEAR
STRANGER BY NIGHT
CRIMES OF PASSION
FEAR THE FEVER
HOT BLOOD X
HOT BLOOD XI:
FATAL ATTRACTIONS
STRANGE BEDFELLOWS
DARK PASSIONS

Published by Kensington Publishing Corporation

DARK PASSIONS

HOT BLOOD XIII

EDITED BY JEFF GELB AND MICHAEL GARRETT

KENSINGTON BOOKS
http://www.kensingtonbooks.com

KENSINGTON BOOKS are published by

Kensington Publishing Corp.
850 Third Avenue
New York, NY 10022

All Kensington titles, imprints and distributed lines are available at special quantity discounts for bulk purchases for sales promotion, premiums, fund-raising, educational or institutional use.

Special book excerpts or customized printings can also be created to fit specific needs. For details, write or phone the office of the Kensington Special Sales Manager: Kensington Publishing Corp., 850 Third Avenue, New York, NY 10022. Attn. Special Sales Department. Phone: 1-800-221-2647.

ISBN-13: 978-0-7582-1413-3
ISBN-10: 0-7582-1413-8

First Kensington Trade Paperback Printing: September 2007
10 9 8 7 6 5 4 3 2 1

Printed in the United States of America

This one's for
Graham Masterton,
who has been with us since the beginning
and has given us so many terrific stories.
Never would we have dreamed when the series began
that someone across the ocean would become such
an integral part of the progression
of the Hot Blood series.

Many thanks, Graham.

Contents

Introduction

Well, we made it.

In 1989, when the first volume of *Hot Blood* was published, little did we think we would make it to a lucky thirteenth volume.

But somehow here we are, thanks to the literally hundreds of writers and thousands of readers who have shown us over the decades that erotic horror isn't just a subgenre, it's an entire universe.

And what a universe! In story after story, our writers have proven that sex and horror can mix in myriad ways we could not have imagined when we first began this series. In fact, the longer the series continues, the more ideas flow from our writers. Erotic horror is a rich vein to mine indeed . . . as you will see in our latest volume!

We live in a society dominated as never before by sex and violence. The *Hot Blood* series turns lustful fantasies into unforgettable if nightmarish fiction, courtesy of some of the very best writers on this planet (or any other). Have they finally mined the ultimate depths of depravity? Find out for yourself! Put on your spelunkers' gear (and other appropriate protection) and join us as we explore all new carnal caverns of lustful terror in *Hot Blood: Dark Passions*.

Thanks to your interest in this series, *Hot Blood* stories have won awards, seen print throughout the world, fathered more volumes than expected, fostered imitations, and had many stories used for various TV series (including "Masters of Horror" and "The Hunger").

Does the *Hot Blood* series now fade into a final bloody red sunset? Keep tabs on us at www.writing2sell.com/hotblood.htm for updates.

Meanwhile, watch your appetite for erotic horror—this stuff's addictive!

A Building Desire

D. Lynn Smith

I come from an illustrious family line, a line of carpenters who took great pride in their work and their tools. But it wasn't until the woman found me discarded on the forest floor that I truly found my place.

It was a fortuitous meeting, her walking through the woods, me under the detritus that had hidden me for so long. My head had finally emerged from its grave, and it was my head that tripped her. She pushed away the leaves and dirt and exclaimed in delight. That warmed me to her right away. She dug up the rest of me and took me home.

There she gently stroked the dirt and debris from my face, my throat, my cheeks, and my claw. She used some steel wool and oil to remove a thin layer of rust that was eating at my metal surface.

Her hand clasped my hickory shaft, worn smooth by time and use. Her grip was firm but gentle. I was made to fit such a hand.

When her husband came in, he saw me resting on the table instead of dinner. He picked me up, his palm soft and damp. He handled me carelessly, as if I were nothing more than an oddity. "Where'd this come from?"

The woman was at the stove, placing some spaghetti into a pot of boiling water. "I found it in the woods today."

He turned me over, feeling my head-to-handle weight distribution. "It's got pretty good balance."

She came over and took me from him. "Look at this." She showed him the engraving on my face that was my family name. She showed him my proper crown that could drive nails flush without marring a wood surface. She stroked my deep throat and strong neck that allowed power strikes even in difficult areas.

He wasn't impressed. "It's pretty old. I don't think I'd trust it to hold up under any hard pounding."

He slipped his arms around her waist, nuzzling her ear. "And speaking of hard pounding . . ."

She giggled, and, as her fingers tightened around me, I felt her pulse quicken. He picked her up and carried her into the bedroom, laying her on the bed and kissing her hard on the mouth. Her body flooded with pleasure, and that pleasure was mine as well. Then he placed me on the nightstand.

She'd held me long enough that I could still feel her ecstasy as his head dipped to her breasts. When her hand slipped into his pants and stroked his hardness, I felt her remember the sensation of rubbing oil into my wooden handle.

"This is our moment," he whispered as he entered her. "Tonight, only we exist."

Her pleasure exploded into me.

The pot of spaghetti boiled dry. The tomato sauce burned.

She was sated.

The same satisfaction filled me when, the following morning, she used me on the addition she and her husband were putting on the house. Her husband had given her a new hammer, one with a fiberglass handle. It was obvious he wasn't a real carpenter if he used a hammer like that.

"This one feels better in my hand," she said about me. "It's easier to use, puts less stress on my muscles and wrist."

"Look, we don't even know how old that thing is. The head could be brittle and throw a chip. Or the assembly could be weak. It could come flying off and do one of us some serious damage."

"It won't."

Clearly he was pissed off, but he came over and rested a hand on her stomach. "This baby doesn't need a one-eyed mother."

Dismissing the comment with a sigh, she put her hand over his. "She's our little miracle. With all the doctors saying I'd never conceive . . . well, we proved them wrong, didn't we?"

She looked up at her husband with tears in her eyes. "Finding this hammer was like a miracle too. I can't explain it, but I just feel like I'm supposed to have it, supposed to use it to build her nursery."

He was angry, and I felt her dismay. For a moment I thought she might put me down and pick up that shiny new fiberglass thing. I sent a little shiver through me, and her grip tightened.

"Have it your way," her husband said as he stalked away.

I became an extension of her as we drove nails and tapped beams into place. She knew some things about carpentry, but as we worked together I suggested some new ways my claw and head could be used. Her delight at these discoveries washed over me, and I almost forgot the trauma of being discarded in the woods. Buried, actually. Hidden.

We were rarely apart. I hung from a tool belt at her hips so that when she walked I tapped lightly against her thigh. At the end of a day's work she took me inside and used a soft cloth to wipe away any debris from the day. She'd caress me, running her fingers down the smooth bevels of my shaft, squeezing me slightly at my belled end, running her hand up to the larger midsection, where she would hold me for light blows, and on up to the eye, deep and tapered for secure head-to-handle union.

As her stomach expanded with the growing child, her husband spent less and less time at home. She smothered her despair by delighting in every movement inside her, with the construction of the nursery, and with me.

But my anger at the husband grew, and with that anger came the thirst. The thirst made me remember.

The powerful swing, sliding easily into the enemy's torso, slicing through rib and lung, penetrating deep. Warm blood and gore glazing me.

The husband said I was old. He had no idea.

Cleaving the hardness of the skull, puncturing into the moist inner sanctum.

I was born as a weapon in a different time and place.

Thrust and parry. A deadly dance until once again I slide into the pulsating wetness.

A blacksmith's fire and hammer reshaped my blade and forged me into what I am today. But the fire of the hearth failed to burn the blood from steel. Instead it fused them, and I was born.

Nights she would toss and turn in her sleep, and I knew she was dreaming my memories. I tried to pull them from her, frightened at first that if they continued, she too would bury me in the woods as my previous owner had done. But my anger at the husband grew in tandem with her despair, and so I remembered, and she dreamed, and she did not throw me away.

She had some morning sickness for a few weeks, but usually it passed quickly and she would throw herself into building the nursery. With my help she became strong and confident. Two blows could drive a nail into a two-by-four. In places where she could not hold the nail, she'd place it in my claw, the head snug against my eye, and drive it into a wall. Then she'd flip me over, and one or two more blows would finish it.

One day her husband saw her doing this. "Where'd you learn to do that?"

She shrugged. "It just came to me."

"Huh. You're really into this, aren't you?"

"Aren't you?"

"Yeah. But not like that. You keep going, you'll be better at this than I am."

She was already better.

Though resentment boiled inside her, she made herself casually ask, "What would you like for dinner tonight?"

"Oh, I'm sorry, hon. I gotta go into town. A client is flying in, and I'm meeting him during his layover."

The lie hung in the air between them. The next nail she drove hard enough to split the wood. The strength of her anger, and her arm, surprised and scared her.

"When do you have to leave?" she asked.

"I'll take a shower in about an hour, then go."

She put me into her tool belt, which was tight around her bulging stomach, and walked over to wrap her arms around his neck. I tapped against her thigh. Her face smiled, but her body was tense and angry. "Just enough time for a little afternoon delight."

He chuckled but pushed her away. "Come on, hon. I'm afraid it'll hurt the baby."

"The doctor said it wouldn't. She said anything we were comfortable doing was fine."

"Yeah, well, doctors don't know everything, and after all the difficulty we've had, I'd never forgive myself if something I did hurt our little miracle."

She didn't argue. She just took me into the kitchen and cleaned me. Flashes of my oldest, bloodiest memories winked through her mind as she did.

The exterior of the addition was complete, and we were finishing the interior when the call came. I remember her struggling to understand exactly what the doctor was telling her.

"Gonorrhea. How could I have gonorrhea?"

I could feel the realization sweep over her. Her mind went to a dark and blank place where nothing made sense and words swept over her without meaning. She thanked the doctor and hung up the phone.

Taking me with her, she went to her car and drove into town.

She found her husband's car outside his favorite bar, the one he'd told her his boss liked so much. She parked where she wouldn't be seen. We waited.

She held me, stroking my shaft, rubbing my head. He came out laughing and stumbling with another woman. They got into his car and drove away.

She followed them to a rundown motel and watched them go into a room her husband had apparently rented earlier. After a few moments had passed, we went to the window, where the curtains didn't quite come together. She saw the man sucking on the woman's huge breasts and teasing her nipples with his tongue. She watched the woman unzip his pants, take his cock in her mouth, and suck until he was moaning. He wrapped his fingers in her hair and held her head down.

"Tonight, only we exist." She couldn't hear the words, but she could see his lips form them. A sickness bled through her and up my handle. She choked on her own bile as she continued to watch.

The woman pulled her head away, then straddled him, hanging her tits in his face, where he sucked them once again. Then he rolled her onto her stomach and pulled her to the edge of the bed. He stood behind and entered the woman, his face alive with bestial perversion.

He wasn't wearing a condom.

She turned away from the window and retched into the bushes, falling to her knees with tears leaking from her eyes. She clutched her stomach where the child slept quietly and rocked back and forth, despair and loss overwhelming her. For a while her mind went totally and utterly blank, and I was left alone with my anger.

When her mind refocused, it was to play the ugliness of her husband's infidelity over and over. He'd jeopardized their child's life for animal lust. He'd thrown away their dreams, their love. *Only we exist,* he'd said to that whore.

She got up and walked back to her car. I lay on her lap as she drove, and I fed her the warm comfort of blood. I fed her the satisfaction of my point slipping into flesh and scraping between ribs. I fed her the deeper thrust where my blade penetrated through to the pulsating muscle concealed within, the cross guard hitting flesh, and my wielder feeling the blood pouring over his hand. I fed her the pleasure of being the conveyor of death.

When he came home that night, she was sitting in the dark waiting for him. He fumbled through some excuse for his lateness. But she was all sugar and offered to get him a beer. He accepted.

He picked me up from the table. "If I didn't know better, I'd think you were in love with this thing."

She brought him his beer and took me from his hands. "A hammer is more than just a hammer, you know. It's such a personal tool that it becomes an extension of yourself. You forge a bond of loyalty with it."

He laughed. "That's the stupidest thing I ever heard."

"Really," she said. "Actually, I heard something even stupider today."

"Yeah?" He took a deep pull on his beer but couldn't keep his eyes off me as she started a hypnotic tapping of my head against her palm.

"The doctor called. Did you know that if a pregnant woman has gonorrhea, then her baby could become infected during the delivery?"

"Gonorrhea. What are you talking about?"

"It can cause the baby to go blind, or have a joint infection, or even a life-threatening blood infection."

He put down his beer. "This is stupid," he said as he tried to get up out of the chair. He fell back.

"Yeah," she said. "It is stupid. As stupid as fucking around without using a condom and then coming home and fucking your pregnant wife."

He was blinking his eyes and trying to stand up. "What did you do to me?"

She smiled and continued tapping my head into her palm. "Not much . . . yet."

I felt the thrill of anticipation. I wasn't sure if it was hers or mine.

She had grown strong while building the nursery. Still it was a struggle for her to strip off his clothes and lift him. She tied him to a ladder, then propped it up in the doorway of the new nursery. The baby kicked and turned inside her.

The first nail was the most difficult. She wasn't used to the soft feel of flesh being penetrated by steel, and she was rocked by horror and doubt. But I fed her my strength, and we drove that first one home.

Waves of pleasure swept through me with each blow. And when my head met the flesh, that pleasure spilled through my shaft and into her hand. She gasped. Revulsion and desire created a tumultuous sea of whirling emotions. Her child shifted inside her. Anger once again rose to the surface and ruled. She drove a second nail through the wrist of his right arm.

We used five-inch nails that went deep into the wood, pounding the protruding part of the nail over and down so he couldn't pull himself free. The final nail pegged his feet to the oak flooring. She removed the ladder when she was finished and let him hang there.

Her husband woke with a moan. He tried to move but was held fast. His eyes fluttered open, muddled and unaware. She watched and enjoyed as understanding flooded into them.

He struggled, trying to pull himself free as he screamed in pain and fear. "What the fuck are you doing?"

She stood in front of him, tapping me gently into her palm. Waves of delicious anticipation rolled over us.

She walked up to him and ran my claw down his chest, pressing a little as it reached a nipple so that I scraped until he yelped and bled.

"Baby, please," her husband begged. "I'm sorry I cheated. I . . . I don't know what got into me. I promise I'll never do it again. Please . . ." He was crying, snot dripping from his nose and across his lips. "Please . . ."

"Cheating I could have lived with," she said as she brought me back up the side of his chest to the other nipple.

"Oh fuck, stop it, stop it," he screamed.

"But you did more than cheat, didn't you? You didn't use a condom." She pulled me back and brought me down hard on one of his fingers. It cracked and smashed into pulp. I shivered with a building desire.

He screamed.

"I thought you cherished us. I thought you loved us."

A second finger collapsed under my head.

After the scream, he begged. "I do. I love you both. I didn't mean to hurt you. Please, please let me go."

"I could have lived with you hurting me," she said.

A third finger went. Her breath was coming in excited pants.

"Stop. Oh please," he wailed as more tears and snot ran down across his face.

She once again stroked his chest with my claw. His skin tried to crawl away from my cold steel, but I reveled in its warmth. She leaned in close to him and whispered in his ear.

"You endangered our child. Our miracle."

I ran down the outside of his thigh, then up the inside. He must have known what was going to happen, because he started to writhe.

"Oh God, no."

The child inside her womb began to kick as she tickled his balls with my claw.

"Please, baby, no."

She ran me between his legs . . .

"No! Stop! Nooo!"

. . . and back between his cheeks.

"And endangering our child is something *you* can't live

with," she said. He screamed. The baby punched at her womb as if trying to escape. She jerked me forward so that my claw hooked on his balls and tore them from their home. Warm, wonderful blood spurted on me as the useless sacks fell away. The sticky wetness poured down my shaft and onto her hand.

He continued screaming, but neither of us cared. Desire ruled us both. She lifted me high, bloody rivulets running down her arm. His skull caved under a stroke we'd perfected together, and I entered the soft gray matter beneath.

His screaming stopped as suddenly as her orgasm exploded upon us.

"Only we exist," she gasped, breathless, her hand resting gently above our child.

Mood Elevator

David Benton
and
W. D. Gagliani

The brownstone's exterior was classic, if a bit tarnished, but from the moment Susan and her husband entered the lobby, she didn't mind at all. Each of the five floors had been split into two apartments sometime in the past forty years, but it didn't matter because, even so, now they would have more Manhattan space than any three of their friends combined. The rent was steep, of course, but now that Artie booked regular gigs both with his band and as a solo act in Village coffeehouses, and her own salary had recently risen to a more comfortable level, they would make it.

Susan sighed as they waited in front of the elevator for the building manager to show them around. He was late, which didn't inspire much confidence in his managerial skills.

She pondered their situation. Sure, she wasn't burning up the advertising-business ladder or anything like that, but her boss at the agency had taken a liking to her, spotting her talent and nurturing her past several peers. Well, true, Susan had taken to wearing tight sweaters and short skirts, often made of supple black leather, but that was her style, and she was finally able to afford it. And if she tended to leave a few of the top buttons undone on her blouses, that was because the office was always boiling hot, wasn't it? The lacy black bras she sometimes wore under those light blouses were just as much an advantage with clients as they were with Harrison Stims, her boss, whose ad agency had developed a reputation for quick and innovative work. Susan was part of that reputation, and she was proud to have her hard work rewarded with more money and a better office, right next to Harrison's. Thanks to her advancement, this apartment wasn't out of their reach anymore.

She took Artie's hand in hers and squeezed it, raising her eyebrows and hoping to turn his perpetual frown into something like a smile.

"You should be happy," she whispered. His rough hand in hers didn't respond to the pressure. "This is a great place."

"We can't afford it," he said. "We're going to have to stop eating out. And we don't cook."

"I'll take cooking lessons."

"Sure. Right."

"We'll manage. My star's rising at Stims, so it'll get even better."

"Yeah, I know."

"You'll get more gigs."

Artie frowned. They both knew he could gig more if he was willing to join a cover band. He wasn't.

Susan shook her head. He just didn't get it.

There was no going back to their old studio walk-up, where you could sit on the pot and make yourself coffee at the same time. Where the heat was more clanging sounds from the registers than actual hot air. Where their friends had to visit in stages because there was only room for a small couch and an armchair (thanks to Artie's pile of equipment, which took up half their living room).

Susan sighed.

Artie made a huffing sound and started tapping his toe.

"Sorry to keep you waiting, you must be the Blanchards, you're gonna love the apartment, let me get my keys."

Susan turned toward the rapid voice, imagining a geeky stringbean type with a frayed sweater and maybe a weak attempt at a mustache. She was shocked at what she saw when her eyes focused.

"Sorry about that, and my motor mouth," he said, extending his right hand and smiling. "I'm Mark Anthony, manager and sometime plumber."

With his left hand he pushed the elevator call button slowly, almost sensually.

Susan gulped and smiled, dumbstruck.

"I'm Art, and this is my wife, Susan," Artie said. The annoyance was still evident in his tone, but he held out his hand.

She let her eyes rove over Mark's fine features as they stood, awkwardly waiting.

Mark Anthony. Yeah, right!

It was either a stage name or his parents had one hell of a sense of humor. But he did look vaguely like she imagined a Roman centurion might—powerful, healthy of body, and possessed of the most limpid dark eyes she'd seen in a long time. Dark hair cropped close to his scalp and yet seeming to flow, lion-like, over his shoulders. His nose had that Roman look, almost too prominent but then not quite, dominating his face but calling attention instead to the full, cherubic lips below. His smile was brilliant and natural, his eyes lighting with sparkles as he shook their hands, Artie's first, then hers, lingering a fraction of a second longer after caressing her skin with his.

Or was she just imagining that?

Either way, Susan hated letting his hand slip away.

The doors suddenly slid open with a slight creak, the car having arrived noiselessly.

The buttons were rounded in the old-fashioned way, three-dimensionally, set in two short parallel rows of three (five floors and the basement, Mark explained). She pushed the top right button and stared at herself in the mirror set just above the panel, noticing that her face was flushed from the heat. At least they wouldn't freeze in this building! Her blouse was opened almost down to her breasts, but her light leather blazer kept her look businesslike. She smiled at her reflection and let her finger linger on the floor button, feeling it yield beneath her pressure. Her breathing quickened.

Mounted on the wall of the car, perpendicular to the controls, was a hinged contraption that appeared to be able to swing down. It was perhaps fourteen inches in length, metallic like a lever but encased in opaque rubber.

Susan felt vaguely unsettled as she examined the lever surreptitiously. When she looked up, she realized that both Artie and Mark were looking at her as if she'd spoken. Or as if she'd flashed her boobs like she had once during Mardi Gras in the pre-flood French Quarter.

A droplet of sweat down the center of her back tickled until it was absorbed by her blouse.

She stared at herself in the mirror. Her lips seemed fuller when she pursed them. Colorful patches dotted her high cheekbones. Her eyes flashed. Behind her, reflected in the mirror, the delectable Mark Anthony was talking to Artie, his hands gesturing.

Susan suddenly wanted one of those hands on her breast. She wanted his fingers to pluck her nipple as if it were a grape on the vine. She raised her hand and caressed the buttons on the board. They were nipples, and she felt them harden under her touch. She placed her other hand on the mysterious lever, encircling it with her slim fingers, feeling it throb as if blood flowed in its veins. It swelled, and she moved her fingers over it teasingly until she thought it would burst. Or she would burst.

"How are the neighbors?" Artie asked.

Susan dropped her hands quickly, guiltily, and turned around to face the two men. Her fingers retained the feel of aroused skin, and she felt wetness between her legs that wasn't sweat.

But she *was* sweating. Another cool trickle seemed to

sizzle down her warm back. She shook her head, hoping to clear it.

"Not bad," Mark said. "Mostly young professionals. A couple of weird artists. Me." To Susan he said, "I see you've noticed the remains of a bygone age. The elevator operator's seat was screwed to that bracket. It would swing down from the wall so the old guy could sit on it."

"Oh," was all she could muster. *Was he leering at her?*

Instead of feeling upset, she felt . . . *tingly.*

The elevator opened, and when she touched the rubber-encased doors, they were like the soft skin of a vagina.

What the hell's the matter with me? she thought, her breath hitching in her throat. *What am I thinking?*

"Fifth floor: beach wear, lingerie, and vacant apartments," Mark said. He smiled innocently as the three of them slipped out of the elevator.

The hall seemed cool and dark compared to the intense swelter of the elevator. Susan suddenly felt self-conscious, almost embarrassed. She reached down and buttoned the top of her blouse.

Down the hall, a young woman emerged from her apartment. She wore a well-tailored business suit that showed off the gentle curves of her slender body. She carried a briefcase in one hand and her keys in the other and smiled at Mark as she passed them on her way to the elevator.

To Susan the smile seemed too friendly, and she felt an unexpected jab of jealousy surge through her.

"This way," Mark said, motioning in the direction from which the woman had come. Artie and Susan followed.

Susan looked over her shoulder at the young woman by the elevator. She seemed to be watching them from the corner of her eye as she stepped through the doors. Or, more precisely, she'd been watching their ruggedly handsome guide.

And Susan was envious, envious of her figure, of her features, of her hairstyle, but mostly she was envious of her apparent relationship with Mark Anthony.

They reached the apartment door just as Susan heard the elevator doors slide closed.

Susan took a deep breath and sighed. She was a happily married woman! And, although she could not deny that Mark was stunningly good looking, she knew she loved Artie despite his sometimes cold demeanor.

Get a grip! she commanded herself.

In the hall, a portrait caught Susan's attention. An old oil painting hung in a gilded frame on the wall.

"Is that Aurora DiLuisas?" she asked.

"Yes, it is." Mark stepped back to admire the picture, a wide smile on his face. "She was known as 'The Greek Marilyn.' She's our official matriarch. This was actually her building at one time. She died in the early seventies, still fairly young. Sexy thing in her prime, wasn't she?"

"Who is this Aurora-whoever?" Artie asked.

"The actress!" Susan declared, latching onto Artie's arm. She had an urgent need to touch him, to reassure herself that things were all right between them. Or just to *touch* him. She stared at the portrait of a lovely woman, lush red lips parted in near ecstasy, dark eyes flashing below deep red hair piled in a single side-braid. "You know, on AMC. She's a late-night, B-movie queen now but might have made it as big as Melina Mercouri, if she hadn't died."

"They say she still hangs around, haunting this place," Mark said, mock fear in his voice. "But I've been here for three years now, and I've never seen any ghosts. It's a great story to tell your friends, though."

Artie grunted.

Mark winked at Susan and slowly slid the key into the hole. He turned the ornate doorknob, opening the place wide for inspection.

Susan gasped. It was better than she had hoped. The floors were all bare hardwood, except for the art-deco mosaic tiles in the bathroom. She walked through it quickly. The rooms were huge, with high, vaulted ceilings and richly embellished plaster crown moldings. A fresh coat of white paint made everything sparkle. The building still used radiant heat, and there were radiators in the bedroom, the kitchen, and the enormous living room. And she instantly fell in love with the old cast-iron claw-footed bathtub. She envisioned herself in the tub, naked in a mass of bubbles, Mark—*Artie*, she corrected, *Artie*—Artie standing beside her, thrusting his erect member into her mouth. She shivered, and . . . the vision faded. She'd never had *that* urge before. She shook her head.

When she looked out the windows, she knew there was no doubt they would take the apartment despite Artie's reservations because the tall double-hungs overlooked the avenue just above the canopy of maple trees lining the street. And after seeing that, there was no returning to the view of the neighboring building's back side she'd had to endure the last five years.

"We'll take it," she blurted.

"The lease is on the counter. I just need you to sign it, and I'll need the first and last month's rent."

Susan signed, and Artie did the same, begrudgingly. It was plain to see that he was unhappy about being railroaded into renting the place. His face was stoic as he handed Mark the check. But Susan knew just how to relax him.

"All right, well, here are your keys," Mark said, setting them on the kitchen counter. "Would you like me to show you out?"

"No, we're going to stay for a little while," Susan responded, giving her husband a devilish smile.

"Okay!"

Was that a leer again?

She led Mark to the door, said good-bye, and turned to face Artie.

"Damn it, Sue!" Artie glared at her.

"Come on, honey. This place is beautiful. It's just what we always wanted."

"It's what *you've* always wanted. At least we could have discussed it before signing the lease."

Susan closed in on him, pulling him by the front of his pants to the kitchen. "Please, Artie, I don't want you in a bad mood the first time we make love in our new home."

She hiked her skirt up a little, teasing, then pulled it up past her hips and hopped onto the kitchen counter, spreading her legs wide. "Like?"

His face turned red. Damn it! He wasn't quite as sexually liberated as she was, and she knew it. What had come over her? She jumped off the counter and went to him. "Artie, I'm sorry."

She hugged him through his discomfort, and they stood like that for a few minutes. She could feel the squelching between her thighs when they headed for the door. Artie still hadn't said much, and she wondered what he thought of her right now. What did Mark think of her?

She hoped she'd see Mark, but the hall was empty. She pressed the call button, and again it was a nipple under her fingers. She shivered. Almost as if it were her own nipple. The doors slid open coquettishly, teasing her with their molded rubber labial folds. When she entered, pulling Artie along, the heat struck her again, and she felt the flush creep onto her face. The Lobby button yielded to her touch like a young virgin, and she almost giggled helplessly at the thought. The doors winked at her as they closed, and she winked back.

She spotted the Hold button, and before she knew it she'd caressed it and the elevator had stopped between floors.

"What are you doing—" Artie began, but she'd pushed him backward into the side and now saw herself in the mirror behind his shocked face. "Susan?"

She knelt down in front of Artie, massaging the crotch of his khaki pants and feeling him stir.

Finally!

Slowly she undid his button and zipper and pulled the cloth down around his thighs. He was straining in his shorts, and now his breath came rapidly above her. She freed and took him gently into her cool mouth and engulfed him, slowly bobbing her head while he grew harder. When Artie reached the point at which she could no longer comfortably fit him in her mouth, she concentrated on his head with lips and tongue, stroking his shaft with her right hand, her left hand gently caressing his scrotum. She pulled away and let him slip out of her mouth with a wet *smack*.

Susan's clitoris tingled, and she started to moisten again. She stood and nearly ripped her black lace panties off with one hand while massaging Artie's member with the other.

"Fuck me," she whispered, her eyes half closed, lids heavy with ecstasy. She saw herself in the mirror and wondered when she'd dyed her hair red. But she hadn't, had she? It had to be a trick of the light.

Even Artie couldn't ignore this force of nature. When she reached up and balanced her left arm on his shoulder and straddled him with one leg up, he slid himself upward and inside her wetness. He thrust slowly and deeply, keeping time with their labored breaths. Susan gasped. He had never seemed so huge. She thought he would scrape the bottom of her ribcage with his erection. She leaned on him, allowing him to surge even higher.

The elevator wall beneath her hands seemed to tremble at their passion, and when her left hand slid downward it naturally found the lever (*the old seat bracket, Mark had explained, Mark Mark Mark*) and her fingers encircled its bulbous head and she groaned as it came to life under her touch and began thrusting out at her in rhythm with Artie's own thrusts.

Susan almost let go of the handle, but it felt so real, so alive, and so urgent in her hand that instead she massaged it as if it were a second lover.

Artie's thrusts gained urgency and seemed to reach up into her chest, making her nipples crackle with electricity even as he approached his climax, taking her with him while she masturbated the metallic hard-on in her hand, until Artie finally exploded, sending jets of his seed deep into her. The phallic lever spurted hot come into her palm, and she groaned and came as she'd never been able to before. She felt Artie's semen sliding along his shriveling member and down her thighs in cooling rivulets.

When she opened her eyes and stared at herself, her hair was its normal color again, and her hand still gripped the lowered seat bracket, but it was dry and not fleshy at all. What the hell had made her think otherwise? She shook her head, dazed, then unstraddled him. They cleaned up as best they could. Artie wouldn't look at her as he jabbed the Hold button and they began to descend. Her body still tingled where Artie'd plunged into her. And the elevator seemed to tingle at her touch as she slowly returned the seat bracket to its upward position, wondering at what she'd felt—how real it had seemed.

Just then the doors opened. Mark stood outside, his wide grin turning into another leer as he saw her hand leave the bracket. Susan knew their disheveled clothing was a giveaway, that and their sweat-stained faces. She took Artie's hand and pulled him docilely out of the elevator, spotting her torn black lace panties in the corner, but too late.

"We'll see you soon!" she babbled as they burst out into the lobby and headed for the street door.

"Nice to meet you!" Mark called out after them as the door closed. Susan thought she glimpsed him bending over to grasp her panties. She laughed until tears came. And, for once, even Artie seemed to think what had happened was one for the books.

Two weeks later their furniture arrived, and after rearranging the couch and armchair seemingly a hundred times, they went shopping for new furniture. As they left, they ran into Mark and said hello. Both of them burst out laughing as soon as they were away from the building. Artie hadn't talked much about "the incident" in the elevator, but Susan couldn't get it out of her mind.

Days, while working, Susan thought about Mark's lips, wanting to crush hers against them. At night, while Artie gigged, Susan fantasized about Mark sliding in and out of her. When she made love to Artie, vigorous, aggressive lovemaking unlike what she'd once preferred, it was Mark she thought of. For his part, Artie had begun to talk less, withdrawing into his music and sleeping later into the day after late-night gigs. He let Susan use his body like a love toy, but his emotions seemed to drift further and further away from his flesh and its needs. She wondered if he could sense her feelings for Mark.

And then, a month after moving in, Susan discovered a fresh need.

She'd been riding the elevator to the basement laundry facilities all afternoon, finding herself becoming more and more aroused. Her lingerie retrieved in a basket, her thoughts turned to the lost black lace panties. She was sure Mark had them. He seemed to smile at her too widely every time he passed her in the hall. And did she catch him winking at her whenever she entered or left the elevator?

Mark rode the elevator a lot, and Susan had started to ride it as much as she could. Even though she had promised herself to use the stairs for exercise, whenever she walked past the elevator to the stairs, she was drawn to the button and found herself calling for the car. She felt a strange tingle every time she touched the buttons inside or out of the car, and today the temptation to ride was too strong once again.

She caressed the button, watched the rubber labia opening to swallow her body, and then once inside turned to see herself in the mirror. Her hair always looked red in the smoky mirror, and she always seemed flush with desire. This time, her mind had already presented her with the solution to her needs. She pinched the Hold button between her fingers like a nipple, then wrapped her hand around the phallic lever and swung it down so it pointed at her like an erection out of a Giger catalogue. Excitement flowed down her inner thighs as she turned and raised her leather skirt, baring her buttocks. She'd taken to skipping panties on wash days, or any days she might bump into Mark. But now her need was greater than she had expected, and she bent over and backed herself toward the rubber-encased phallus, feeling it meet her lower lips at exactly the right height. And angle. She skewered herself on its fist-sized head and felt herself slide over its length as if it had been created for her.

Perhaps it was, a voice spoke within her, but she dismissed it as her own sense of humor.

Her first orgasm rocked her within seconds, and she rode it and felt the second and third building even as the first crested. She let the elevator fuck her until the sweat poured down her cheeks and pooled on the carpeting below, watching herself the whole time in the mirror. Seeing someone else smiling in the reflection, and not caring.

Rumors spread that the elevator wasn't working, but Susan knew it was her trysts that kept it out of service. Mark winked at her every time he saw her, as if he knew. Artie grew colder and more distant every day. And nights he'd once stayed home he now found gigs to fill.

Susan felt herself splitting apart—one side wanted to repair her relationship with Artie, while the other wanted to do lewd things in the elevator, with or without Mark. Like most people locked in self-conflict, Susan wished she could do both. While it tore her apart, she found herself irresistibly drawn to the elevator. And once there, she surrendered to her desires in ways she could barely admit to herself were unlike her. Yet she felt so good, she couldn't stop.

They had moved in weeks ago, but she had only recently noticed the machine-whirring sounds coming from behind the wall in their spare bedroom. This was the farthest wall from their front door, and she'd heard it late one night when she'd been working at her desk as post-gig Artie snored the sleep of the half-drunk in their bed.

The whirring wasn't continuous. It started and stopped irregularly, and soon Susan realized that it sounded like the elevator being called and traveling like a phallus up and down in its enclosure. Just thinking about it made her wet.

The intensity of her excitement easily overwhelmed any guilt she might have acknowledged.

She opened the closet and leaned in, hearing the motor turning nearby.

So near!

She found a seam in the drywall and used her sharp letter-opener to pry off a large triangular portion of painted drywall, which split and tore, becoming paper and chalk in her hand.

Flickering light shimmered in the darkness beyond.

Susan felt a deep shiver work its way down her back. For some reason, she felt hot wetness begin to gather between her thighs.

Without hesitation, Susan reached into the hole and tore out another chunk of drywall.

She *had* to get into that space, whatever it was!

Ducking, she crawled through the hole and found herself in some sort of shrine. The shimmering light came from dozens—*no, it had to be hundreds*—of lit candles of all shapes and sizes. Melted wax had crusted along the length of most, but she could clearly see that many of the tapers had been phallic in nature. Flickering dildo-shaped candles covered every flat surface, their flames dancing in the rush of air caused by her entrance. As her eyes adjusted to the gloom, she realized that the extensive shrine had been carved out of the elevator mechanical room, which apparently butted up against the rear of their apartment.

Everywhere hung or leaned paintings and photographs of the lusty Aurora, some clearly taken from old movie magazines. They were ringed by ranks of shimmering candles by the light of which she saw numerous vases as well as Greek urns and pottery that might have been imitations but which she somehow knew were quite ancient. She approached one and gingerly picked it up, her fingers tracing the erotic design of women bent over and being penetrated from behind by well-endowed males. The next vase showed a ring of figures entwined in an orgy of genitalia and mouths. A set of ornate platters portrayed various sexual positions between various combinations of genders. One included a pair of hounds. She picked up a cracked pitcher and found that the handle she grasped was an enormous phallus complete with scrotum.

She turned, and on another surface stood a collection of wooden dildos, from three inches long to about fifteen. She touched the tip of the largest, and a spark jabbed her fingertip.

Voices seemed to whisper in her head. She felt the urge to reach under her skirt and swallow the gnarled phallus with her moist flesh. Her fingers encircled the sleek wood.

In the center of this phallic collection sat a bowl, Sapphist in design. A bit of black cloth resting in the bottom of it tugged at Susan's attention. She reached in and pulled out a pair of black lace panties, *her* panties.

She whirled when she heard a loud *click*. A column of light dispelled the gloom and broke her trance.

"Who—who's there?" Her voice cracked. Then she gasped. She could see Mark's profile in the doorway.

"Relax, Susan," he said, a smile in his voice. "You're the One. You're the Chosen."

"Wh-what?" Susan felt an equal mixture of fear and lust, both fueled by the grotesque shrine to Aurora DiLuisas and its ancient erotic artifacts.

Mark came slowly closer, his hands reaching out to her.

"Aurora herself selected you from the many we have seen come and go," he said, his voice soft and musical. "And come," he added. "You've noticed that your urges have been on the rise, yes?"

Susan thought she heard Mark's New York accent peel away like dead skin flaking off a snake.

"Aurora left us while in the elevator and has been using it as a temporary domicile until a more suitable vessel could be found. *You* are that vessel, Susan."

A part of Susan wanted to run back through the hole in the wall and rouse Artie to help her. But an unnaturally strong desire, tenfold stronger than any longing she had ever experienced before, held her fast.

Suddenly Mark dropped his pants in one fluid motion and stood near, his erection pointing straight at her, and his lips—of which she'd dreamed so long—now only inches from hers. Her mouth slowly came to touch his, and down below her hand guided his scalding-hot penis toward her flesh. She felt his glans tease her outer labia and start to penetrate, and her thighs turned to butter and melted into him.

"Aurora has waited a long time, a very long time," he said, speaking directly into her mouth as his tongue reached out to hers. "I have tested so many and found them wanting." He nuzzled her neck and drove himself another inch into her. The position would not have worked, but Susan's suspicions had been correct and Mark's erect penis was enormous, for she could feel that he still had length to give her. Now his mouth was on her nipples, driving her wild even as another inch of him slid into her folds.

"Oh Mark," she whispered.

"Aurora, I have brought you the One." His teeth nipped a nipple; then he withdrew from her and turned her around. He flicked the skirt up and with his hands spread her labia apart. With the longest dildo from the collection, he prepared her to receive his burning flesh. The wooden phallus was cold and yet radiated heat, and it seemed to melt her insides.

Then Mark withdrew the ancient artifact and entered her. Susan gasped with pleasure and pain, almost fainting, her eyes glazed. And when he drove farther into her, she wondered for a moment if she could possibly take his entire length. But then he pulled her head back toward him and doubled her pleasure by thrusting even deeper within her. Her orgasms began to roll in waves and she barely heard him. Her vision failed, and the room became a blur.

"Aurora, I have brought you a Vessel worthy of your lust and of your ambition, and I give her to you as a gift of gratitude for the immortality you will grant me."

Susan heard, but her ears were muffled by the roaring of her blood singing through her veins like floodwater through a canyon. She felt as if Mark's erection was splitting her open from top to bottom, and suddenly she felt another presence—another presence inside *her*. How could this be possible?

How?

Susan heard a voice. "You will need the final offering, Marcus! You must have an offering to complete the transfer . . ."

Susan gasped. It was her own voice, but she hadn't spoken the words.

Just then she heard a crashing, tearing, and pounding coming from the hole she had torn in the drywall.

"What the fuck is going on here?"

Artie! Artie had found her and was coming to rescue her.

Susan opened her mouth but emitted no sound other than a lustful purring that she knew—*knew beyond any doubt*—must have been Aurora's.

"Welcome, Artie," said Mark from behind her. And suddenly he withdrew from her and she saw him leap like a panther over her and toward Artie, whose eyes could not have yet adjusted to the light. In Mark's hand, a curved dagger glimmered in the dancing candlelight.

Oh no! Artie!

The broad slash slit Artie's throat and almost severed his head, sending a great curtain of blood gushing over her bare flesh. He crumpled into a heap. While Artie's feet still twitched, Mark went to work with the dagger and one of the erotically designed dishes. Susan could barely make out the butcher-shop sounds that came next. She was receding: the sound of blood rushing in her ears had become a din of white noise, and her glazed vision had tunneled and was now fading into darkness.

"You must move quickly, Marcus!" Aurora's whisper was a hiss.

"The blood sacrifice is done, my Aurora," said Marcus.

When he turned, he saw Susan rising to her feet.

But now her hair was flaming red in the candlelight, and her eyes were no longer glazed.

Aurora had returned, and now her mood needed an elevator. "Come to me, Marcus," she purred, and he brought his blood-splattered flesh to her, letting her sink to her knees before him.

There was nothing left of Susan but the Vessel. But that was the last thing on Marcus's mind.

The Thirteen Locks

Dave Zeltserman

A hand clapped me on the back of the shoulder. I could barely believe it when I turned and saw Roger Hormsley's round, pink-cheeked face beaming at me.

"Jack, Jack McFarssen," he exclaimed as he held out a damp hand. "Jesus, of all places to run into you, downtown Manhattan. Last I heard you were skulking around the banks of the Euphrates. Would you mind?"

He was referring to the empty chair at my table. I have to admit seeing him was a shock. As casually as I could, I signaled for him to join me. Hormsley, of all people. Such rotten, putrid luck. If that's what it was.

"Roger, quite a surprise," I said. "And no, I don't know what you've heard, but I haven't been near the Euphrates. Too dangerous these days with what's going on in Iraq."

He smiled thinly, then looked past me to wave over the barmaid. When she came to the table, Hormsley smiled broadly at her, showing off his perfect white teeth, and told her that he was guessing I was drinking my usual, twenty-four-year-old Macallan.

"Yes, sir," she said.

"Well, then, set me up with the same and bring another for my old friend."

He watched her as she walked away, his smile fading and his small eyes turning dull. When he looked back at me, his round, jolly face was lifeless. "Jack, rumor has it you've been searching for the Scrolls of Hazaa."

"Roger, I've been stateside the past six months. San Francisco, if you must know. What made you think I was in Iraq?"

"Charles Lutton. He saw it with that glass of his."

The barmaid returned with our drinks, and I was grateful for it. Charles Lutton! I should've expected as much. Spying on me with that glass dragon's eye of his. A shriveled prune of a man, more gristle at this point than flesh. If he were broken open, there would probably be nothing more than rust in his veins. How old was he? A hundred years? Two hundred? All I knew was he'd been in the occult game longer than anyone could guess. Hormsley and I had both been in it for over twenty years and were novices compared to Lutton. Of course, as experienced as Lutton was, as far into the dark shadows as he may have slid, he didn't have in his possession the Scrolls of Hazaa. I did.

My hand shook slightly as I brought the scotch to my lips. Hormsley noticed, and it showed briefly in his eyes. I waited until the barmaid left and then told him that Lutton must be playing with him.

"Must be."

"Or maybe that damn dragon eye of his has been clouded up by cataracts. Making San Francisco Bay look like the Euphrates."

"Hmm-hmm." He took a slow sip of his scotch. "So, Jack, what were you doing in San Fran?"

"I heard there was a copy of *L'Occulto Illuminato* hidden there."

"And did you find it?"

"No."

"Of course not. All known copies were destroyed in the sixteenth century."

I shrugged and made a weak excuse about how I'd been tracking down a bum tip. Hormsley stared at me intently as he sipped his scotch. He leaned forward, his tongue darting out and licking his lips.

"I believe what Charles told me," he said. "He was quite earnest."

I could imagine that. Anyone would be *quite* earnest knowing the Scrolls of Hazaa had not only been unearthed but had fallen into the hands of a skilled occultist like myself. I forced a laugh. "This is ridiculous," I said. "If I did have the scrolls, what would I be doing in New York?"

"Akkadian is a tricky language. Outside of you, myself, and Charles, there are maybe a handful of people alive who could decipher it. One of them is Professor Tappani at Columbia. My guess is you've come here for his help."

"No, Roger, I'm not here to see Professor Tappani. I'm here to rest a bit and take advantage of Christmastime in New York. Nothing more."

His eyes bored into me as he edged closer. He said, "Look, Jack, I can help you with the scrolls. The nuances of Akkadian are immense, but together we could translate them without error. There's no reason the two of us couldn't enter the Hall of Hazaa. As one man, you'd have to solve all thirteen locks by yourself. Why not do it together? Both of us could have what the scrolls promise. Immortality. Agelessness. Virility of a god. Why not, Jack?"

It was pitiful watching him demean himself like this. Why share something that I could have all to myself? Especially since he failed to mention the most treasured of the rewards for solving the thirteen locks. The eternal services of the Furies. I would be like a god. And share them with this whining, wretched excuse of a man? Was he insane?

"No, Roger," I said, struggling to keep the pity from my voice, "I don't have the scrolls. And I am not here in New York to see any professor from Columbia."

I looked away and drank my scotch. From the corner of my eye, I could see his round face deflate like a punctured tire. He stood up, placed some money on the table for the drinks, then nodded toward me and, with his shoulders slumping, trudged off to an empty table.

Of course, while Hormsley had been right about the scrolls, he had no clue as to why I was in New York. It wasn't to see Professor Tappani or anyone else. I was quite confident in my own translation of the scrolls. But my reason for being here—as bizarre as it may sound—was that the Hall of Hazaa was right here in Manhattan. As the full moon reached its highest ascendancy, and if I were standing in the prescribed spot, the gate would become visible for a mere few seconds. After that it would be another seven years before entrance to the hall would be possible. According to my calculations, the gate would be able to be seen at exactly two thirty-one this morning, giving me a little over three hours to wait. I had gone over the scrolls a hundred times, and I was sure of this—as sure as I was of anything. After I gained entrance to the hall, I would have twenty-four hours to solve the thirteen locks. If I failed, well, I didn't want to think about the consequences. All I could do was trust that I wouldn't. The rewards were too great to do anything else. Anyway, while the scrolls didn't spell out how to solve the locks, they hinted that if I asked I would be told. Whom I would ask, I didn't have a clue, but I would cross that bridge when I got to it.

I ordered another drink, and after finishing it looked over and saw that Hormsley had left. He had to have known I wouldn't share the scrolls with him, but I guess desperation can make men do foolish things. Or maybe he was simply trying to get a read on me, to see whether or nor Lutton hadn't lost his mind and that I actually had the scrolls in my possession.

I ordered dinner and black coffee. The next twenty-four hours were going to be long ones. After I finished eating, I hung around until twenty past one. The location of the Hall of Hazaa was no more than an hour by foot, and I wanted to get there close to the time that the gate would show itself. I didn't want to have to loiter in case Lutton or anyone else was spying on me.

It was nippy out. My breath showed in front of my face as I exhaled. I held my overcoat tightly by my throat and pushed forward against the wind, dropping my head as I walked. The cold air was quite a contrast from the blistering heat of Iraq, but after a while I got used to it. Soon the numbness in my ears faded, and I could hear the footsteps keeping pace with my own. I walked a little farther and then turned down the next alleyway and pushed myself against the building. Sure enough, Roger Hormsley followed me into the alley. He seemed surprised to see me standing there waiting for him, then shrugged weakly.

"Jack," he said, "how could you blame me? We're talking about the Scrolls of Hazaa, for Chrissakes—"

I stepped forward and punched him hard in the throat. His face purpled as he gasped for air. His eyes searched out mine, begging me, pleading with me. I kicked his legs out from under him, sending him to the pavement.

"That's right," I told him. "We're talking about the Scrolls of Hazaa."

I kicked him in the mouth, knocking out several of his perfect white teeth. With the force of the kick, his head banged against the brick building, and as he lay still I stomped down on his throat, pushing hard with my foot until I was sure he was dead. I was staring at his dead, half-opened eyes when a beam of light hit me in the face. I looked up and saw a patrol car had stopped by the alley and a police officer was shining his flashlight at me. Then the light lowered to Hormsley's body. I started running. The shattering high pitch of a police siren followed.

I raced down the alley, cut across two others, then through a building until I was able to backtrack to the street I needed to get to. All the while I could hear the cops chasing after me. Adrenaline pumped through me, pushing me faster than what I thought humanly possible. I spotted the alley where I would find the gate to the Hall of Hazaa. There was a parked car mostly in the shadows of the streetlights. I dove under it, rolling as far back as I could. My breathing was ragged from the hard run, and I tried desperately to control it and to keep from making any noise. The two cops ran by, both of them panting hard. I heard them yelling at each other, asking if they saw what direction I had run off to. Their voices grew more distant. I waited until I thought it was safe. Then I pulled myself out from under the car. Squinting hard under the streetlight, I saw I had two minutes before the gate would show itself.

As quietly as I could, I made my way down the alley. Earlier in the day I had found the exact spot to stand using a GPS tracker. I now stood there. In front of me was a dumpster. If I had properly translated the scrolls, the Gate to Hazaa would unveil itself to me. All of a sudden I heard yelling, and then the beam from a flashlight hit my chest and then my face. One of the cops yelled at me to get down on my stomach. I heard them running toward me, but I ignored them.

All at once I could see the gate. Massive in size, a tarnished silver exterior with carvings of the Furies decorating it. They were hideous, horrific creatures, and if I solved the thirteen locks they would be in my service.

I moved quickly, placing my hands and fingers in the positions that the scrolls had outlined. It was a complex series of movements, but I had them memorized, and as I completed the last one, the gate swung open. While I never looked in their direction, I could feel one of the cops reaching toward me as I slipped through the open gate. Then it swung shut behind me.

I was in a narrow hallway illuminated by an eerie green light, maybe fifty feet or so from the Hall of Hazaa. My heart pounded in my chest. So close. So damn close.

Immortality. Agelessness. Virility of a god. The service of the Furies.

It would all be mine if I could solve the thirteen locks.

The hallway bent to the right. When I made the turn, I could see it. I could see the Hall of Hazaa. And then I could see them.

I almost stumbled into the hall, dazed, as I stared at them. And they just stared back at me, their eyes shining brightly. I counted them. There were thirteen of them. Thirteen girls, all naked, all heart-stoppingly beautiful, all of them looking no more than eighteen years of age. All of them thin, petite, with just barely perceptible bulges to their bellies, all with pert, champagne-glass–sized breasts and perfect pink nipples. Each of them only showing bare traces of pubic hair—more like peach fuzz than anything else—making the lips of their pussies visible. I remembered a passage from the scrolls, how the key would be an *arrow made of flesh and blood*. It all started to make sense. I knew how to solve the thirteen locks.

All their eyes were on me. I walked farther into the room. One of them—a girl with long red hair that fell past her shoulders—moved toward me. The others, their eyes were blue or gray, but hers were an emerald green. Absolutely dazzling. She stopped five feet from me and then lay on the ground. One of her hands crept down to her pubic area. She had her legs spread wide as her hand rubbed her pussy, and then using two fingers she pushed through the opening, going deep inside herself. And she moaned with each thrust of her fingers. I heard more moaning, and as I looked around the room, I saw more of them on the ground, moving in ecstasy as they fingered their pussies and pulled at their pink nipples. Several of them had paired off and were rubbing their breasts against each other as they touched each other. My mouth felt dry as I watched them. I could barely swallow.

The redhead rolled onto her knees so her ass was facing me. It was about as perfect an ass as I'd ever seen. Small, tight, with just enough to it to make the blood rush through my head. I could hear it pounding in my ears. Her hand snaked between her legs, and I watched transfixed as she rocked rhythmically back and forth, each thrust from her fingers into her pussy bringing a soft moan from her lips. Her head turned back to face me, her eyes rolling upward in orgasmic delight.

I shook myself out of the trance I had fallen into and asked her if I would solve the locks by entering each of them. She gave me a puzzled look, all the while thrusting two of her fingers back and forth into her small, tight pussy, her small hips gyrating and shivering slightly with each thrust. Of course it was stupid asking her in English. I tried again, this time in the extinct language of Akkadian. I had never spoken the language before, and my dialect sounded unnatural to my own ear, but she seemed to understand me. In a throaty purr, she answered me back in the same dead language, telling me that penetrating them wouldn't be enough—that I needed to ejaculate in each of them to unlock them.

So there it was. Thirteen girls in twenty-four hours. I would have to fuck each and every one of them. If I failed, I would be eaten alive by the Furies, fully aware and conscious as they sucked the marrow from my very bones. Thirteen girls in twenty-four hours . . .

If I was a teenager, I could've done these thirteen in an hour. At forty-two and after those four scotches I'd had only hours earlier, I wasn't so sure. But what choice did I have? According to the scrolls, I was safe from the Furies until I tried to unlock the first lock, but how could I walk away from the treasures that the Hazaa offered, especially now that the police would be looking for me for Hormsley's murder? But if I did it . . . If I fucked all thirteen of them, I'd be like a god. With the services of the Furies, I'd have no need to worry about the police or any of man's laws.

I looked from the redhead to the others. All of them writhing on the ground, either thrusting their fingers into their own pussies or into the pussy of a girl next to them. This was like some sort of pornographer's wildest fantasy. Thirteen absolutely gorgeous girls, all moaning in ecstasy as they pleasured themselves, all waiting for me to enter them. I didn't know if I could fuck each of them in the twenty-four hours I'd be given, but I didn't care. As I stood watching them, as I felt the hotness of my blood pounding through my head, I didn't care. It didn't matter. All I wanted was to fuck them.

My hands shook as I took off my overcoat, then my boots and my clothes. As the girls saw my erect cock, they started moaning even louder than before, which made my cock even harder. I looked down at it. It hadn't been this hard in years, if ever. It was far more than any arrow: it was a fucking battering ram.

I looked at all of the girls once more and felt dizzy, felt like my heart was going to explode out of my chest. The pounding in my head was like island drums. The redhead was still on her knees. I joined her, taking hold of her small hips, and as she removed her fingers from that perfect tight pink opening, I slid myself into her.

Things changed instantly then. Instead of the warm, tight pussy I was expecting, it was more like I was fucking a swamp. Something primevally foul. And it unleashed the most rotten stench imaginable. Like decomposing corpses and sickness and vomit. And her skin that just moments before had been so smooth and firm to the touch was now more like some squishy, gelatinous substance. She changed too, no longer a beautiful girl but becoming a hideous creature, her flesh bloated and an awful gray, her form misshapen and bulbous. She still had the same red hair and green eyes from before, but that was all that remained of what she had been. Her hips were now wide and grotesque, and as I held them my hands sunk into her flesh as if it were mud. Then I looked down and what had been so perfect before was now more like a cow's udder. I stared in horror as it moved as if a living thing, the lips of that udderlike genitalia sucking on my cock, making the most godawful unearthly slurping noises.

I wanted to scream. I looked around and saw they all had changed, all of them becoming these hideous mockeries of the female form. What had once been small but perfect breasts were now large drooping, oozing sacks of flesh, and those beautiful pink nipples had transformed into massive purplish wartlike things. But it was their bodies that were the biggest horror, no longer slender and lithe but bloated as if they were waterlogged corpses and now the shapes and colors of nightmares. They were still all pleasuring themselves, shoving their clawlike fists up their holes, but they were no longer moaning in ecstasy. Now it was more of a caterwaul of screeches and cackles and other ungodly sounds.

These thirteen creatures were the Furies. The same that were carved on the outer gate. The same that were illustrated within the Scrolls of Hazaa. While there was no mention in the scrolls as to how many Furies there were, there was no doubt that these were them. And I had to fuck each and every one.

I wanted to scream. I tried to pull out, but those slurping lips held tight to my cock, and then I remembered the scrolls. If I failed to open any lock that I started on I would be instantly feasted on by the Furies. My resolve hardened. I'd be damned if I'd let these foul creatures slobber on my flesh and lap up my blood.

Somehow I kept going, pounding into that swamplike hole, all the while her gelatinous haunches pushing into me and seeming to melt around my body like slime. I tried to think of the way she had been before the transformation, but I couldn't hold on to that image. All I could think of was the hideous creature she now was. I forced my thoughts to the last girl I'd been with, a Chinese girl I had paid for in Iraq, and with a soul-deadening horror I ejaculated into the creature before me.

Those lips still held firm to my cock, and I had to pry them open as if prying open a clam. Exhausted and sick to my very core, I fell to the ground. Then the others came crawling toward me, their clawlike hands grabbing for my limp cock, their bluish purple tongues—as rough as sandpaper—running over my body, darting into my ears, pushing into my ass. I tried to ignore it; I tried to ignore them. Otherwise I knew I'd go insane.

One down, twelve to go.

I lay there with my eyes closed and tried to conjure up other girls I'd been with, all the while trying to ignore the feel of their claws and their tongues on my body. Somehow I was able to bring Emily to mind. She was this dark brunette I had slept with for nine months in Florence, Italy. I tried to picture myself taking off her panties and then studying that wonderful black bush of hers, all the while playing lightly inside her with my finger. After that I reversed positions so I could lick my tongue around the lips of her pussy and then her clitoris while she sucked on me. As I thought of that, I pushed those foul claws and tongues away and stroked myself until I became hard again. Then I grabbed the nearest of those foul creatures. I couldn't get her on her knees and instead had to go at it missionary. God knows how I did it. My body sank into that gelatinous mass, and with horror I realized that her pubic area was more alive than I could've imagined. While they had only had a small amount of peach fuzz when they were girls, now it was more like steel wool, except each strand was living. They were like little thin worms that slithered and pricked at me. Somehow, although it seemed to be an eternity, I came once again and, like before, had to pry open those lips to free myself.

I checked my watch. Over two hours had elapsed. With each one it was going to get harder and harder. As it was, I knew it was going to take years to forget this nightmare I was now living. How many flesh-and-blood women would I have to be with to rid myself of this foul memory? How many years would I close my eyes at night and have to relive this horror? I knew the answers to both of these questions would be in the hundreds, but I would have all of eternity to cleanse myself. Eventually I would. Then I remembered the passages from the scrolls recounting how the Furies would feast on me if I failed. I couldn't allow that to happen. The thought of that was beyond horror.

I fucked four more of those creatures, each time first bringing to mind a woman from my past and then making myself hard enough so I could penetrate that vile, ungodly hole. Each one was more horrific than the last. Instead of fucking a swamp, it was like I was fucking a pool of congealed blood, and their bodies were even more grotesque, with lumps that moved and crawled under their skin. The last one, God, the last one—it was like fucking a vat of mucous, and all the while those hideous lumps under her skin sucked on my body as I pounded inside her.

When I finished with those four, I collapsed on the ground, and then I must've passed out. A cold chill shook me awake, and I became aware again of their claws and tongues slithering over my body. With a start I looked at my watch and saw that I only had five hours left. Five hours to fuck the remaining seven monstrosities. I almost gave up then, but as I lay there with my eyes closed, listening to their cackles and screeches, I imagined them flaying the flesh from my body and then the greedy and obscene looks that would form over their faces as they sucked my flesh down their throats. That thought forced me to keep going. Somehow, I forced myself to become hard again.

Fucking them had gone beyond horror. Their screeches as I thrust myself into them, the way those monstrous udders sucked and slurped at my cock, it was enough to drive any man insane. But I kept going. I had to. I had to survive this nightmare so I could be with a real woman again. I had to feel human flesh instead of this gelatinous obscenity. I had to feel the warmth from a female mouth and tongue again. I had to touch the delicate curve of a woman's belly and trace my fingertips down her thigh and feel the moistness between her legs. My last experience couldn't be this. It couldn't be this horrible stench or the slimy feel of their bloated, gelatinous bodies or the fetid sourness from those hideous mouths. And worst of all, the touch of those eel-like tongues along my skin. Somehow I had to get through this. Fucking these living nightmares couldn't be the last experience I had.

Somehow I kept at it. Somehow I would force myself to become hard and ignore their horrors as I pounded away inside them. I knew I was on the edge of insanity, but I kept it up until I had ejaculated into twelve of them. Twelve of these unholy locks unlocked. I looked at my watch. I only had ten minutes left. I steeled myself. I had gone through too much already to give up now. *Hell and back* was no longer an abstract concept.

Over the last twenty-three–plus hours I had endured horrors that no man should ever have to imagine. One last of these horrors to endure, and then I would be free.

I closed my eyes and tried to remember what it was like to be with a flesh-and-blood woman again. As I imagined it, I stroked myself until I was hard, and then I entered the last of the thirteen Furies. Pushing myself again and again into that dank creature while listening to her insane cackling. As I did this I recognized patterns on her back and lumps and indentations along her thighs and buttocks and realized that I had already unlocked this one. Staring bleary-eyed at my watch, I saw I only had six minutes left. I had to pry myself free, all the while with that creature cackling hysterically over the joke she had pulled on me.

They were all on me then. One by one I pushed them away until I found the last of them. Then, wrestling her to her knees, I forced myself into her. Inside, though, it was cavernous, and as I pushed my cock into that hideous creature there was nothing for it to rub against, no way for me to unlock that thirteenth lock. She started cackling then at my situation. Less than two minutes were left. Out of desperation, I forced those lips open and pushed my fist deep into its hole so I could stroke myself as I rocked back and forth within that creature. With only seconds left I ejaculated a drop into that horror. Spent, exhausted, I pried myself loose and collapsed onto the ground.

The redheaded creature crept over to me and smiled with something that could only be described as contempt. I asked it whether I had unlocked all thirteen locks.

"Yes."

"So I now have immortality?"

"Yes."

"Agelessness?"

"Yes."

"Virility of a god?"

"Of course."

With that answer, I noticed my cock had started to throb,

growing hard, erect. It felt like it was on fire. I looked away and back at the redheaded Fury.

"The services of the Furies for all eternity?"

A look of confusion twisted her shapeless face. Then she started making a sound like glass being scraped together. She was laughing over a private joke, and when she could she repeated to the other Furies that I thought I had their services for all eternity. They all started to make that same sound. Of glass being scraped together.

A panic overtook me as I tried to remember the text from the scrolls. "I have the services of the Furies for all eternity!" I insisted.

"No," she corrected me. "You will service the Furies for all eternity."

I remembered Hormsley warning me about the nuances of the Akkadian language. About how easy it is to make a mistake.

I remembered the text, realized the mistake I made. Then in a blind panic I scrambled to my feet, but before I could make it to the hallway they were on me, grabbing me and dragging me back to the redheaded Fury.

"No!" I yelled.

"You will service the Furies for all eternity. As written in the Scrolls of Hazaa."

"No! God no!"

She ignored me and sunk her claws deep into the back of my thighs, then pushed me into her so my now rock-hard cock slid into that monstrous hole of hers. She then used me as a human dildo. There was nothing I could do to break free. Nothing to do but be pushed over and over again into that foulness. To have that sour, fetid breath against my face. To feel that ungodly tongue poking into my ear. All I could do was scream, but their own orgasmic screeching drowned me out.

For all eternity.

Beauty and the Beast

Richard Wilkey

don'tlookatmelikethat

Someone seemed to be scolding him. The voice was faint, hazy, almost distant. It sounded like a woman, but his mind was cloudy and his head ached so badly that it was difficult to concentrate. Where was he? What was going on?

don't-look-at-me-like-that

There it was again, but, hell, he wasn't looking at *anyone*. His fucking eyes were closed; he felt too dizzy to open them.

"Don't look at me like that!" her voice screeched again, intensifying his headache.

Jason Walker struggled to open his eyes to a wavering blur. Could this be the worst hangover of his life? The room seemed to sway to the left and then to the right, rocking as if he were on a distressed steamer on a stormy sea. As his senses gradually improved, he realized he was naked from head to toe—and strapped to a straight-back wooden chair. His worst hangover became his worst nightmare.

"Are you happy now . . . *stalker*?"

He almost did a double take when his vision finally focused on her. She was stunningly gorgeous, with long brown hair that tumbled over her shoulders and a dark, even tan everywhere that he could see. She had sparkling blue eyes and was packed inside a light blue cutoff T-shirt that was at least a couple of sizes too small. She obviously wore no bra, because the nipples of a pair of what seemed to be grapefruit-sized, near-perfect breasts strained against the thin fabric. She wore ultratight, supershort shorts and looked like one of those Dallas Cowboys cheerleaders in black spiked heels. Few women in his life had taken his breath away, but the sight of this one could damn near put him inside an oxygen tank. But what the hell was she talking about? He hadn't been staring at her; his fucking eyes had been closed!

Jason tried to focus. A dog barked from another room of this scarcely furnished apartment. "Wh-what?" he managed to mumble. The nightmare was now transforming into his wildest fantasy. Here he sat, naked, his clothes obviously having been removed by this virtual goddess. Could it be some kind of twisted, sexy role-play that she wanted? But something felt wrong. She was almost a dream come true—except for her demeanor. She was fidgety, like she was either high on something or was suffering from withdrawal. She paced back and forth, taking short, quick steps, mumbling beneath her breath. Then she stopped and stared directly into his eyes.

"You were *gawking* at me, you asshole," she hissed.

Jason expelled a burst of pent-up breath, becoming more aware of his nakedness. Who the hell *wouldn't* stare at her? But what the fuck was she talking about? He tested the tension at his bound hands and found it uncomfortably tight.

"Hey," he began, "help me out here. I'm—"

"SHUT UP!" she yelled, her face a reflection of mounting anger. Jason realized that his perception was shifting once again, this time making a sharp U-turn from Fantasy Boulevard back to Nightmare Junction. The damn dog, still unseen, continued to bark incessantly.

This was crazy. He vaguely recalled meeting this sexpot in a bar. She'd been overtly flirtatious, and he thought he'd struck gold when she invited him to her place. They had made out on the sofa, but he couldn't remember much beyond that. It seemed she had made him a drink, and then . . .

"You were leering at me," she spat. "At the bar . . ."

Jason swallowed hard. "What? No!" he defended himself. "I wasn't leering at *anybody*. But you put something in my drink and—"

"Liar!" she interrupted him.

Jason slowly shook his head, but even the slightest movement amplified his headache. "Lady, I was just minding my own damn business at that bar when you—"

She stomped her right foot, the tip of her high-heeled black shoe slamming against the hardwood floor. "SHUT UP!" she yelled again. "Don't lie to me." Her voice almost echoed within the sparsely decorated walls.

Jason struggled against the ropes and glanced around the room for any hope of help. He could barely see a worn-out sofa ten feet or so away, but the lights in that area of the apartment were off. He thought about yelling to get the attention of neighbors, but her own loud voice hadn't called attention to herself. Anyway, this bitch obviously had something evil in mind, and she could do whatever she wanted long before anyone could come to his assistance.

She stepped directly in front of him and bent over toward him, yielding a close-up view of her ample cleavage. "You wanted to *fuck* me," she whispered.

There was definitely something wrong with this bitch. She was incredibly beautiful and sexy on the outside, but there was something dark and wicked within. How should he respond to her? Which answer did her twisted mind want to hear? "What?" he finally answered. "No, I didn't—"

She backed away and glared at him again. "You're all alike. You're *disgusting*," she interrupted him again.

Now he was angry. Of course he'd wanted to fuck her. She'd baited him from the beginning, and he'd swallowed her hook.

What the hell did she expect from him? Wasn't that what it was all about? "Listen, bitch," he snarled, "I don't know who the hell you are or what you're trying to prove, but I want *out* of here."

She smiled for a split-second, then hissed, "I told you to *SHUT UP!*" She stared at him through narrowed eyes and slowly shook her head in apparent disgust. "Besides, my name is *not* Bitch. It's Carla. You're thinking so much about fucking me that you can't even remember my name."

Carla. The name did seem familiar. But she had obviously drugged him and wiped out much of his short-term memory.

"But I remember *your* name . . . *Jason*." She pronounced it like it was a fresh pile of horseshit. "But names aren't important now." She backed a step farther away and eyed her prey like a cat stalking a mouse, playing with him, taunting him. "Do you honestly think you can just lie your way out of this?" she said, finally in a calmer voice.

Jason shook his head again. The headache was clearing, and his senses were rapidly returning. He knew he had to do something. "You're fucking crazy, lady. I want out of here . . . *now*."

Carla strutted seductively toward him, laughing. "You're not in much of a position to tell me what to do . . . *pervert*," she said slyly.

Jason tried to calm himself. She was right. He shouldn't be so demanding. He'd have to be diplomatic to get out of this mess. The air conditioner kicked on, and a vent directly above him blew cold air across his exposed skin, raising chill bumps. No matter how he tried to lower his pulse, however, he couldn't control the anger in his voice. "I told you, dammit, I was just trying to get to know you. Sure, I was looking at you, but I never leer at *any*body. The way you were dressed, everybody in the whole damn place was giving you the eye."

"Oh, so it's *my* fault now?"

Jason slowly shook his head and exhaled in frustration.

Now, suddenly, her attitude shifted again. She smirked at him, pursing her lips and batting her eyes seductively. "Do you really expect me to believe that you didn't want to fuck me?" she said. She ran her fingertips through her hair and jutted her breasts out farther. "Think you could pass a lie-detector test?"

Jason groaned and shook his head harder. She was crazier than he'd imagined. He struggled against the ropes again, but they were as tight as ever, offering little hope of escape. Should he play along with her? Maybe she'd loosen the ropes for whatever she had in mind, and he could make a run for it then. He was at a loss for words as the air conditioner chilled him even more.

"I'm not stupid. I knew all along what you were up to," Carla said. "I know *exactly* what you want."

Jason groaned in exasperation. "No, that's not—" He stopped in midsentence, reminding himself of her lie-detector question. "Yeah, yeah, I could pass a test," he finally said. "Like you just happen to have a fucking lie detector in your closet, huh, bitch?"

She smiled, and her nerves seemed to suddenly calm. "Oh, no, not at all," she cooed. "There's a lie detector right *here*."

She was staring at him as she said it. What the hell did she mean? She wasn't making any sense, and he couldn't figure out what to say next. He swallowed hard, then said, "Okay, okay, so let's see your fucking lie detector."

She stepped directly in front of him, bent to her knees, and stared at his crotch. "Oh, it's not *my* lie detector, honey. It's *yours*. Right there . . . between your legs."

She seductively pulled the tight T-shirt up and over her head, her breasts springing free with the most erotic jiggle he'd ever seen. Her dark pencil-eraser–sized nipples were erect and bobbing directly in his face. Her perfection seemed even more flawless than before. Jason was captivated.

She leaned closer, and he could smell her perfume, her mint-flavored breath. "If your lie detector doesn't move, I guess you really *don't* want to fuck me." She slowly glided around him, her hip lightly grazing his naked arm. Then she leaned in close against the side of his head, nibbling at his ear and neck. "But if it points straight up . . ." she whispered as she stepped back in front of him and slowly peeled her shorts down to her knees. She was wearing no panties.

Jason leaned as far back from her as he could get and closed his eyes. "Oh shit, this isn't fair." He gasped. The familiar tingle began at his groin.

"*Look at me!*" she hissed. She pinched his bare thigh sharply as she stepped out of her shorts and stood totally nude in front of him, revealing her smoothly shaven snatch. She slowly ran her fingertips down her body to her crotch, enticingly running her fingers between her legs. "If you're lying and your lie detector points straight up," she repeated, "I might just have to . . ."

His eyes expanded as she reached behind him, dangling her breasts in his face and bringing back a long, menacing knife. "*Cut it off!*" she spat.

Jason momentarily held his breath in shock, then pleaded, "No! *No!*"

She grasped the knife in her right hand and took in several deep breaths, thrusting her breasts forward, then slowly approached him. His dick responded as it normally did, as any heterosexual male's would. She smiled and wet her lips with her tongue, then carefully straddled his knees, facing him, leaning against him to whisper in his ear as she gazed down at his manhood. "Uh-oh. Your lie detector says you're lying," she whispered.

Jason summoned all of his strength, trying to rock the chair to knock them both to the floor. "Oh God, no, lady—*please!*"

She laughed in his face and slid the blade of the knife against his cheek. Sensually she ran the fingers of her left hand through her hair again and softly moaned.

She's completely over the edge, Jason realized. He leaned away from her again and felt his erection lightly graze against her pussy lips. It was maddening.

"When Pinocchio lied, his little nose grew," she said in a lighthearted tone. "Looks like something *else* grows when *you* lie."

"My God, lady, what the hell do you want from me?"

She brushed her breasts against his face, and he fought the

urge to take an erect nipple into his mouth. "Just the truth, fucker," she hissed. "I only want the truth."

Jason's heart pounded against his chest, his skin tingling now with fear. "Please, lady. For God's sake, I've never done anything to you."

She smiled wickedly and leaned in closer, pushing her breasts against his chest. "Oh, but you *want* to do something to me. That's all that men like you *ever* want, isn't it?"

His mind was spinning now. His dick stood at attention, and there was a sharp blade only inches away. He was at her mercy. "Listen, we can work this out. Do you really *want* me to fuck you? Is that what this is all about?"

She laughed and stared blankly into space for a brief instant, then kissed him long and passionately. When she pulled away, he saw an expression of lovely hatred, beauty and the beast all in one. His erection began to wilt, far too late. Terror consumed his consciousness. She glanced down at his crotch again and slowly shook her head. "Oh, too late for that," she said. "The truth hurts."

Carla smiled at him seductively, appearing almost normal again. Then she slid back along his lap to straddle his knees, making room to reach down between his legs. "Looks like I'll be adding another one to my collection. . . ."

Jason screamed and rocked the chair back and forth, but she hung on like a cowboy on a wild steer. She grabbed his now-flaccid dick with her left hand and lowered the knife. "It'll be worse if you fight me," she whispered. "A clean cut will be better for both of us."

He swallowed hard and sat perfectly still, sweat beading across his forehead, willing her to please stop, praying that this was just a bad dream, when he felt the knife blade slide underneath his balls. Tears streamed down his cheeks. "Please, lady," he begged. "I'm sorry . . . if I—"

Without warning she pulled his dick straight up and began to saw through tender skin. Left to right . . . right to left. Jason shuddered, feeling the motion at his groin a split second before the pain registered. Too horrified to scream, too frightened to even move, he closed his eyes tightly, unable, or unwilling, to watch. A warm liquid flowed down his legs, and with his eyes shut he didn't know if his manhood had been severed or if he'd pissed on himself. A short while later, lying on his side but still strapped to the chair, Jason's breath ceased, his movement subsiding amid a spreading pool of crimson.

His final conscious sight was a pair of bloody footprints leading away into the next room.

Clad only in a bra and bikini panties, Carla stood at the kitchen stove gently stirring the simmering contents of a small saucepan. From the nearby living room her roommate called out, "I guess Trixie had another accident last night."

"Oh . . . right," Carla answered.

Trixie, their seven-year-old golden retriever, padded into the kitchen just ahead of Marsha, who still wore her faded and baggy flannel pajamas. Marsha was of stocky build, about Carla's age, with short-cropped brown hair. She yawned, then stepped behind Carla and gave her a kiss on the neck. "Good morning, sweetheart," she cooed.

Carla glanced at her watch. "Actually it's two-fifteen. What time did you get home last night?"

Marsha exhaled deeply. "I had to work a double shift. I'm not quite sure what time it was, but the smell of bleach on the living-room floor almost knocked me to my knees when I opened the door."

Carla shrugged. "Trixie gets nervous sometimes. She can't help it."

"Well, at least she didn't do it on the rug."

Carla smirked. She always made sure there wasn't a mess on the rug.

Marsha stretched her arms and took in a deep breath, apparently awakening more by the minute. "Mmm, something sure smells good," she said, easing behind Carla and peeking over her shoulder into the saucepan. "What's cooking?"

Carla stirred the contents a bit more rapidly. "Meat balls," she answered.

Marsha looked closer at the saucepan's contents, a confused expression sweeping over her face. "Only two?" she asked.

Carla groaned in disgust. "They're for Trixie."

Marsha laughed. "You're kidding, right? That's hardly even a mouthful for her!"

Carla slowly raised her head and stared blankly ahead, then pivoted to face Marsha, glaring at her. "Don't get started with me. I'm not in the mood," she growled.

Marsha touched Carla on the shoulder and said, "Honey, please. I didn't mean anything by it."

Carla's look of anger grew worse even after Marsha leaned forward and gently kissed her on the lips. "We need to talk," Marsha said.

"When I finish this—"

"*Now,*" Marsha interrupted. "I'm serious."

Carla prodded the simmering contents with a spoon and shrugged. "They're almost ready anyway." She turned the burner off and flashed a grim expression at Marsha.

Marsha took Carla's hand and led her to the living-room sofa. The two sat together, and Trixie occupied the far end of the sofa. Marsha began to gently massage Carla's neck, but Carla flinched. "Your shrink called yesterday," Marsha began.

"So?"

"He said you've missed some appointments."

Carla looked away. "He has no right to talk to you about me," she said.

"You signed a release, remember?" Carla sulked and turned away. Marsha squeezed her shoulder. "Have you been skipping your medication too?" Marsha asked.

Carla slammed a foot against the floor. "You don't understand me!" she shrieked. "*Nobody* understands me!"

Marsha tried to hold her, but Carla jerked away. "Leave me alone," she shrieked. "Don't *touch* me!"

Marsha's expression suddenly faded. She reached for her cell phone, glanced at Carla, and pleaded with her eyes. "Calm down, honey," she whispered, swallowing hard. "I'll get you some help. It'll be okay, I promise."

As Marsha punched numbers into the keypad, Carla grabbed a nearby lamp and swung its base hard against her roommate's head. Restricted by the length of the electrical cord, the blow only stunned Marsha but sent her tumbling to the floor. By now, however, Carla raised the straight-back chair in which Jason had been recently strapped and brought it down hard against Marsha's head, promptly muting her screams. "No. You. Won't," Carla repeated over and over. When she stopped swinging the chair, little was left of her roommate's head other than a bloody lump.

Carla shook her head. This time the rug *was* a mess.

Trixie whined and plopped to the floor, taking a quick lap of Marsha's pooling blood, then staring sad-eyed at Carla.

She'd never attempted this before, and it proved to be more difficult than she'd imagined. Marsha's lifeless corpse lay faceup and naked on the floor, legs spread far apart. The jar of pickled penises rested just to the right of Marsha, and Carla fished out another one, a larger one this time.

Even after adding a lubricant, this one was still practically impossible to jam inside Marsha. It was like stuffing Jell-O through a keyhole.

"Damn," Carla muttered. She considered applying a makeshift splint to the flaccid member when another thought occurred to her. Was it possible to preserve an erect dick? She recalled her Uncle Ed, who had molested her repeatedly as a young teen. He could never get it up, so he used some kind of pump device to get hard. He'd stick his dick into a tube, then pump out the air to draw blood into his dick, forming an erection. When he was totally hard, he'd slide a tight rubber band over the tube to the base of his dick to trap the blood inside. *Purple penis . . . purple penis . . .* She stared blankly ahead and shuddered at the thought.

Perhaps if she clamped something tightly around the base of the next pervert's dick and somehow sealed it as she cut it away, she could preserve the boner. It was worth a try.

Carla dropped the shiny, severed penis back into the jar of alcohol with the others. She replaced the lid, then shook the jar, watching the various-sized penises swirl against each other. Carla smiled. Looked like she'd soon have to find a bigger jar.

It wasn't supposed to be like this.

Carla paced nervously in front of her latest victim. He was beginning to awaken, and she didn't know what to do. She took a deep breath and looked him over once again as he slumped in the chair to be sure she wasn't missing something. There was a bald spot at the crown of his head that she hadn't noticed before. Streaks of gray in his hair had been virtually invisible until now. Perhaps she *had* overlooked it.

A thick mat of chest hair looked like a bearskin rug stretched over his husky, masculine body. His legs were open but—

No. It just wasn't right. How could this be?

His head rolled from side to side. His eyes slowly opened, then blinked repeatedly. He seemed to be focusing his attention on her now. Carla continued to study him carefully.

His eyebrows arched. As his senses apparently returned, he showed little concern over being naked and bound. He swallowed hard, and a grim expression washed over his face.

"Don't look at me like that," he hissed.

Carla stood speechless. Wasn't *she* supposed to say that? He glanced down at his crotch, then made eye contact with her again. "You hot bitches are all alike," he said. "You only want perfection. You don't have even an ounce of sympathy for guys like me."

"I . . ." she started but then was at a complete loss for words. She swallowed hard; then her mouth hung open.

He slowly shook his head, glanced down again between his legs, then grimaced at her. "I wanted to prepare you. I meant to say something before I passed out." His eyes narrowed as he scrutinized her. "You spiked my drink, didn't you?" She stood motionless, and he laughed unexpectedly. "I thought only guys did shit like that," he said.

For the first time that she could remember, she was self-conscious about her appearance, but it seemed that no matter how she moved, he stared at her harder.

"That hot body of yours is hazardous material," he said. "You should put one of those yellow labels on your ass." He smiled broadly and pursed his lips. "But I know what you're wondering," he said. "And the answer is yes." He tested the rope at his wrists and shrugged. "You've heard of phantom limbs before, haven't you? A guy loses an arm in an accident, but it feels like it's still hanging there?" He hesitated briefly. "Well, babe, I'm hard as a rock right now."

Carla stared blankly at the vacant space between his legs.

"Arms aren't the only body part that can be lost in an accident," he said. "But guys like us? We still gotta live. We still have urges, but we learn to compensate."

An uncharacteristic sense of sadness washed over Carla. Perhaps she'd been wrong to judge all men so harshly. Maybe there were actually some out there who couldn't think with their dicks.

His face turned to stone. "I've already felt a fucking Rottweiler clamp his teeth between my legs. There's nothing you can do to me that could be any worse, so go ahead and get it over with."

She stood speechless. He slowly shook his head and grinned.

"Never seen a dickless guy before, huh?" he said. "You're no different from any other bitch. They're all curious . . . but no compassion." He took a deep breath, then exhaled hard and swallowed. "I can still piss through the little tube you see down there." On closer inspection, she saw what he was referring to. "I can even have an orgasm if someone will take the time to lick around the scar tissue." He rolled his eyes and laughed. "But there ain't many bitches around who'll bother." He gave her a cold, hard stare. "You bitches are all alike. You're only out for yourselves."

Carla trembled as a wave of emotion overcame her. "I . . . I'm sorry."

"Yeah . . . sure you are," he smirked.

A tear trickled down Carla's cheek. It felt odd. How long had it been since she'd felt such emotion?

Following a moment of awkward silence, he said, "So, what the hell happens next? Sorry I disappointed you."

Carla slowly shook her head. "I was wrong. I didn't know."

He exhaled deeply. "You're not making any sense."

She quickened her pace. How could she have been this mistaken about men? Was it possible that some were not sexual predators? She felt her skin tingle. The familiar restless feeling swept over her. Should she take her medication? No, not yet. She had to do something with this guy first.

"It's getting cold in here. Can't you at least throw a blanket over me?" he complained.

What should she do? She had been so wrong.

And then the thought occurred to her. Maybe a gesture of kindness could make everything right. Perhaps through one simple act she could turn her life around. In her twisted mind it made perfectly good sense.

A smile crept over Carla's face as she stepped across the hardwood floor to her bedroom. Trixie barked and jumped all over her bed as she retrieved the jar from her bedroom closet. Everything would be fine, she felt certain. She would untie him and let him have his choice of any of the jar's contents. He could feel whole again.

He would thank her, she was sure.

She couldn't wait to see the look in his eyes when she handed him the jar. . . .

Tres Hermanas

Roberta Lannes

The men huddled together in the Minneapolis bar so they could hear each other in the din. One, haggard and lean to the point of gaunt, gulped down his fourth scotch. His heavyset friend in the Hawaiian shirt wiped his face with his hand as he shook his head.

"I don't get you, Jim. You were separated five minutes when you got involved with a hot babe a year older than your daughter who just wanted to fuck you twenty-four hours a day. You spent every free minute with her, stopped sleeping, and started having hallucinations. Your dental practice went all to hell, and you didn't give a shit. Now this woman disappears, and you're begging for help . . . now, after you told us all to fuck off? Explain why I should even try."

Jim cocked his head. "Okay. Look, Benny. You understand how it is when you *have* to have something. When you're living for it, thinking about it every second you're not tasting it. Hell, I don't know how you can sit in a bar and watch me drink and it doesn't bother you."

"So, you think you're . . ."

"An addict? Yeah. Addicted to Carmen. To the sex." Jim nodded. "I even miss the fucking hallucinations! I can't tell you how many times . . . in the beginning . . . I prayed she'd dump me so I could get a full night's sleep. Shit, I was terrified I'd drill the wrong tooth, fit the wrong crown, but she took me over, man!" He elbowed his friend. "You *know* what that's like. . . ."

Ben snorted. "Okay, so you see where you're at, that's important. Find a twelve-step program for love addicts, sex addicts. They have them, you know."

"Yeah, yeah. I know. Anything you can get hooked on, they got a twelve-step thing for it." Jim motioned for the cocktail waitress. "But until then, you'll help?"

"You have to help yourself, man." Ben looked at his watch.

"Yeah, I hear you, Benny, but look . . . you're a detective. You can find Carmen for me."

Ben pulled his two hundred and sixty pounds up off the stool and slapped a ten-dollar bill down on the table. "You're completely fucked, Jimbo. Find a shrink, get professional help. The one thing I'm not going to do is find the bitch who put you here."

Jim trembled. His eyes were the color of watery cream-of-tomato soup. "Please. Her name's Carmen Almanza. Twenty-six years old. Five feet ten with short, wavy black hair and chartreuse eyes. Born in Guatemala."

"You need help, man, not *her*." He stared into Jim's eyes and saw only desperation. "I got to go, buddy. I'll call you."

Ben did his best to walk out without turning back. His friends had gone through the same anguish with him when he was a gutter drunk. When they turned their backs because Ben could only love the bottle, he hit bottom. It took years to win back the trust, to learn how to help other guys who were falling down. When Jim was ready, he'd walk the walk with him.

Still, when he got into his car, he pulled out his notebook and jotted down the name and description Jim had given. Maybe this woman had a sheet; maybe she was a con and had left a trail. He'd check her out. At least that.

* * *

Esme braided her sister Yolanda's thick, dark hair into one long plait as their middle sister, Carmen, stroked lotion over her shapely brown legs. Their party dresses for the evening were draped across the back of Esme's sofa.

"Why am I nervous?" Yolanda, the eldest, patted gloss onto her full lips. "I always worry we'll give ourselves away."

Carmen wiped the last of the lotion onto her forearms. "Once we're there, we're strangers. We're practiced at this."

Esme laughed. "Yoli's nervous we won't find a ripe man."

Yolanda turned and swiped at her sister. "Don't be ridiculous! We are each the light on the porch to the moths. They always flutter to us. We will find many."

Carmen stood. She was the tallest and thinnest of the sisters. She wore golden green contact lenses which, with her olive skin and wavy black hair, gave her the most exotic look. "You have a way with words, sister. It's *moths to a flame.*"

Yolanda turned to Carmen. "What's the difference? They're drawn to us. We are the lights." Yoli had the most naturally Latina appearance, with her black eyes and dark skin and voluptuous figure.

"And we'll all be lit up tonight!" Esme giggled. "I'm getting dressed. I promised Julian I'd get there early to help set up." Esme, the lightest skinned, whose pale blue eyes belied her heritage, began brushing her long, red-streaked brown hair.

Esme had promised her boss all the beautiful, smart, single women he wanted for his wealthy, intelligent, and nerdy software-designer friends. Julian warned her: many of the men weren't socially adept, none looking for one-night stands. Esme invited half her yoga class, some of the girls at her hair salon, some from her art class, but the sisters had lived in LA only three months. Yolanda, a nurse, met sick kids and worried parents, and Carmen did research at the Getty Research Institute, cloistered in a cubicle. Neither could offer Esme much help finding women.

Carmen slithered into her dress. It clung like pale water to her skin. "Come, my fellow porch lamps. We have some moth hunting"—she chortled—"I mean, man hunting to do."

Michael's hand trembled on Carmen's lower back, rustling the fabric of her silk blouse as she opened her front door. She turned to him, her eyes wide, smile mischievous.

"Are you okay with this?" She leaned into him, put her arms around him, and let him kiss her. He was awkward, pushing his tongue in, swallowing her. "No, Michael, like this." She took his face in her hands, put her lips softly to his. Her tongue was gentle, playful, sensual on his lips, parting them. When his tongue darted at hers, she pulled away. "Let me . . . just relax."

The man was shaking. It was their first date. "I guess you can tell I haven't done this much." His shrug was sharp. His every move rigid.

Carmen, laughing playfully, turned to open her door. "We need a lot more wine."

They had been out for dinner, where Michael nervously dominated the conversation with grueling details of his work for Julian's software company. Carmen half listened, half observed. He was just a bit overweight; no exercise, she guessed. He was handsome in a boyish way. Someone dressed him, because he wore nice clothes but didn't inhabit them. He told her he lived with his sister and brother-in-law since he spent most of his time at work. He'd been alone since moving to LA. Carmen considered him "ripe."

It took an entire bottle of wine to relax him. Carmen turned off the lamp, lit some candles, then excused herself to use the bathroom. She returned in a red satin robe and nothing else, then draped herself over him on the couch.

"Kiss me now, Michael." Carmen stared into his eyes, her lips but a few inches from his. She arched her back. The robe slipped slightly from her shoulders. His eyes went from the curve of her breasts to her lips, then closed. She felt his hard-on beneath her.

His kisses began less awkwardly, and soon he forgot himself. Michael breathed in Carmen's spicy scent, felt her long fingers move along his shirt buttons, plucking them open.

"Yes, that's better. Let me show you what I need and make you a very happy man. . . ." A low purring sound rose from deep in her throat as she peeled off his shirt. He was pale and doughy but not flabby. Her fingertips went to his small nipples and began to knead them gently. She stopped kissing him on the mouth, moving to his neck, then to his chest, where her tongue took the place of her fingertips. Michael gasped sharply, giggled.

"Tickles!"

"Shush. Let me show you . . ." She worked her hands to his belt, undid it, then his zipper. She felt the waistband of his briefs, and his cock pulsed under her palm.

Carmen pushed him back onto the couch. She knew her men, never choosing cunning, macho types who would not be led. Michael let her pull off his slacks, his briefs. She stood and let the robe fall to the floor as he lay back.

"You're beautiful, Carmen." He grinned, taking her hand.

"Yes, here." She placed her hand with his on her taut belly. "Do you know how a woman likes to be touched?"

Michael blinked, nodding weakly. Carmen went onto her knees, taking his hand to one breast, then took his other hand to her mouth and began sucking on a finger. His hand was rough on her breast. She stopped him, took both his hands, showed him what she wanted—gentle and soft caresses. Her nipples were large, and his fingers went easily over them. She purred louder. "Very *good*."

She maneuvered onto the couch, straddling him as her breasts brushed over his lips. "Suck on them, Michael. Make them hard. Put your fingers here. . . ." She guided his hand to her pussy. She knew her body, that with the right manipulation, he would get her sweet syrup flowing.

This was the point when the man often balked; when he felt how wet she was, when he parted her labia and felt the huge clitoris coming unsheathed as she grew aroused. Carmen thought of her sisters lying together in Esme's bed as Michael's fingers slipped inside her, slid up and felt the taut bud. He grunted, and his body went rigid. She reached for his prick and began to stroke it. He relaxed some.

She cooed to him. "It's all right, Michael. It's just how God made me. Unique. So sensitive. Like you . . ." She moved her hand expertly over his cock until he moaned.

He touched her clit tentatively, then tried to enter her. Carmen was in charge and pulled back, sliding away. She lay opposite him on the couch, her head on the other armrest, her legs apart. He got up on his knees.

"Kiss me here, Michael. A woman loves for a man to take her sex into his mouth and softly move his tongue over it. Just as a man enjoys this." She sprang toward him like a cat, her mouth over his penis, her hands on his surprisingly firm ass. His cock went down her throat easily, and she nodded slowly, feeling his back arch, his hips come forward. She teased him until she tasted the silvery tears that arrive just before a man orgasms, then slipped away.

She lay back, opened her legs. As he came to kiss her mouth, she took his shoulders and pressed them down. He hesitated, resistant.

"I don't . . . I've never . . ."

Carmen knew this wouldn't do. She began massaging her nipples, smiling up at him. He watched with one hand on his prick, the other on her thigh. Then he looked down at her mons, at the one-inch-tall clitoris, red and thick.

Her voice changed as she spoke through the purring, seductively: a hypnotic, haunting sound. "Suckle on me, as I did you . . . please . . ." Michael responded, arranging himself so that he could put his head between her legs. She continued to purr to him until his mouth went around her clit, his tongue going over it, investigating. His inexperience showed, but he aroused her nonetheless. And he would learn.

As he suckled, he swallowed her sweet liqueur. Soon it would have its profound effect on him, turning him into a living talisman, connecting her to her sisters. Then the magic would take over, and he would no longer need her guidance.

Carmen closed her eyes, waiting for her elixir to do its work on Michael, and concentrated on Yoli and Esme. Miles away, in the candlelight of Esme's bedroom, their nude bodies were entwined. They embraced so that their mouths were on each other's clits, hands reaching up or down to the other's nipples. Carmen smiled as she caught mental glimpses of her sisters throwing back their heads, equally aroused, their clits crowning. Everything was moving along well, timing ahead of expectation.

We're synchronous, the connection growing. Her thoughts traveled out to the women. Esme moved her hair so that Carmen might see her mouth moving over her sister's clit. Yoli's lips moved, but Carmen read only her thoughts; their union was without sound. What she told Carmen was, *We're close.*

Carmen opened her eyes and glanced at Michael. His head moved rhythmically with his lips and tongue. He was drunk now with her liqueur, off in the darkness that was created as he became a conduit. It was time.

She licked her fingers and put them to her nipples. She milked them softly, increasing her arousal. She closed her eyes again and let the scene miles away flash back into her head. The sisters had shifted position, Yoli straddling Esme's head, her fingers pulling her labia wide. Esme's tongue and lips went over and over the swollen clitoris, moving faster, evenly. Yoli shivered, her nipples dark and hard in the candlelight. Esme's hands grasped Yoli's breasts, her fingers reaching for the rigid nibs. Just as she grazed them with her feather-light touch, Yolanda climaxed, her hips bucking against Esme's face.

In that moment, Carmen felt the swell of pleasure and climaxed as well. Her guttural moans, body shuddering beneath

Michael's suckling, continued in waves. As the vision of her sisters ebbed and winked out like an extinguished torch, she took Michael's head in her hands and held it still.

Slowly, as if coming out of a trance, Michael blinked up at her. She beamed down at him, bliss evident on her face. "I want you inside me, *now*." Her mesmerizing voice, purring resonantly, reached down into him until his spine vibrated like a tuning fork.

As he moved her so that she was on top of him, he stared down at his cock. Carmen enjoyed this moment as her man noticed his cock had expanded to a size much larger than he'd ever seen—thicker, longer, and destined for one place alone. The men tried to hide their awe, fear, and delight for a moment; then the enchantment took over. Carmen slipped over Michael's cock and down. It was a tight, sure fit. He would hit the unique spot that released more fluid, assuring a secure, closed circuit.

Michael pumped himself into her, moving easily at first, respectfully. But the link he provided was electric, powerful. So much so, the synaptic firing in his head opened the sisters' conjoined passion and hunger to him. Michael's face changed from boyish pleasure to that of lust-driven madman, possessed. He sat up, grabbing Carmen by the neck with one hand, the other on her ass, and began thrusting wildly. His eyes rolled up into his head, and his mouth fell open. Time stopped as he became the conduit to the sisters' delight and basked in it himself.

Carmen shut her eyes. As if she were there beside them, she saw Yoli's head between Esme's lovely legs. Their eyes were shut as well, seeing Carmen in Michael's lap, getting fucked hard, his enormous cock thrusting in and out of Carmen's pussy. Tonight, the magic was at its pinnacle.

The precinct was operating at a low hum around him at eight in the evening. Too early for the night shift to be out; everyone on paperwork, interviewing suspects or witnesses. Ben sat at his computer inputting everything Jim had told him about Carmen. He got hits right off. First, most recently, Carmen Almanza had been a research assistant at the Walker Museum of Art. Another reference had her as a research fellow at the Guggenheim Museum in New York. She specialized in Latin American artwork. For a couple of Google pages, she impressed Ben as a competent if fickle art historian and researcher. Jim said she was in her mid-twenties. Ben's gut-warning bells started going off. Who got to where she was, accomplished so much, at such a young age? She never stayed more than a year in any position. No surprise. Ben's guess, she left when a guy got too obsessed. She must be a looker, he mused.

He googled for a photograph without success but found bulletin-board postings about her. Strange world—bulletin boards, newsgroups. People who might otherwise never meet or speak shared their interests and lives with frightening detail. It took a while for Ben to get past his tendency to read for minutiae to scanning more holistically. Once he did, his evidence detector began flashing brightly.

Jim wasn't the first guy obsessed with Carmen Almanza. At alt.LoveAddicts, a newsgroup, he found a thread started by "Woody" back in 1998 that described how, with Carmen and his hallucinations, he went from successful banker to living out of his car in ten months. 1998? When she was seventeen? Ben's warning bells clanged so loud he flinched.

Woody wrote about his hallucinations. "I'd see two gorgeous women making love to each other; sometimes they did things with different guys. The hallucinations always came when I was fucking her. One minute, I'd be in bed with her, and then I was in a kind of darkness, like a cave that swirled around me. Then the hallucinations came. I was looking through a keyhole or tunnel until I was inside another room, close up. At first, I thought the hallucinations happened because I wasn't sleeping. She had me going at it every night, twice, three times! My shrink pointed out the visions were situational, which was weird."

Ben blinked. Jim described the hallucinations the same way. Sleep-deprived visions. Carmen had the same effect on *any* guy she was with. Poor Jim. Fresh from a milked-dry, sexually dead marriage, he was easy prey for whoever came along. Jim was the perfect rube for a soul-sucking bitch like Carmen.

Ben found out far more than he'd been looking for. There were other men in similar situations with women other than Carmen. Some wrote about a Yolanda; a few wrote of an Esme. Each surnamed Almanza. It didn't take a Yale Scholar to put it together: these three women were sisters. Different places, big cities. But in every one, there was a nurse, or an office worker of some kind, or a researcher. Ben got the manic thrill of finding evidence—circumstantial so far, but evidence. He had to fight himself to quit, log off, get home, and go to sleep. Time had flown past. His shift began in six hours, but he couldn't turn off thoughts about Jim and these guys who'd fallen prey to the Almanza sisters. Stranger still, for the first time in fourteen years, he wanted a beer.

The sisters sat at Yolanda's dining-room table having breakfast. Esme scooped an omelet from the pan onto Carmen's plate. "You've never found a man so malleable on a first night. He did whatever you asked, no questions, no resistance!"

Yoli weighed in. "This Michael . . . He didn't strike me as experienced enough, yet when I watched him at the party, I sensed an open heart."

Carmen sipped her orange juice and grinned. "We got very lucky. Michael shows promise. He worked the first time . . . and I like him. He's kind, not ego-driven like the last one."

"Oh, those doctors or lawyers, any man with a God complex. They're the ones who turn into the compulsives, the stalkers. What is it about control freaks when they lose control of a substance, or sex?" Yoli laughed. "I hope Michael will be more balanced. I *like* it out here in LA."

Esme pushed a large, brightly colored dish full of sausage and bacon to the center of the table. "I agree. If we choose better, we stay here longer."

Carmen nodded. "I'm calling Michael later to arrange another date. I expect he'll be at my house by dinner. Is everyone up for more lovely sex?"

The others purred. Yoli clapped her hands together. "After last night and this morning, he qualifies as the quickest fully invested talisman Carmen has ever found us. Hell, I still feel him, and it was Carmen he fucked! So no matter what Mr. Computer Genius's job holds for him, he will be with us tonight."

Carmen slipped her bare feet into her trendy sandals. "Well, did either of you find someone interesting who might fit us?"

Yolanda leaned across the table to fidget with the flowers in a vase. "I did."

Esme grabbed her sister's hand. "Who? I still have the guest list in my head!"

"He is the older man with the silver hair and deep tan. Holden. He wasn't a guest. He's head of company security. I got the sense he is fearless, truly loves women. A good combination, no?"

Esme laughed. "I know who you mean. He reminds me of the actor Cesar Romero."

Yolanda shook a finger at her sister. "Be careful . . . that observation dates you."

Carmen shushed her. "We can be careless with each other. Let her be."

"Do you think these men know each other?" Esme looked to each sister.

Carmen put her hand to her mouth, then swallowed. "I hadn't considered that. Can you check it out?"

Esme nodded. "Sure. They work on different floors, I know that."

Yolanda walked to the window overlooking the small garden of her house. "You know, we've been doing this since we were very young. Sometimes I forget what compels us, why we continue. I seldom think of how Papa protected us and how now it is up to us to protect ourselves. It's simply our lives. We work, we love each other, and we have our unique sensual magic. But perhaps we've become too sure of ourselves, and we'll make a mistake. It didn't occur to me that I might find someone at the party who would know another of the men. Like at a bar, I was just thrilled that we had so many possibilities."

Esme came up behind her. Her hands went around her waist and up, cupping her breasts. She breathed in the clean scent of her sister's hair. "We'll keep each other from making mistakes."

Carmen huffed. "You two worry too much. It's good to be careful, but our magic is powerful stuff. The men don't believe what they're seeing because it's impossible that they do."

Yolanda and Esme turned to Carmen. Yolanda shook her head. "Maybe. Magic is commercialized and homogenized into everyone's lives to the point that it's Saturday morning cartoons and children's party themes. Little girls have unicorns and fairies painted on their walls, and boys pin on towel capes for superpowers available only in comic books. Then they grow into disillusioned adults. Childhood's mystique is destroyed by reality. So when something supernatural actually occurs, they deny it's anything but coincidence or a psychological trick."

"So we can just relax and expect the magic to protect us? All it takes is one man to question . . ." Esme folded her arms. "Can we control that?"

Carmen went to her sisters and embraced them, kissed each deeply, passionately. With their heads touching, arms about each other, Carmen said, "As long as we have this, we have control."

Ben put in a call to Jim's cell phone every day for a week. He left voice-mail messages but got no return calls. He finally tried Jim's dental office. The receptionist recognized Ben's voice.

"He's with a patient, Detective. I'll have him call you when he's between appointments."

"So he's got appointments coming in again? That's good."

"Yeah, well, he's a great dentist. He was just going through a rough period. Getting separated and all that. . . . His patients understood."

"Does he seem better to you?"

The woman chuckled. She told Ben that Jim was smiling, putting on weight, focusing. He was seeing a "specialist," a Dr. Posner.

"Dr. Posner?" He put the name into the police database for physicians. Posner was a psychiatrist. Ben was relieved. "He'll be good for Jim, thanks."

Even if Jim was still struggling, he wasn't avoiding his problems. Ben decided when Jim was ready, he'd share the information he'd amassed on the Almanza sisters. The printouts sat in a big binder, hundreds of words from wounded men, full of caveats, anger, whining: real witness reports. Evidence. Ben loved evidence.

Carmen watched Michael get out of his car and amble to her door. The awkward geek was gone in only a month. He seemed taller—probably because he'd lost fifteen pounds—and more confident: he definitely knew what he wanted. *Her*. She checked herself out in her long mirror. Her dress was tied at strategic spots to keep it on, but otherwise, it was barely there. Her brown skin was glowing. And tonight, her sisters were going to join them, with Yoli's Holden joining their circuit. A threesome.

"Carmen. You're amazing!" He kissed her long and deeply. Just right. "Mmm, let's eat this takeout before it goes bad like last night." He laughed. The pizza had gone cold and hard as a Frisbee when they finally remembered it at six in the morning.

"Yes, let's be strong." Carmen took the bags to the kitchen and laid out the boxes of various Asian dishes with chopsticks. She was hungry.

They talked about her work cataloguing thousands of prints in the Getty archives. It was unusual for one of her men to show an interest in her life outside her bed. She liked that Michael did. They laughed over restaurant horror stories and most embarrassing moments. She asked about his family. He told her about his parents: his father a high-school physics teacher, his mother a social worker. He wanted to bring Carmen over to meet his sister and brother-in-law one day, when she was ready. He asked her about family.

She hesitated. "I suppose it's time I tell you our story." She glanced down, then back into his eyes. Would Michael understand her history, what made her what she was? If only. There was so little of it she could tell. She gave him the sanctioned version.

"Back in Guatemala, my mother, father, me, and my four sisters lived in a thatched-roof hut in a very poor village. Our father was drunk every night, spent all his laborer's pay on drink, so my mother began to take in men along with laundry and other odd jobs during the daytime, so that we girls wouldn't starve.

"One day, when Yolanda, Esme, and I were at the small church-run school in town, one of the paying men saw my two youngest sisters in the back room, playing on our straw mattress. Ana was three, and Yesenia almost five. He raped them both, then told our mother he'd be back for more. He swore he would shoot her if she told anyone. Though she was terrified, she told Yolanda, who was twelve at this time. Yolanda told our drunken father, who did nothing. The next day, when we returned from school, Ana and Yesenia were gone. We found Mother shot, dead. Father made us sleep in the same bed where this horror took place. We huddled together every night quaking in fear the man would return and take us, do to us what he had to Ana and Yesenia. It was during this time we found our fear disappeared when we pleasured each other. It was a nightmare we survived only by relying on each other. Eventually, Father brought us to the United States." Carmen waited. How the man responded told her whether it was safe to go on. Those who found the story sexually exciting made her sick, and she made them leave.

Michael looked horrified and angry at the same time. "Did they ever catch the monster that did this? Were your sisters ever found?"

Carmen shook her head. The sadness of it caught her voice a moment. "No. But there was good that came out of it. Our father got sober and learned to protect us. He found the strength to move us away. He died four years ago. Now the fear stalks us. The monster is still out there. Maybe it's silly to be afraid after so many years, in a different country . . ."

Michael wrapped his arms around her. "Silly? No. Let *me* protect you."

Carmen's mind went blank. She was surprised—a man offering to protect her when he heard her story? The others usually told her she *was* silly to be afraid. *It happened in a foreign country. You're safe now. Let's go to bed.* Michael was different. She had no idea how to react. Her heart opened to him. In a little voice, she said, "Please."

He picked her up off the chair and took her to the bedroom. He just held her, still clothed, rocking her. How she wished her father had chosen to do this with his daughters to help them heal instead of the choices he made that scarred them still. Carmen felt tears brim, then recede. The Almanza sisters didn't cry. Not anymore.

Carmen turned her face to Michael's and began their choreographed dance with a kiss. She sucked his cock to near coming, made him sup at the font of her womb and suckle her nipples and clit until she climaxed, driving him into the dark void that provided the connection with her sisters. Carmen smiled when she closed her eyes and saw the silver-haired man in bed with the two women. He had a wonderful body, big, deeply tanned, and ripped. Yolanda seemed well-pleased by him as Esme was about to have him.

Michael commanded her, moving her roughly, his cock ready

to jam inside her. "I want you on your hands and knees, Carmen. I want to hold your tits while I fuck you from behind." He bent over her ass, then took a nipple between his fingers and thrust into her.

Carmen loved the thickness of his cock filling her, the thrall that came over her as he touched her just right. Moments passed as he got his rhythm, then the effect of her liqueur kicked in. His hands went from her breasts to her shoulders to get the best leverage as he began banging her hard. His head went onto her back at the nape of her neck as the darkness took him over.

As Michael fucked Carmen, the scene that played through her into his mind was exquisite. Yolanda was on her knees, bent over Esme, licking her clit, while Esme, propped up on pillows, was sucking on Holden's prick, a long finger up his anus. Esme quit on him just as he was about to come. She climaxed heartily. Rock hard, Holden pulled Yoli onto the bed beside him and flipped her onto her stomach, maneuvered her into the same position Carmen was in. He pressed himself into Yoli, his hands on her hips as Esme slid under Yoli to suckle her nipples and finger her clit.

Time hovered still as the five of them took each other to sexual exhaustion some twelve miles apart, each seeing the others in the warm haze of their thaumaturgy.

Carmen was awake as Michael slept in the early morning hours before sunrise. The twinge of sadness from the evening before returned. Michael had become much like the others—sleeping seldom if at all, wanting the union two and three times a night, more on the weekends. She was deeply fond of him. She didn't want him to end up a zombie, constantly hungry and desperate for her. Perhaps, because he was different, he'd find a balance, stay with her awhile, with them, and not self-destruct. But the only way that would happen was if she helped. With no idea how to do that, she had to find faith in Michael and a part of herself that magic had not usurped.

* * *

Jim looked much better when Ben saw him sitting at the bar. He was drinking Pellegrino and had the color in his cheeks, not his eyes.

"I almost didn't recognize you! Here's the Jim I remember." They shook hands.

"Feeling much better. Seeing a shrink. Found a support group for dumpees. I'm seeing my son and daughter, trying to mend fences. I even started going on regular dates with women my sister sets me up with. Low expectations all around. She tells them I'm 'Rebound Guy'!" He laughed. "Means I'm attractive to women with fear of commitment or rescuers, but I'm learning boundaries."

Ben patted Jim on the back. "You've got the jargon down pat, buddy. I have to say, I didn't think you'd be this far along in five months. I think you're ready."

"Ready? Ready for what? I'm handling all I can handle!" Jim smoothed his cocktail napkin. His hands still shook a little.

Ben pulled his briefcase up onto the table. He patted it as if it contained the Holy Grail. "Inside this case . . . is your Carmen Almanza."

Jim froze, blinking furiously. "What?" He stared at the black briefcase. "You found her?" He squeaked out a quick, hysterical giggle. "No. No, Benny, I can't. Dr. Posner . . ."

"Hey, I don't know where she is, I'm glad to say." He flicked open the clasps. "But I've got over five hundred pages of notes on her." He explained the blogs, bulletin boards, newsgroups, the professional information gained from his police database.

Jim touched the case tentatively. He spoke in a monotone. "So I am not her first . . . the only one she had an effect on. It's the same with every guy she fucks. And not just her. Her sisters too."

Jim motioned for Ben to open the case. He took the bulk of the notes and set them down on the table. "I don't know if I want to read it, but I want to have it. I'm dumbfounded. I never thought you'd do anything."

Ben grabbed Jim's wrist. "There's more, buddy. Can you take some more crazy shit about these sisters?"

"This isn't crazy enough?" Jim seemed to test a hidden gauge inside a moment, then nodded. "Go on."

"Okay. Let me know when you want me to shut up. It gets pretty weird." Ben took a deep breath and sighed. "I kept coming up with huge discrepancies in time. For instance, I found Internet stuff on her employment going back to 1993, when she was a staff researcher at the Frick in Boston. If she's twenty-six, maybe twenty-seven now, that would have made her thirteen years old at the time. Not likely, eh?"

Jim shook his head. "It's getting weird."

"Yeah. So I decided a month ago I needed a vacation in Guatemala. I went to Antigua, which is a well-preserved colonial city with libraries filled with historical stuff. I met a journalist in a bar who would make a rag like the *Enquirer* proud. With a few bottles of whiskey and an interesting story to investigate, Jorge Domingo was ready to steal whatever information he couldn't get legally.

"In less than a day, he got us into an archive where they house newspapers back over two hundred years! They have computers and shit, but I wanted to go back. Way back. Possibly before they had microfiche. Jorge brought in some of his gofers, and we went through every newspaper that might have the story you told me Carmen told. About her sisters and mother.

"It took five days and a lot of whiskey, but in a little local paper we found articles about the murders."

"Murders. I thought the sisters were kidnapped and only the mother was killed."

"Look, I had to consider that if the timelines were off, Carmen might have lied to you about more than when this story happened. Turns out it's *Twilight Zone* stuff."

Ben moved the stack of information in its binder in front of him and flipped it open to the back. He found copies of the articles and their translations separated by a red acetate sheet. He poked at them with his beefy finger. "You said she was afraid to sleep in the dark . . . something about the guy who killed her mother still out there, maybe looking for her and her sisters. Well, if the perp is still alive, he's too old to hurt anyone."

Jim glanced over to the first translation, then moved the binder so he could read it.

Seguila is a quiet town where the United Fruit Company has improved the rustic living conditions of the poor. Hardworking people with families, like the Almanzas, wouldn't expect trouble, especially from the company that had helped better their conditions. But yesterday, it was learned that their peaceful lives had been shattered by a week-long brutal rampage by itinerant UFC laborers who broke into homes in their somewhat remote area.

The four men, who had been rumored to have dropped in on innocent families for meals and to torment them, found the Almanzas particularly easy to overtake. Hector Almanza and his wife, Manuela, were sought out by locals as gentle healers. Hector is still considered a respected brujo. Their five beautiful daughters were bright, the eldest three in the church school.

Over a three-day period, with Hector tied to a chair, denied food or water and forced to watch, the four men repeatedly raped the girls and their mother. The females were made to cook and bathe the men, cater to their every need, and were whipped and beaten. By the end of their siege, little Ana, age three, and Yesenia, age five, were dead. Then the men, believing their fortune in not being detected would soon end, threatened the remainder of the family with the loss of their lives should they tell of their ordeal. As they went to leave, Manuela Almanza grabbed a knife from one of the laborers. When she attempted to cut him, the knife was fatally turned on her.

The ravaged family was discovered by a nun who had grown concerned when the girls had missed school for two days. "It wasn't like them at all," she told this reporter.

Jim put his hand to his chest as if struck. "Oh, man. This is worse than she said."

Ben patted him on the back. "Take a look at the date on the article."

Jim flipped back to the copy of the original article. August 12, 1921. "Nineteen twenty-one? Hell, this can't be about her, then. Eighty-five years ago? No way. Carmen is twenty-seven now. Her sisters, one a couple of years older, the other a few years younger. No. Not possible, Benny." Jim stared at his friend.

Ben shrugged. "I'm not a guy who believes supernatural bullshit, Jimbo. I go with the evidence, always. But I start with my hunches. And my hunches tell me there's a connection with the father being some kind of witch, and some bad magic here. I don't want to believe you got yourself hooked on having sex with an eighty-six-year-old woman any more than you do. But think about those hallucinations, seeing the other women . . . her sisters? They find some guy just out of a relationship, dumped, lonely. A beautiful, sexy woman comes along and wants *him*. Then they do something to him, slip him a potion, some drug: do a spell. Before he knows it, he's jonesing for it."

Jim closed the notebook and shivered. "Whatever this was, it's over. Thanks, Benny. This'll help." He pushed the binder aside.

"Just be glad you're not their type. And you know their scam. You know, I worry about guys out there right now . . . guys heading where I was. You think there's a way to stop them?"

"I've got some ideas. When I get some time between cases, I'll see about locating them. They're not hiding, changing their names.

Maybe they're lazy." Ben's mind whirred with "next steps." "But hey, you're moving on!" He grinned. "That's what counts."

Their one-year anniversary was six weeks away. Michael dreamed up a private dinner on the roof of Julian's company headquarters. The view took in the ocean, mountains, and glittering city lights. He found it boring staying in every night having sex. He wanted to romance Carmen, to share his world. Reluctant at first, in the last month she'd become open to new things, meeting his sister and brother-in-law, a weekend in Santa Barbara. This would be his first surprise for her. It felt exhilarating.

Since he couldn't get access to the roof for the setup without security clearance, he made an appointment with the head of security. Michael had only been on the top floor to see Julian. He liked the highly polished woods, marble floors, and atrium garden with real plants. The receptionist had the starchy reliability of security department personnel.

"You here for . . . ?" She touched the tightly wound hair at the nape of her neck.

"Holden Alsop. It's Michael McCrary."

Buttons were pushed, ear piece adjusted, hushed words spoken, then Michael was ushered into Alsop's office.

Alsop stood. He looked through Michael more than at him. Michael recognized the guy but couldn't place him. The man looked haggard, wan. They shook hands. Alsop motioned for Michael to sit down. Michael explained why and when he wanted to use the roof.

Alsop's voice came raspy, and he coughed. "Sorry. We don't do roof parties, Mr. McCrary. Private for two or forty-two. Too many security issues." Alsop locked eyes with Michael then. Something sparked there in his deeply set, shadow-ringed eyes. "Have we met before?"

"I practically live on seven, but I work out in the gym on the third floor. You?"

"Used to. Have trouble sleeping lately. No energy. You eat in the cafeteria?"

"No, I go out with my partners to the Promenade. Maybe I met you at one of Julian's parties." Michael remembered that was it, then suddenly realized where else he'd seen Holden Alsop, up close and personal. His blush started under his arms and turned his face bright red.

Alsop raised an eyebrow. "You okay?"

Michael nodded. "Yeah, it was that party a year ago. The one at Julian's new house?" Michael stared out the window. It was also the night Carmen had bewitched him. "So, no roof celebration."

"No, sorry. But good luck with whatever you put together."

Michael stood, started to walk out. One word to Julian and the roof was his, he could bypass Holden Alsop. Why hadn't he considered it before? He'd never have to see Alsop again. At least willingly. "Hey, I'm going to go through Julian on this, just to give you a heads-up."

Alsop stood. "Knock yourself out." Then he frowned, concentrating, staring at Michael. He looked away, sighed. "I remember now."

Ben, in his Hawaiian shirt over what he called his Midwestern tan, a shade of white mushroom, sat at a table practically on the beach. His old friend from the police academy was late meeting him for lunch. Not that he minded. LA was pleasantly different from Minneapolis, with its ocean, fantastic weather, and beautiful women every two feet. He liked it a lot better.

He thought he saw his pal shuffling through the crowd but doubted it. This guy looked eighty years old. Then the man waved. Ben's warning bells clanged. He'd seen that worn-to-the-bone look before. It was Jim all over again.

"Hey, Benny, looking like a man on a vacation."

"Hey, my oldest friend calls and says he needs me, I'm here.

It doesn't hurt that you got a beach in your backyard." Ben bear-hugged his friend, so thin now. "Still with the permanent tan, hey, Holden? I guess being out here in paradise, you can have one of them."

Holden Alsop fell into his chair. "Yeah, Benny. You can have just about anything out here. Sometimes too much of it."

Ben motioned for the waiter to come over. His mineral water with lime was warm, and his friend really needed something stronger. "What are you still drinking, man . . . wait, scotch?" Holden waved him off, shaking his head. "Okay, another one of these for both of us."

They sat in silence awhile, watching the waves roll in. Ben waited for the story to come. He guessed Holden was considering how anyone, even his oldest friend, could believe what he was about to tell him. Impossible.

But Ben would tell him how he could believe it, about Jim and all the others he found in his research. He'd tell him about his plan—that he found the sisters and now had photographs of them. How he hired guys to put up a website that linked to dating sites warning men online. About the informal blue line of friendships that ran through every police station in the nation, where there now were flyers with the sisters' faces on them, and thousands of officers and detectives talking to each other, warning men in bars, doing socials, and using dating services. He'd let Holden know that wherever these women went, the word was getting out, and while he couldn't warn every man, a wave of caution was building. And he'd ask his friend to help make sure no one else would fall prey to the sisters. He hoped Holden Alsop would be strong enough to do the right thing.

Alsop downed his drink and cleared his throat. Then the story flooded out, like long-simmering bile. Julian's party. Yolanda. Mind-blowing sex. Losing sleep, seeing things. The sisters. Michael.

* * *

Carmen paced behind her front door. Michael was due an hour ago. It was their first anniversary. A big surprise, he'd said. He was never late. Her phone rang. Michael!

She purred into the phone. "Hello, darling, what's keeping you?"

"It's me, Yoli. I know we're not connecting tonight, but I'm still getting strong feelings from you. Something's wrong."

"Yoli, he's late. I don't think he's coming."

"I know you're anxious, but when has a man of ours let us down once we have him? Something happened. A flat tire. Work. He'll call soon. Relax. Have some of that wine you're chilling for him."

"Yes, you're right. I'll call you later."

Carmen sat down and opened the wine. She was *scared*. For the first time, she thought she might trust a man enough to love him. For months she felt twinges of shame that her sisters and their men watched her and Michael making love. She hated that she was losing control. It was nearly a foreign sensation, except when she remembered those horrific days when she was nine years old. It took her father's witchcraft, his spells and years of teaching the sisters the ways of enchantment to protect themselves, to regain a semblance of control. Sitting, hugging herself on her couch, she felt herself hurtling back so many decades, stifling a whimper.

She forced herself to think of her sisters, her allies. The bargain they had made as children was mutual. All these years, men were nothing more than the vehicle for the union that brought them pleasure and protected them. Now they were learning not every man was a crazed UFC laborer, the beast, the enemy. Their father had done everything in his power, and that of the dark arts, to keep them from harm, but in doing so, he'd kept them from something precious and good. With their father gone, perhaps it was possible for them to find a man worthy of love. Did her sisters suspect that Carmen was considering it now?

She finished the first glass and gave in, called him. Voice mail.

She couldn't leave a message. And say what? "I'm sitting here desperately waiting for you, my love, to come complete me?"

Three hours later, panic set in. Her sisters arrived, consoled her, and worried a little too. This could mean starting over again. They liked the climate. They wouldn't have to go far. And Carmen would get over Michael. He was, after all, just a man.

San Diego sparkled just as Santa Monica had. Yolanda took a position as a private nurse for a little girl with a genetic disorder. Esme took over as an office manager for a real-estate conglomerate, which helped find the sisters a house and two condos. Carmen decided she needed something that would take her out of herself and went into sales in Mayan and Aztec antiquities for a gallery in La Jolla. They began to rebuild.

Four months passed, and it was time to search for new men. Esme learned of two new kinds of dating services: The 3-minute Date Night and The Rotating Lunch, where an equal number of men and women were in a situation that allowed them to meet many prospects in a short amount of time. Esme set the sisters up in all she could find.

Carmen was the first to notice something "off," as she put it. One evening, Carmen did The 3-minute Date Night at an Italian restaurant called Trastevere. The participants were kept in separate sections; women got nametags and instructions from an overweight psychologist named Tracy, and the men received theirs from a gangly Mensa geek named Max. The women sat at eighteen small tables, the men lined up ready, and a timer bell indicated they were to move from woman to woman through the circuit, with only three minutes to chat up each one.

It was clear to Carmen that she was the most beautiful and sensual woman in the room. The women were in their late thirties, some older, most with weight issues, bad hair, and fashion challenges. For tonight, she was certainly "the light on the porch." The men, except for two, appeared more matched to the other women.

When Terry sat down, Carmen grinned widely. His tag said he was thirty-two, originally from New York, and an attorney. He was handsome and well-dressed. She wondered why he'd submit himself to The 3-minute Date Night.

His accent was deep Brooklyn. "So, gorgeous, it's obvious we're the only two lookers here, so let's just cut the chit-chat and exchange numbers." He pushed one of his business cards across the table. "I can picture us horizontal already!"

She shook inside. Her Creep-Meter was off the charts.

Later, Phillip sat down. He seemed exhausted by the experience. He looked at Carmen as if he were trying to remember where he'd seen her before.

"I feel like I've met you before. Maybe you've done the circuit dinners in Mission Bay?"

He was nice looking, reminded Carmen a bit of Michael. She shooed his memory away. "This is my first foray into the dating-service world."

"You look familiar. Maybe because you've got a Jennifer Lopez thing going."

Carmen smiled. She actually knew who she was. Saw her photograph in a magazine at her hairdressers' in Minneapolis. "Thank you, I think. So you're a claims adjuster for a car insurance company . . ."

"Boring . . . Tell me about the gallery. We only have two minutes!"

As Carmen spoke, Phillip's face went from exaggerated interest, to a frown, then his eyes slid away from her. When she tried to get him to tell her about his family, he mumbled and looked at his watch. The bell sounded, and everyone was instructed to get up and hand their list of "interested" participants in to Tracy and Max, then mingle over drinks.

At the bar, Carmen waited for the usual flurry of men, but the only interest she garnered was from a woman who wanted to know if her eyes were really that color or she wore contact lenses.

Later, sitting in Esme's living room, the sisters lamented their bad luck. They all experienced a sense that men looked at them as if they knew them, or that their initial interest seemed to wane rather quickly. The men hesitated, made excuses. Those that showed an avid interest weren't the kind of men the sisters wanted. Yolanda mentioned she thought that some of the same men seemed to show up everyplace they went, not just at mixers or parties or dating-service get-togethers. These men were watching, smiling sometimes, but never approaching. Once in a while, they spoke with the lonely men around them, their eyes jittering over the sisters and then away.

Then Esme found David at a seminar. He wasn't attractive, but he was fit and eager. His last girlfriend had been when he was in college, and he graduated ten years ago.

"I can't believe my luck. The prettiest woman in the room approached me! So, what made you seek me out?"

Esme considered his question. The desperation that had begun to plague them changed everything: eroded her confidence, expanded her range of choices into unfamiliar areas. David had attracted her because of his guilelessness. Had that been a factor before? What did it mean that a man was "ripe"? She couldn't be sure anymore.

"You have an innocent quality. Not jaded."

He laughed a nice, clear laugh. "You mean my lack of experience shows. I'll take that as something, if not a compliment. How about a drink, and we can talk. I'm looking for intelligence in a woman, and conversation tells me everything." He winked, or perhaps his nervousness made him blink erratically.

Two hours later, they were getting their coats and going back to Esme's. She asked him to wait while she went to the ladies' room. She called Yolanda from her cell phone.

"I think I've found someone. He's not our usual . . ."

"Still, I am glad. If tonight goes well, we'll join you tomorrow night."

"Yes." The thought gave her a thrill.

"Oh, by the way, did you see any of the creeps that have been following us?"

She had. One. But he hadn't approached David. Yet. "I have to go, Yoli. I left him alone!"

The hulking man with a crew cut and bad-fitting suit moved away from David as Esme approached. She stifled her anger, banished the fear from her face. Watching David, she searched for the doubt that had crossed the faces of the others in months past each time a disturbing man had spoken to them. David's eyes went to her, the carpet, back to the retreating man, then to her.

She smiled at him then, hopeful, though she sensed the light on the porch was flickering, and the moths were going elsewhere.

He held out his arm for her, returning her smile. Grateful for any moth at all, Esme grabbed his arm to take him home.

The Mile-High Club

Trevor Anderson

She caught him looking at her as they boarded the Air Express 3:45 PM flight to Las Vegas. He was not exactly handsome, but there was something in his rough features that appealed to her. He was looking at her, so why shouldn't she look at him?

He was about six feet, steel-gray eyes, longish hair, good build, leather jacket, black T-shirt, snakeskin boots tucked under jeans. A very noticeable bulge in his pants.

She felt a familiar little tickle in her groin. She smiled just a bit and scratched her thigh, raising her already-high miniskirt another several inches so "Boots" could really get a look at her long, tanned legs. Let him stare all he wanted. She was well aware that her legs were one of her best features, though not the only one.

Actually, she had been blessed with beauty from head to toe. She'd used that gift her whole life to get what she wanted, first from the boys she'd played with, and now from the men she toyed with.

As she entered the plane, she made sure she brushed against the guy's shoulder so he could get a whiff of her perfume. He could also get a better view of her breasts through the flimsy T-shirt she was wearing, which barely covered the top half of her stomach, leaving her pierced navel showing.

She noted that, to alleviate the summer heat outside, the plane's air-conditioning was running at full blast, which was sure to make her nipples hard in a few more seconds. That would enhance her appearance even more, as she was often complimented by her bedmates on her "gumdrops," as she called them. Guys liked pulling and sucking on them. She figured it was because they were weaned too early from their moms' tits. Men were all such babies. She figured they got what they deserved.

She saw "Boots" putting an overnight bag into the overhead bin and slipped hers next to his. He sat down by a window, and she immediately sat next to him. Air Express was a commuter airline, and there were no assigned seats. Perfect for her. And for him.

"Do you mind?" she asked as she arranged her short skirt to his best advantage.

His laugh was more of a grunt. "Not at all," he said. She offered a well-manicured hand. "Tawny."

She noticed the strength of his grip and the scratch marks on his hand. Either he had cats or a tough gig, though he didn't look like a day laborer. "Eric," he answered, holding on to her hand for a bit longer than necessary before releasing it.

The warmth of his handshake activated her tickle response again. She crossed her legs and let him catch a glimpse of her purple panties, then smoothed her skirt. She looked him straight in those steel-gray eyes and smiled, almost daring him to respond. His lips parted in a slight grin, showing uneven but white teeth.

This guy was something different for her. Obviously interested and yet, for some reason, not responding to her usual signs. He wasn't wearing a ring, but then not all married guys did these days.

A bit flustered, she asked, "You get to Vegas often?"

He shrugged. "When I get the urge."

Now she was back on more solid footing. "The urge for what, Eric?"

"Depends," he said, staring more directly at her flawless legs. She felt his stare as if he were Superman and his X-ray vision was penetrating to her bones. Damn, she was making herself horny. But then, that was par for the course for her.

The plane started taxiing back from the gate, a full flight of Vegas tourists en route to play out their dreams and schemes.

His eyes rose to meet hers. "Sometimes I gamble," he said.

"Are you a high roller?" she asked.

He considered for a moment. "I've been known to drop a bit of cash—for the right reasons."

Excellent, she thought. "So you're not afraid to pay money to have some fun, huh?" She eyed him for his reaction.

"Depends on the circumstances," he said cryptically.

Then, as the plane started to increase its speed for takeoff, she grabbed his arm. "I'm kind of scared of flying," she explained. "Hope you don't mind."

He regarded her with a bemused expression and said, "Go for it."

She squeezed his rock-hard bicep. "Mmmm," she purred. "You must work out."

"Oh, I do all sorts of exercise—on the job and off."

The plane shot into the sky, and she gave his arm an extra squeeze for effect.

"What do you do, Eric?"

He hesitated. "A little of this and a little of that."

"Ooo . . . mysterious," she cooed. "I'll bet you're in the FBI and can't admit it."

"Hardly."

"A cop?"

"Hell, no. Let's just say people hire me to do certain things for them."

She allowed her hand to rub his leather-jacketed arm a bit, up and down and up and down, before releasing her grip. Was she being obvious enough?

"Really? What a coincidence . . ." She let the sentence trail for effect, but he didn't go for the obvious follow-up. In fact, he started to reach for the airline magazine in the seatback in front of him.

Tawny grimaced. He was one tough customer. She decided to try a more direct approach. After all, there was little time to waste.

"There is one thing I love about flying," she admitted. He cocked a groomed eyebrow as he placed the magazine on his lap. She smiled—she had his attention again.

"The Mile-High Club," she purred and paused for effect. He did that odd but sexy thing with his lips again, something between a smirk and a smile.

She leaned toward him until her nipples, through the thin fabric of her T-shirt, brushed his leather jacket. "Are you a member, Eric?" she whispered.

Now he did smile. "Can't say I have had the pleasure."

She put her hand on his. "Listen, the flight to Vegas takes forty-eight minutes. That means we have about thirty-five minutes before they start the descent . . ."

"Sounds like you're an old pro at this."

"You might say that," she said.

"Well . . ."

Was he waffling? "Hey, I'm sorry. I thought you liked me."

"Oh, listen, I like you all right. I just . . ."

She took his hand and placed it on her bare thigh. "Can you feel how hot I am right now?" She slid his hand up under her short skirt and into her underwear. "And how wet?" She looked around, but the people on the other side of the aisle were looking out their window. And anyway, it was none of their business. If they wanted some, they could stand in line.

She maneuvered his fingers until one was settled on her clit and another was about three inches inside her.

"I guess so," he laughed as he slowly pulled out. His finger, they both noted, was glistening. He licked it and grinned, "Just like candy."

"There's more where that came from," she cooed as she placed a hand over his pants where the bulge had gotten noticeably larger. She gave it a squeeze. "Feels like you're ready."

"Oh, I'm ready all right."

"And I have condoms with me," she offered. "So we'll be safe."

"Safe?" Again with the bemused smile. She liked it but found it disconcerting as well. Strange guy, but now she was totally turned on and ready to go. And so, she hoped, was he.

She said, "You buy, we fly."

"What?"

She made a face. "You gonna make me spell it out for you? Most guys get it pretty quick when I start squeezing their . . . arms."

"You're a call girl?"

Tawny twitched. "Keep your voice down! Shit!"

"Sorry!" He spread his hands out in mock apology. He seemed to be enjoying making her feel uncomfortable.

"Anyway," she continued, "twice a month I fly to Vegas because I can make more money there in a weekend than I can in LA in a month. Actually, I'm planning to look at some Vegas real estate this weekend. LA's a shithole, you know?"

"It has its charms."

She looked at her watch. It was time to cut to the chase. "Listen, if you want me, you'd better pay me, because this plane's landing soon."

"Well, you drive a hard bargain," he said, grinning. "I don't like to pay for pleasure . . . not that kind of pleasure, anyway. . . ."

"Oh, I'm worth it."

"How much?"

She considered. "Depends on what you want. Standard fuck starts at five hundred dollars. You want the whole shot, a grand."

He whistled. "Man . . . you must be some hot shit."

"Try me."

"You come with a money-back guarantee?"

"No one's complained yet."

They remained silent for a bit after that, as she watched him consider her offer. She hoped he'd agree—she was hot for this guy, and his cash. Fucking him had become a mission for her.

She watched as he finally reached inside his leather jacket, retrieved his wallet, and pulled out ten hundred-dollar bills.

"I knew you had money the minute I saw you," she said, a happy lilt in her voice.

He handed the cash to her. "Keep these someplace safe," he said.

"Oh, don't worry, I never lose a nickel. Or a customer." She slipped the bills into a small pocket in her miniskirt. "Trust me, you'll be back on this flight in two weeks."

"We'll see."

She stood up, taking his hand. "So—you ready to 'join the club'?"

He nodded. "I'm betting your scenery beats that scenery," he said as he glanced at the Sierra Nevada mountain range some 25,000 feet below them.

She motioned him to follow her to the back of the plane. When they got to the restroom, she looked around to see if anyone was watching. The coast was clear. The attendants were busy passing out soft drinks and peanuts to greedy hands.

They both slipped inside the tight restroom space, and she locked the door behind them.

He asked, "What if someone has to go . . . ?"

"There are three restrooms on this plane. No one will bother us. If they do, I'll groan and make like I'm throwing up."

"Lovely image," he said, and they both laughed. "So now what? There's not a whole lot of room in here. . . ."

"We don't need much room for this," she said as she unzipped him with one hand and simultaneously slipped her purple panties down her legs with the other. Then she sat on the closed toilet lid and took him into her mouth, lubricating him with her tongue and then downing his entire shaft in one long, fluid gulp. She was pleased to hear him actually gasp. She slid him in and out of her mouth while he stood, hands against the wall of the tiny room, and they both watched her stellar performance in the mirror. This was one of her specialties.

She let him pull out of her mouth and smiled when he noticed that she had somehow slipped a condom on his penis while giving him head. She motioned for him to sit where she was. He sat down, and she straddled him.

"Feel that?" she asked breathlessly.

"You're so wet I could use an umbrella down there."

"No, I mean the way the plane's engines are vibrating. Adds to the thrill of the ride, doesn't it? Gawd, I love this feeling," she enthused as she rode him, back and forth and up and down, arms around his neck, smelling his fresh-washed hair, feeling his nails dig into her back.

Suddenly she stood up and faced away from him, hands on the restroom's door. "Now you get to be the pilot," she cooed, and she felt him enter her from behind.

He laughed in obvious pleasure as he hammered into her. After a minute, someone knocked at the door, and Tawny yelled, "I'm sick in here, use another restroom," and faked a barf. That made them both laugh as he continued to pound into her soft flesh.

A few ecstatic minutes later she asked, "You ready to cum?" as she backed away and he slid out of her.

He nodded. She took off the condom and placed her face in front of his massive member, then grabbed it and jerked it hard until he splashed her face with his semen.

Then he was finished and drying himself off and handing her paper towels to wipe off her face.

"Satisfied?" she asked. Now she was smirking.

"One hundred percent," he said, and she was pleased to hear none of the cockiness in his voice that she'd noted before.

She'd tamed another one. Men were all alike, once you licked their dicks.

Another knock came at the door. "Are you okay in there?" This time the voice sounded more official; obviously an attendant.

"I'm sick, but I'll be out in a minute," Tawny yelled as she continued to dress.

She let him slip out first and slapped his butt as he went past her. She peeked through the door, and the coast was clear, so she exited the restroom as she continued to adjust her skirt. She felt great, as she always did after her mile-high adventures.

When she sat back down, she was pleased to see that Eric's face was flushed.

"Feeling better?" she asked as she patted his crotch.

"Sure. So—how much do I get back?"

"What do you mean?"

"You know—from the grand."

"Are you kidding? I just gave you the premium pussy prize."

"*That* was a thousand-dollar fuck?" He laughed ruefully. "I don't think so."

"No? Okay, let's see," she said and raised her closed fist. "First I let you finger me at the seat. That was fun, huh? Really got the juices flowing, didn't it?" She raised one finger.

"Then I gave you the best blow job of your life. Deep throat costs extra, of course." Two fingers.

"Then the straight fuck, and then I let you do doggie-style. Arf arf!" Three fingers.

"And then, of course, the happy ending—right on the smacker, remember?" She touched her cheek. "Adds five hundred dollars right there." Four fingers.

She looked at her hand as if it were a calculator. "Any way you look at it, you just got a thousand-dollar Mile-High-Club experience."

His laugh was darkly menacing. "I don't think so. In fact, I think you just fucked me for free." He raised his closed fist and offered her his third finger.

"Listen, asshole," she said, aware of trying to keep her voice down, "I am being met at baggage claim by my six-foot-seven boyfriend, who's a bouncer at one of the clubs on the Strip. One word from me, and you're in an emergency room."

An attendant alerted the passengers that the plane had started its descent into Las Vegas.

"You don't say?" Eric responded, the bemused look back on his face. He looked around at the surrounding seats. People were sleeping or staring out the windows, watching the ground reach up to meet the plane. "Better buckle up—we're landing, and I wouldn't want you to get hurt. . . ."

As he finished the sentence, he punched the side of her head. It whipped back, and her eyes slipped to the top of her sockets. She was unconscious for the landing.

After the plane taxied to its gate and people were starting to get off the flight, a flight attendant noticed Tawny, now groaning and barely conscious. "Sir, is your . . . friend all right?"

"Oh, sure, you know how it is—she started partying at a bar at LAX and was sick all the way out here."

"Oh, so she was the one in the restroom," the attendant noted. "Should we call a wheelchair?"

Eric shook his head. "She'll be fine. The fresh air will revive her. Right, honey?"

Tawny gave a garbled response, and Eric shook his head. "How many times have we had this discussion? That's the last time I let you drink before getting on a plane."

The flight attendant clucked his tongue and moved on. Eric got Tawny to her feet, one hundred pounds of near-deadweight. He picked up both of their overnight bags with his free hand and half walked, half carried the still-stunned woman off the plane.

When they hit the loud, colorful gate area, with its endless rows of slot machines, waitresses, and thousands of noisy tourists, it was easy to cuff her again without anyone noticing, so that she was barely conscious as he guided her out of the airport.

As they walked, he chatted to her. "So where's that bodyguard boyfriend of yours, huh?" He gut-punched her to keep her from resisting or responding. "Oh, that was just another one of your lies, right? Gee, what a surprise."

They crossed the busy street in front of the terminal and headed toward the parking garage. "I'm here often enough," he explained, "to keep a car parked in long-term parking. It's a Lexus. You like Lexuses, 'Tawny'? I hope so, because we're gonna take a nice long drive in one." They got to the black Lexus, and he looked around. No one was within eyesight. He cuffed her chin, and she slumped in his arms. He retrieved some rope from the car's spacious trunk, trussed her, shoved her into the trunk, and slammed the lid.

He turned the AC on full blast as he paid the parking attendant and pulled into traffic headed out of the airport.

He yelled, "I know it's warm back there, especially this time of year. Sorry about that. But I've got the AC on—can you feel it back there? I kinda doubt it. But I'll bet if you were up here, those cute nipples of yours would be hard as rocks." He heard muffled screams in response, and he laughed.

Within an hour he was well north of Las Vegas and in a deeply forested area of Mt. Charleston. He parked the car at a vacant trailhead and popped the trunk lid. Tawny was dazed and gasping for air, her clothing drenched in sweat. He pulled her out of the trunk, and she slid to her knees.

". . . . bastard," she gulped as he pulled her to her feet. There was not a soul in sight. He tore a T-shirt and tied it around her mouth to keep her from screaming and then pulled a shovel out of the backseat of the car.

"Most folks don't think of woods when they think of Vegas," Eric noted conversationally as he pushed her ahead of him. "I like it up here. Real peaceful. Cooler too—at least thirty degrees cooler than Vegas is this time of year. I come here often . . . for pleasure and business.

"I like making my own trails," he continued as he led her off the well-marked path and deeper into the woods. Aside from chirping birds and the buzzing of flying insects, there were no sounds of life other than their crunching footsteps on the dirt and leaves. Finally he stopped moving.

"Well, this is it." He looked around. "Nice place, huh?" He kicked at her legs, and she fell to her knees in front of him.

He regarded her struggles and whimpers and offered his sweetest smile. "That's quite the scam you had going there, 'Tawny.' By the way, I doubt your real name is Tawny, is it? Well, no matter. Of course I knew you were a pro the second you brushed your tits against me. You're as obvious as a neon sign in a desert.

"But hell, I like a good fuck as much as the next guy, maybe more. And if you didn't ask for money, you wouldn't be here right now. You really shouldn't have pushed me on that." He shook his head slowly. "Not a good idea at all."

She made more noises, and he kicked her in the stomach. She started crying as he continued talking. "You think you were the only pro on that plane, 'Tawny'? I told you people hire me to do certain things for them. Specifically, I guess you'd call me a hit man. And just your luck, I'd been hired to take out some little punk here in Vegas who owes the wrong guys way too much money.

"He's gonna end up here too," Eric noted. "As others have, over the years. It's kind of a favorite place to me."

He looked around, taking a deep breath of the fresh air. "Say, weren't you looking for some prime Vegas real estate? Well, here you go—how does six feet long, two feet wide, and four feet deep suit you? A nice view of some trees. Good breeze."

Before she could answer, he raised the shovel high above his head and brought it down forcefully on hers. The crunching sound echoed between the trees as she flopped a few times, then was still.

He went to his knees and retrieved his money from her miniskirt pocket.

As Eric started digging, he kept up his conversation. "I do have to thank you, though, for initiating me in to the Mile-High Club. Very entertaining."

He worked silently for several minutes, building up a sweat despite the cool mountain air. "Just getting my exercise," he muttered. "Gotta keep these biceps in shape, eh, 'Tawny'?"

Finally he stopped digging and dumped her body into the shallow grave. He covered the corpse in dirt and then camouflaged the gravesite with the many nearby leaves and branches.

Eric breathed in the fresh Nevada air. He stared down at the gravesite, now invisible to any eyes but his, and addressed it. "Allow let me return the favor, 'Tawny.' I've heard this is the highest point in Southern Nevada . . . over ten thousand feet, I think."

He spread his arms wide, addressing the gravesite and the surrounding forest. "Welcome to *my* Mile-High Club."

Care and Feeding

Christina Crooks

My hand trembled as it swished the cup of lukewarm bathroom tap water. A handful of floating sea-egg blue sleep gels slowly dissolved and sank. Another handful of chalky Vicodins dissolved even faster. I eyed the small bottle of Maximum Strength Drano on the bathroom counter. There was a reason I was doing this, and doing it this way.

I drained the cup of water. The dregs tasted bitter. I stared into the cup. I told myself I shouldn't feel regret.

"Valeria? Are you well?"

His voice, sex on velvet. He sounded concerned. I hyperventilated, pulled myself together. Then replied, "Yeah, babe. Just give me a few minutes." A few more minutes would be all it would take. I felt the concentrated brew hitting my bloodstream, leaching away pain.

How would he react?

Would he react at all?

My vision got kind of blurry for a moment. Of course he would. And that made it all worthwhile.

I steeled myself.

Then I grabbed the bottle of Drano and poured the caustic contents down my throat.

* * *

Two months earlier. Consider: Twenty-three years old, plump, a suicidal blood-fetishist and blow-job queen. Me. Not much to look at. But I had a good heart, I liked it kinky, and I could suck the brass off a doorknob. It was my strong neck muscles and sturdy gag reflex.

It'd have to be sturdy after all the times the emergency room rammed a tube down my esophagus to vacuum my stomach. Otherwise known as gastric lavage. Those nurses and doctors had long since stopped hiding their contempt. Last time this surly resident shouted "Valerie, you have a cast-iron stomach" and then muttered about how I should try a gun next time. He had a point. I guess I just liked the attention. He got my name wrong though. It's Valeria.

I was one night-clubbing goth girl among many looking for vampire love. I had cleavage corseted out to there, jiggling my way across Belfry's dance floor, swinging my bracelet of well-oiled razor blades and licking my bloody red lips. I didn't believe in false advertising.

I was starting to think my elusive soul mate did, though. Lovelier specimens than myself draped themselves over wrought-iron railings, posed on zebra-striped divans, leaned against Grecian columns, posturing and exuding sex and distracting any halfway decent guys from noticing me. Did I mention that I was a little overweight? It made a difference.

Then Adrien happened.

"I like to play with sharp objects." I felt fingers roughly fondling my blades.

I turned toward the deep voice, mostly worried some poser was damaging himself. And promptly forgot how to breathe. Tall, dark, delicious.

As if his hypnotic eyes and chiseled bone structure weren't enough, he immediately traced his warm, wet fingertips over my lips. I tasted the slits where he'd cut himself.

I think I came.

It got better at my place. Surrounded by gothic crosses and vampire art, I felt even more eager. Once niceties like names and clothes were out of the way, he teased and pinched and spread me as if he had a hundred years and then proceeded to give me the most supernatural fucking of my life. His cock, a weirdly tapered grayish thing, had to be the size of an elephant's trunk, with the same flexibility. But I'm an accepting sort, and it paid off. I showed off my famous oral skills and heard him give these little grunts of surprise and pleasure. And then later, I swear I felt part of the thing caressing my G-spot even as the monstrosity seemed to split me in half, driving so hard and deep I saw stars and passed out.

Needless to say, I was at Belfry's right at opening time the next night.

Banzai was a lesbian drug dealer, but not at all butch. She lurked just inside. After exchanging hugs, the first thing I asked her was about my amazing find.

"Adrien? Handsome creature of night? Sure, I've seen him around. At every goth, industrial, and fetish club in Los Angeles. A real love 'em and leave 'em type." Banzai's usually cynical twist of a mouth formed itself into a frown.

"Heard something else?" I wanted to know everything about Adrien. All we'd had so far was vanilla sex, and already I felt hooked on him. I tried not to tip my hand just how truly into this mysterious stranger I was, but from the keen look she shot me, I didn't think I succeeded.

"He's got quite a reputation. A friend of mine from the Dungeon—Selene—hooked up with him. They lived together for a few months. She had it bad. By the time he moved on, she was an anorexic wreck. Claimed he was a real vampire. Ended up in a psyche ward."

I shifted impatiently, scanning the incomings. I'd seen Selene at the Dungeon, talked with her a few times. Plump girl like me. Could stand to have lost a few pounds, also like me. So she couldn't keep her man and got herself a broken heart? I felt bad, actually. But what was I supposed to do? It's not like I was in a position to help her. I smiled about Adrien's ex calling him a vampire. He hadn't bitten me. Had he? I fingered my neck. No wounds. I smiled sheepishly when I caught Banzai's smirk.

She rolled her eyes. "Aren't I glad I like girls."

I saw Adrien. "Gotta go."

She grabbed my arm as I turned, her long fingernails sinking into the flesh above my blade bracelet. "Be careful. That one gets around. He really lays waste."

"Vampires will be vampires," I told her, keeping a straight face. What did I care if he had a disease, AIDS even? Suicidal, remember? But I patted her hand and then spontaneously squeezed it. "Thanks."

And then Adrien was there, eating me up with his eyes, and I know I was gobbling him too, and we went back to my place to have at it.

We talked, and screwed, and talked some more. I went down on him and got him to make those pleasure-grunts again. And he made me feel very much out of the world. At one point, after the third time but before the fourth, I kissed his fingertips, grateful. That's when I noticed.

The razor-blade wounds I'd given him? They'd vanished.

He noticed my noticing. "I heal quickly."

"Vampires do." I grabbed the nearest cross and pressed it against his chest. I made sizzling sounds.

I was close enough to hear the way his breathing stopped for a second. His voice was much chillier when he spoke again, gathering his clothes. "I should get going."

I reached for him, bereft already. "What's the big deal? Vampires are cool."

"No!" I recoiled from his emphatic denial. "No, they're not. They're the most miserable of leeches."

I wasn't sure how to respond. "Do you want to bite my neck?" I offered in a small voice. He looked so sexy standing there.

Adrien shook his head, but he smiled. "I like blood play. But really, I do have to go."

"Sunrise, huh?"

"Work. And, I probably should have told you this before, but . . . I have a girlfriend. But I'm planning on breaking up with her," he added. "Just as soon as she's stable and out of danger. You know."

I did. My heart felt like it was plunging all the way down to hell. Which was stupid, so stupid. So weak. So very like me. But what I said was, "I understand. Maybe I'll see you around."

"Count on it," he said. I could have given him the script.

I kept the smile on my face until the front door closed.

Then I swallowed all my Elavils. I called 911 at the last moment, when the seizures started scaring me. I'm so weak. How could I be so stupid, I kept thinking. To fall for someone like Adrien. I knew he was too good to be true.

Most of all, I just wanted to see him again. It was my stupid heart's fault, fixating on a guy like that. Caring too much. I think I got a defective one. Heart, I mean.

Three days later, when the psychiatric hospital let me come home, I found that my favorite corset fit much looser around my waist. Had to be the heartbreak-and-stress diet. Weight loss was the one purely good thing to come of the recent festivities, I told myself.

Of course, I went back to the Belfry.

I had to have him. I felt addicted.

I found him swapping spit with some girl and dragged him back to my place and all but raped him. He didn't seem to mind. In a weirdly romantic way, it seemed as if he'd expected it.

He moved in.

His strange, long, elephant-trunk-flexible penis rocked my world, and my oral talents rocked his. He was as addicted to my blow jobs as I was to his cock. When I sucked it, I swear I could feel it all the way down into my stomach. I enjoyed those little sounds he made. We hardly ever even exchanged blood.

The issue of vampirism didn't come up for months.

I kept losing weight, though. I ate all the time but kept shedding pounds. All that vigorous sex, I thought. Adrien liked my hearty appetite, my stamina, my deep throat. He liked everything about me, he said.

I sure liked him. I was even contemplating the other "L" word.

Then one night I passed out while blowing him.

I revived right away, but he was pulling out and backing up and tucking it away into his underwear. Then pants. And then putting on his silky black shirt and leather jacket.

"You're going out?" My voice sounded sluggish and confused. Hell, I was confused. Men don't leave blow-job queens. Did they?

"I'm going out."

"Don't go."

"I have to." He jingled his keys, one of which fit into my apartment's lock. "I don't want to hurt you. I'll explain when I get back."

I cried for a while. Then I shut up. I'm a self-sufficient girl, I thought. I'd get by. When I went into the bathroom, the mirror reflected a blotchy face and swollen eyes. It also showed my newfound planes and angles. My lips looked like lush, ripe fruit in the middle of all that lovely bone structure.

I'll be a pretty corpse, I thought as I gobbled a bottle of aspirin.

Three days, one deliberately clumsy stomach-pumping, and a couple of exasperated psychiatric professionals later, Adrien sat me down. "We need to talk."

I'd just finished a huge dinner, trying to make up for the nasty hospital food I'd been subjected to.

"About your other girlfriends?"

"Yes."

I did a double take. He'd just admitted it. How could he just admit it? Didn't he care I was suicidal? Maybe he wanted me to die.

I guess I was feeling a little bit of shock, because he shook me slightly. "Valeria. Are you okay?"

I started laughing. "Peachy. Now give me my key and get out."

He looked at me with admiration. I'm sure that was it. He heaved a big sigh and held up both palms: wait. Then he did a strange thing. He started unzipping his fly.

"Whoa, buddy, I don't do good-bye gobbles."

"I'm not saying good-bye."

"I'm the one who's saying good-bye!"

"No, you're not. You want me. They always want me. Hundreds of years, and nothing changes but the names. I think it's something in the semen. It's truly a shame they get so skinny, so quickly. Even the overweight ones usually die."

"You aren't making sense." I felt cold.

"I'm talking about being a vampire. The most miserable of leeches."

He didn't seem all that miserable to me. I tried not to look at what he pulled out of his pants. "The cross . . . the blood. You're a vampire like I'm a werewolf. Exactly why do you feel the need to fuck with me?"

He sighed. "You're not going to believe me unless I show you. Suck my dick."

"Fuck yourself."

He grinned coldly at me, adult to child. In that moment he seemed every bit a vampire. Or some kind of predator, anyway. I wished it didn't add so much to his appeal. "Okay, Valeria. Watch and learn." His cock, which had always been strange looking, suddenly got a whole lot stranger. It writhed, like a grayish cobra dancing, and folded over on itself and then rose stiff and straight toward me, straining . . . and then the head, with its G-spot–rubbing, wide-load helmet, shifted, and a new head pushed through it like a baby crowning and extended, tubelike.

I froze.

It extended. And extended. I shut my mouth with a snap when it nudged against my lips. I couldn't tear my eyes away from its ruby red tip. It was a small, pursed mouth. The mouth puckered up. Kissed.

I realized I was shaking my head in denial when his hands cupped my jaw. His cock was back to Adrien-normal now. Even in the middle of my hysteria, I remember looking at the way it lay there so thick against his leg, ready to spring to action and pleasure me the way only Adrien could.

I felt my nonexistent gag reflex trying to come back to life. I felt like I might blow chunks all over that alien cock. I'd had that thing in my *mouth*.

My retching sounds had the most galvanizing effect on him. He sprang forward, slapping me across the face. "No! Don't waste it!"

"Waste it." I rubbed my cheek. He was going to pay for that. "Explain."

"Vomit contains enzymes and acids that I need. Puke's the price I have to pay for immortality." Adrien laughed, bitter. "Anything else besides the very specific, balanced brew found within a stomach would give me great discomfort and possibly kill me. Real vampires—not the romanticized Draculas—are truly the most miserable of leeches."

"Why . . . puke?"

He shrugged. "Something to do with needing to destroy old tissue so the new can be regenerated. That's as much as I can determine without subjecting myself to unpleasant scientific experiments for the rest of my long, long life. Which brings me to you."

My thoughts were whirling madly, all the recent memories rearranging themselves. It made sense. Veteran of so many stomach-pumpings, I couldn't fail to recognize the sensation of a long tube vacuuming out the contents of my stomach, now that I thought about it.

His long tube and my weight problem. Former weight problem.

Of course.

My mind finally caught up to the present. "What about me?"

"I've chosen you for my companion. I can't make you immortal, but I can partake of your stomach contents only sometimes. Just enough to keep you beautiful. Besides, you do have a delightful way with your mouth."

"And if I say no?"

"Then I'll leave you to get back to your fat and happy life."

I flinched. He could be brutal, my vampire. I couldn't believe I was considering it, but the setup had undeniable benefits. Then I remembered.

"What about the other girls?"

He stroked my forearm soothingly, misunderstanding. "They won't be missed, don't worry. With so many women dropping dead from anorexia in this city, a few more each year won't be noticed."

I shuddered, even as my skin pebbled under his soft caress.

"I have to feed, or I'll die. But eating isn't cheating. I would be true to you in my heart." His cock stirred. I looked at it warily, and Adrien laughed. "I can control it, Valeria. I look forward to making you scream with pleasure, night after night."

God, I was tempted. He was a beautiful, alluring, evil demon. My very own vampire.

I tried to blank out the thought of all his other victims, those girls not as favored as myself. Their deaths. I tried hard, imagining myself with the best lover in the world, one who was a built-in Weight Watcher. But did he care for me personally, or was I just a meal ticket?

When he started moving against me, my body itched for his.

"I can tell you want me, Valeria. I love you."

Love? All my internal alarms went off. I was a self-sufficient girl, with a too-caring heart. It was a curse, that heart.

I let his tongue and hands and rhythms seduce me even as I hid my tears. His cock was a miracle, and Adrien showed it had even more miracles to perform inside me, now that his secret was shared. I knew that the things he made me feel, as he worked between my legs, would make any lover after him pale spectacularly.

After a while, I excused myself to go to the bathroom.

When I came out, I grinned and licked my lips clean of Drano. His cock was hard and ready.

Before I took him into my throat, I announced, "Dinner is served."

Magna Mater

Cody Goodfellow

It wasn't in the nature of the place for anyone who worked at the Tender Trap Adult Books & Video to notice what went on in the #9 coin-op video booth. Real human contact was not what anyone came for, and of the perverts who frequented the porn shop, those who lurked and groped themselves in the booths were the most furtive, like ghosts sure to vanish under a good, strong stare. Violet was a quick study, having learned early in life the connection between vigilance and not getting hit, but she had her own problems, and it was only when those began to fade into the background that she noticed that many patrons who used the #9 booth simply never came out.

The Tender Trap was the last growth industry on J Street, the embattled border where urban renewal had given up the ghost and the stately Gaslamp District degenerated into seedy downtown.

When Violet walked in a month ago, drawn by the Help Wanted sign, one of her eyes was still too swollen to see out of. She looked like what she was, but while waiting to speak to the manager, she caught a shoplifter stuffing EZ-Whip cartridges in his pants and was hired on the spot.

Violet came in on the bus from Riverside. Wade would be gone a week, maybe a month, and when he returned, tearful and pleading if he remembered what he'd done at all, she had planned to be set up in a new town with her own home, job, and life. She had run away before and always came back to the trailer park within a day or two, so this start had gone better than most.

She found no room at the Salvation Army Women's Shelter, which was packed with women worse off than her and crawling with children. Wandering the streets, weighing the relative merits of going back to wait for Wade or sleep on the street, she found the Tender Trap. The rest—a room above the store to sleep in and a few people to talk to and money to save for something better—had come with it, and she began to feel safe.

Then she began to notice about #9.

The booths were a holdover from the pre-home–video era, when porno theaters and hookers thrived on the sailor traffic. While all kinds came into the store, only a few virtually invisible types used the booths. Those who had no home in which to watch porn often begged outside all day and night and used the booths as a kind of coffee break. Illegal aliens, filthy and shaking from exhaustion, often had to be chased out because they tried to catch a nap inside. Then there were the businessmen, the upright, solid-citizen types whose wives would never tolerate such filth in their homes.

They were as broad a cross-section of masculine humanity as could be found in the city, but once they came in the door, they adopted uniform customs, darting past her roost at the elevated cash register to duck into the back of the store, stopping only to get quarters from the change machine. They stayed inside for a few minutes or an hour, then darted out just as quickly, while Lupe, a hunchbacked Latina crone who sat on a stool at the end of the row of booths, cleaned up the dregs of their ardor with paper towels and 409.

Violet had no inclination to pry into the lives of the customers or the store, but just keeping her eyes open, she soon noticed how, every so often, one would fly into the booth alley and never come out. The Tender Trap had no back door, but Violet didn't ask questions. She watched a little closer when she saw a customer go in. She came out onto the floor to straighten the bargain VHS carousel closest to the batwing saloon doors that blocked her view, glancing over them at the retreating masturbator. It took several of these spying expeditions to discover that only #9 held on to its suitors.

After an hour or so of whatever went on inside, Lupe went to the booth and opened it with a skeleton key, sprayed down the interior, and shuffled back out, always carrying a bundle wrapped in towels in the crook of her arm, which she brought back to the closet that was her workspace and where, for all Violet knew, she slept. Lupe, the manager told her, was a Mayan Indian and didn't speak a word of English or Spanish. Whatever language she did speak, Violet never once heard her use it, no matter how many times she tried to draw the cleaning woman out.

She asked the other clerks about it but got nowhere. Merle, the defrocked carnival-ride operator who ran the counter through the dinner hours, eyed her warily and snapped, "What're you, a cop?" Crayonne, the ugliest, gayest, blackest man Violet had ever seen, told her there were peepholes, if she wanted to watch them jerk off, then laughed at her the rest of the night. Judith, the early morning cashier, sighed in obvious relief. "Do you see them right now too?" she asked, sweeping her shaking bird-claw hands and jangling silver jewelry around to accuse the whole empty store. "I do . . ."

Violet did not ask the manager, Zoe, about #9. Zoe hired her and set her up with the studio apartment upstairs, asked no questions but seemed to understand everything. When she thought of bringing it up, Violet began to doubt that there was anything amiss but her own fucked-up nerves misfiring. Besides, every time she got deeper than surface chatter with Zoe, she was pressed against the ceiling of her own ignorance. After a few days of the job, Zoe had asked her how she was doing.

Violet stuttered, "Doesn't any of this stuff, you know, ever make you feel, you know, weird?"

"How do you mean, honey?"

"You know, being a woman," she said, feeling a flush of shame fill her face. She wasn't offended by the wares, but she failed to see what the pixilated video couplings and sterile rubber prosthetic plumbing they sold had to do with sex. Not that what passed for sex in her house would come any closer to a romantic ideal. "Doesn't it, you know, *objectify* women?"

"Oh gods, Vi, where'd you ever get such a big, dumb word?" Squat, doughy Zoe was about as sensuous as a garden gnome and acted like they were selling plumbing fixtures. "Men objectify women, Vi. They look at us and see machines to make them come, to fill their bellies, and we see them as machines to make us feel special and safe. This stuff—well, we should all breathe a sigh of relief that some men whack off to it and leave real women alone."

"I don't mean, well . . . You know, Wade, he used to—" And she shut up when she found she could not articulate her feelings or thoughts without Wade stories.

"Men come in here for all kinds of reasons, Vi. We don't judge. Nobody is beyond forgiveness."

So she let it lie. But night after night, she caught glimpses out of the corner of her eye, when she rang up a gross of nitrous chargers for a gay biker couple, or rousted drunken frat boys who tried to climb into the Swedish Swing, or when Cowboy Chuck Berry or one of the other street people came in to beg bus change or read her a poem. She would see a man dart in the front and vanish through the saloon doors, or she would only see them swinging.

And then one day, she caught one.

Above the sounds of sweat-slick hands pawing rubber and neoprene and leather, the whisper of licked lips and spastically blinking eyes, the idiot music of the door sensor jerked her out of her trance. He was already halfway across the floor to the booths, and Violet slid off her stool and banged her knees on the counter. She followed the phantom into the dank corridor and peered around the corner and, yes, the hunched figure stood before the door of #9 with a roll of quarters in one shaking fist.

The full weight of the stupidity of her obsession sat upon her chest and struck her dumb. The plans she'd hatched as she lay in bed in the morning, wishing she'd had the brains to bring the TV from the trailer, scorched and fell away like film stuck in the gate of a projector.

She reached out and touched his grubby flannel shirt, but the man jerked away as if her aura burned him. Only when he turned and faced her did she realize that she'd feared, hoped, he was someone else. "Excuse me, mister, you can't use that one—"

He was Hispanic, old drunk's face like piss-cured leather, eyes bloody, melting marbles. He blinked at her as if she'd awakened a sleepwalker. His fist balled, his arm cocked and stopped inches short of smashing her face in. She looked long and hard at it, seeing just who she'd thought he was. Big as a billboard, the wall of knuckles before her eyes was scarred and swollen, bruise-blue and black, and red, red, red with blood and lipstick.

If she was startled by the man's reaction, he was thunderstruck. He looked at his poised fist as if it were only the last and least of his countless betrayers, then let it sag against his drooping gut. She thought he was hyperventilating, but as he grasped himself, she heard the razored breaths as prayers, though in what language, or to whom, she couldn't tell. "I know what I want, *puta*," he mumbled and ducked through the door into #9. The door music sounded again, and she retreated to her post.

He never came out.

Crayonne sat at the counter, shaking his head at her. Zoe called her into the office. "You'd think you would know to steer clear of that type."

"What type?"

"You know."

"How do you think you know—"

Zoe pointed to the signs on the mirrored ceiling, where only a shifty customer would look, that said SMILE! YOU ARE ON CAMERA!

"I–I," she stuttered, making the truth feel like a lie, "I thought he was someone else."

"And if it was him, what would you have done?" Zoe's round face was all laugh lines. She had rhino-hide skin: trouble never penetrated. *But she must know what happens back there, in that booth—*

"I don't . . . You don't even know me!"

"So tell me what makes you different. Why did you run away, Vi?"

She defended herself and attacked Zoe until her manager grumbled "Fuck it" and dismissed her.

Maybe Violet had to be yelled at or blown off to open up, but she sat down and started talking about Wade and kept talking until Zoe told her again to get out. Shaky, Violet rose and went to the door, stopped. "What happens in there?"

"You're not ready to ask that yet. Ask yourself this first. If he came back tonight, could you forgive him?"

Violet bought a little TV, some groceries, and a discreet, minimalist vibrator with her first paycheck. But when she tried to fall asleep watching her shows in the morning, Zoe's words banged against each other in her head.

She kept watching. In the week since their talk, four men had gone into #9. Neither of them brought it up. Once, thinking she'd caught Lupe in the act of cleaning up #9, she snuck back. She was not at her perch at the center of the labyrinth, and none of the booths were occupied.

The other booths bore obscene placards on their doors, advertising the nastiness within—BLACK GLADIATOR STUDS IV, DIAPER PAIL HIJINX, SLEEPING WITH THE ENEMA, and so on.

There was no placard on #9, but someone had tagged the door with a black permanent marker. The ritualized graffiti flare was so dense the words were an abstract picture, but as near as she could tell, they said MAGNA MATER.

She thought she heard someone stir inside, a whisper and a hiss of wet flesh against sticky plastic. She drew in a deep breath and grabbed the edge of the door, threw it wide open and prepared to get hit. But the booth was empty.

It looked like a porta-shitter with a molded plastic seat bulging out of one wall and a twenty-inch screen with a coin slot at lap level on the other. The blank screen was indifferently smeared with a streaky antiseptic that made raw chlorine smell like sugar cookies.

The booth had a dim, stuttering fluorescent bulb that flickered more on than off. The interior crawled with spiders of black ink, every battered inch of the green plastic walls, floor, and ceiling swarming with insect initials in Magic Marker, pocketknife, and blood: tags, symbols, and names, most rendered with no flamboyant gangster style whatsoever but in the unaffected, palsied script of the drunk, the drugged, the beaten down, and the beaters.

So many names.

There was the musky reek of ancient jism, but aside from the names, there was no sign that the booth had ever been used. None of the sticky, omnipresent ooze here that coated even the outer floor despite Lupe's relentless chemical warfare. No trapdoors, no secret entrance to an underground railroad for damned masturbators, no scent of brimstone, no scorch marks or fresh blood. Nothing but whatever Lupe took out wrapped in towels, and she had foiled Violet again.

Shivering, holding the door open with one foot, Violet put a quarter into the slot. If this was some sort of trap, then surely this was how to spring it, and the thing had chewed up Violet's brain too much for her to care whether she sprang it on herself. When nothing happened, her sigh of relief was sour with disappointment.

Lupe was back at her perch in the cleaning closet when Violet came out. She must've been there all along, but the door had been closed while she disposed of whatever she took out of #9. Her eyes bore right through Violet as she asked once again about the man who went in, about all the men and where they went.

She learned nothing more, and tried to forget what she knew, until the night she'd feared and hoped for finally came.

She held down the counter at half past two, head propped up on her sweaty hands, glassy eyes turned inward as she sat watch on the empty store, when he came in.

She told herself at first it was just her eyes playing tricks like before, because none of the men she'd thought were him bore any real resemblance to him, except in the way they walked like a losing boxer leaving the ring. When she saw him come in the door, she believed it was only a fantasy, a waking night terror.

But it was Wade.

He looked to be at the ragged end of the bender that had driven her away almost a month ago. His eyes were bloodshot, his skin oily and oozing alcohol dregs and less healthy stuff. His fists flexed at his sides as he stood there in the doorway. Violet opened her mouth to call for Zoe or Crayonne, but her teeth clamped on and bit through the tip of her tongue.

She leaped off her stool. One leg pulled her toward the back office while the other simply buckled. She caught herself against the frame, rattling the beaded curtain screening the office.

Wade just stood there, looking. She knew what he expected. She'd been collected before, and though her terror was never greater, neither had she ever missed him so much. She hated herself for it, but what else, who else, did she have?

"Wade," she managed, "how did you find me?" She made herself look up and meet his gaze, recoiled as if slapped when his eyes roved over her. He didn't recognize her at all. Or if he did, the rage he burned her with where other men felt love had guttered and gone out. The walls he'd built to keep her out were smashed and smoking ruins, and deep down inside where he'd let her in, there was no hurt little boy, no bestial transfigured prince, only a howling vacuum.

Looking into him was like putting her ear to a big conch shell, the rumbling silence of a ghost-ocean where his shouts of love and hate came from echoes without a source. He knew her, but he was past hitting, past begging, far past any words or feelings. He looked like a man bound and determined to drown.

He fed the change machine, then turned and went through the saloon doors into the maze of booths.

"Wade," she cried out, "don't."

A hand reached through the beaded curtains and clutched her shoulder. Surprisingly strong, it tugged her off balance as she tried to rip free and go after him. "Don't, honey. He's not here for you."

She got away and ran for the booths. She hit the saloon doors so hard one of them broke off its hinges and flapped in her wake. She hit the locked door of #9 even harder, screaming, "Wade, come out, baby, I'm sorry, it's my fault, come out of there, they're gonna kill you—"

From inside, she heard a choked sob.

She turned to Lupe, inscrutable on her stool in the closet. "Open it," Violet shouted in her face, taking hold of the cleaning woman's smock and shaking her like a doll. "Open it, or so help me, if he's not okay, I'll fucking—"

"So you forgive him then?" Zoe's reasonable voice pricked her panic and instantly flattened it. The manager stood behind her, massaging Violet's white-knuckled claws off Lupe and pulling her back down the corridor. "His life is not in your hands, honey."

Violet trembled so hard her words wouldn't come out in a string. When she could shape them, she let them pour out. Even now, she couldn't be of one mind about it. She knew nothing about what went on in #9, but she knew what it meant.

All the men who came in here were of a type, Wade's type, the kind who hit women, and none of them came out.

How many times had she wished him dead? How many times had she seen his type defiantly roaring at a talk-show audience mob and wished for all of them to burn and hang and be blown straight to a special Hell run by battered women? This too Zoe must have known when she hired Violet. She knew everything. She must have known that, sick as it was, her love for Wade was still strong. "You set him up, you bitch!"

"I told him nothing, honey. He came here, but not for you. Sooner or later, when there's nowhere else to go, that type of man always finds his way here. It's just a sort of coincidence, or maybe the Goddess brought you here to see."

"You kill them! What gives you the right? You're not the one to judge him—"

"No, none of us can judge, any more than we can change them. You still think you can change him, don't you, honey? Well, come into my office, and I'll show you—"

Numb, she let herself be led. Crayonne had locked the front door and stood outside, pointedly watching the street. They went through the curtains and into Zoe's cluttered office. Zoe crossed the room and took down a row of binders on a shelf above her desk.

There, on the stained formica-paneled wall, was a single fish-eye peephole. Zoe beckoned her closer, bade her put her eye to the hole. "There's security cameras in every booth, but they don't capture what really goes on inside. You have to see it with your own eyes. Go ahead and look, honey . . ."

Violet pushed back, but again Zoe's soothing hands squeezed the resistance right out of her limbs. "You want me to watch him get—"

"It's what he wants, Vi. It's all he wants now, and it's all he ever wanted and couldn't have, so he hit you and every other woman who tried to give it to him and couldn't. Watch . . ."

She put her eye to the hole. She saw only black but heard

rustling and the familiar cadence of Wade's half-snoring, drunken breathing. Clicking, and the booth leapt into sharp silver-blue light as he fed the slot. A fine blur of wire mesh before her eyes told her she was looking through the ventilation gills behind and above Wade's head.

She cursed that she couldn't see his face or the screen, but the set of his shoulders, the galvanic twitches that wracked his neck, told her all she needed to know. He had gone past the point where he broke and begged forgiveness, and she had not been there. What was going on inside him now, she couldn't begin to guess.

She wanted more than ever to go to him and pull him out, but the screen blinked and syrupy electronic music snapped on, and she was pinned to the spot.

"Go back to your bitch, then, asshole! Go beat her up and eat her fucking food!" The voice on the soundtrack was her own. She was so angry and hurt and wired that last night, she knew there probably never was a bitch; he barely had the strength to beat *her* up—

She listened to the sounds and remembered how Wade cornered her against the sink and yanked her baggy sweatpants down around her knees, bent her over. His cock, knobby and brittle like driftwood, knifed into her to the root, though she was dry as Egypt down there. She screamed into the dirty dishes, and flies swarmed up out of the swampy scum. She screamed and whooped with no pleasure, but something deeper, the painful thrill of being needed, made it all right.

When he came, he shivered and let out a strangled growl and zipped up, disgusted with her again. He went all cold and sneered, shifting gears, changing games so fast she was speechless, frozenly pulling up her soiled pants.

"Yeah, I got another bitch." She mouthed his words as they came out of the tinny speaker. "She's hotter than you, she's cleaner, and her insides aren't all fucked up, either. She can have babies, Vi, and she's gonna have mine."

If she could find a knife in the mess, she'd stab him. Her arms whipped out at him, and nobody was more surprised than she was when they slapped and scratched his face. "You want to make babies, Wade? You want to make a baby with her? You can't be a fucking father, you're not even a fucking man, you—"

And Wade said "That'll be enough of that" and threw her right out the door like garbage. Into the garbage, in fact, which had piled up outside their door for two weeks, his seed leaking out down her leg, dying inside her, circling her scarred, scraped womb like kamikaze pilots with shitty directions until the acidity of her burned the last one up.

Violet blinked away tears, watching Wade's silhouette pumping at his cock. God help him, he was hard and whacking off at the impossible replay of his cruelty, but he was sobbing too.

"Oh, Vi, baby," he choked, "I'm so sorry—"

His hand froze on his dick and jerked away as if it shocked him. "What the fuck . . ." he grumbled as he stared at a new scene.

The music regressed, sax flatulence, junkie-funk guitar, and canned moans seeping through the wall.

"What did you see?" a woman rasped, lighting a cigarette.

"Nothing, Mama," a boy mumbled, and Wade's broken whisper echoed him. Popcorn popped on a stove.

"He wants to watch TV, so you make yourself scarce."

"But Mama, it's Monday Night Football night—"

She cuffed him across the right ear with her silver Zippo lighter clenched in her fist. He yelped and ducked away. The Jiffy Pop's pregnancy came to term, swelling foil belly splitting open to ooze steam. He rolled away from her kicking legs and ducked for the door.

"What the fuck, Ruth?" A man's bleary voice.

"You want to be his daddy? You want the duty? No? Then shut the fuck up!"

The ghostly cathode light went murky as the screen before Wade became a mirror. The music changed too, subsiding into a deep bed of whispers and moans, soft, edgeless cries as of a dozen girl-girl scenes playing at once.

Wade leaned forward to feed the slot more quarters, cursing his reflection in subsonic hisses, when Violet spooked and jumped back from the peephole.

In the screen, she thought she'd seen herself through the wall, as if the camera in the booth had X-ray vision. But when she went back to the hole, her heart pounded as she saw that Wade wasn't alone in the booth, and what was in there with him looked nothing like her at all.

Zoe grasped her shoulders, held her up to the hole. "This has to happen, sweetie," she murmured in Violet's ear. "He wants it, he needs it—and so do you."

She looked again, daring it to be real, but it was still there, more *there* than ever. On the screen, someone rose up behind Wade, but she knew this was a trick, because nothing blocked her view. Wade stared into the screen, transfixed.

All she could tell was that it was a woman. She stood taller than Wade so that the screen cut off her head, but her alabaster body was so enormous as to defy the physics of the booth. Absurdly voluptuous breasts dwarfed Wade's head, while her belly smashed and overflowed around his skinny, shuddering form. Her elephantine hips rutted against the walls and blocked the door. Her arms floated up and stretched out to the screen, shockingly dainty little hands reaching up to the thin film of glass that separated her from the flesh-and-blood Wade, all but claiming his stupefied TV ghost.

"Please, Mama," he wheezed, "please take me—"

On the screen, Wade closed his eyes and went limp as the arms closed over him.

In the booth, something rose up between Wade and the screen. It bloomed and swelled and enveloped him, the glow of the screen shimmering through its molten form as it filled out and became a liquid replica of the headless woman on the screen.

As it grew, she saw rancid white slime oozing out of the seams in the booth's walls from all sides, all the spilt seed of a million meat-beatings conjuring itself out of the cracks and congealing in #9 to form the Magna Mater.

Violet bit back a scream.

The liquid thing took Wade in its arms and cradled his head. His sobs broke into seizures he smothered between her mammoth breasts. She guided a dripping nipple to his mouth, and he locked on to it for all he was worth, sucking convulsively like a newborn.

The milk soothed him, and he subsided in her arms, anguished cries subsiding, deflated into a fetal ball. His limbs sagged bonelessly as his belly filled.

Violet groaned and tried not to vomit. The thing grew still larger and rolled over Wade, oblivious, delirious, at the teat. His clothes peeled back, shredded, melted away. The thing rolled up onto the bench and settled down around him, his rigid cock swallowed by slithering mouths of fluid flesh.

He moaned loudly around the monster teat, but the thing flowed through his fingers and rearranged itself so breasts and belly lolled backward, and he sat facing the oleaginous grotto of a sopping, cavernous vagina.

Wade uttered an infant's piercing whine and leaned back from the maw. Her cyclopean thighs clenched him and drew him closer by a hideous peristalsis, like food going down an esophagus into a bottomless stomach. Finally, Wade gave in and put his face into the gaping, flowery mouth.

Violet's revulsion spilled out over her lips, and she threw up on the box of domination supplies between her feet. Through her tears, through hot flashes of oncoming faint, she could not stop looking.

As the thing lowered itself onto him, Wade leaned face first into her, and she parted, unhinged, like the mouth of a python to kiss, then devour him. The labia closed over his whole head, then flexed and strained to gobble up his shoulders, chest, and abdomen.

Violet shoved Zoe back, ran to the booths. Lupe stood before number 9, but stepped back when she saw Violet coming fists first to save her husband. Violet grabbed the skeleton key from around Lupe's neck and jammed it into the door. The Occupied light still glowed above, but she could hear nothing inside—no music, no moaning, no Wade. She threw open the door and lunged inside with her fists cocked, but the booth was empty.

"No! No, goddamit, Wade! Where are you, baby?" She whirled on Lupe and the approaching Zoe. "Bring him back, you bitch! How dare you judge him—"

"We don't judge here, sweetie," Zoe said. "We just help them get where they need to go. Take another look—"

Violet looked inside the booth again, eyes straining in the dim half-light. All she saw was a pile of rags on the bench—Wade's clothes. They were no dirtier than when he came staggering in, but they were all torn and wet and wound up into a tight, owl-turd bundle that stirred as she came closer. Stirred and gave a tiny cry.

"*Her* people come for the ones nobody claims," Zoe whispered in her ear. "Why don't you go home early, sweetie? He's beautiful now, and he needs you."

Violet stumbled and bumped into the remaining saloon door on her way out. She didn't even notice Crayonne holding the front door open for her as she wandered out into the night cradling her newborn baby.

Change of Pace

Steve Vernon

Forty-year-old white men just shouldn't try to rap. It was a shame nobody told the house band before they slid into their third attempt of the evening. Malcolm hated rap. The same damn beat, the same damn lyrics. How many times could you find a rhyme with "pussy"?

The band didn't help matters. A quartet of three fat, balding country crooners, along with a lead singer that they'd undoubtedly found in the wreckage of a condemned piano bar, vainly struggled to morph themselves into the twenty-first century.

Malcolm tried his best to get used to it, willing his ears to close up. It didn't help or matter. The band was the least of Malcolm's problems.

The problem was Maria.

"Women change," Malcolm said. "That's the hell of it. You think you've got things figured out, and they go and change on you."

"The old missionary isn't working for you anymore, eh?" Seymour said.

"It isn't that. It's her. She's changed. What worked before just isn't working now. No, sir, it isn't that at all."

Seymour shrugged and grinned. "I dunno, Malcolm. It sounds like that to me. Have you tried ginseng?"

Malcolm had expected this. Seymour was a holistic healer this year, or at least that's what he called himself. Last year he'd been a cab driver. The year before he worked in a call center. Seymour liked change.

"I've tried ginseng, vitamin E, pheremonal antiperspirant. I've tried it all, and nothing works."

The band eased into "Margaritaville." It didn't sound much better than the rap, but at least Malcolm knew most of the words. It was a damn shame the band didn't.

"Maybe it isn't physical. Maybe all you need is a little changeup. Have you thought about another woman?"

Malcolm shook his head. "If I was to get myself another woman, I'd have to get myself another man to keep her satisfied."

"That bad, huh?"

"Seymour, I'm tiptoeing up to the fifty-year mark. I don't need or want another woman. I'm just trying to keep the woman I want happy."

"Well, okay, maybe not another woman. But maybe you just need a little change of pace."

Malcolm stared at his beer, wondering if it was possible to read your future in the foam. He peered as hard as he could, but all he could see was a cluster of tasty bubbles clinging to the side and bottom of the glass.

Seymour kept talking. "You need to loosen up. Invite another woman over for a threesome. Go to a key party. Try new positions."

"Change your tune," Malcolm said. "You're starting to sound like a damned fortune cookie."

"Well, damn it, Malcolm, you can't just ignore it and hope it'll all go away. You've got to try something."

"Try something?"

Malcolm snorted.

"Seymour, I've tried everything. Last June I surprised her

with a romantic bedside banquet of oysters. Flew the fuckers right in from Florida."

"Oysters are good," Seymour allowed. "High in zinc, long on libido. Sounds like just the thing to poke the ashes of a dying fuck-fire."

Malcolm snorted even louder.

"You'd think that, wouldn't you?" He poured another beer. "How the fuck was I supposed to know she was allergic to shellfish? Hell, I can't even spell anaphylactic."

Seymour sat there, stone-cold silent, but Malcolm could see he was fighting hard not to let the laughter slip out. Truth to tell, Malcolm didn't blame him. It was funny.

Except he wasn't laughing.

"Then you know what she said? Right after the slurred speech and vomiting let up? 'Honey,' she said, 'stop trying to build a relationship with a ball-peen hammer.'"

"Damn," Seymour swore. "That's cold."

"So then I tried green M&Ms. Everybody knows they make you horny, right? I bought a whole carton of jumbo bags and damned near turned myself color-blind sorting the green ones out of the assortment. Then I blended all of the green ones, must have been nearly a thousand. I blended them up into a giant chocolate smoothy. Chocolate is sexy, isn't it?"

"Can't go wrong with chocolate," Seymour agreed. "Did you know the Mayans invented it?"

Malcolm couldn't resist.

"Google?"

Seymour shrugged.

"*Survivor: Guatemala,*" he confessed. "So what happened? Did the M&Ms work?"

"What happened? It turned out that when she isn't being allergic to shellfish, she's busy developing an allergy to green food dye. Her hives swelled up like orgasmic puffballs, and she spent the whole night in the emergency ward, damn near choking to death."

"Maybe you need to try some different positions," Seymour suggested. "There's lots of varied techniques can add a whole lot of jungle to your loving."

"Kama Sutra, you mean? I tried that last spring. Found a how-to video at a yard sale. Talked the guy down from five bucks to two."

"So what happened?"

"I'll tell you what happened. Halfway through positions one through six, with Maria's right leg hooked somewhere around my left ear, and her right elbow jammed deeply into an erogenous area of my inner kneecap, I discovered my fucking lumbago. I still limp when it rains."

Seymour just shook his head, but Malcolm was on a roll.

"Last month I hooked up a set of speakers in the bedroom and tried piping in 'Bolero,' like in that Bo Derek movie? All it done for Maria was bring on one of her migraine attacks."

"Shit, sounds like you've tried everything."

"You ain't just whistling William Tell's overture. Last week I tried voodoo. I sacrificed an entire bucket of Kentucky Fried Chicken to Damballah, the god of bad ideas. Then I stripped myself naked and danced a quick one-man tango of desire about Maria while chanting out the only chant I know."

"What chant was that?" Seymour asked.

"Ooo eee, ooo ah ah—ting tang, walla walla bing bang."

"Walla walla bing bang?"

Malcolm shrugged. "It was the best I could come up with."

"Did it work?"

Malcolm laughed. "Oh, it worked all right. Worked so well Maria had a panic attack thinking I'd gone and developed a shivering case of jumped-up St. Vitus jitterbug fever."

Malcolm tipped back the glass of beer and drained it.

Seymour worked up enough nerve to talk. "Well, hell, Malcolm. It sounds as if you've got the right idea."

"What, that I need to scare my wife to death? Poison her with shellfish and green M&Ms?"

"Hell, no. The trying-new-things part. That's just what you need to be doing. Only problem is you haven't found the right thing to try."

Seymour pushed on. Once he'd latched his problem-solving muscles onto a situation, it was harder than juggling fresh scrambled eggs to get him to let go.

"It's like baseball, you know?" Seymour said, grinning like a skinny, buck-toothed Socrates.

Oh hell. A sports metaphor. Malcolm should have known better. Seymour always turned everything into sports. Ever since he'd joined the high-school football team. You'd think he'd have grown out of it by now.

People never change.

"All of the best batters know how to changeup. Otherwise, you get predictable. Even Babe Ruth knew how to bunt. What d'ya think?"

Malcolm did his best to look like he was considering Seymour's explanation.

"What do I think?" he asked, tilting the beer to get the last few drops of barley from the bottom of the glass. "I think it's your round. Ante up, big boy."

Seymour flagged down a waiter.

"Look," Malcolm said. "I don't want another woman. I want Maria. I just want things to jazz up a little. I'm not talking sex toys. I don't need any blow-up dolls or his-and-her vibrators. I just want a tune-up, y'hear what I'm saying?"

Seymour nodded, thinking about what Malcolm had said. The waiter showed up with another pitcher. Christ. Maria was going to kill him.

"Well, maybe it is physical. I think I know just what you need," Seymour said. "I think I know how to fix things up. What you need is a little dose of Spanish Fly."

Malcolm laughed. "There ain't no such thing."

"Is too. I know where to get some. Get you laid faster than shit."

"I don't want to break it to you, Seymour, but most of the shit I've ever known doesn't move that fast or get laid at all. It mostly just lays there and grows maggots until somebody flushes it away."

"Look," Seymour said. "I'm trying to tell you this stuff is freaking legendary. I'm talking the real deal. I can get it for you."

"Sure," Malcolm said. "I've seen that stuff in the sex shops. Spanish Fly. Quicker Pecker Upper. Fire In The Hole. You know what all of that stuff is? Just a little sugar, a little food coloring, and a big old price tag. The only kind of hole you'll get is the ones that grow in your teeth."

Seymour shook his head hard. "I'm not talking about anything store-bought. I've got a guy who can get you the real thing. He brings it in from South America or something like that."

"Something like that?"

"I don't know. He makes it special, you know? Out of certain ingredients."

"You gonna hook me up with a pusher, Seymour? Man, you've been watching too many *Miami Vice* reruns."

"What do you have to lose, Malcolm?"

Malcolm thought about it. Seymour was right.

"You've got to try something," Seymour said. "If you don't use it, you surely will lose her."

Seymour was dead right. Malcolm was scared he was going to lose Maria. There was no way he wanted that to happen. She was the best thing that ever happened to his fucked-up life.

"What do you say, Malcolm? It's the bottom of the ninth."

Why the hell not? Maybe it was just what he'd needed. He just needed to change his swing.

He just needed a good pop fly.

Yeah, that was it.

He just needed to pop Maria a little Spanish Fly.

* * *

They climbed into Seymour's primered-over '83 Thunderbird right after they'd finished off their second pitcher of beer, just as the house band hip-hopped over from rap and began disemboweling an old MC Hammer tune. They couldn't touch it.

"You see," Seymour said, swinging the big car around an overturned garbage can and a snoozing wino, "Spanish Fly isn't really made out of houseflies."

"So what's it made out of? Zippers?"

Seymour wasn't bothered by Malcolm's sarcasm. He was in full oration mode, showing off his holistic healing skills. Seymour was proud of his job, and a good friend besides, so Malcolm did his best not to let on that he knew full well that Seymour learned most of his skills and technique from reading the labels at Sister Marriedwell's Holistic Health Food Emporium and a stack of *Mother Jones* magazines that he'd picked up in a paper drive.

"The actual drug is made up of dried and crushed carcasses of green blister beetles."

"So let me get this straight. You're advising me to feed my wife bugs?"

"Couldn't do any worse than the green M&Ms."

Seymour had a point, but Malcolm couldn't help wondering just what a blister beetle might look like. He kept getting this vision of funky, slime green beetles crawling out of the blisters and bunions of Juan Valdez's dirty sandaled feet.

Ten minutes later Malcolm and Seymour were standing in a sleazy bodega in the sleaziest corner of the worst side of town.

A fat Puerto Rican clerk with a long, greasy moustache stood behind a counter stuffed full of unnameable cuts of meat. Long ribbons of yellow flypaper dangled down like streamers on a prom night from hell. There were flies of all shapes and sizes hung and stuck on every inch of the paper, like a treasure trove of fat, buzzing crystal.

Seymour spoke to the clerk in a language that sounded a little like Spanish. Malcolm had never known that Seymour knew Spanish. Come to think of it, he didn't know that much about Seymour at all. He was just some guy he'd known since high school. He threw a good football, he'd been divorced twice, and the two of them called each other best friend.

That was all he knew about the guy. For all he knew, Seymour could have been a double agent from Alpha Centauri sent to infiltrate the simmering ranks of lower-class trailer trash.

The clerk pointed.

Malcolm reached for a package resting between a bin of habanero peppers and a basketful of bootleg porno DVDs.

"This is Spanish Fly? The real stuff?" he asked.

"I make it myself. The real thing. Very special," said the clerk in a voice that sounded like it was bubbling up from the bottom of a quarry.

Malcolm paid him.

Then Seymour drove Malcolm on home to Maria.

In the morning, Malcolm crawled out of bed. His head felt like it was stuffed with cobwebs, crepe paper, and creamed Crisco.

"Oh shit," he whispered.

He'd gone to sleep in his jeans. He hadn't even bothered changing into his pajamas.

In the kitchen, Maria banged a couple of pots together in fire-alarm fashion. She was enjoying herself, but it wasn't doing much for Malcolm's skull. It sounded horrible, way worse than last night's rap music.

He stumbled out into the kitchen and glared at her backside, watching it jiggle as she made like Buddy Rich with a ladle and a pasta pot. She was having fun. Fucking bitch. He'd like to give her a banging.

Then he grinned. It was funny. He wasn't really angry. He

was just displacing his feelings of frustration with anger. Like turning one emotion into another. He'd learned all about that shit from Dr. Phil.

No, he wasn't angry, but he still wanted to bang her.

He thought about it for just about ten seconds. Just go for it, grab her and throw her down on the kitchen table, and let her have it.

To hell with that. She'd either turn him down or go dutifully through with it to be nice. One was as bad as the other. Besides, they only had three more months of payments to go on the table.

His smile turned rueful.

Time was she would have welcomed it.

Right now she was mad, and he just couldn't blame her. He knew he'd be in trouble. He knew he shouldn't be out that late, drinking on a work night.

Fuck it. He and Seymour had been getting shit-faced together since high school. Why the hell should he change now?

Yeah, Maria would understand that. Shit. He didn't have a leg to stand on.

What the hell. He might as well go to work. A change was as good as a rest, wasn't it?

She'd cool off by the time he got home.

He took one last look at her before closing the front door behind him, as if he wanted to fix her image in his memory.

"Good-bye, honey."

That damn Spanish Fly had better work.

He clicked the television off at nine PM sharp.

"What'd you do that for?" Maria asked. "*Law and Order* is coming on."

"It's probably a repeat."

"I want to see it anyway."

"My back's killing me, babe. We can watch it upstairs, can't we?"

He resisted the urge to drop any hints. He didn't want her to see this coming. That'd kill the mood for sure. It definitely had to be spontaneous.

She didn't argue. It was more comfortable upstairs for watching television.

He remembered when they'd moved the old television upstairs. For the first six years of their marriage, they had resisted the idea of watching television in bed. There were too many other things to do in bed.

Then one day he'd bagged a big bonus and treated the household to a new television. Rather than bother with trying to sell the old one, or worse yet just dumping it on the curb, Maria suggested they move the old television upstairs. How quickly things change.

"I'm going to the kitchen. Make some cocoa."

"That'd be nice," Maria said. "But I thought your back was hurt. You sure you don't want me to make it for you?"

No, damn it, Malcolm thought. *I want you to make it* with *me.*

"The moving around will do me good," he told her.

And that was that.

He heated the pot of milk, stirring the cocoa in with heavy spoonfuls to mask the flavor of the Fly. He read the instructions.

Then he poured two cups, one in Maria's favorite mug. Then he added the Spanish Fly to Maria's mug.

How much? Shit, there were no instructions. What kind of a dosage did this involve?

He shook in a handful. It looked pretty, kind of a cross between powdered Emerald City and fine dried parsley.

"Somewhere over the rainbow," he sang to himself.

"Honey, hurry up. You're going to miss the beginning," Maria called down.

"Coming, sweetheart."

He added some baby marshmallows. They melted and clustered together like wet fungus.

Then he went upstairs, carrying the mugs.

That ought to work, shouldn't it? Chocolate was supposed to be an aphrodisiac, wasn't it? And besides, hadn't Seymour said the Mayans invented chocolate? To Malcolm's way of thinking, that made for a perfect blend.

He walked into the bedroom, nearly tripping over the throw rug and spilling the cocoa.

"Hey, babe. I made it just the way you like it."

She reached for the mug.

"Thanks, honey. You're the best." She smiled up at him. "Don't ever change."

For an instant he nearly changed his mind.

And then she reached up and took it from him.

Before he could say anything, she took a sip.

It was done.

"Hmm, this is good," she said.

"Drink it down while it's warm."

He felt like shit, but he hoped it would be worth it.

The stuff worked fast. By the time Arthur had finished his first tough talk to Jack McCoy, Maria had her panties off and three fingers buried up her steaming pussy. She was hotter than a week of foreplay.

Malcolm leaned over her. He could feel the heat radiating off her skin. She was damned near burning up. Her flesh seemed to move, like it was molten lava. Christ, she was hot.

He touched her lips with a sweetheart kiss. She clamped hold of him and dragged him down to the bed, sucking her mouth onto his with a pressure that was damned near pneumatic.

Her tits were high and hard and hot, the nipples like ruby bullet branding irons scorching into his skin. He ran his hands over her. She arched herself against him, grinding her pelvis against his groin.

His cock stiffened to attention beneath his pajama bottoms.

He didn't remember getting naked. It happened that quickly, as if she'd grown an extra set of arms in order to tear his pajamas off.

And then he was inside her. He'd never felt her so warm, so wet, so damn tight.

"Fuck me hard," Maria begged.

He didn't need any coaxing. He rode her hard, humping it into her. With every thrust she rose up to meet him, grinding her clitoris hard against his pelvic bone.

She came like she couldn't stop.

He pushed up, pulling himself free, struggling to catch a breath. He figured he'd catch his breath and then get his turn at coming.

Maria had other plans. She grabbed him hard by the ears.

"I hope you've got gills," she said before pulling him face first down into her pussy.

Malcolm licked for dear life.

After a time, he thought he could hear the sea.

She fell asleep something like a quarter after her fifteenth volley of orgasms. Malcolm had never seen the like. He'd known a lot of women, at least three, and never had he seen such passion. It was like having group sex, like living in a *Penthouse* magazine, so wild and uninhibited.

It had pretty nearly killed him.

He lay there, slowly catching his breath. He was totally happy but totally depleted. How the hell could he keep this up? He'd have to invest in some serious vitamins.

Or maybe the Spanish Fly might work for him as well.

He watched her lying there, her chest rising and falling, rising.

Shit.

Her chest wasn't rising.

It was growing. Rising and swelling from sensible handfuls to high, ripe melons. Her hair was lengthening and changing color.

More disturbing were the tiny tentacles growing from various parts of her abdomen.

What was in that Spanish Fly? She was turning into some kind of a monster.

She opened her eyes. Looked straight up into his.

Oh hell.

"Maria," he whispered.

He lay back down onto their bed. This was crazy, but she was his wife, damn it. And besides, she was hot.

He was amazed to find himself growing another erection. He thought he was finished, but when he looked into her eyes, everything changed. He slipped his erection into her. He felt tiny fingers inside her pussy, skillfully manipulating his cock, bringing him to an even higher pitch of excitement.

They fucked like a platoon of oversexed minks. She continued to change in mid-fuck. And each new Maria incarnation demanded more and more sex.

Malcolm kept trying to please her, trying every position he could think of. Between lovemaking bouts he choked down vitamin tablets and protein shakes and ginseng tea to keep up his energy level. Nothing seemed to last for long.

And then finally he took the Spanish Fly.

Six weeks later everything had changed. Malcolm and Maria barely left the bedroom. The two of them were screwing like the world's largest free love commune. He hadn't seen hide nor hair of Seymour since that night in the bodega, and he didn't really care. Malcolm the Multiple was having a great time with Mondo Maria, trying hard not to think about that cluster of throbbing eggs hidden in the bedroom closet, jellied beneath the shoeboxes and slippers and lost socks.

Hot Hot Hot

Ed Gorman

So what if there wasn't that old turning of heads when he walked into a bar or café anymore? So what if the ladies didn't send him drinks and smiles now that he'd reached his mid-fifties? And so what if men didn't glare at him when they caught their ladies glancing his way every chance they got?

Welcome to the world of Dr. William Carlyle, neurosurgeon, a millionaire many times over, Bears fan of the most neurotic kind (absolutely toxic for at least twenty-four hours when they lose, especially a close one), father of two grown sons, husband of the most beautiful woman in his undergraduate years, "Cam," short for Cameron Ames, and president of the county medical association, which often resulted in one of the local liberal rags running his stock photo. About a year ago, one of them had committed the unforgivable sin of running a current picture of him. He had called the publisher, whom he knew from several of his clubs, and made his point calmly while repressing white-hot fury. He wanted all photos of him to be from a set he'd had taken when he was thirty-eight. And no fucking Jack Benny jokes, either, asshole.

The bar was one of the new clubs that catered to what the marketing lads called an older demographic. For men, an older demographic. The women, late twenties, earlier thirties, running the gamut from divorcees to never-marrieds and husband-out-of-town cheaters. In other words, perfect for picking up.

To win this evening's freedom he'd had to call Cam and tell her he had an emergency staff meeting at the hospital. Seems there was a chance that they might be hit with a malpractice suit thanks to something a dumb-ass nurse had done in the post-op of a fellow doctor's patient. She had sympathized, of course. A good, true woman. A man couldn't ask for better. He hadn't had to strain to sound contemptuous when the subject of nurses came up. He was of the belief that nurses were for doctors to have sex with; medically, they were useless.

All fine with Cam, who in fact worked at a free clinic two evenings a week, this being one of them. She'd see him later.

The good doctor was now free to roam.

Cam followed Bill from the hospital to the club. She needed to be sure where he'd be drinking and trawling tonight. She gave him fifteen minutes inside, making sure he'd be there when she got back, and then hit the expressway, using the directions the young woman had written down for her so carefully.

Amy Todd was the young woman's name. Cam had seen the potential immediately. There was real beauty there once the vulgarity was scrubbed away and suitable attire covering the elegant, slender body. They'd spent four hours shopping earlier that day. Half the time Amy was fascinated not only by the clothes but the casual way Cam spent so much money. The other half of the time she worried aloud that she was nervous about this whole thing. The nervousness was quelled when Cam went into the bank, leaving Amy in the car, and returned with nine thousand dollars in cash and six thousand dollars in traveler's checks.

When she slipped into the car tonight, Amy was almost unrecognizable from the trailer trash posing as middle-class she'd been forty-eight hours earlier. She'd insisted on some sort of disguise, so Cam took her to her personal hairdresser, and the elegant blonde was now the elegant brunette. Shania Twain with a hint of Jackie Kennedy. God Almighty, how could Bill resist?

"I'm still nervous, Mrs. Carlyle."

"I thought I was Cam."

"Okay, Cam. I've never done anything like this."

"You've never met a man in a bar and gone home with him?"

"Just a couple of times. I was always afraid he'd be a serial killer or something."

Cam laughed. "Well, Bill is no serial killer, believe me. Serial other things, yes, but not a killer."

"I know, but—"

"But what?"

"I guess it's just the sneakiness."

Cam pulled away from the curb and shook her head. "Think about where we're going. You don't think he sneaks around on me? The only way I can get the divorce settlement I want is to have absolute proof that he's cheated on me."

Amy shrugged the shoulders of her ice blue silk Donna Karan blouse.

"This way, we both get what we want. You'll have the money you need to get out of the city. And I'll have my freedom."

Amy stared back at the apartment compound where she lived. Severely designed and laid out as starkly as a prison. All it needed was a guard tower. The cars lined up at the curb were old and dirty in the moonlight.

Amy turned back to Cam. "I just hope I can hire a lawyer who'll help me get my kid back when I get to LA. That's all I care about, Mrs. Carlyle. Getting my kid back."

"Well, Amy, you'll have thirteen or fourteen thousand dollars to hire him with even after you pay for your air fare."

Amy gave her one of her rare smiles. Ravishing. Poor Bill wouldn't know how to say no.

* * *

There were three or four of him in the bar tonight. He'd always been fascinated by the idea of doppelgangers, and this was in a way that very thing.

Three or four men, gray haired, classically handsome, well dressed—but without the sagging, fleshy jowls and the loose, protruding belly. They reminded him of him—several years ago.

They glided up and down the bar like sleek predatory birds waiting to swoop down the street. And they had no hesitation about escorting stunning young women to the dance floor, something Dr. Bill had stopped doing when the belly couldn't be restrained anymore. He hated the sight of lumpy old people on the dance floor looking silly, pathetic. Hated the idea of other people looking at him and thinking those exact same thoughts.

These doppelgangers were as good as he'd once been. They were after top-grade sex and would settle for nothing less. He wished he could hear their conversations, be reminded of how much fun it had been when the very best let him escort them home. Anybody could take home a lesser woman. Top grade was another matter. But top grade had eluded him for several years now, which is why he'd ended up at one of those knee-banging little cocktail tables with two public relations women, one of whom seemed offended by his presence (she must have rolled her eyes at every second thing he said) while the other one, the one he'd likely end up with, was interested and pretty but in no way top grade.

Ms. Eye Roller finally excused herself, saying, "I hope you and Gramps here have a good time."

Donna, for that was her name, a name he'd inexplicably never cared for, said: "She hates older men ever since she got dumped by her boss."

He wasn't sure that he liked the older men reference, but he said, scarcely believing his own words, "Would you like to dance?"

And knew instantly that he'd said something profoundly foolish. "Really?" she said as if he'd just suggested something insane. Which, in fact, it was.

* * *

Cam found one of those coffee bars where you could rent a laptop. She couldn't write the letter at home. Too easy to trace.

On the drive over, the letter had been perfectly composed in her mind. But now that she sat in the quiet, near-empty place, the words weren't the right words at all. Writing had always been difficult for her—despite the fact that she read three novels a week, her own words never seemed to convey the meaning she wanted—and so she faced some serious time with the computer.

Half an hour later, her coffee cup empty, she stood up and got herself a refill. The place was getting crowded with twenty-somethings. They were so fresh and vital, they seemed to be of another species, a decided improvement on the previous edition. She too had been a member of that species for a time, but she'd been kicked out early because of her age. Actually, she thought, her cowardice had gotten her kicked out. She should have had the strength to leave Bill when she first caught him cheating. God, this was back when he was still an intern in New York. He'd promised never again, never again.

She always thought that she might have left him if the boys hadn't come along so quickly. But there she was, wanting the best for her sons, and how could she get it if she divorced Bill? The years collapsed one upon the other, and in the course of that collapse—the Tudor-style-estate house; the summer home up on Lake Michigan; the European trips she took with girlfriends who were in the same marital predicament; and—face it—the social importance of being attached to a man of Bill's stature—no guts, no glory, just an endlessly luxurious, endlessly empty life.

Bill, of course, led a life full of accomplishments and riches. And not just his surgical triumphs and not just his enormous income. She estimated that over the years he'd had six serious mistresses and God alone knew how many one-night stands. Not including tonight. Yet.

They slept in separate bedrooms, they took only a few meals

together, they conspired to put on a show of Happy Mommy and Daddy for the sake of the boys, who knew better anyway, and they continued the fiction of him working late so many nights and her gently chiding him for being such a dedicated medical man.

But about a year ago, when some whore he'd met somewhere had started calling her late at night and drunk—ironically when he was out with some other whore—she knew she could no longer live like this with even a pretense of dignity.

Was this a five-drink dream?

The other men along the bar, bartender included, had to be wondering the same thing. Because they were in the dream too.

The young woman—if she was even that—had appeared half a drink after the doctor's public relations woman had deserted him for a different dancer. Young, slender, mesmerized by her breasts. He'd retreated, sullen, to the bar. Never mind Grade-A material. She'd been B material at best, and even then he couldn't hang on to her.

He had been sulking when the bartender interrupted his orgy of self-pity and set a fresh drink down in front of him. "I didn't order that."

"No," the bartender said, "but she did."

And then he saw her. And then the notion that this was all a dream came to him. Because she was beautiful in a simple, fresh, startling way that a man his age shouldn't even dream about. This was beyond even Grade-A material. He was so shocked by her gesture, he couldn't fully appreciate the curiosity and jealousy of the other men at the bar—losers like him; the successful ones were on the dance floor or at one of those knee-knocking little tables.

And the dream continued. . . .

A slow song played now, and everybody in the place knew what that meant. Universal dry-humping on the dance floor, a few couples so excited that they would slip from the dance floor into the shadows where they would have sweaty standing-up sex in the booze-and-coke delusion that they were suddenly invisible.

But there was none of that with her. They danced closely but not intimately. But he held her, and for now that was enough, almost too much, really. It had been quite a few years since his fingers had felt flesh this taut but supple and he'd seen a face so pure in its elegance that it inspired not merely sexual fantasies but memories of real romance. For just a moment there on the dance floor of couples groping each other, he was living in a past time, back when he was still interning and numbingly in love with a night nurse on his floor. He'd almost left Cam for her and would have too if Cam hadn't gotten pregnant.

She kissed him then—she, she, she; he didn't have a clue about her name—a gentle kiss, with her long, slender fingers brushing the back of his head and the subtle scent of her perfume making him weak with the memories of that long-ago night nurse.

And the world he had inhabited only moments ago fell away. He had no idea of how many songs they danced to. Not even if they were fast or slow. He was all need—need of her specifically and need of what she represented. He was a man reborn, a man who had not felt this vital in a decade or more. And somehow, then they were in his car. And somehow, then they were in the catacombs of the parking garage attached to the hotel where she was staying. And somehow, then they were in bed.

The taste of her sex threatened to make his mind burst into joyous insanity. He was drinking the very elixir of immortality. He came even before he entered her, but it didn't matter. He was ready again in minutes, recalling his fraternity days when he had Olympic-class hard-ons. And this time he lasted for longer than twenty minutes, shifting positions so that he could plunge his miracle rod into her every way possible.

And then, after many minutes that seemed like glorious hours, they were spent.

* * *

"I've never felt like this."

She had a Mona Lisa smile. If it was a smile. Her beauty was enigmatic, timeless. She would have been as lovely in the time of Rome and King Arthur or the Renaissance or Winston Churchill. Lovely, but always difficult to read in any satisfying way. He sensed enormous secrets in her, but had no idea of how to dislodge them.

"I could stay the night."

Rule one, according to all his friendly fellow philanderers: always go home to mama. You pull an overnight, your ass is grass.

"I really need to get up early."

"That wouldn't bother me. I have to get up early too."

"You're married."

"I didn't say I was married."

The odd, unreadable smile again. "You didn't have to."

"That obvious?"

"Afraid so."

They lingered apart. When he touched her hip with glancing fingers, he felt a tremor race up and down her body. Or was it a shudder? Did she find him repulsive suddenly?

"You're a consultant, you said?"

"Yes. Office design."

He was watching her, eyes unwilling to leave her face for even a moment, when a shudder of his own troubled his stomach. He'd been holding off a bowel movement but could hold it no longer.

"Much as I don't want to, I have to excuse myself for a few minutes."

"I'll just lie here."

Nice if she'd said, *I'll just lie here and think about you*. In the old days he'd been not only a trusty cocksman but a trusty heartbreaker too. Hard to say which gave him more pleasure. The sex or knowing they'd fallen in love with him.

"Be right back."

No, *hurry back* or *I'll miss you.* Just watching him. Watching.

And when he finally did come back—much longer in there than he'd hoped, and God, he hoped the toxic odor had quelled by the time she needed to go—she was gone.

Her clothes. Her purse. Her person.

Gone.

Cam was no more or no less pissy with him than she usually was in the days and nights following his time with the mystery woman in the hotel. He had cautiously explained that his important medical meeting had run late, but she didn't seem interested one way or the other. For the next week of nights, he dutifully stayed home, the irony being that for three of those nights she was gone to her various meetings and social gatherings. The duties of a prominent man's wife.

He hadn't forgotten about the woman. That would have been impossible. He tried to find out her full name—Jane was all he had—but when he phoned the hotel, their computer information indicated that 605 had been registered that night not by a Jane but by a woman named Beth Whitney. The information indicated that she was a press officer for the state government and resided in the state capitol. Which turned out to be bullshit. No Beth Whitney listed on the state employment rolls, no such occupation as press officer except to the governor . . .

Who the hell was she, and where had she gone?

The letter arrived on a sunny Saturday morning. Cam had long ago been told never to touch his mail, to leave it on a small table outside his study.

It was the only piece of mail he received that morning. She propped it up against the wall behind the table. Impossible to miss. She wondered how many times she'd rewritten it since the night her faithless husband slept with the mystery woman in the hotel. Over and over she'd polished it.

"I think I'll play handball this afternoon," he announced at lunch.

"Very good exercise."

He looked at her then, something he rarely did. And it was more than merely looking. It was *studying* her. She felt her right hand begin to tremble, something it always did when she was nervous. Did he know that she'd hired the young woman? Did he know that his faithful wife had dummied up the letter? Had the young woman betrayed her, told him everything?

"You all right?"

"Fine, dear. Why?"

"You just sound—funny, I guess."

She smiled. "Afraid not. Same old grumpy lady I've always been."

He gave her the rote kiss before going to his den. The one on the side of the mouth. The only kind of kiss she'd had from him in a long, long time.

She sat and listened. She knew his temper well. After opening and reading the letter, he might well begin to smash up a few things in his den. He'd done that quite often. Some of the things had been impossible to replace. But he didn't value gifts any more than he valued his marriage.

And then it came. The entire house, enormous and all too showy (just the way he wanted it), seemed to tremble, much like her right hand. My God, she'd never heard him like this—this loud, this furious, this obscene.

But Cam supposed she would be just as enraged if somebody she'd slept with sent a letter a few weeks afterward saying that they had just been diagnosed HIV positive.

Bill would get himself tested, of course; he was vain, arrogant, even idiotic in his own way, but he wasn't stupid. When the test came back negative, he might chalk up the letter as a mean-spirited prank. But Cam hoped that the fear he was feeling now would have a sobering effect on him, that he would realize that he wasn't a thirty-year-old lothario anymore. That he looked ridiculous prowling the bars at his age. That it was time for him to settle down for good.

But if not . . .

Cam opened her purse and removed the dirty syringe that she had taken from a junkie dying of AIDS at the free clinic. She held it delicately in her hand while listening to Bill rage and swear in his office.

There were always other ways.

Miss Faversham's Room

Chelsea Quinn Yarbro

"And this," said the housekeeper, "is Miss Faversham's room." She indicated the door on the broad landing halfway up the staircase as the two of them climbed the wide, carpeted stairs. "Actually, it's three rooms: a sitting room, a bedroom, and a dressing room. The bathroom is through the interior door and isn't considered a part of Miss Faversham's suite since it has access to the swimming-pool area, although the interior door makes it seem private." She used her key-card to open the door and stood aside to permit her companion to enter ahead of her.

"I've been told every Faversham hotel—all fifteen of them—has a room just like this, a suite, really, although they don't call it that," said Harold Bright, speaking into his Thumbnail recorder as he walked into the room, the housekeeper behind him. He noted the room was a bit cold, as if the heat hadn't been turned on yet; shrugging against the pull of his luggage strap, he dismissed the chill as the result of the room being used rarely.

"Surely you've already seen a few of them," the housekeeper said with an air of remonstrance.

"I've seen some," he said without missing a beat. "But not all."

"Well, then I suppose you know as well as I that Miss Faversham's room is an intrinsic part of every Faversham hotel," she said.

"That's what all the PR material says," Bright told her. "But I like to check on such things for myself."

"I suppose that's a reasonable precaution," the housekeeper agreed, going to the thermostat and turning it up.

"You know how these things are," said Bright, turning to look directly at the housekeeper. "Sometimes it's hard to sort out fact from publicity."

"I'm sure the Board could provide you with the information you need—accurate information," said the housekeeper.

"They've been very helpful so far," said Bright, trying to stifle a sudden yawn, for although it was three-thirty in the afternoon, he had been traveling since ten the previous morning and had only arrived in Belgium from Buenos Aires two hours ago.

"Then you will know whom to ask for more material," said the housekeeper.

Bright decided to change tactics. "You must get many inquiries about this place, given the history of the chain," he prompted, reminding himself how important it was to chat up the staff, particularly since he did not truly fit into his surroundings. The leather duffle slung over his shoulder, although of excellent quality, seemed a bit shabby in this gorgeous room. Even his tweed jacket, silk shirt, and flannel slacks were a trifle too down-market for the suite with its museum-quality furnishings.

"Yes, we do," the housekeeper said, her answer well rehearsed. "And yes: there is such a room in all our hotels. Every one of them on the landing of the Grand Staircase, as this one is; they're modeled on this room, of course. The Empire House is the first Faversham hotel. But I suppose you know that." She patted the back of a swan-armed Empire sofa as if it were a spoiled pet. "They are furnished to complement the hotel, of course, which is why this one is in the Empire style. I'm sure you've seen the styles for each of them." She went on automatically, "The hotel in London is Tudor, the one in Geneva is Art Deco, the one in Buenos Aires is eighteenth century classical, and the one in Montreal is—"

"—Louis XV," said Bright, unable to resist showing off to the housekeeper. "The one in Tokyo is Art Nouveau, the one is Moscow is Russian Imperial, and the one in Washington is Federalist. The Roman hotel is Renaissance; the Berlin, Grand Baroque. The one in LA is Spanish Colonial. The Faversham room is always decorated to match the stylistic theme of the hotel, and always in superb taste." He smiled at the housekeeper. "I've seen the American and European Favershams but not the Tokyo hotel; I'm scheduled to fly to Japan next week to see their Faversham. Then on to Melbourne for the opening of the newest in the chain, making sixteen. Edwardian decor, all the pre-opening releases say, with a great deal of crystal and fine wallpaper. Then just four to go, and I'll put the article together for publication next November, which is our annual top hotels issue."

"So I understand from the CEO; Monsieur dePuy has said to extend you every courtesy, "said the housekeeper primly. "I trust you'll enjoy your stay, and that your article will reflect well on the Faversham chain." She touched the soft collar of her cream-colored blouse that set off her navy blue wool suit. Her smile was professional—more teeth than goodwill—in contrast to her neat, self-effacing demeanor.

"So far so good," said Bright, taking in the handsome room with its elegant furniture and beautiful appointments, including a tall porcelain vase on an ebony highboy and a dragon-motif lamp that looked as if it had escaped from Brighton Pavilion.

"It's most unusual, allowing a journalist to stay in Miss Faversham's room. Usually only corporate guests are permitted to use the room, no matter which hotel it may be in. Your publication must be more widespread than I had supposed," said the housekeeper in a tone of polite inquiry. "How did you happen to get such an assignment?"

"It's my editor's idea," said Harold Bright. "He couldn't set it up for Moscow or Rome, but Montreal was fine, and so was Washington and Vienna and Buenos Aires, which opened the doors to all the rest of the chain. This one is the prize." He tried not to look smug but failed. "If all goes well, I'll get a book deal as well as the article out of it. It's a real incentive. And I get to stay in these wonderful hotels." He swung his free arm to take in not only Miss Faversham's room but the whole of the Empire House.

"A very *nice* assignment, if I may say so," the housekeeper observed. "I haven't been to the Moscow hotel, nor the one in Hong Kong. Grand Victorian, with Chinese accents."

"Overstuffed chairs and a lot of wicker, large mirrors and portraits in heavy frames, along with Ming vases and Chinese carvings," said Bright. "Beautiful carpets, polished wood, and brass." He paused. "This is the flagship hotel, isn't it?"

"Yes. Horatio Faversham built it in 1874. It was ten years before he built the London Faversham, the Tudor House."

Bright hoped to keep her talking, so he said, "Wasn't it risky—an Englishman opening a hotel in Brussels?"

"This hotel was originally intended for British travelers to the Continent. Brussels was often the place they began their journeys, and Horatio's Faversham gambled that this would be the kind of establishment they would want before they moved on. The next hotel was built in Paris—I trust you know that."

"The Grand Epoch House," Bright confirmed, recalling that Faversham had wanted Louis XIV, but that proved impossible, and so Faversham had gone for another kind of grandeur. "Then Vienna in 1901. His son Percival inherited four hotels in 1909; he expanded slowly and still almost lost all he owned during World War I, but he hung on and made a fortune before the end. I don't know much more about him, but I've found a couple of troubling references to him," Bright added to show he knew the basics and to encourage the housekeeper to enlarge upon his knowledge. "I don't know what to make of him." He noticed the heating had begun its soft, warm whisper.

"He *is* a bit of a puzzle," said the housekeeper. "He was a prudent businessman, beyond question, and he laid the foundations for the entire chain in spite of setbacks, but his private life was . . ." She cleared her throat and went on more carefully. "There were many rumors at the time he owned the chain, some quite . . . unsavory, as I infer you have discovered. But Percival was not a well-liked man, and some of what was said about him might be nothing more than a reflection of that dislike, which one should bear in mind when reviewing the reports. At the time, nothing could be proven, but the accusations made . . . I was shocked to read a few letters from the thirties and forties. If half of what they hinted was true, I can only pity his poor wife, having to live with such a man."

"And daughter," Bright suggested.

"Certainly she had a great deal to handle—assuming the worst of the rumors were true, which they may not have been." This last was accentuated by a turndown of her mouth, as if in realization that she had said too much about Percival Faversham. "Miss Faversham took over the chain—then seven hotels—in 1947, the year after her father's . . . death."

"The final decision was suicide, wasn't it?" Bright asked, making note of the housekeeper's wince at the suggestion.

"That was the ruling; there wasn't sufficient evidence for the coroner to find it was murder. Given the taint of scandal, and the politics of the time, it was the most justifiable conclusion that could be reached, or so Miss Faversham decided." She coughed delicately, lifting her handkerchief to her mouth. "No one thought a girl of twenty-four could possibly manage such a huge business, but she not only managed, she enlarged and improved the chain to what we see today." The housekeeper shook her head, signaling the end of her forthcoming remarks; she returned to her prepared spiel. "The hotels were her whole life. You probably know that she died in the Istanbul hotel?"

"The Ottoman House, in 1994."

"August ninth," the housekeeper supplied and turned away.

"I understand she wanted to be preserved cryogenically, or

cremated and her remains put into the foundation of her hotels." Bright almost made it a question—one to which he was yet to have an answer.

The housekeeper pretended not to hear this last. "The bellboy will bring your bags up directly. You are familiar with the arrangements of this suite. Your computer can be connected any number of ways; there is a book describing the various links and lines we offer. The room-service menu will be brought up to you. We don't keep one in Miss Faversham's room; she never needed one." She put down the room key-card on a splendid little occasional table standing not far from the door and started to leave, not quickly enough to seem rude. "I'm not available from seven until ten AM, and five until nine-forty PM, but otherwise you need only call my office and have my assistant page me for you."

"Thanks," said Bright, nodding as he looked around the room again. "The place is pretty impressive. It wears its age well, doesn't it?"

"You could put it that way," said the housekeeper.

"I seem to remember there was a major renovation not long ago—is that right?"

"In 1998," she said, preparing to depart. "Everything was modernized and made energy efficient. The whole chain will be energy efficient in four more years."

"Well, it looks great," said Bright, taking care to put his duffle on the floor instead of on the butler's table next to the elegant sofa.

"Thank you. Enjoy your stay," said the housekeeper as she let herself out of the room.

Bright nodded to the empty room. "Thanks," he said and shoved his hand into his pocket to find the five-dollar bill he had put there. He also touched his cell phone and wondered idly if he should use it to let his boss know he had arrived. "Not yet," he said aloud as he continued to take stock of the room; he often talked to himself when there was no one else to hear him. He coughed as a suggestion of a smoky odor went through on an unexpected breeze; a window must be ajar—he would have to find the source and close it. "Then something to take the edge off," he said aloud, stretching to relieve his muscles from the hours of travel he had endured yesterday and today, truncated though they were. Strolling around the suite, he had to guard against the sense of déjà vu that took hold of him—too many nights in eerily similar rooms. If it weren't for the different styles of furnishings, this suite might have been in any number of Faversham Hotels, and he could be in any one of fifteen cities. He began to look for the opened window and discovered that the side door in the bathroom leading to the hall to the swimming pool was open a crack. He closed it, wondering why it wasn't locked. He returned to the sitting room and tried to make up his mind whether he should get out his laptop or continue to use his Thumbnail.

His cogitation was interrupted by a short rap on the door, and the call, "Bellhop."

Bright went to open the door, ready to hand over the bill in his pocket. "Just bring them in and set them down. I'll sort them out later," he said as the bellboy maneuvered the handsome brass trolley through the door and into the center of the sitting room.

"If you like, sir," said the bellboy, a lanky fellow about forty whose face showed almost no emotion. He lifted Bright's large, wheeled duffle off the trolley, then hefted the large Gladstone bag and set it beside the duffle, and in a single motion took the five-dollar bill and slipped it into his tip-pouch. "Thank you very much, sir," he murmured as he made for the door, pulling the empty trolley after him. "I've been told to bring you a room-service menu. It'll take me about ten minutes to do it, if you don't mind the wait." His accent was basic British but smoothed down to a regionless clip.

"Fine," said Bright. "But could you ask them to send up a cognac, at least twelve years old?"

"Certainly; I'll have the waiter bring you the menu." He

stopped. "Doesn't this room have a private bar?" The question was out before he could stop it.

"None of the others have had," said Bright.

"Oh," said the bellboy. "I'll tell room service, then." He opened the door and swung the trolley out of the room. "Ten minutes, sir."

"I'll be here," said Bright, stretching again as he felt the knots in his shoulders start to loosen. He ambled around the room, taking in the beautiful layout, the fine appointments that punctuated the splendor of the setting. The room was quiet, but the activity in the hotel was obvious. In his travel from Faversham hotel to Faversham hotel, Bright had come to appreciate the strategic location, for the pulse of the hotel thrummed along the Grand Staircase. From this suite, Miss Faversham had been able to monitor the place without having to open her door. He shivered once as he pulled off his jacket and dropped it over the arm of the sofa.

Room service arrived with a snifter of excellent cognac; Bright signed for it, accepted a room-service menu, tipped the waiter, and set out to enjoy his stay. He went from the sitting room into the bedroom and found the forty-two-inch television in the larger of two armoires. Taking the remote, he plopped himself down on the bed and turned the set on, allowing the disasters and riots to wash over him as he supposed Miss Melantha Faversham had done. It was hard to think of war and ruin in this beautiful room. Sipping his cognac, he got out his Thumbnail recorder and began to recite into it all the beautiful items he had noticed in this suite, starting with the bed and lighting fixtures, then going around the room. "Two Empire armoires," he ended up. "One for television, one for clothing, I guess. They say Miss Faversham kept a complete and appropriate wardrobe in each of her rooms in her hotels so she wouldn't have to travel with more than a single suitcase." He had looked in the wardrobes and closets of all the other rooms he had stayed in and resolved to do the same here, but later, when it would feel less like snooping. "Fine quality antiques, as per usual, excellent state of preservation, and everything useful as well as elegant." He paused, then said to the recorder, "Miss Faversham must have been quite a character. Bit of a dragon but very ladylike. They say she never raised her voice. Women of that generation put a lot of emphasis on their femininity." He stared up at the ceiling, noticing the decorative plasterwork consisting of an oblong medallion in the center of the room with ball-and-lozenge accents at the corners. "I hope that's original. These days, it would cost a fortune to put in."

He turned off the Thumbnail and let his mind wander; he was a bit jet-lagged, although he didn't want to admit it, and it was pleasant not to have to concentrate on his work. He blinked and glanced at the television, where the screen was filled with milling crowds in Chinese clothing in front of two large buildings going up in flames; a skittish reporter stood at the edge of it all, trying to describe what was happening behind him.

Bright got up and found the leather-bound room-service menu, turning to the central page for the most utilitarian listing of available food. As he had found in other Faversham hotels, this one had an eclectic offering for hungry travelers. He selected the spring rolls, the endive salad, the sturgeon in pastry, and the grilled eggplant accompanied by a half-carafe of five-year-old Côtes du Rhône. As soon as he called this in, he decided he had time for a quick bath—Miss Faversham had never had a shower installed in her bathroom, not in any of her hotels—and loosened his tie while he programmed his watch to buzz in twenty minutes, time enough to bathe and be out of the tub by the time his meal arrived.

This bathroom was a wonderland of pink marble, tall mirrors, golden fixtures, and an elevated tub of lavish size. After turning the gold-plated spigots to fill the tub, Bright hung his garments on the silent butler, then opened the closet to remove one of the Turkish cotton robes he knew would be hanging in it. He set this on the seat of the silent butler, stepped out of his shoes, and bent to remove his socks, then stopped as he felt another draft slither through the room. He stood still for a moment, a sock in his hand, waiting for something to happen. Surely the door hadn't opened again. When nothing more occurred, he removed his second sock and went to the bathtub, tested the water with his hand, and, satisfied with the heat, climbed into the hot water, reaching for the nearest packet of soap as he did. He knew it would smell of lavender and violet—all soaps in Miss Faversham's room had that aroma—but he did his best to ignore it. The bath was polished marble, five feet long with sloping sides that made it easy for the six-foot Bright to recline without sinking. He sighed and closed his eyes for a couple of minutes before reaching for the large, natural sponge set in the basket-shaped soap dish at the side of the tub and set to lathering it up. Little as he wanted to admit it, his thirty-nine-year-old body was beginning to feel the wear and tear of a life spent traveling. He made a point of massaging the tightened muscles in the backs of his calves and his shoulders.

Emerging from the bath just before his watch hummed, he toweled himself lightly, shivering a little in another unexpected breeze, then shrugged into the luxurious Turkish bathrobe, tied the belt, and wandered out into the sitting room to fetch his bags. He was just unzipping the large duffle when the rap on the door announced the arrival of his meal. He found six Euros tucked into the pages of a book he had been reading on the plane, then went to admit the waiter with his rolling tray.

"Just put it in front of the sofa," Bright requested, pointing. "Move the butler's table if you have to."

The waiter complied without having to move the butler's table, accepted his tip, and left the room in less than a minute.

Bright wandered back and sat down, lifting the covers off the dishes and inhaling deeply. He set aside the lid from the spring rolls—three of them, laid on a bed of shredded cabbage; a small serving of sweet-and-sour sauce, and another of hoisin sauce accompanied the appetizers, which he ate with his fingers, licking the sauce off his hands when he was through, feeling a bit gauche but enjoying himself. Then he picked up his salad fork and began on the endive leaf by leaf, each of the five leaves bearing a dollop of sour cream topped with caviar. "To think Miss Faversham dined like this every day of her adult life," said Bright to the room as he finished the salad and gave his attention to the sturgeon, watching the pastry flake as his fork went through it.

A sudden ringing of the phone jarred Bright so much that he almost dropped his fork. He frowned as he reached out to pick up the receiver, wondering who might be calling him. "Harold Bright."

"Harry," boomed Jeremy Snow, the managing editor of *World Traveler* magazine. "How was the flight from Buenos Aires? How's Brussels?"

"Pleasant; it's supposed to drizzle tonight, but just now it's cloudy," Bright answered, glancing toward the window, where the light had turned a tarnished silver color as the day wound toward its close. "The flight was uneventful. But you're not calling about the weather, or my traveling. What can I do for you?"

Snow laughed aloud. "There you go—business first, last, and always."

"That's what you pay me for," said Bright, putting his fork down and reaching for his napkin.

"Truth, truth," said Snow. "Okay, here it is: we need you to stay on for an extra day. We'll get your new plane tickets before nine tomorrow, but it's important that you attend the semi-annual Faversham's executives' luncheon on Thursday. They're supposed to be discussing two new hotels planned. I want to be the magazine to break the news about where and what theme these new Favershams will have."

"Okay." Bright looked around for a pen. "What time and where?"

"At the Empire House, of course. I'll e-mail the pertinent information before I go home this evening; make sure you log on to get it, and use tomorrow to prepare for the meeting. Make sure you go over it before the meeting. I've cleared it with dePuy, who'll be expecting you." Snow chuckled. "Remind me to tell you how I finessed the invite."

"Yes, please," said Bright because it was expected of him.

"So you make sure you make the most of it. I want to know where those two new hotels are going to be. My bet's on Cairo for one, maybe Mexico City for the other. I know the New York hotel is still on hold." He made it sound as if he didn't want to be wrong. "I'll want details, of course, and schedules."

"I'll make sure to talk to dePuy," said Bright.

"And get as much information as you can out of the rest of the executives. They all probably have plans and projects we'll want to put in the story." He paused. "I'm upping your article to 18,000 words. I'll push it as high as 20,000 if you get an extra scoop."

"That's great," said Bright, contemplating the prospect of filling eighty pages with enthusiastic puffery.

"I want you to call me after the meeting. Right after. No half-hour delays. Use your cell phone—why else do we pay for international connections? I'll be waiting." Snow didn't wait for a response but hung up without farewell.

Bright looked at the receiver in his hands and shook his head slowly before putting it back on the cradle. "Thanks," he muttered, returning to his meal with mixed annoyance and fatigue. The food had lost most of its savor, but Bright knew that was because of the pall of tension that had come over him, not anything in the meal itself. Three bites of the sturgeon in pastry, and he was done. He poured himself a glass of the wine he had ordered and drank it down too quickly. He debated ordering a second carafe when he remembered that he had a little of the cognac left in the bedroom, so he tossed off the last of the wine, moved the rolling tray toward the main door, picked up his Gladstone bag, and made for the bedroom, determined to do his utmost to relax. He hung up the Turkish robe and scrambled into his pajamas, noticing again that there was a draft in the room. Pulling back the duvet, he got in between the sheets and pulled the duvet up to his chin as he reached for the television remote and toggled the sound back on.

"—ooding has claimed the lives of at least a hundred people in the town of San Tomas," the anchorman intoned while pictures of a torrential river filled the screen. "Authorities are concerned that with two bridges and three roads wiped out, rescue workers may not be able to reach San Tomas for at least thirty-six hours."

A suggestion of a pop claimed Bright's attention; he sat up and felt a cold finger of air trace along his arm and shoulder. "Shit," he said and got out of bed to fetch his laptop: Snow's e-mail might be waiting for him, and he wanted to look it over. The air was chilly as he crossed the bedroom, and he took a little time to conduct a search for the source of the draft and once again found the bathroom door into the outer hall ajar. Now he was bothered. He closed the door firmly and made a point of locking it. "I forgot before," he said aloud, as if to reassure himself that he had. Returning to the bedroom, he turned on his computer, made his e-mail connection, and saw that Snow hadn't yet sent the information. He conducted a desultory check of the rest of the e-mails, added one to Sheryl, telling her of his changed schedule. As he sent his e-mail to her, he admitted to himself that their relationship had probably cooled past saving. She no longer worried when he traveled and didn't fret when he was delayed. Her own career was thriving, and increasingly she put her attention on her work rather than on him. He was startled to realize how much this saddened him. "Maybe if we'd married . . ." he said, closing his laptop, setting it on the nightstand, turning down the lamp, and getting back under the covers.

The television was showing a fast-moving twister cutting a swath across southern Missouri, flinging buildings and vehicles into the air in crazed abandon; then a pasty-faced middle-aged man describing how his wife had vanished into the eye of the storm. "I couldn't b'lieve it. I just couldn't," he said, his expression blank. "Up she went. Up. I couldn't stop her." This was followed by a weatherman with maps and charts, talking about activity zones and possible new tornados.

Bright took the last of the cognac in a single gulp, put the snifter aside, then lay back to watch the rest of the news. Almost at once the screen filled with a shot of central Bucharest, where two large mobs were locked in street fighting. The sounds of gunfire mixed with shouting and sirens. "—began when two Moldavian men were convicted of killing three youths of the pro-Turkish Reconciliation Party last year," the announcer droned. Bright shook his head, glad he wouldn't be going to Istanbul again any time soon. He watched the images flickering and tried to organize his thoughts as the first, welcome nudge of sleep came over him. He reached for the remote to turn it off, but it eluded him, and he sank back on the pillows, already in the twilight between slumber and wakefulness.

Strange how much this room was like the one in the Grand Colonial House in Buenos Aires. Or perhaps it was more like the Grand Victorian House in Hong Kong?

"—estimated the number of students protesting at six thousand. Early reports say that several hundred were arrested, and dozens sent to hospital—"

Student riots? Not in Hong Kong, surely. But there were men in threadbare clothes howling in the streets and sporadic gunfire from somewhere. Two men in uniforms that looked old-fashioned stood at the foot of the bed in what looked like the Grand Baroque House in Berlin, but with elements of other Faversham hotels mixed with it. They spoke eagerly, apparently preparing for a night of pleasure, for one of the men removed his tunic while the other took a silver cigarette case from somewhere and lit up, willing to wait his turn. On the bed, a woman reclined, her eyes half closed and smoky. Bright had the dismaying sensation of being permeated by the woman, so that he and she were trans-

fixed by this partial dream. He tried to twist free, but her presence held him where he was as the men at the end of the bed prepared to have sex with her. Bright felt drugged and realized that the woman was high on something. Again he attempted to break free of her, and again he failed.

"—with the German chancellor saying that he would oppose funding for such a wasteful project—"

One of the men was naked now and caressing the woman on the bed in a perfunctory way before he climbed onto her and shoved between her thighs. Bright squirmed in disgust and sternly told himself to wake up. The men faded, and he seemed to be in Miss Faversham's room in Los Angeles at the Spanish House; he recognized the exposed black beams and adobe-finished walls. A slow wind flapped the draperies on the far wall, and the noise of traffic was loud in the room. Bright strove to wake up but was left to flounder on the bed while a tall, lean man with a pistol in his hand approached the bed, the barrel leveled at the occupant, who Bright realized was a middle-aged woman in a lavish peignoir. He felt more than heard her say, "You don't want to do anything so stupid, Ronald, now do you?" and then she extended her arm toward the man. "You don't have to be a fool." The decor, Bright realized, was at least one renovation ago, and the clothes were those of the 1950s; the man looked like something out of a gangster movie. Bright squirmed, but only mentally, as the woman reached out for the gun. "You can put it down, Ronald. And put something better up." No matter how corny this sounded to Bright, the man hesitated, and the woman smiled.

"—the penalty phase of the trial. Since Hammond was convicted on eleven counts of first-degree murder, it's likely the jury won't need much time to decide on the most severe—"

Now it was the Geneva hotel, probably in the eighties, Bright supposed. The room was dark and smelled of scented oil. He felt the woman, now noticeably older, stretched out through him, in spite of aching shoulders and hips. She was stroking her thighs and belly, murmuring, "Too bad about Ronald. Poor man. Too bad about Paul and Ernst, too bad about Demetrios, too bad about Jaime, too bad about Trevor, too bad about Papa, too bad about Claude, too bad about Sergei, too bad about Tazuki, too bad about . . ." The names went on in a dreamy litany as Bright began to share the old lady's arousal. He shuddered and tried to break free of the hold she had on him, but to no avail; her need possessed him, and he was inextricably bound to her presence. He shivered, unable to banish the cold that engulfed him even as the old woman suborned his body. He could share her memories, the faces and locations for each of the men. "One for each hotel," she crooned as she shook in ecstasy, and Bright was seized by his own orgasm. "Each hotel a shrine, and a tomb." She swallowed a pill and drifted into profound sleep, still reciting the names of men she had—had what? Had killed? Had seduced? Had—Bright moaned even as he lapsed into sleep.

"Before the dam collapsed, mandatory evacuations saved more than six thousand residents from drowning. Present damage estimates are at sixty million dollars and climbing. The premier of Alberta has already dispatched four hundred aid workers to the area most damaged by the dam failure, has ordered an investigation of the explosion that caused it, and has set up an identification and relocation office in West Frazier—"

Bright sat up with a cry, his eyes wild as he stared around the room, and saw only the television set, still turned to International CNN; the first pallid, pre-dawn light filled the room and made everything look slightly unreal. He lunged out of bed and staggered toward the bathroom, wanting nothing so much as to wash himself. As he stumbled through the door, he felt the draft again and noticed the outer bathroom door was once again ajar. "What the fuck—?" he muttered and went to lock the door again. He was about to fill the tub when he hesitated. So much of this bathroom was *hers* that he could not bring himself to expose himself to her again.

"That's just silly," he told his reflection and said, more forcefully, "You've been immersed in this story. You're saturated with it. You were worn out. You fell asleep with the news on, and you made up things about Miss Faversham from what the TV said. Come on. You've got an assignment to finish." He stared at himself, doing his best to ignore the breeze that went through the bathroom, and the old, old eyes that looked back at him from his reflection in the mirror.

Axis

Gary Lovisi

"The blood spatter spoke to me of love and obsession and was born in violent sexual release."

I turned off my mini-recorder, put down my notes on the case, and thought again about what I had just discovered about the latest victim. That was Jennifer Kelly, murdered in a similar manner to the first victim, Wanda-June Esposito. But the Kelly murder scene showed some differences. The blood spatter was markedly different. I had to think over what that meant.

That was all before Ron was with me. He'd insisted on coming up.

"Julie," he'd called so forcefully. "I have to see you."

"Can't it wait? I'm in the middle of a new case, a second homicide that appears to be connected to the Esposito murder. That may mean a serial murderer. . . ." I tried to keep the excitement out of my voice, not really appropriate under the circumstances. However, that excitement was because I was a too-young, too-pretty, and too-new bloodstain analyst working for the police on a contract basis. I hoped this could be the case that made my career; you know, got it going to the big time. Maybe even TV spots with Greta and Geraldo. Ron's insistence and negativity about my chosen profession only complicated an already complicated relationship. He was a hot-shot Wall Street trader on the way up, and he didn't like what I was involved in.

"No, it can't wait, Julie. I haven't seen you all week. . . ."

"But I'm on this case . . ."

"I know. You're always on some kind of case. Look, I'm coming over." Ron was like that; he never took no for an answer. Sometimes I really liked that about him, but tonight I didn't.

I sighed, collected my paperwork, and prepared to put it away for the night. I tidied up the place, and then I took a shower and waited for Ron. I knew he could be possessive and obsessive, but the sex was totally incredible. Wild animal sex!

I waited in anticipation, wondering just what Ron had in store for me this time. Our first bout with rough sex had gone far over the limit. Ron had slapped my buttocks raw, calling me a mean, bad bitch, punishing me, humiliating me. However, instead of making me angry, it just got me excited, building me to a frenzy I'd never known before. Ron and I went on from there. He never slapped my face, and he always told me he loved me as he hit me. As long as he told me he loved me when he hit me, I figured that was okay. I know it was *out there*, but we liked being *out there*.

When he got to my place, he attacked me like a rabid beast whose lust hadn't been sated in months. I loved the attention, perhaps even required it. I melted under his power and let him take me hard and often. We both liked it rough. We often did it like this, so fast and furious. I realized that all the pent-up emotion these last two cases had brought out in me was coming out in our sexual bouts. If anything, once Ron initiated our rough foreplay, I continued it and even brought it into even more intense areas we'd never explored before.

Ron was surprised by my unleashed passion, and it brought us both off like we'd never experienced with any of our previous lovers.

After our bout of animal sex, lying in bed exhausted, I massaged my welts. My only hope was that they wouldn't show or become black and blue. I got an antiseptic from the medicine cabinet for the scratches I'd dug with my nails into Ron's back. Many of those cuts were still bleeding, and, as I wiped up the blood, I noticed the small drippings and spatters that ran down his back, onto my pillows and sheets. He was pretty badly torn up, and I gasped, then smiled, hardly believing I had done that to him.

Ron didn't mind though. He never complained about anything I did to him; he said he liked it all. He said he enjoyed the pain. He liked to get it, and he liked to give it. Ron told me he wanted us to go further in our sexual adventures, and I was intrigued. I didn't know what that meant, but he left it purposefully vague, a delicious and erotic surprise that I could fantasize about when I was alone and missing him.

When I awoke later, I discovered that Ron was gone from my bed and noticed that the light in the living room was on. I figured he was watching TV, but I heard no sound. Instead, I walked in on him sitting on the sofa looking over the Esposito and Kelly crime-scene photos.

"What are you doing?" I asked, more than a bit perturbed that he was looking over my private notes and personal papers on a case.

"Couldn't sleep; found these and figured they'd be more interesting than TV, so I took a look. Hope you don't mind."

"Well, no, of course not, but . . ."

"Interesting case," Ron commented quickly. "So you interpret the blood spatter at crime scenes. What does it tell you, Julie?"

"A lot of things, sometimes," I said.

"These crime-scene photos, they're"—he looked up at me, smiled wickedly—"very graphic. Very bloody. Are they always like this? The woman naked, so vulnerable, so much blood all over . . ."

"Look, Ron." I knew he wasn't used to such things in his day-to-day Wall Street world, and his prurient mind could turn anything onto a sexual angle. But this? "These women were murdered, bludgeoned to death. I don't think you should be looking at the photos in *that* way. It's not pornography, Ron."

Ron smiled. "Of course, Julie, I didn't mean anything by it." He put the crime-scene photos down, looked up at me, and said, "Come over here, you."

Then he took me again on the couch, then on the floor. It was harder than previously, more brutal. It hurt me a little, but I actually enjoyed it. When it was over, Ron left and I went to sleep, exhausted.

The third murdered woman showed up next morning. Clarissa Roberts. She'd been murdered the same way as the other two.

I was busy for the next few days and didn't see or hear from Ron until the murder was written up in the papers in a new article that used leaked information to connect the Roberts murder with the previous two. A task force was now formed, and it took most of my time. I ended up having to do more extra work when I discovered I'd somehow lost or misplaced some of the photos of the two previous murders. That really annoyed me.

I was dog-tired and ready for bed when Ron called that evening and said he had to come over. As tired as I was, I became wet with lust for him, anticipating our games. I told him to come up, but just for a little while, as I had an early day at work the next morning.

Ron and I went right to it as soon as he entered my apartment. This time he brought handcuffs, and he was wearing a mask. I didn't like it at first, but I was too excited to worry about it, and right away we were onto—and into—each other with a frenzy I'd never known before.

The problem was, I could see where, sometimes, Ron seemed to get carried away with things. The cuffs were too tight on me, but his wearing of the mask seemed to bring out a hidden part of him I'd never seen before. Some of it I liked; it was beyond kinky. But some of it was weird . . . scary. But I guess I liked that part too. And Ron wasn't the only one, because I got carried away with these new games. I wondered if either if us knew how far to take things before we stopped, how much pain was acceptable or not, and *if* we could stop.

Ron's newest kink was posing me. He'd force me down into various positions, bind me, then, when I was helpless and scared, he'd penetrate me in all three orifices. It was rough, even brutal, but I liked it most of the time. The last time, when I'd yelled at him to stop, I had to tell him to leave.

"What?" he shouted, annoyed I was breaking the fantasy. "The magic," as he called it. "Come on, you like this just as much as I do!"

"No! Stop! No more!" I shouted, angry now.

I was nervous, fearful of the look I'd seen in his eyes just then, a lust I saw that was not sexual any longer; it was only violent. You see, I had the strange feeling that Ron was posing me in scenes from the Kelly and Esposito murders. Some of the positions were eerily familiar from my crime-scene photos. That was just too much for me.

"I don't think I like this," I said, but when he asked me and I told him what I thought he was doing, he just laughed.

"Julie, what's the problem? It gets me off, I find those photos . . . interesting."

"I think they arouse you!"

"All right, so what if they do? It's nothing any different from some of the S&M porno we watch, stuff we both enjoy sometimes doing."

"Those are movies, fantasies. You're posing me like the killer posed Jennifer Kelly's body at my crime scene. She was a real person, a murdered woman. How could you? That's . . . disgusting!"

"Oh, come on now! You do the same thing. You tell me to do you this way, that way, stand or sit in a certain position . . . like you don't pose me! You don't hear me complaining, Julie. It's no big deal."

"Well, I don't think I like it," I said softly, thinking that maybe I'd been too severe with him. After all, Ron wasn't in law enforcement, or a victim, so he couldn't really understand.

Ron huffed about it. He looked angry, even hurt, but I think he was secretly pleased. I asked him to leave again, but mostly because I had a big day tomorrow. I had to give my presentation to the new serial-killer task force. I had more evidence connecting the third murder victim to the previous two. Ron left, and I prepared for bed.

Lying in bed alone that night, I thought about Ron and our relationship. It wasn't exactly right, I knew that, but I liked a lot of it. I don't know why I bothered with Ron sometimes. I'm sure really, down deep, he didn't like women—maybe not even me. But in spite of myself, I couldn't resist our games. I liked them too much. In a way, I may have been too much like Ron for my own good. Anyway, it was just too deep and complicated to try to figure out that night, so I just decided to go to sleep and allow myself to enjoy it as long as it lasted. After all, it was just sex and games, and that was just too much incredible fun for me to pass up.

The next morning I looked over my notes before my presentation like I always did. I noticed that some of the crime-scene photos for the third victim, Clarissa Roberts, seemed to be missing. I thought I'd had twelve 10 x 12 glossies in the file, but there were now only ten. I looked through all my files and papers, and the more I looked the more frantic I became. These were two of the most graphic photos of the lot. I never found them, and a cold chill struck me, so I called Ron. There was no answer at his office. I left a message and then left for work and gave my presentation to the police with the information I had on hand.

"The blood spatter on the first victim, Esposito," I told the detectives, "was projected—it was gushing blood, mostly in arterial spurts from a blow or blunt-force trauma. The blood spatter in victim number two, Kelly, created high-velocity bloodstains.

The pointed end of the bloodstain, the tail, indicates the directionality of the force. This victim was attacked from behind."

There were questions from the detectives, and I answered them as best I could.

"And that brings us to victim number three, the latest one, Clarissa Roberts. Again, we have projected blood. Most of it is as I have already described in the previous victims, but I also found something else. Something totally different. With this victim we have projected blood spatter, but of a unique pattern in one area of the murder scene: the wall behind the corpse. This blood was projected through a syringe."

That created an uproar, and the cops wanted to know what the hell that meant. So did I.

"I'm waiting for the DNA report on this blood sample, but I am sure it will indicate this particular syringe blood is not—can not be—from victim number three. I assume it will be found to be blood from victim number one or number two. If that proves to be the case, then we are not only faced with a very devious and brutal serial killer, but one who is apparently taunting us with his crimes."

The DNA report confirmed my findings. The detectives were not pleased. The press had to be notified, and more manpower was authorized for the task force.

I went home exhausted. When I got to my apartment, Ron was there waiting for me. Inside.

"Hope you don't mind. I let myself in," he said matter-of-factly, the usual charming Ron.

"I wasn't aware you still had a key," I replied testily but too dog-tired to argue. He'd obviously made a copy of the key I'd asked for him to give back to me. "What do you want?"

"Just to be with you, Julie. This case, your work, is building a wall between us. I don't want that. You may not believe this, but you're very special to me. And I know I'm special to you too."

He came over to me and caressed me with a softness I'd never seen from him before. Then he smiled his winning smile and added, "And besides, the sex is great."

"Yeah," I muttered quietly.

"Oh, come on. You like our little games as much as I do. I don't hear you complaining. Sometimes you even egg me on with your own ideas. Maybe I went a little overboard the other night. Can't we put that behind us? I have some new ideas, something I think you'll really like."

I looked up at him. He looked so sincere, so little and lost, and in spite of myself I couldn't help thinking about what was now on his mind. What new games had he planned? My juices began to flow with anticipation. I could feel the area at my crotch getting wet and saw Ron had noticed the tiny stain that had appeared between my legs now. He was smiling. In spite of myself I ran into his arms, and in a moment we were naked and rolling around on the carpet.

Ron's new kick was ritual bleeding. He wanted us to bleed each other, then mix small amounts of our blood together, rubbing it all over our bodies as we had sex. Ron knew me, see. He knew I was up for almost any freaky thing, especially if we'd never done it before. Well, we'd never done this before. Soon we both lost ourselves in the frenzy of it all. The cutting. The bleeding. Not deep cuts, but a lot of blood. We did some drugs, and that made it all easier, painless, all so dreamlike. I don't know what the pills were that he gave me. I never asked. Ecstasy, probably. I felt like I was somewhere above us, watching from overhead, like in a film. It was ethereal, unreal. I never felt any pain. I don't remember too much of what happened. In the end I must have passed out.

When I woke up the next morning, Ron was gone. I was alone. That was so much like Ron, like most men I guess, to leave after he'd taken what he wanted.

I got up and showered. I was covered in dried and caked blood. I looked like one of my own murder scenes, for chrissake. I was also weak, exhausted. I cleaned my wounds—most were nothing but mere superficial cuts, but a couple needed Band-Aids. My arm was also sore. I thought it was from a muscle pull—we'd been pretty crazy last night—but then I noticed a small black-and-blue bump that looked like an injection site on the inside of my right arm, by the vein.

Had Ron injected me with something? Some kind of drug? Meth? Heroin? I panicked for a moment, but I was a scientist after all, and I knew the signs of those drugs. It wasn't meth or heroin. Probably some kind of muscle relaxant or barbiturate cocktail to put me in that dreamy state I remembered. Something Ron gave me to feel no pain, only pleasure.

I was called to the task force early that morning for an emergency meeting. There had been another murdered woman discovered the night before. The woman, Shelia Smith, had been killed like the others. However, "Number Four" had been written in blood on the wall behind her corpse. I studied the blood spatter with dread, because it was projected blood and it appeared to have been done through a syringe!

I knew we had a serious problem with this killer. He was vicious, intelligent, and now taunting the police to catch him. The DNA report on this projected blood from the syringe, however, had me stumped. This time it was not blood from any of the four victims we knew about. So who was the blood from? The killer? It seemed improbable. We could never be that lucky. Or was it blood from a fifth and presently unknown victim? That possibility sent a chill through me—the realization that we could have another, unknown victim. I informed the police of my findings.

That night Ron was not in my apartment when I came home. He wasn't waiting for me inside or outside. I was almost thankful he was not there, except I was so full of pent-up emotions at what I had discovered at the fourth crime scene that a good, hard dose of wild sex with Ron would have been the perfect drug to set me right. Something to get me to sleeping like a baby that night.

Then Ron called. He was nervous, edgy. "I need to see you, Julie," he said forcefully.

"Ron, can't it wait? I've had a hectic day, and I'm totally out of it right now."

"I'm coming over," was all he said.

"Ron . . . !" I replied curtly, but he wasn't on the line any longer. I sighed, put down my phone, resigning myself to the fact that he was coming over.

It was late, and I was tired, but the more I thought about him and what he might have in mind for us, my anger lessened and my libido grew. And that sexual appetite became a massive hunger, fueled by my fantasies of all the delightfully wicked things we had done in the past—and what we might be doing soon.

By the time my doorbell rang I'd showered and was dressed in sexy silk pj's, ready for my man to take me any way he liked. I know it was wrong, sexist, slutty, maybe even dangerous, but that's what excited me about it. I felt the wetness between my legs growing, my anticipation building, as the bell rang. I knew it was Ron at the door. As I got off the couch to answer the door, I shivered from the tickle of one warm, solitary droplet of moisture that ran down my inner thighs. I knew I was ready for Ron. I just hoped he was ready for me.

He was.

No sooner had I opened the door than I felt the force of a large body pushing me backward, hard. Powerful hands held me down and covered me with something—a dark blanket—or large plastic garbage bag.

My head hurt. I struggled, terrified, but Ron didn't pay any attention to my pleas. Or was it Ron? I could not see his face. Maybe it was someone else? The killer? I began to grow fearful now. I tried to cry out, but my face and mouth were covered so tightly I couldn't make a sound. Whoever it was, he was so much bigger and stronger than I.

Now it was getting hard to breathe!

Then I felt my pajamas ripped away with rude force, followed by the hard joy of penetration. Now I knew it was Ron. He was mounting me from behind. I screamed in agony—joy—fear—lust—I couldn't even tell you what I felt just then. I lay back helpless as my body spasmed with multiple searing orgasms. Then I heard Ron scream wildly as he climaxed into me with a force I'd never felt before.

Finally we both fell to the floor, the bag removed from my head, the gag taken from my mouth. I gasped in exhaustion.

"Surprise!" was all Ron said, looking languidly into my eyes from beside me.

I punched his chest twice with my small, balled-up fists. "You bastard! You scared the hell out of me!"

He laughed. "But you liked it. I know you liked it."

I never answered him, but the truth was I did like it. It had been great, incredible—and just a little sick. I began to fear that I had become a slave to my desires, and Ron was my addiction.

I watched him as he got dressed to leave. After all, he'd gotten what he wanted. He gathered his things, looking so confident, so superior. I watched as he collected his rope, duct tape, plastic garbage bags, a hammer and screwdriver.

Then a dreadful chill took me. I knew what I saw. It was quite plain. Ron had his own rape kit! The realization had my mind whirling.

And this kit of his hadn't been the result of our spur-of-the-moment sexual games either, quickly throwing together a few things, but a well thought-out plan. Or even scarier, the result of long practice and experience!

"Ron?" I asked quietly.

He looked over at me as he continued to collect his things. He put them all in a large black gym bag near me on the floor.

"I think we should stop this. It's not right, not . . . healthy. I'm afraid we're going to go too far some day, and one of us will lose control."

"Isn't this what you want, Julie? What you crave? I know it

is. I know you only too well," he said, coming toward me now with that confident winning smile of his. "You live a well-ordered, logical life in a well-ordered world ruled by science and reason. So do I. We need to escape, and our games give us that escape."

"I don't think I want to do this anymore," I said slowly.

Ron just looked at me and laughed.

That got me angry. I shouted, "I'm serious, dammit!"

"Sure you are. You don't know what you want, and now you're acting like every other damn bitch with a bug up her ass about sex."

"This isn't sex! This is . . . sick. It's not right what we do."

"You like it. I know you do."

"Maybe, but I don't want to do it anymore."

"You don't know what you're saying."

"Don't tell me I don't know want I'm saying, dammit! I'm telling you—"

Then Ron slapped me hard. Twice.

I screamed and cursed him. "Get out! I want you out of here now!"

"You'll change your mind," he said with a confident smirk.

"Fuck you!"

His eyes focused on me then with an animal rage. Suddenly he came at me, pinning me down on the floor so I couldn't move. His hand grasped my throat and squeezed tight. This wasn't fun and games. This wasn't sex now. I was having trouble breathing.

My God, he was going to kill me!

I became frantic, and from somewhere, somehow, I gathered the energy to push him off me. He fell over to my left, and I bolted to my right and fell into his gym bag. I remembered the hammer I'd seen him put inside it and frantically pulled it out. When Ron came at me again, I hit him full on the forehead with the ball-peen hammer, and he dropped down like a felled ox, unconscious or dead. I didn't care which at that point.

I got up shaking, angry, infuriated with a rage I had never felt before, but surging through my body was another feeling I knew well but had never realized I could feel from such an incident—the release of incredible sexual energy.

I quickly looked at the other things inside Ron's gym bag. There I found my missing crime-scene photos. And others from the crime scene, Polaroids not from the department, but his own personal photos of *his* crimes. Ron was the killer! My mind reeled at the knowledge. Then I saw a vial of blood with a label marked with my name on it, along with a syringe. It was all clear now.

I looked down at Ron; he was moaning softly but apparently unable to move. He was so helpless. The memory of my previous outburst of violence had turned me on like nothing else ever had. Now, seeing Ron helpless on the floor only stimulated my sexual desires even more. I touched my nakedness. My most intimate area was moist, soon dripping wet. My nipples were hard and sore, hypersensitive and burning to the touch. I was on fire. Now I was anticipating doing something with Ron that we had never done before.

I picked up the ball-peen hammer and hit Ron once on the head. The dull thud caused him to moan loudly. As he did so, I moaned louder in my sexual frenzy, hitting him again and again and again, faster, faster, faster—screaming in an orgy of sexual release, culminating in a bloody orgasm of sheer violence.

I looked at the members of the task force and concluded my report. "This latest victim, a male, Ron Jackson, was a dump job. He was killed somewhere else and then left at the edge of the park. Blood spatter indicates blunt-force trauma. I'd surmise a hammer of some kind." I smiled slightly. "Probably a ball-peen hammer."

[illegible]

[illegible] another thing [illegible]

[illegible] some other kind of thing.

[illegible]

[illegible] the same sort of look [illegible] into the [illegible]

[illegible]

[illegible] along with [illegible]

[illegible]

[illegible]

[illegible]

[illegible]

The Bonfires of Humanity

Jeff Gelb

When the zombies came, it was nothing like the movies. It was much, much worse.

I was driving home from work when my wife, Alissa, called my cell.

"Hi, honey," I said innocently. "How's the love of my life today? The 405 is a nightmare, but I should be home in—"

"Jack," she interrupted breathlessly, "something's wrong with Derek."

My heart skipped a few beats. "What do you mean, 'wrong'?"

"They called from his school and said he was sick, and needed to be picked up. In fact, most of the school was sick, and most of the kids went home."

Now I was getting really distracted. I was a chemical engineer, so my brain started considering the options. "Something in the water, I'll bet. The school's water system . . . those old, lead-lined pipes . . . I've warned them they should be replaced."

"Jack, just shut up," she screeched, "and meet me at Torrance Memorial!"

I nearly slid into an SUV being driven next to my Camry. "Derek's in a hospital? What . . . ?"

"He's in the ICU, Jack! He's on fucking life support!" Alissa shrieked.

My synapses were not capable of absorbing this much negative input in so short a time. My darling wife was screaming obscenities into my ear. Worse, our amazingly bright and handsome eight-year-old son was in some hospital, tubes running up his nose and down his throat?

I pulled off the freeway at the next exit and moved to the side of the road. I slid the Camry into Park to catch my breath and let my brain try and absorb the last two minutes' conversation. "Did they . . . where is . . ."

Nothing was making sense or coming out right. I suddenly felt like I might be getting whatever sickness had overtaken my son.

"Jack, honey, just meet me at the hospital. Please hurry!" She hung up, and I stared at the cell phone as if it might provide some answers to this sudden insanity. Finally I pulled back into traffic and headed toward the hospital.

The waiting room of the ICU at Torrance Memorial was like open house at Derek's elementary school—half the parents were there. The place was a zoo, with people shrieking and crying, demanding to see their sons and daughters. The hospital staff could barely keep things under control. I noticed numerous obviously nervous cops at each elevator bank and at the nurses' station.

Finally I found my wife. "Oh Jack, thank God you're here!" She ran into my arms and smothered me with kisses, which made me feel that all was right with the world again—at least for that second.

But then I noticed that her tears had ruined her eye makeup. She looked like she was wearing Alice Cooper's stage makeup. It was a ghoulish sight, especially on her pretty face. "Honey, please . . . What can you tell me? How's Derek? Where is he?"

She held my arms in a viselike grip. "They won't let us see him. They won't let anyone see their kids. Jack, the cops are keeping people in the waiting rooms until the doctors know more. They think it's highly contagious." She started bawling in my arms, and I was too stunned to respond emotionally.

Finally her tears subsided, and she pulled away a bit. "Why aren't you crying?" she asked accusingly.

"I . . . I need some answers," I said as I let her go and headed to the nurses' station. A cop beat me to my destination. He was big and burly, wearing a surgical mask over his nose and mouth. The overall effect would have been comical except for the circumstances. "Please step away from the station, sir."

"I want some answers," I said in my most authoritative voice, which sounded so phony to me. I heard others behind me agreeing, encouraging me, taunting the cop. He blinked away the abusive words.

"I understand," he said, literally holding me at arm's length.

"Don't touch me," I warned him, brushing off his hands. He held them up, acknowledging my anger.

"The nurses and doctors are doing everything they can," he attempted to explain. "And as soon as they know whether this is contagious, they'll make a determination about visitation rights."

"Rights!" I shouted. "My son is in there." I pointed down the hall. "For all I know, he may be dying, or . . ." I couldn't bring myself to say it. "I want to see him right now!" I started to move around the cop.

"Sir!" I saw the cop's hand reach for his holstered gun. "Step back into the waiting room, or I will have to arrest you. Now!"

Reluctantly, I retreated, the sting of defeat reddening my face. Others around me sighed and went back to their conversations. I heard a lot of crying. My wife ran to my side and pulled me back into the cacophonous room. I knew these parents from my son's soccer and basketball games, from their kids' birthday parties. Everyone was nearly hysterical. I felt like I was on the verge of hyperventilating.

Alissa had wiped her eye makeup on the sleeve of her flower-print blouse, but her eyes were so red from crying she still looked like she was wearing some sort of macabre makeup. I just wanted things to look and be normal again. "Alissa, what have you been told?"

She shook her head. "Just that most of the school had to be sent home midway through fourth period. And halfway home, Derek was panting and throwing up so bad, I knew I should bring him to Emergency. When I got here, half the school was already in the parking lot. Jack, I'm so scared . . . Our family has always been so close. What if . . ."

I looked around. "This is bad," I muttered. "Real bad." My brain tried desperately to figure out some reason for this nightmare. We were good, religious people. Why was this happening to us?

Just then a doctor came rushing out of the ICU, looking worse than any of the parents. He started coughing, and a rush of blood spit out of his mouth as he threw up on the shoes of the cop guarding the nurses' station.

Everyone looked at him with horror, and I heard someone scream, "He's gotta be contagious! Get him out of here!" In fact, it was obvious the doctor was in terrible pain. He was on the floor, writhing in his own vomit and blood, body spasming, screaming in a high-pitched squeal. It was shatteringly frightening. Half the parents ran screaming out of the waiting room, some toward the elevators and others past the stunned cops, toward the ICU. I saw one cop raise his gun threateningly, pointing it at a shrieking mother, and then lower his hand to let her pass. Some even went along with the parents. Hell, some of the cops probably had kids back there.

Suddenly the doctor stopped screaming, and I could see a puddle of urine form under his trousers. I knew, even from halfway across the room, that he was dead.

I grabbed my wife's arm. "We've got to get out of here, or we may get what he has . . . had."

Alissa looked at me in stunned surprise. "Jack, we can't leave.

Derek's in there. We have to get him, we have to bring him home with us . . . ."

I shook my head. "Something's beyond wrong here. Something really terrible is happening. We can't help Derek. And if we don't leave now, we won't be able to help him or ourselves."

Just then I heard a horrible scream. I turned to see one of the fathers walking out of the ICU with what must have been his young daughter in his arms. I recognized both of them as neighbors on our block. "She's dead," he shrieked. "Liana's dead! They're all dead back there. They're all dead!"

The room turned into utter pandemonium as parents ran around like the proverbial headless chickens. Alissa started bawling, and I knew she'd totally lost it. Somehow I hadn't—yet. I slapped her hard across the cheek and grabbed her and went running for the stairs. "We have to leave—now!" I commanded, and she obeyed, obviously in total shock.

Somehow we made it back to our car, only to see the parking lot transformed into a fun-house version of an amusement-park bumper-car ride. Cars were plowing into each other right and left as panicked parents tried desperately to distance themselves from the horror hospital. Smashed cars already blocked in my Toyota Camry. It was obviously going to be impossible to get out of there by car. I took my wife's hand, and we made our way out of the parking lot as cop cars, sirens shrieking, zoomed past us toward the scene of carnage. I watched cops with riot gear jump out of vans and head toward the hospital's main entrance, their rifles raised.

We weren't more than a mile from home, but even that mile added to the nightmare as we saw dozens of accidents. I heard snippets of newscasts on car radios telling of similar scenes playing out through LA, and the entire country. Something had gone wrong, horribly so, and now everyone was in a panic. The cops were totally incapable of stopping the wholesale lawbreaking as people ran red lights, went down one-way streets in the wrong direction, drove down sidewalks, did anything to get away from the city or to get home.

But why assume our homes were safe? If it was something in the water . . . None of this made any sense, of course. But why should it? Who said that the world had to go from day to day the way it had the days before? Who said that nature, or terrorists, or Lord knows what, might not change life forever in an instant, the way those meteors had killed the dinosaurs virtually overnight millions of years ago? Who said life was always going to be fair or just? Who knew what justice really was anymore?

But in the end there was nowhere else to go, so we went home. Our street was almost deserted, as we'd seen most of our neighbors at the hospital. Walking turned out to be the fastest way home that day, some three months ago, when everything changed.

Our son died, of course. Or so we were told by the medical authorities, who would not let us see him, or even pick up his body, once he had succumbed to the effects of the horrible mystery disease. In fact, about a third of the population of the entire world had died over the next ninety days or so, and the staggering numbers were showing no signs of slowing down. The scientific community was at a loss as to whether it was an airborne virus or a water-bred one. Nor did anyone seem to know whether it was a terrorist plot gone awry—or perhaps a highly successful one. Despite claims of credit from dozens of terrorist cells, there was no proof that anyone human had engineered this ultimate nightmare. There seemed to be no cure for the horrible disease that had spread globally in a matter of days. All we knew for sure was that the world had been decimated in the most horrible way imaginable; billions had already died.

And then come back to life.

Usually they returned to some semblance of life within hours of dying. But not as flesh-eating ghouls, not as somnambulant walkers, but just as apparently brain-dead vegetables whose hearts somehow still pumped poisoned blood even while their bodies continued to rot. Limbs literally decayed and fell off as the zombies watched in numb fascination. It was not uncommon to see errant flaps of skin floating in the summer breeze.

The zombies all had to be incarcerated, of course. Their rotting bodies were full of diseases that even the still-healthy could die from. So at first the various worldwide governments had filled up prisons, then schools, then army barracks and airport hangars, until it became obvious that the legions of the living dead would have to be destroyed. They simply could not be cared for without fatal risk to the caretakers, and besides, we were running out of room and food (not that they ate much). So ultimately the United Nations, or what was left of it, had voted to kill them all. They were first shot with narcotics that numbed them to the pain to come, or so we hoped, anyway. Then they were herded to open fields where they were burned alive, in huge pyres whose pillars of smoke could be seen from anywhere you looked, and whose ashes turned the skies permanently gray.

We'd never seen our son again, and that had driven poor Alissa around the bend. She was living in the guest bedroom at our home, and I was taking care of her. I used my engineering skills to rig up an air-filtration system in our house that was second to none, so that no air from outside could reach her room. I modified our water-filtration system in many subtle ways to do everything possible to keep any waterborne spores from affecting us.

But it was all a giant crapshoot. No one knew what had turned the planet Earth into a giant bonfire of human souls virtually overnight. We were forced to confront our mortality and our faith in the worst ways imaginable. Many of faith felt that the Lord was finally repaying us for screwing up His greatest gift—life itself—for so long. Others used their faith to somehow maintain a semblance of sanity in the midst of the carnage. Still others, like Alissa, simply went mercifully crazy. I guess the only thing that kept me sane was my desperate search for a chemical or biological solution, something that would keep the crisis from killing off every living human on the planet. It was suddenly the only goal worth living for.

Plants and animals had not seemingly been affected, for some unknown reason, so we could all still eat, at least. But the worldwide economy had ground to a halt, as the only viable remaining task was a search for answers and solutions. I was part of a Los Angeles task force assigned to experiment on tissue of living-dead subjects who had been donated to our facility by surviving family members. We were never in the same room as the zombies, of course, but we pumped altered air into their rooms and altered water and chemicals into their bodies and then watched how they responded, hoping against hope for some sign that they might stop dying on us.

But nothing worked. The world was dying, the numbers beyond staggering as city after city fell to the bonfires of humanity.

I awoke to my wife's screams. I jumped out of bed and ran to her room and unlocked the door. Weeks back, I'd decided I would have to lock her in the guest bedroom to keep her from going into the kitchen, grabbing a steak knife, and killing herself, which she had tried on more than one occasion.

The darkened room stank of sweat and shit. She'd probably lost control of her bodily functions sometime that night, and it wasn't the first time.

I ran to her side and reached for her. Her body was drenched in sweat, her eyes wild, breath rank, panting like a woman about to give birth.

"He was here—right next to the bed! I saw him! I touched his face!"

It was a familiar monologue. In fact, it was the only time she ever spoke anymore—when she would tell me about her recurring nightmare.

I brushed sopping strands of hair off her forehead. "Who, Alissa?"

She looked at me like I was the one who was crazy. "You know who—Derek! He came again. He comes every night. He's looking for us. Crying. Asking why we didn't rescue him. Why we let him die in the fires . . . ." She broke down completely in my arms, and now I did too. My emotional resolve had long-since crumbled, and I spent what seemed like hours every day crying into my beakers and microscope.

She cried. "His face . . . Oh Lord, his face. Derek's face was burned to a crisp. I could barely recognize him. He only had one eye . . . ."

The dream was getting worse by the night. "Don't, honey. Don't torture yourself. It was just a dream . . . ."

"Then kill me," she shrieked. "Kill me so I never have to have that dream again!" Her cries were screams of soul-pain, and I pondered her request for a more than a moment. Perhaps the only humane thing to do would be to give her a lethal injection. And then turn the needle on myself.

Then I felt her hand at my groin. Initially I pushed it away, but when she grabbed at me even harder and more forcefully, I realized she was trying to reach beyond her insanity and connect with me in the only way she could still somehow manage. I sighed and slipped out of my pajamas, then laid her back on bed-sheets that were soaked in tears and sweat and Lord knows what else, and we made love.

At first I was an unwilling partner, turned off by the rank smells, the wetness of the bedsheets. But her utterly animal sexuality overtook me, and I realized I needed the release of tension that only sex could bring to me.

But it wasn't just sex; no, not at all. It was not just two human animals grunting and grabbing, thrusting and gasping in ecstasy. It was the only expression of our lost love we could still share.

I wanted desperately to please her, to reach her, hoping against all hope that perhaps by making love I could bring my wife back to some semblance of sanity. That perhaps by connecting on this physical level, becoming truly one, I could somehow transfer some of my sanity through my sperm into her bloodstream and ultimately into her brain.

I slipped inside her, gently moving back and forth, in and out. She sighed in what I could only hope was pleasure as I grabbed her breast and kneaded the soft flesh as it fell apart in my hands.

I stared at the glistening pink blob in my hands in utter horror. Her nipple and a good third of her breast had actually fallen off her body and were now dripping gore into my own hands.

"Oh Lord," I shrieked as I threw the putrefying flesh to the floor and disengaged from my wife. I scrambled off the bed and backed up until I hit a wall. Alissa started crying again, and in the shadows of the room I could see her reaching out for me.

"More," she begged me, " More. I need you . . . inside me . . . . Come inside me!"

I gasped, tears flowing as I ran for the door, slamming it behind me, locking it with shaking fingers. I ran down the hall to my bathroom and took a long shower, standing under the blistering water, crying my eyes out.

Just hours ago I'd fed her dinner, some kind of tasteless chicken-and-peas slop I'd managed to put together. She'd eaten a tiny portion without any emotion, which was not unexpected. She'd barely acknowledged me as I wiped the food stains from her still-pretty face. I looked in her eyes in vain for a sign that she still knew who I was, still cared for me, still wanted to live.

And now, despite all my best efforts at maintaining a perfectly controlled environment, she'd gone through the Change, as the remaining scientists called it. She'd become one of the living dead. My wife was a zombie.

I dressed and went to my office. At my desk, I turned on the computer, searching for any news that someone had found a magic bullet of some kind. But there was no news on any of the blogs of any progress. In fact, many of the bloggers and their sites were now dormant, and I suspected their owners and caretakers had succumbed to the disease. They too were undoubtedly now zombies, and computers would mean no more to them than the people with whom they used to correspond. But there would be no more miracles.

The Good Lord had apparently decided to pull the plug on humanity, and it was up to us to decide how to deal with it. I looked at the computer, and all the anger I'd bottled up for the past ninety days bubbled to the surface, overflowing. I grabbed the monitor, ripping the cords out of it, disengaging its life support as it were. I flung it across the room against the far wall, where it smashed in a noisy mess.

The whole world was a noisy mess, and I couldn't see a reason to keep going. The only thing that meant anything to me anymore was a living-dead woman whose sobs I could still hear from the room down the hall. Her cries ripped my soul to shreds.

I knew tomorrow I'd have to call the authorities. It was the law—I'd be incarcerated if they found I was secretly harboring a zombie. They would come for her in their hermetically sealed white spaceman suits, first pumping her with some narcotic that immediately rendered her unconscious. Then I'd have to sign some papers releasing her to them, and then they'd take her away. And then my own bonfire nightmares could start.

I walked down the hall, unlocked her door, and entered the room. She was still crying, though whether it was from physical pain or something beyond that I could not say. I went to her side and she grabbed for me. I allowed her to touch me and then pull me to her, and I felt her cold body against the heat of mine. The place where her breast had been oozed against my own chest, but I did not turn away. I held her like that for longer than I'd held her since our son died.

It might have been minutes or it could have been hours later when I got up and smashed open the nailed-down bedroom windows with the butt end of a lamp, allowing fresh air to circulate through the room for the first time in months. I kissed the tears from her eyes as I carried her shivering body into the bathroom. Where my hands held her weight, I could feel them literally sinking into her flesh, where her muscles and organs caressed my fingers and oozed their mysterious fluids into my pores.

I placed her naked body into the bathtub and turned on the warm water. I disrobed, stepped into the tub, and lay next to her. In a fairy-tale past now all but forgotten, we'd used this oversized tub many times to make love, our wet bodies slipping and sliding against, in, and out of each other. Now, in the soft glow of the moonlight, I could see fingernails and other body parts and flesh floating in the warm water. I felt no pulse from her, but I could hear her breathing, her body defying all logic as it decomposed while remaining semifunctional, at least on some subatomic level. I held her tightly until I felt myself drifting off to much-welcomed sleep.

In my dream, Derek, Alissa, and I were at a park, having a picnic. The day was bright with the warmth of the summer sun, and I could smell fresh flowers in bloom all around me. Derek and Alissa were playing tag and laughing. Their laughter was contagious, and I joined in, absently wondering why my laughter was punctuated with sobs and tears.

Even in my dream I realized laughter was a sound I had not heard for many months, and the strangeness of that sound woke me up. I blinked as I came back to the present.

I looked at the tub. Virtually an entire layer of Alissa's skin had seemingly slid off her body, now floating in pieces in the tub all around me. I smiled through my tears as I held her against me, feeling the inner muscular structure of her back against my fingers as I slowly ran my hands up and down her back. She sighed, or some such sound escaped what was left of her lips, and I kissed her, long and hard. As her remaining teeth hit mine, I was surprised to feel one of my teeth loosening and then falling out of my mouth.

So it had started.

I kissed her with greater intensity and felt her come to life, or a semblance of it anyway, as she once again grabbed at my manhood with hands that were now more bone and sinew than flesh. The effect was breathtakingly erotic, as she rubbed me, pushing my foreskin up and down, up and down, until I felt the skin of my penis split apart in her hands.

"Quickly," I whispered into my wife's ear, "put me inside you. I want to be inside you. I want to come with you one last time."

I felt her guide me into her moist vagina, and I closed my eyes, remembering all the times we had shared this exact intimacy in this tub. Then it was pink with bubble bath; now it was red with our mixed blood, as the life juices of my own decomposing body were melding with Alissa's in one last erotic painting.

My penis slid into her vagina, and I started slowly pushing in and out. Without the foreskin, the effect was maddeningly intoxicating, and it didn't take even a minute before I screamed in pleasure and felt what remained of my life force pumping into her.

I stayed inside my wife, slowly moving in and out, back and forth, until I felt my entire penis crack apart. I disengaged, leaving an intimate piece of myself inside her.

I felt no pain. In fact, all feeling was starting to slide away from me, like fading memories of a long-lost life.

Alissa was completely still, perhaps already dead, perhaps just somehow enjoying the afterglow of the last orgasm we would ever share.

In the dim recesses of what remained of my brain, I knew they'd come for us in the next day or two. Some colleague would report me missing, and they'd find us here, or what was left of us. I just hoped when they did, there wouldn't be enough left to identify which body part belonged to which person.

I had connected with my wife one last time, and this time was for all eternity.

But now it was time to go back to sleep and return to that picnic, and the sunshine, the smells, and especially the laughter of my family.

What Scares You

David J. Schow

Loneliness scares me. There, I've admitted it. Not being alone—that's something else entirely. If you can't enjoy your own company, why expect anyone else to? Isolation doesn't scare me. But the impingement of loneliness, which always leads to some form of despair, remains a scary thing.

This story probably isn't what you wanted to hear when you came in. You were in the market for a fine little fright; I know that—some little backsnap in the tail to make you smack your forehead and go *Oh wow—never saw that coming*. A digestible kind of unease. A black midnight snack. But if I'm to be completely honest with you, I won't do that stunt; it's too much like being a party robot that flawlessly replicates the same trick every time you push the button or slap a coin into the slot. No.

Nor will I spiel off bullshit (or endure yours) until you "allow" me to fuck you. Before tonight, things might have gone differently, more like the long yawn you call seduction. Now, when I think of seduction, I think of what happened to me on the most basic level, and it still frightens me, because it forced me to stand alone. It infected me with a dread that never goes away. Being startled is not being scared. Being genuinely *afraid* is quite different. No wonder sane people choose the former, when it comes to safe risk.

When I think of what *you* call seduction, all I can see are parasites eating each other to death.

Since you won't let me escape without talking, I'll instead tell you the story of Niall Otheringame, who succeeded in scaring me with the things he said. When I met him, I was flat on my back in a puddle of beer, watching an enormous boot swoop down to smash my face. I saw Clarity that night too. No, don't roll your eyes—Clarity is a name: Niall's female half. But that's jumping ahead of the story.

About forty mostly sleepless hours following my latest and final "discussion" (so-called) about "our relationship" (double wince) with the notably blond and usually perceptive Giselle—you probably know *that* whole bitter drill, am I right?—I forced myself back into a nearly forgotten pattern and decided to visit a lounge called the Back 40, having just turned forty myself. Numerical symmetry insisted. I pretended to ignore the sharky, trolling atmosphere of the place and lied to myself that I was just going for a drink or two, pretending my eyes were not laser targeted for fresh females, pretending there was not a whole universe of new people to engage and bodies to newly unwrap.

I pretended I was a normal human, when in fact I was an alien from some planet of misanthropes, observing Earth mating culture and finding it lacking, sad, futile. I smiled at strangers, thinking of that oldie about the smell of desperation. I smiled once too often and wound up on the floor facing the boot heel of a bald behemoth in a leather vest. I had smiled at the wrong blonde, and now Ook the Caveman was going to mulch my skull.

I should have taken that as a warning. A sign that I should not be in this place at this time. When such thoughts occur, it is usually too late for thinking beings to benefit from them, like the French notion of staircase wit—you know, *l'esprit de l'escalier*—thinking of the right rejoinder too late? A lot of people don't know that expression was coined by a guy named Denis Diderot, a freethinker and encyclopedist who advanced a very early version of the theory of natural selection in the mid-1700s. Never mind. The strong prevail. I was about to get my head crushed as proof.

Ook withdrew. I missed it. I was too busy shutting my eyes and reconsidering prayer. Bracing for impact and calculating hospital costs. Completely pathetic, am I right?

When I opened my eyes, I saw Ook talking to a man in a white topcoat. Ook was easily a foot and a half taller, but he wore a penitential expression akin to that of a chastised child. The gentleman in the topcoat smiled and spoke in a low, even voice. I could not hear what he said, but whatever it was, it humanized my assailant, who seemed mildly confused. I thought the man had Ook in some sort of nerve grab, squeezing his armpit hard enough to immobilize him, but no, that wasn't it.

The big man nodded in understanding and helped me up off the deck. "Sorry, dude," was all he said, and he melted back into the bustle of the Friday night bar biz. When I saw him half an hour later, he was sitting by himself and weeping.

Great, now I was obligated to a benefactor. Swell. I know that makes me an ingrate, but it was what I really, truly thought at the moment. But people rarely say what they're thinking, and that was kind of the lesson of the entire evening.

The man in the topcoat wore a tailored three-piece suit. He had modest pattern baldness and a smile full of dentures. Paternal, with interestingly wrinkled hands. Now he was smiling at me. He introduced himself as Niall Otheringame and idly added that the rescue for which I complimented him was nothing, really.

Great, I've managed to attract an old fag, I thought. Swell. He sees a semen mouthwash followed by an asshole-widening. Outstanding.

"You were thinking about silverware," he said. "Just before. That's the first intriguing thought I've encountered all week. I'd like to hear more."

I'm afraid I made a ridiculous face. "Silver—?"

"Flatware," he said. "Knives, forks, spoons. You were trying to explain it to that young lady at the bar when her escort interceded. I fear he thought it was some sort of pickup line, you see?"

Oh, right. I once invented this perverse notion that people were largely the same, divisible into the three major kinds of eating utensils. It was an adequate rap to displace anything like genuine conversation. I was unenthusiastically explaining it to the cleavage of the now-vanished blond lady, already knowing it was the same as talking modern art to a throw rug. For the benefit of Mr. Otheringame, who had done me a kindness, I reeled off the story.

At length. I should have just shut up.

"You know that expression about how someone was 'born with a silver spoon in their mouth'?" I began, feeling guilty for having refined my story to a speech. "Well, I'll tell you something: everyone is born with a spoon in their mouth, and sometimes it's silver, and sometimes it's wood. Sometimes it's golden or platinum; imagine a black diamond spoon. But it doesn't mean the individual is spoonish per se. Some of them are born with spatulas in their mouths, or shovels. Or, considering their sloth and girth, ladles. Soft, plastic ladles, molded in urethane so as not to harm or impede the delivery of double shares. You know which people are spoonish, and which are soup-spoonish. Think about it."

"'Spoonid,'" said Niall Otheringame with an indulgent smile.

"You are what you eat with. You know knivish people are aggro, direct, and all the adjectives—sharp, edgy, keen, pointed—all say the same thing. Handle with care. Forkish people try to have it both ways. They can say one thing and mean, or do, another. They have lots of utility. Politicians and actors enjoy forkishness. Sometimes they are knives or spoons masquerading as forks, or those multipurpose tools that deploy from a Swiss Army knife.

"It is very important for knifely people to make love as though they are attacking one another. They strop themselves to sharpness on others. Fork people service themselves while appearing to service others. And you already know about spooning.

"Look at a fork. Now look at a human hand. Add an opposable thumb—intelligence—and there you are. It is important to remember that you can take out a human eye with a knife, a fork, or a spoon. Or a chopstick, for that matter. The only operative differences are in degree of efficiency, level of sadism or pain, and available time. Spoons can kill, and frequently do. Do not underestimate the spoon. Spoons can clean up what knives or forks leave in their haste. Think of Dr. Frankenstein as a fork, his monster as a knife, and Igor as a spoon, and you can figure out most human relationships.

"Life is a meal. Knives, forks, and spoons are useless without the concept of consumption, and humans consume each other in order to amass what is called 'a life.' They chew each other up, spit out the bits they dislike, pick and choose, refine their appetites. They snack, gorge, and starve. Bulemics and gourmands all use the same basic tools; it's all a matter of desires, objectives, and tastes.

"Roll the idea around on your palate. Knivish people, forkish people, spoonish people. Spoons secretly want to be knives. Forks pretend to be spoons. Everyone wants to be something else, and a lot of furious biological activity is devoted toward presenting a personality that may have admirable aspects of all three, with no downside. In truth, there is no such person. But that doesn't stop them from trying to be silverware."

I took a long drink to signal my break. Niall Otheringame had paid polite attention. Around us, the patrons of Back 40 continued to swarm, but now it was as if we were inside our own hermetic bubble.

"Now, that's amusing," he said. "You see? Much better than sitting in a bar, boring each other to death with chitchat. Better to say what is on your mind than erode your audience with business, politics, or religion."

"What people mean when they chat you up and say 'What's your story?' and you tell them what you do to earn money."

"Exactly. I give not a tinker's damn what people do for money. There is no rational point to discussing politics—none. About religion I care even less. All that"—Niall Otheringame groped the air for an appropriate word—"*noise pollution* about some invisible skygod."

"Bertrand Russell," I said.

He shrugged. "You see? I sensed you were a person I could talk to usefully. You would not waste time in yammer about family, friends, who you know. It all boils down to embarrassment, or worse, name-dropping. As if I could be impressed by that. So I ask you, here and now: does that smooth story about silverware actually get you laid? Tell me what's *really* on your mind."

He'd had my character nailed from the start. He just let me prove it by flapping my lips. Maybe it was the liquor, but I told him what was on my mind. It was that perverse, flash impulse, the kind you always blame on drink. That's what alcohol is for.

"That woman by the jukebox, the one with the copper-colored hair? That's what's really on my mind."

She was also on the mind or within the cognizance of 70 percent of the males in this zoo, and three other women I could see from my seat. I almost said, "I want to make love to her," but that was a lie too. I wanted her bent over my sofa, spread wide, panting, begging. Indelicate, but closer to true.

"Tosh," said Niall Otheringame with a snort. "Look where we are. Look at the behavior of these animals. Rampant ego, seeking to amortize self-abasement by rocking and rolling in each other's flesh. All propped up by cliches and fantasies, with booze to fuel dishonest passion. Besides, she's not for you."

"You're going to tell me she's really a guy, right?"

"No, she's real enough. You have but to meet her to fall for her. Can you imagine being that desirable? I can't. But watch how every time the door opens, her antennae go up, scoping the talent of the room. She won't go home with any of these failures, because she's not cruising. She's coming here for her self-image.

If any of these guys got a photograph with her, they'd make up stories. They'd lie about how she was some past girlfriend. They'd invent a fake name for her. Whole delusional histories, fabricated by people who have no imagination to begin with. People ask if she's an actress, a model, a dancer. She has one of those long body-pillow things she hugs with her legs when she goes to sleep, alone. She actually feels comfortable that she has set standards for herself no human being could hope to meet. She cries a lot between binges and purges. She's fiery and attractive and ready to snap. She will not end well."

"How do you know all that?"

He made a dismissive gesture. "I just know. That's my curse."

This was already fun. "What about the guy in the mock turtleneck?" I said.

Niall Otheringame looked the target over. "Factless, hopeless, and useless. He's circling that woman at the bar like a fly trying to figure out a landing vector on a really choice turd. Look at her, ignoring him. They deserve each other so much they're practically grandparents already. Look closer at her: if you were to lean in and whisper the words *biological clock* in her ear, her blood pressure would blow the hair out of her scalp. Now look closer at him: middle management, awaiting a full partnership. Pretty soon he won't have any time left to shop for an arm doily or life mate; every night he comes in here is like a pop quiz where one wrong answer means failure. The two of them will talk about not using lines while disdaining this bar for being a meat rack. They'll rattle on this way until they're sufficiently lubricated to attempt stupendously boring sex. She'll keep her eyes closed and teeth grit for most of it. He'll be lost once he's inside her. It'll be over relatively quick, like a car wreck, and then they'll lie to each other about how good it was, how long since they've felt that way, et cetera, et cetera, while all the time eyeing the nearest exit door. Each of them will lie to themselves about what just happened to them."

"You're making this up," I said.

"Am I?" He gave me an odd little tilt of the head. "By the way, I admire the way you flung in that tidbit about Red being a man, disguising it as both a joke and a question."

I think I blushed, just a teeny bit.

"Very sneaky," he said, signaling for a refill. "You were trying to goad me into reaffirming that I am not a homosexual myself, in order to bolster your acceptance of me. You see? People never *say what they're thinking.*"

I decided to ambush him with it. "You're not . . . are you?"

"More pansexual, if you'd like a mere word," he said, with the air of a prepared answer. "But let's consider some of our other candidates."

I did a quick scan-and-sweep. "Boots," I said. "Long brown hair. Standing next to the booth by the restrooms."

Niall Otheringame scrutinized her for exactly five seconds. "She knows most men in the room want her and most women in the room hate her. It's that good length of leg, heft of bosom, the aqua eyes that doom all comers, and she is aware of her armament. She puts on makeup the way killers load shotguns. She tries to present a tough exoskeleton, but inside she's a terrified aesthete, so she marginalizes all contact and tries to play the rowdy freebird by fucking bikers and car mechanics—anyone pitifully easy to control. It's child's play, literally. She's got great excuses for avoiding any real commitment and can talk anything into a fight; hence, it's simple to shuck the tough guys and maintenance fucks she accumulates, because when it comes to real conflict, they're hopelessly outclassed. She runs through enough of them to amass a backlog of anecdotal drama galore, plenty to float her to the next diversion. People are fast food to her; interchangeable protein units that burn at variant rates, in assorted seductive colors, and she couldn't work up genuine despair even if she had a manual and a how-to video. That's the tragedy of her existence. She trolls one night per week. The rest she sits at home considering methods of suicide suited to what she believes is her personality."

"So what you're saying is . . . 'not for me' too?"

He smiled, nodded. "Most of these creatures don't have the grace or honor to just kill themselves, which is what they should really do. Save our gene pool. As for imagination, well, decanting wine from crushed marbles would be easier. You're dealing with delusional beings who've talked themselves into mock-life. Listen to them right now—you'll intercept all sorts of prattle about lifestyles, spiritual delusions, and half-baked horseshit homilies usually shoplifted from the pages of someone else's book. All kinds of reasons why they should live or dodgy justifications as to why the world at large owes them any damned thing; a menu of felicitous philosophies at lunch-special prices; discount dreams; bargain-rack, second-hand aspirations. Most were more honest when they were children: I want to be a firefighter; I want to go dinosaur-hunting. Now that's all polluted, and we're looking at children, spouting childish nonsense from adult mouths, in adult bodies governed by childish intellects. Listen to them rationalize themselves long enough, and you'll start to hear a melody in the buzz of a mosquito."

Niall Otheringame held up a finger to emphasize his point. "I'm not trying to brag, or shock you, or redefine your boundaries, or anything like that. I'm just telling you what I know, and from your expression, you want me to keep talking. Guess that means *you're* not gay, right?"

I blushed, or blanched, or both, and it seemed to please him.

"Joke," he said.

"The guy with the corporate buzz cut," I pointed out.

"Violent," said Niall Otheringame. "The thinnest veneer of humanity. A yeller, a hitter. Beneath his lacquer of health and fitness he conceals a sadistic need to infect women with various diseases as punishment for their being female. Chlamydia, yeast infections, urinary-tract inflammation. He has this sensitive face he whips out for Phase One, but his real orgasm comes from seeing that glint of fear in the eyes of his victims when he whips out Phase Two."

"Jesus," I said. "This is getting a lot more complicated than *all women are crazy, all men are stupid.*"

"You want crazy? Check the guy-magnet in the corset and fishnets." Niall Otheringame tipped his recently refilled glass to single out a dark siren with crystal green eyes, definitely dressed to threaten as a primary culling filter. She had the rapt ear of no fewer than three male candidates and could assuredly pick and choose at any time.

"What am I not seeing?" I asked him.

"That the façade is all there is," said Niall Otheringame. "As far as relationships go, she behaves according to a very strict playbook that no one else has heard of, let alone read. The word *relationship* to her means *menu of assumptions*, which means *rules*, which she holds as immutable *law*. Any of these rules can be invisibly violated at any moment, to the eternal regret of the transgressor. Basically, her life is a howling void of nothingness. She wants someone to *complete* her, as the movie phrase goes. To fill the gap in her life. Unfortunately, in her case the gap is 95 percent of the life. You could pour your entire identity into hers and reap no reward save the privilege of being drowned second, after her, as she pulls you under with her. So . . . who's stupid, or crazy?"

"You mentioned relationships," I said. "I don't think that's what most of the people here are after. I mean, look at them."

Niall Otheringame smiled as though to spare me from the chagrin of having my thin attempt at foxing him exposed again. "No? You're still just seeing the surfaces, not the clockwork. Believe me when I say nearly everyone in here radiates the need, the craving, for an architecture they mistakenly *call* a relationship. They muck through these clumsy couplings with an eye out for something better. They delude themselves they can meet their soul mate in a bar. Then, if luck prevails—they always depend on luck—the candidate must pass a previously inapplicable set of standards; what if you meet your soul mate but they don't fit the templates of position or power? What if one wants to breed and the other doesn't? If they're not the right race or the correct age, there are a hundred variables further down the ladder that all handily disqualify the potential soul mate if one can't find a realistic excuse for saying no. So they all know they're going to flush and try again, but they delude themselves and presume a mental faculty beyond their reach. They're born to wallow about but won't admit it. I'll give them this: they're willing to keep on trying. Isn't that why you came in here in the first place?"

"Wow," I said. "Busted, I guess."

"Look at that bubbly, effervescent one, the woman just coming through the door," he said. "Attractive, yes?"

My tongue got thick in my mouth. "Yes, indeed."

"You want to run as fast as you can in the opposite direction," Niall Otheringame said. "She got so preoccupied with the idea that men only wanted her for her sex that she actually stabbed herself in the vagina with a coring knife, the custom kind that costs nearly a hundred bucks at Williams-Sonoma and is made from Japanese stainless steel? Out, damned G-spot! She wound up in the hospital and had to indulge a bit of plastic surgery. Now she has a shopping list of "special needs" she inflicts on anyone unlucky enough to get her clothes off. It's designed to drive lovers away, their horror proving their unworthiness and justifying her own self-mutilation. Her identity had localized to between her legs, and when she cut that up, she found that there was not a lot else to recommend her to the world at large, so it became self-prophecy fulfilled, in a sense."

"Now you're *definitely* making this up," I said.

"If you say so."

That was an alarm phrase; it meant *Oops, I've succeeded in scaring you off*. The kind of thing you say as a verbal prybar to begin the process of working free and scooting out the door.

Niall Otheringame merely smiled again, as if he had just reached some sort of satisfactory decision or conclusion. He excused himself and headed for the restroom. I thought perhaps I should stop trying to read everything he did for deeper motive. He had me thoroughly swoggled.

Always remember that past a certain point, a smile is just teeth.

Not long after that, a woman came barside to introduce herself as Clarity. She had very long, dark hair and violet eyes. She looked to be in her mid-thirties. Young enough to know; old enough to know better. Her hands had long-pianist fingers, and everything about her seemed precise. But she was the sort of beauty that defied pinpointing. You could focus on details, but they were insufficient to paint the whole picture—that kind of latent mystery. The first thing she said to me was: "So, what do you make of Niall? According to him, each person in here has enough neuroses for six."

"I just knew somebody like that couldn't have come here stag," I said, a little too flippantly.

"He likes you," Clarity said. "He usually doesn't talk that long to anybody."

"He was frighteningly perceptive."

"He wants me to kiss you. How do you feel about that?"

Clarity had an inviting mouth. Above that, a saucy frankness to her gaze, as though we already shared a secret. The timing was impeccable. I was just about to blurt something about needing to make contact, to participate instead of just languidly observing.

"Is he watching us?" I said.

"What do you think?" Her mouth was already on approach, homing in.

And I thought, to hell with it, let's give ole Niall a show.

Her kiss was a powerful flood of resurgent memory, the kiss you fantasize when you're a teenager, loaded with portent and hot with hormonal flood. The kiss you crave before the grown-up world scotches your dreams. The kiss you see as your hope for redemption once the world stomps on you. The kiss that ruins you for all other kissers.

Plus, something extra: an amorphous weight, a kind of sliding heaviness that caused my heart to take on gravity. It came from her and settled into me; that's the best way to describe it.

Clarity smiled again. Teeth. "That was very pleasant," she said, indicating no desire to continue. She collected herself as though her task was done. "By the way, that was really a corker, your story about the silverware."

Bang, adrenaline; a rush that screwed up my breathing.

As she made ready to excuse herself, her expression said, *You should see your face.*

Either: Women are crazy, and Clarity had done something crazy to me. Or men are stupid, and I was so stupid I did not twig.

They're the same, I thought. Niall Otheringame and Clarity are the same person. Niall ducks out and Clarity appears. I would kiss a woman who looked that good, but not a man. Somehow, Niall had slipped undercover, changed skins, and renewed his assault on me as a lady. It was the trick ending, the disposable scare, easily predictable. You probably guessed they were the masculine/feminine flipsides of the same coin. But I also think that Niall Otheringame read my psyche from the moment we were introduced and somehow conformed Clarity to reflect my inmost desires. So I would kiss her back. The supernatural snap in the tail, story over, my, wasn't *that* fun?

The part Niall omitted was what he saw when he looked at me. What I saw when I looked at myself in the mirror, just a few moments ago.

Don't ask me about the crippled and terrified monsters in here. From where we stand I can see a man who murdered a woman and got away with it. Tonight he's using a little pick-me-up called D10, short for D4B toxin 10, discovered at Stanford, a quantum leap over roofies. It has bee venom among its constituents. It mildly intoxicates while amping the female reproductive urge. The morning after, she'll apologize instead of filing a lawsuit. If she survives.

That trio of women I noticed earlier? They're top-skim hookers who work the Plaza, having a day-off night out. They'd rather be fucking each other, and they came here to mock the amateurs and destroy egos the way you'd toss back a cocktail.

I say all this, yet I know a little less than nothing about prostitute psychology or metabolic chemistry. I know it the way I now know that stud over there has calf implants and a face full of botox. *That* one, the one being seduced by the woman who scratches herself to let the pheromones out. You can virtually smell her lubricating from here.

You think this is all risque patter: man-ramble as preamble. Then you'll say you don't see the relevance; you thought I was going to tell you a horror story.

You haven't been listening.

Loneliness?

What I was really thinking, before you stopped me at the door, was *don't even speak to me*. Don't risk it. I met some lifeform to whom our inner selves are a naked, open book, and somehow the son of a bitch infected me with the same perception, and what I see makes me want to kill myself to stop the pain. But I can't even escape, not now. Especially not by just running out a door. Because I already know what you're going to say. Because I look at you, and all I can think of is cutlery—knives, forks, spoons. Nevertheless, I linger.

Because you smile at me, and you say, "How *interesting*."

The Last Resort

Lisa Morton

"I can tell you how to get what you want."

Emmie dries her eyes and listens, intrigued. "You can?"

The woman with the brittle hair and bad teeth grins and starts talking.

It was just a few minutes past ten when Emmie came home and found George eating out some other girl's pussy.

Emmie was tired when she parked the car before her tumble-down shotgun house (that looked just like about a million other Florida shacks); she'd worked a ten-hour shift down at the supermarket today, and everything below the knees ached. She was moving slowly as she headed up the walk toward the front door, and she thought later on (while nursing a beer in the bar) that her hearing must have been tired too.

Because that's the only way she could have missed the moans and squeals of pleasure coming from her own bedroom.

She stopped for a moment, forgetting her sore feet as she focused on the sound, first in disbelief, then in growing anger. She couldn't hear George, but she thought the neighbors three houses down could surely make out the woman.

She strode through the unlocked front door and stopped

again to listen. *Who the fuck is that? Jesus, I think it's Tessa from the beauty parlor. . . .*

She was walking down the hall toward the bedroom when she caught herself and stopped. What was she going to do? Scream, demand they stop immediately? Order George to move out? Tell them both how disappointed she was? Tell Tessa she'd be finding a new manicurist?

Instead she ended up gawking.

The bedroom door had been left open, and as Emmie approached she could see a couple on the bed, their figures outlined by the flickering glow from the bedroom television set. Now she could make out a second layer of sound, more moaning voices and a cheap musical accompaniment. It took her a few seconds to place it.

It was that sleazy porn flick George always tried to get her to watch. Apparently he'd found someone else to share his interest.

Except they weren't watching the movie. The woman, who Emmie could see now was definitely Tessa the manicurist (she could tell by the teased blond hair spread across her pillow), was naked and spread-legged on the bed, her eyes closed, head thrown back in ecstasy. George was sprawled near the end of the bed, his head bobbing up and down as his tongue worked on Tessa's crotch.

He never did that with me, Emmie thought.

Then she ran, all thoughts of confrontation having vanished. She slammed the front door on the way out, hoping they'd heard it, wiping tears from her eyes as she stumbled to the car. She gunned the engine too strongly and then peeled rubber as she shot down the street, heading for the interstate and . . .

. . . she didn't know.

A quarter hour later she found herself in a lowlife bar.

She'd picked it completely at random. Or maybe she'd liked the name—the Last Resort. That felt right, tonight.

Normally it wasn't the kind of place she'd ever go into, but it'd been open and there'd only been a chopper and two pickup trucks in the dirt lot (it was a Tuesday night, after all), and there'd been an empty table near the rear. She'd ordered a beer (or three), taken a chair facing the wall, and cried into the solace of a cocktail napkin.

"That bastard," she'd muttered, uncaring of what anyone thought about the sobbing woman alone in the back muttering obscenities to herself. "That lousy, stinking sonuvabitch."

She'd supported him for the last six months, and she thought they'd been a good six months. He was so handsome, with his easy grin and wavy brown hair, that at first she couldn't believe he cared about her. Their life together had been for the most part easy, and he seemed to like the sex, even if Emmie secretly thought it was a bit dull and found his interest in porn embarrassing. Sure, she didn't like all of his friends, and he had a tendency to drink too much, but she'd believed him when he'd sworn (with that gorgeous grin) that there'd be no other girls for him.

Jesus, what an idiot she'd been.

And now . . . they hadn't even tried to hide it, hadn't even had the decency to go to a motel. And right when George had known Emmie would be coming home from work—had he wanted her to find them? Or had they just been so lost in their sexy hijinks that they'd lost track of time?

And what would she do now?

She couldn't picture herself facing him. She was still burning in shame from the customer at the store who'd called her a bitch when she'd told him they were out of his favorite cigarettes. She hadn't even been able to respond; she'd just fled to a restroom, locked herself in a stall, and cried for ten minutes.

She hated herself.

"Don't hate yourself, honey, it's that dickwad's fault."

Emmie looked up, surprised to find a woman now sitting at the other side of the table. Emmie was already on her third beer, a little drunk, and so it took her a few seconds to wonder: *How did she know I was thinking that?*

"Caught him with another chick, huh?" the woman asked.

Emmie nodded, then wiped her eyes again and looked at the woman more carefully. She wasn't attractive—in her thirties, with bad skin, worse teeth, and dirty blond hair—but there was something about her, something familiar, as if she was a movie star that Emmie had seen once in something, or . . .

Then Emmie gave up on trying to place her and asked, "How'd you know?"

The woman grinned and waved a hand about the room. "Please, you're a young girl sitting by yourself in a biker bar and crying. You don't have any bruises, so I know it's not that he beat on you; so what's that leave?"

There was a strange sympathy in the woman's tone, and Emmie relaxed, even smiled herself. "Yeah, I guess so. He was . . . well, he was in bed with the woman who gives me my manicures."

The woman threw back her head and roared. "Hey, that's good—he was nailing your nail expert!"

Emmie chuckled, bitterly, then thrust out a hand. "I'm Emmie."

The woman took it, and Emmie was shocked at the strength in her fingers. "Lori."

Her grip was also cold, and Emmie pulled her hand away before it froze. "I don't know what to do now," she confessed miserably.

"This hasn't happened to you before?"

"Nope," Emmie said, shaking her head. "Although I suppose I should've seen it coming."

"Yeah, you fuckin' should've." Lori leaned in closer and held Emmie's gaze with her own, which jittered slightly and left Emmie less comfortable. "There's only one question to ask yourself at this point: do you want to stay with this guy?"

Emmie thought for a moment and finally answered honestly, "I don't know."

"Well, that you gotta fuckin' decide for yourself. But if you want to keep him"—here she lowered her voice and cocked an eyebrow at Emmie—"I can tell you how to get what you want."

Emmie dried her eyes and listened, intrigued. "You can?"

"Oh, hell yes, honey, it's easy: you gotta take control. You know—in bed."

Emmie's jaw dropped a half-inch. Then she looked away, her face hot. "Girls don't do that—"

"Fuck they don't!" the woman exclaimed loudly, causing Emmie to look around nervously. No one else in the bar seemed to have noticed. "Your boyfriend—"

"George," Emmie obliged.

"Right, George," Lori continued, "he's got a dick, right? Then I guarantee you he wants you to lead him around with it. It's up to you, honey. Take the lead—or spend the rest of your life crying in bathroom stalls."

Emmie shook her head, tilted it back for another swallow of beer—and when she looked again, Lori was gone. She turned and scanned the bar, but there was no sign of her.

And how the fuck did she know about the crying-in-bathroom-stalls thing?

For a few days, Emmie wanted nothing to do with George.

She avoided him around the house, and he acted as if nothing was wrong; apparently he and the nail-filer really *hadn't* heard the front door slam as Emmie had stalked out.

But even while she was hating George and his smiling, happy deceit, Lori's words kept rolling around in her head.

Take control . . . in bed. . . .

Emmie would look at him working out in the mornings, with his muscled body lightly covered in musky-scented sweat, or the way his white teeth glistened as he played videogames, or the endearingly silly way he bounced his head to that one Eminem song he listened to over and over, and she realized that she really didn't want to lose him. At least not right away.

Take control . . . in bed. . . .

It was twelve-thirty the night George staggered into the bedroom, pleasantly drunk . . . and found Emmie waiting for him in bra and panties.

She hoped he was drunk enough that he wouldn't notice how nervous she really was.

He didn't notice. Instead, he actually stopped in the bedroom doorway and gaped, an expression which made Emmie both more anxious and happy. She tried writhing slightly against the sheets, tilting one hip up, and a slow smile started to spread across George's fine face.

"Well, girl . . . what's this?"

He looked good lounging there in the doorway, and Emmie began to think maybe she really could do this. She motioned him forward, crooking one finger. "Get into this bed *now.*"

He had his shirt and pants off in record time.

He tried right away to lower himself onto her—like usual—but she put a hand against his chest and pushed him back. "Uh-uh," she purred, "not like that."

He stared at her for a moment, and Emmie nearly let out a scream as she saw that he was plainly waiting—waiting to be told what to do.

She suddenly realized she had no idea what to tell him. "Lick my feet" popped into her head.

To her astonishment, he obliged all too happily. His tongue on her tender soles brought delicious tickles of pleasure that drew out slowly as he began to work his way up her body, pausing behind her knees, at her belly, and along her neck.

Finally he was kissing her, just as his fingers found their way under her panties, and he groaned when he felt her wetness. "Oh, baby . . . whatever this is that got into you, I like it."

"Shut up and eat me," she ordered. If it was good enough for Tessa, it was good enough for her.

And it was good. Very good. His tongue and fingers worked the places between her legs until she was bucking like a jackhammer and making Tessa sound quiet by comparison. The first orgasm shook like none had in years. The second came when she finally allowed him inside her, and even though he was on top of her it wasn't like it had always been in the past: it was sweaty and hard and had them both screaming. The third came later that night, when she'd demanded he stay awake and hard long enough to fuck her again, slower and quieter this time.

Sometime toward dawn, as they finally exhausted themselves and were drifting toward sleep, Emmie thought she owed her friend Lori a beer. Hell, maybe a whole keg.

"C'mon, honey, don't be a fool. They all fuck around, all the time," she says, her strange, twitching eyes jumping from Emmie's to the house and back again. "The only question is what you're gonna do about it."

The sex with George was equally great for the next three nights. They tried things Emmie had imagined when she was horny and by herself but that she'd never thought she'd actually have the nerve to attempt for real. She rode atop George. They nearly tore the house apart with a sixty-nine. He even let her tie him up one night, and he finally had to tell her to stop because he couldn't come again.

On the fourth night, George was out of town helping a buddy who was a stock-car racer, and Emmie went back to the Last Resort, looking for her new friend, Lori. She sat at the same table, in the same chair, ordered the same beer . . . and waited.

She waited for an hour. For two. She finally realized Lori wasn't coming, and it'd probably been stupid of her to assume she'd be there. But Lori had looked so at home in this bar, as if she'd always been there.

Emmie finally asked the bartender if he remembered seeing her and the woman from last week. She mentioned she'd been crying. The bartender, a huge ex-biker named Big Joe, with tattooed arms the size of Emmie's waist, scratched at his grizzled beard and said he recalled seeing her, but he'd have sworn she'd been alone all night.

She finally left, slightly disappointed, and got into her beat-up old Honda. She was just starting up the engine when she heard, "Hey, girl."

She jumped and jerked to the right, where she saw Lori sitting in the passenger seat. "Where did you—?!"

Lori cut her off. "You tried that thing, didn't you?"

Emmie sank back, tingling at the memory of George's mouth and fingers and cock. "Yeah. That's why I came here tonight—to say thank-you."

"Uh-uh," Lori corrected, "that's not why you came here. You came to ask me what you should do next."

"No, I . . . I know what to do now," Emmie replied, confused.

"That's what you think. Start the car."

"Why?"

"Because we're going for a little drive."

Emmie nearly told the woman to get out of her car right then and there, but she remembered the strength in Lori's fingers (and the cold) and realized the other woman could easily overpower her. Emmie's stomach churned as she turned the keys. "Okay. Where to?"

"Easy: home. Your home."

Oh God. Is she going to do something to me right in my own home? Even if she doesn't, she'll know where I live—

Lori interrupted her thoughts with: "Georgie-boy's fucking a waitress in your bed right now."

Emmie put the car in gear without a second thought.

Ten minutes later she found out Lori was right. They stood outside Emmie's bedroom window, and this time they could hear both George and a woman whose voice Emmie didn't know.

Emmie felt her throat fill with bile. "He told me he was going out of town! He lied to me! Motherfucker!"

"Nah, Emmie," Lori corrected, "right now he's a waitress-fucker."

"I can't fucking believe it!" Emmie hissed, her hands balling into fists.

"Believe it, honey, because it's happening. And it's going to keep happening, because that's just how Georgie is."

"But . . . ," Emmie said and was ashamed at the hot tears spreading over her cheeks, "I thought we were back on track. We were doin' great—"

"C'mon, honey, don't be a fool. They all fuck around, all the time," Lori said, her strange, twitching eyes jumping from Emmie's to the house and back again. "The only question is what you're gonna do about it."

"I don't know," Emmie said, pacing a few steps, feeling her nails chip as she ground them against her own palms. She suddenly turned back to Lori furiously. "You were the one who told me to take control—"

"Yeah, but you couldn't keep it. There's only way to do that, Emmie: kill that fuckin' bastard."

Emmie felt both a chill of revulsion and great, obscene glee sweep through her. "What?!"

"Wait until the girl leaves, then take that old pistol of his in there and blow him away."

Emmie stared at the woman in disbelief, and for the first time she realized:

She's crazy.

"I'm not going to do that—"

"C'mon, he needs to fuckin' pay for this."

Emmie backed away, scared. "Yeah, but . . ."

Lori stepped closer to her, and Emmie suddenly realized she'd backed up against the house and there was nowhere else to go. Lori reached out, and her arms went around Emmie . . .

. . . and Emmie felt something like fire, and like ice, slide into her. It entered through the spine, and Emmie stiffened as it curled up through her guts, her head, and finally settled into her heart.

The next thing she knew, she had George's gun in her hand, and it felt *so good* there, so right, and she burned as she walked down the hallway toward the bedroom, and George was alone (When did the waitress leave? She couldn't remember.), and the gun went off (more than once), and for a moment Emmie was deafened.

George was dead.

He'd taken at least three bullets at close range, and his blood had spattered everything in the room, including Emmie. Emmie lowered the gun and stared, feeling something wild rising in her, something primal. She let it come . . .

. . . and then she felt cold hands on her shoulders, and there was a voice in her ear, whispering:

"It's good, isn't it?"

She nodded, absorbing the smells of the gun and the blood, and then the chill fingers were around her and gripping her breasts, kneading them, and Emmie was almost instantly perched on the edge of orgasm. One hand slid down to her crotch, under the hem of her jeans and panties, and Emmie gasped as something icy slithered into her, pumping at her, and then Emmie screamed as the orgasm took her, but this one went beyond simple sex into something Emmie couldn't name, something so deeply at her root that it felt like she'd just fucked God.

And when the last wave of pleasure passed, the voice behind her murmured again: "So you listen to me now . . ."

She did.

It was hard work, cleaning up after the murder.

Fortunately it was late, and none of the neighbors gave any sign that they'd heard the shots. Lori said getting rid of the body was first, so Emmie used the blood-soaked sheet to drag George's heavy body down the hallway and out to his truck. She drove the truck two miles to a heavily wooded area, then tried her best to settle him in the driver's side. She used a towel to wipe the truck clean of her fingerprints.

By the time she'd walked back home, the first hints of dawn were in the sky, but she still had a few more hours of work in front of her, wiping down the walls and the floor, putting the rest of the bedding in a big black plastic trashbag that she'd dispose of later.

She'd have to buy new sheets.

And through it all, she felt only that needle of icefire that now inhabited her heart and a grim satisfaction at knowing that George got what he deserved.

"They'll get easier every time, from now on," Lori says with a grin that reveals her stained and crooked teeth.

They did get easier, and Emmie got good at it.

The first one (after George, that is) was a truck driver she met in the parking lot of the Last Resort. He cornered Emmie against his truck, and in the past a moment like this—with his arm over her, virtually pinning her into place—would have terrified her.

But tonight George's pistol was in her purse.

They crawled into the little space behind the truck cab, where the driver had a bed, complete with photos of spread beavers tacked to the walls. Emmie tore his shirt buttons off with her teeth, and he cackled with glee. The thought of what she was about to do already had her nearly dripping, and the driver couldn't believe his luck as she tore off first her jeans, then his. He was already hard, and although he was disappointingly small, she lowered herself onto him eagerly. His hands reached up and held onto her breasts as if they were handles while she rode him, groaning. They both came quickly, in minutes.

Then Emmie reached back into her purse, got the gun, and shot him.

Only one shot this time, through what she guessed was the heart, and there was blood, but it was flowing around his convulsing body, and she quickly raised herself off him and grabbed her clothes.

She was dressed and back in her own car two minutes later. No one else had been in the parking lot. She hadn't even gone into the bar.

No problem.

She did five more over the next two months.

After the fifth one (a short-order cook who'd followed her out of the supermarket one night), Emmie realized she hadn't seen Lori in a while, so she headed over to the Last Resort.

Lori was there, at the same table near the back—and deep in conversation with another woman.

Emmie froze and felt the (now-familiar) rage rising.

The other woman's back was to the door, and Lori could see her shoulders shaking slightly, her head bowed. She was crying. And Lori was smiling at her.

Emmie stalked forward until she'd reached the table, where she glared down, first at Lori and then her companion. The other woman.

"Who's this?" she demanded.

Lori looked up at her and smiled casually—but her eyes still had that old tremor, the one that used to leave Emmie so unnerved. "This conversation doesn't involve you, so fuck off."

Emmie didn't move, except to finger one of the empty beer bottles that littered the table. "I think it does involve me."

The other woman was very young, maybe not even twenty yet, and Emmie felt a quick pang of sympathy as she saw several large bruises splayed out across her face. Then Lori was rising, slowly, and Emmie's pity changed to wariness. "You know, I can take back what I gave you, you stupid cunt."

Emmie flinched and felt the shard in her heart tremble. "What are you talking about? You didn't give me anything—"

Lori suddenly stepped forward, and her hand was *in* Emmie's chest, and Emmie could feel something impossibly cold moving around in her . . .

. . . and suddenly the icefire was gone from her heart, and she saw what she'd done, and the strength went out of her. She fell to her knees behind the other woman's chair, gasping, clutching at her empty heart.

"Oh Jesus . . . oh fuckin' hell, what did I do . . ."

The truck driver . . . the soldier on leave . . . the fat guy with a picture of his wife on his visor . . . the bald one who liked to talk . . . the cook . . . and George, oh Christ, she'd loved George and she'd killed him. . . .

She was wailing, and the bartender, Big Joe, rushed out from behind the bar and knelt next to her. She grabbed on to his massive arms, clinging to them desperately. "Lori told me—she told me to, and I—"

Big Joe tried to calm her down, stroking her fingers. "Hold on there, gal, who's Lori?"

Emmie nodded at the woman standing three feet away, grinning madly. "Her! Lori! Right there!"

Big Joe followed her gaze, then turned back to her, puzzled. "There ain't nobody there—"

Emmie turned wide eyes on him. "Lori, right there, are you crazy?!"

Then Emmie realized the other woman, the young one with

the battered face, had turned and was eyeing her, perplexed. "Her name's not Lori. It's Susan."

Suddenly Big Joe's jaw worked for a moment, and he stiffened. "What's this 'Lori' look like?"

Emmie laughed once, harshly. "What do you mean, just look at her! She's got blond hair, bad teeth—"

Big Joe finished: "—skin's kinda red and leathery?"

"Yes," Emmie said.

Big Joe pried Emmie's grip off him and backed away. "I'm gonna call the cops."

"What . . ." Emmie started but didn't know what else to say.

Big Joe turned back once before he stepped behind the bar to get the phone. "'Lori' and 'Susan' were both aliases she used. . . . Jesus, I figured we'd finally seen the last of her when they executed her. For all those men she killed. . . ."

Emmie's eyes jerked back to the woman she knew as Lori, and the woman was laughing, great gales of insane, howling laughter that Emmie knew only she and the young woman could hear.

That other woman suddenly stood and turned, and Emmie saw she wasn't crying anymore. Instead she smiled, and there was a strange jitter to her eyes. "I gotta go home and fuck my husband," she said.

Later, Emmie was still screaming in the back of the police car as it drove away from the Last Resort.

Secret Admirer

Steve Armison

I'm waiting outside in the parking lot. Headlights stream steadily down the nearby thoroughfare. A few people walk toward their own cars, some with companions and others alone, but none are more lonely than I am. I take a deep breath, then exhale. I can't believe my life has come down to this. Never in a million years would I have expected it. I flex the fingers of my right hand and scour the area once again before grasping the loaded revolver on the passenger seat. I check my watch; it will be over soon.

There could be witnesses, of course. But that's of little consequence. My world ended the moment Sharla decided to be unfaithful.

A tear trickles down my cheek. I recall the start of it all just a few weeks earlier. It was the beginning of the end. . . .

Across the desk from me sat Dr. Tannerbaum, Sharla's psychiatrist. He was a caricature of a man, and I couldn't understand how she could take him seriously. He was slightly plump, with a handlebar mustache and thin strands of dark hair slicked back over a mostly bald head. He looked as if he should be singing in a barbershop quartet a hundred years ago. Despite the serious nature of the meeting, I found it difficult to keep from smiling when I faced him. I couldn't help but imagine him wearing a striped jacket and a straw hat.

"As you already know, Mr. Leach, your wife consented to this meeting," the doc began. "However, I remain limited as to what I may reveal to you regarding her condition."

I nodded. "I understand completely, but please call me Edmund."

He leaned back in his heavily padded leather chair. "Of course," he answered.

There was a moment of awkward silence. I glanced at the multiple diplomas gracing his rich hardwood walls. I had hoped he'd be more proactive, that he could offer some kind of instant solution to Sharla's psychological slump. Growing impatient, I said, "So?"

The doc cleared his throat. "There are several contributing factors to your wife's present state of mind—"

"Sharla," I interrupted. "Please call her Sharla."

"Yes, of course." He shifted in his seat. "She's postmenopausal, as you know. You've recently relocated here, where your wife has no friends, and she's yet to recover from the tragic death of your only grandchild last year."

That last one really stung. The truth is, I hadn't gotten over little Brandi's death either, and I doubted I ever would.

"Your wife's—Sharla's—self-esteem has been shattered," the doc continued. He paused briefly, then added, "Over the last several sessions, I've discussed her past with her in depth. I've delved into your relationship with her, and I've honestly been unable thus far to detect any basis for the deepening of her depression."

"She's never been like this before," I interjected.

The doc nodded. "To be perfectly honest, I initially suspected that *you* were part of the problem, that you were berating her, that she was suffering some kind of psychological control or mental abuse, but I could find no specific evidence of that. From my perspective, you two seem to have had a happy marriage."

I stared at him blankly until I could get the word out. "*Had*?"

The doc cleared his throat. "Yes?"

"You said *had* a happy marriage. Shouldn't that be *have*?"

The doc appeared to give it some thought before answering. "I suppose only you and she can answer that question."

Now I was getting angry. I had done everything imaginable to make Sharla happy, and how dare anyone infer that I could be at fault?

"Listen, Doc. Did she tell you how many surprise gifts I've given her recently? Did she mention how often I tell her that I love her? Did she say how many times I've complimented her appearance? Did she—?"

"Now, hold on, Mr. er, Edmund, I haven't accused you of anything. But in answer to your question, no, I'm unaware of any of that."

I couldn't believe it. I slowly shook my head. I had been driving myself nuts thinking of ways to cheer her up. I had gone way beyond the call of duty, and she hadn't even recognized the effort. "Are you telling me that she never even noticed anything I've—" I began, but he interrupted me again.

"Keep in mind, Edmund, that it's simply human nature to discount gestures such as those from our loved ones."

"What the hell does *that* mean?"

"Well, we *expect* that kind of behavior from people we love."

"So?"

"So, we unfortunately tend to undervalue it."

I shook my head. I was about ready to just get up and leave. "That makes no fu— That just makes no sense." I was steamed.

"Let me explain it this way," the doc continued in a softer tone, obviously trying to calm me down. "Would you tell your wife to her face that you no longer find her attractive?"

"Of course not!"

"Would you tell her that she looks great when in fact she looks no different than before?"

"Sure!"

"Well, there you have it."

"*What*?" This seemed to be going nowhere.

"We know that those who love us will protect us, even from the truth. We have a tendency to sometimes back away from reality, perhaps even lie, to protect the feelings of those we love. It's an unwritten rule that we subconsciously expect from those we're closest to."

It finally began to sink in. "So compliments from a complete stranger could have more impact on Sharla than anything I might say?"

"That's correct."

I slumped back in my chair. "But that just isn't right!"

The doc smiled and lightly nodded. "Ah, but I'm afraid that's the way it *is.*"

And I thought about what he said all the way home. I trusted the doc's judgment; I took it quite seriously, and it hurt, if you want to know the truth. But I loved my wife, and I would do anything for her.

Sharla Leach booted her home computer and prepared to sift through her daily influx of e-mail, deleting the usual accumulation of spammed messages that typically jammed her in-box. Sharla yawned and took in a deep breath. Spam filters were not yet trustworthy, in her view. She had tried several, but each had mistakenly screened out important messages. Sorting her mail would only take a few minutes, but beyond that she didn't feel like surfing the Internet today.

When the downloading was complete, she saw that there were nineteen new messages, probably no more than three of which were legitimate. She quickly scanned the list, automatically marking for deletion the notifications for winning lotteries she'd never entered and the requests of foreigners to help safeguard large sums of money. Then she hesitated at the sight of one message in particular. Its subject line read *Your Secret Admirer From the Appleton Days.* She'd seen somewhat similar headings from spammed messages before, from matchmaking or sex sites, and God only knew how she had ended up on their mailing lists. But this one was different. This one specifically mentioned Appleton, the small town where she and her husband first met in a singles group almost twenty-five years ago.

She stopped for a moment to reminisce. As Charles Dickens had said, *it was the best of times, it was the worst of times,* the two years following the divorce from her first husband. She'd never been so lonely and heartbroken in her entire life, but after she became heavily involved with an Appleton group of single adults, everything changed practically overnight. Her phone began to ring so often that she bought her first answering machine. There was always something going on, and she had an opportunity to date several men, some of whom she quickly wrote off and others who apparently did the same to her. But that period of her life had always carried a certain mystique, and here appeared to be a message from one of those men from whom she hadn't heard in a long, long time.

Secret admirer, huh? Could it be someone she liked but never dated? Or someone she dated but subsequently dumped? Perhaps it was one of the two or three with whom she later regretted having severed the ties. She started to open the message, then hesitated. Its sender was identified only as *Mystery Man,* and she wondered if it was truly the right thing to do. Could the message actually be legitimate? And if so, why was he being so secretive? She could easily hit the delete key, and the whole thing would be behind her. But what would it hurt just to take a quick look? She took a deep breath, then clicked.

Hi, Sharla!
I hope you're the right Sharla. If you're not, I apologize, but if you're the same Sharla who used to belong to a great Appleton singles group, I just wanted to say hello and tell you that I've been thinking about you all of these years.
You were always my favorite.
MM

Hmm, not a hint of who this mystery man might be. Should she respond? Curiosity was killing her, and if she was totally honest with herself, she had to admit she hoped the message was from Lewis Michaels. She and Lewis had spent a lot of time together, but for some reason a meaningful relationship never developed. She'd sometimes wondered why. So what would it hurt to respond? She clicked the Reply button, and an e-mail template popped onto the screen. Choosing her words carefully, she typed:

Well, hello, Mystery Man!
You've found the right Sharla; and now I'm dying to know who you are.
Won't you tell me? Pretty please?
Sharla

The improvement in Sharla's attitude wasn't what I'd call miraculous, but I definitely noted a change. I saw a faint smile here and there, and she was a bit more talkative. We sat at the dinner table quietly eating taco salads when I broke the silence.

"Anything special happen today?" I asked.

She hesitated briefly, then sighed. "Not really," she said.

So I left it at that. Any improvement at all, even at such a minor level, was significant at this point.

Mystery Man had proven to be quite frustrating. Sharla had exchanged several brief messages with him, and he steadfastly refused to identify himself. More and more she suspected him to be Lewis. Few men had known her well enough to be privy to some of the incidents to which he referred in his messages. And now she began to feel nervous, perhaps a bit guilty about what she was doing. After all, she was a married woman. Happily? Well, that was subject to debate.

Mystery Man had suggested that they IM each other. She hadn't a clue what that meant, so he patiently explained how to download the free software for instant messaging. Through it, they could have live, interactive online conversations.

Part of the process required registering a screen name, for which she chose SecretSweetie. That name had already been taken, so she added a number and became SecretSweetie319. Mystery Man had wanted the screen name of MysteryMan007, but that one was too good to be available still, so he had to alter it to MysteryMan7007.

They had met for brief chats on a few occasions, and she had gotten no further in determining his true identity. She had quickly grown comfortable with him, however, as a definite connection appeared to be developing. Little by little, Mystery Man pushed her to stretch her limits. Each time she felt more guilty and uncomfortable but couldn't resist the urge to continue. Should she make him angry, Sharla couldn't stand the thought of losing him. Booting her computer would never be the same if there was no possibility of communicating with this mysterious man from her past.

Life was getting better. It was nice to see my wife smile every now and then, even though I knew it wasn't actually directed at me. I was beginning to feel a bit restless myself.

One night as we lay in bed I rolled over and put my arm around her. "You awake?"

"Mm-hmm," she grunted without movement.

I put my arm around her and worked my hand underneath

her flannel pajama top. I nestled closer and squeezed her breast. "Not now," she muttered.

That wasn't a good sign.

Little by little, Mystery Man convinced Sharla to try online sex. Without a doubt, that was crossing the line, but she reminded herself that it was only a computer and far less personal than anonymous phone sex. Reluctantly, but also with a twinge of curiosity, she agreed to log on at the specified time for her first encounter with cybersex.

I must admit that by this time I was enjoying the charade. Sharla was feeling noticeably better every day, and I was getting a kick out of experiencing an online relationship like I had heard others talking about. I was feeling a higher level of confidence knowing that I had the power to sweet-talk my wife all over again after all of these years. In hindsight, however, I failed to realize that as I got closer to Sharla online, we were growing more distant in reality.

In both e-mail and IM sessions she continually prodded me for my real name, but I was careful about every detail I revealed. I did tell her that I was married, happily in fact, but that my wife sometimes didn't understand me. And I admit it stung when she said that her husband was distant and inattentive. She was, in truth, describing herself. And every time she prodded me to admit that I was, in fact, Lewis Michaels, I felt a growing anger.

Our online encounters always occurred during the day when Sharla thought I was busily at work. Being my own boss afforded the opportunity to close my office door and enjoy these temporary liaisons. I carefully planned our upcoming sexual escapade in advance. I wanted to give her a powerful performance, as much for myself as for her. All of this was feeding my ego on one level and completely destroying it on another, though I failed to recognize it at the time. But the fantasy was intoxicating. I could readily understand how people got addicted to chat rooms and such.

Sharla had logged on and said hello to Mystery Man. She felt nervous, with a twinge of guilt over what was about to transpire, but she'd been haunted by images of herself with Lewis. Funny how she'd never thought of him in physical terms way back then, but now . . . now her life was different. Perhaps the timing had been wrong before. Now, who knew what the future held?

MM: ready?
SS: i guess so

She glanced at her watch. Edmund wouldn't be home for at least a couple of hours. That should allow plenty of time.

MM: imagine we're on a deserted beach
SS: ok
MM: we spread a blanket in the dunes
SS: mmm
MM: i kiss you long and hard
SS: yes
MM: i can feel your heartbeat pounding against my chest

He paused briefly.

MM: can you hear the surf?
SS: yes
MM: can you feel the breeze?
SS: yesss
MM: our tongues intertwine
SS: mmm
MM: take a deep breath

SS: ok
MM: touch yourself
SS: what?
MM: touch yourself for me

She hadn't realized this would be part of it. For a moment she felt a bit dim-witted; after all, this was what it was all about, right? She glanced around the house, then slid out of her jeans. Off went her panties as well.

Sharla relaxed in her chair again and slid her middle finger below the wireless keyboard in her lap, past her stomach to her pleasure zone. God, she was wetter than she'd been in years. She closed her eyes and let her imagination run wild until the computer's audible alert informed her that Mystery Man had IM'ed her again.

MM: u still there?
SS: oh, YES
MM: just relax and read what i say
SS: why?
MM: i don't want u to be distracted by typing. just keep your hands off the keyboard and do what i say
SS: ok

Sharla felt like a teenager in the backseat of her boyfriend's car. The sexual energy was indescribable. She continued to stimulate herself as she followed Mystery Man's lead, imagining the possibilities . . .

MM: i carefully peel your swimsuit away. you're beautiful.
MM: your nipples are hard, pointing to the sky
MM: i watch you breathe
MM: then i start at your lips and kiss my way down
MM: between your breasts
MM: way down

MM: past your belly
MM: between your legs
MM: in the distance we hear thunder
MM: a light sprinkle of rain begins to fall
MM: but we don't care

Sharla paused to exhale deeply. Mystery Man was quite good at this. She wondered how many times he'd carried on this way with other women, but the thought only excited her more. She was being adventurous, stretching her admittedly limited boundaries, and it felt dangerously exciting.

MM: you like this, i can tell
MM: you're so fucking wet
MM: my tongue traces lightly around your vagina
MM: then it slowly pushes inside
MM: my tongue slips up and down, in and out
MM: it tickles your swollen clit
MM: i suck your clit, using my lips to massage it

She couldn't stand much more of this. Sharla set the keyboard on the floor beside her chair, closed her eyes, and imagined what he would describe next, oblivious to the audible alerts of more and more lines scrolling down the screen. She didn't care what he was saying; her mind had now taken control. Her clit was so sensitive that it wouldn't take much longer. She imagined Lewis Michaels's head between her legs tenderly administering to her needs. She tensed; her legs shook. She applied the pressure and adjusted the frequency of her touch to the optimum level, and then she exploded. "Oh my God!" She moaned. Waves of pleasure rippled as her head rolled from side to side. She moistened her lips and maintained the contact, slipping into orgasm after orgasm. She lost count of the times she came.

* * *

I eventually admitted to myself that I had taken the ruse as far as it could go. My original goal of lifting her spirits had been accomplished, and, quite frankly, the erotic thrill was gone for me. I suppose it had much to do with the realization that Sharla thought I was someone else, that my dear, sweet wife, my soul mate and the mother of my children, was imagining herself fucking another man. It should have dawned on me earlier, but I had allowed myself to get completely caught up in self-gratification. By the time we had graduated to online sex, Dr. Tannerbaum's words had faded into the distant past.

I admit, the cybersex was fun, but only to a point. Sharla tried to reciprocate, but the truth is, she wasn't very good. Jacking off at my computer just didn't work for me. After all, I wasn't exploring uncharted territory here; there was none of that electrifying passion that comes with a new partner—I was having online sex with my own wife. The fact that she thought I was someone else weighed heavier and heavier, so I was thinking of different ways to put an end to the whole ploy when she dropped the bomb on me. I was stunned. We were in the middle of a casual IM session when it happened:

SS: i want to have u for real

I stared at the screen, numb, for God only knows how long.

SS: u still there?

I exhaled a burst of pent-up breath.

MM: i'm here and i'm real. you've got me for real already
SS: u know what i mean

I swallowed hard. My wife wanted to fuck her old buddy Lewis Michaels. How could she do this to me? How could she betray me after all I had done to make her happy? And what the hell would happen if Michaels suddenly appeared out of nowhere? They would wonder who the hell had impersonated him, then realize they were all-systems-go for a roll in the hay.

MM: gotta run
SS: wait!
MM: catch you later

And then I signed off.

Superman, the so-called "Man of Steel," is practically indestructible until he stumbles across kryptonite. Pussy is the kryptonite of the heterosexual male. Even the biggest, toughest muscle-bound macho freak turns into a mass of jelly when the right pussy rubs against him. The owner of a pussy can make a man feel like the king of the world or the lowliest leech in the food chain. The latter best describes me as the truth sunk in that my beloved wife's heart was beginning to betray me too, even though I was the secret object of her desire.

I knew Lewis Michaels way back in Appleton. He was a loser. What the hell did she ever see in him? And how could she throw twenty-three precious years of marriage away for a roll in the fucking hay with him?

My anger grew exponentially and brought me here. Grasping this gun as I wait in my car, I'm determined to put an end to this whole sick mess, starting at its source. When I think of Sharla in the arms of someone else, especially Lewis Michaels, I practically lose control. I want to smash something, and that's exactly what I'm about to do. I started this whole charade to lift Sharla from a deep depression. In the process, I made her feel better but threw myself into a bottomless pit. There's only one way out.

* * *

Sharla regretted hitting Lewis up so suddenly with the idea of meeting in person. Although she'd been thinking about it for days, it had still been a spur-of-the-moment decision when she typed those few fateful words. She'd hesitated before hitting the Enter key but then threw caution to the wind and went for it.

She had grown increasingly attached to Lewis. She loved his personality, his playfulness. She wondered if he would be the same in person, however. Some people were far more open and carefree online than they were in reality, she'd heard. And she loved Lewis's passion when it came to sex. Edmund had never shown such creativity in the bedroom. No matter the cost, she had to get things back on track with Lewis.

She hadn't expected this reaction, however. She'd left her computer on all day, logged on to instant messaging, hoping to hear the sound of an opening squeaky door signaling that Lewis had logged on. *Nada*. She would now have to resolve this through e-mail.

Dearest Lewis:
Please don't be upset with me. I know that in the beginning we agreed that this would only be short-term and that it would never go beyond the Internet but something special happened between us, honey. I don't know what it is and I can't explain it but I truly believe we were meant to be together. We can't just throw something this precious away. Please write to me. You don't have to tell me that you love me. I'm not asking for that. I just want us to be online together again and discuss the possibility of a whole new life with each other. Can't we at least do that, honey?
You don't have to say it back to me, darling, but . . .
I love you.
Sharla

* * *

You're probably wondering how I felt when I read Sharla's confession of love. Well, imagine having your balls removed by a chainsaw. Or perhaps a cactus enema. You get the picture. I would have much preferred a bullet through the heart or an arrow through my skull. Instead she attacked me with something that simmered inside, that slowly ate away at me like an injection of weak acid into my bloodstream. I felt the pain slowly creeping throughout my body, gradually ripping me apart. Isn't that enough to justify an extreme act? Wouldn't just about anyone understand?

I've been a decent man: a good provider and great father to my kids. I've given Sharla everything she's ever needed, and yet she wants to piss it all away. And without realizing it, the man she's fallen in love with . . . is *me*!

I know where Lewis Michaels lives. Yeah, he's still around, and I've parked along his street and secretly watched him come and go. He looks much the same, only older. He has young kids living at home, and his wife isn't much to look at. His life looks incredibly boring. He would jump at a chance to nail Sharla. If it was that easy for me to find Lewis, Sharla can look him up with no trouble at all. In fact, she probably already has. Chances are better than good that she's with him this very moment. They've probably been fucking all of this time and playing me for the patsy. Sharla probably knew it was me from the start. But this whole thing isn't Lewis's fault.

My headache is killing me. There's a roaring sound in my ears. I'm shaking all over as I grip the steering wheel and the gun. I wipe beads of sweat from my forehead and put down the window for a breath of fresh air. Every woman I see looks like Sharla. And every one of them frowns and looks the other way.

I'm not sure that I can go through with this; I'm not a violent man. But the thought of the two of them together is more than I can bear. I take a deep breath.

Gun in hand, I quietly open the door and step outside.

My heart is pounding; my hands are trembling. I feel helpless. But we must all accept responsibility for our actions. I'm not a confrontational man, but I know what to do.

A familiar figure exits an adjacent office building and walks away from me toward a parking lot on the other side of the complex. I follow, the revolver at my side. "Hey, home wrecker!" I yell.

He turns, and fear washes over his face. He stands perfectly still, puzzled. It's been a while since he's seen me. Does he even recognize me?

"He's got a gun!" someone yells, and dark figures begin to scramble for cover. It's him and me now. He sees the revolver. I try to prevent it from shaking as I hold it in place.

I step closer. Breathing becomes more difficult. I see the panic in his eyes. He knows who I am now.

"Wh-what is this about?" he stutters. His briefcase slips from his right hand and tumbles to the pavement. The latch breaks, and papers spill across the asphalt.

"Let me explain it *this* way," I say as I tighten my grip on the revolver.

The fear in his eyes alone is worth what I'm about to do. "No!" he says. "This is never the answer." He takes a careful step in my direction, arms out straight toward me, palms open wide.

"You deserve this," I mumble. "You destroyed my marriage."

"No," he begs. "There are always better options."

The gun shakes in my hand. I pull back the hammer.

"Please," he pleads, "think of what this will do to your wife!"

And that's exactly what I think about as I focus on his disgusting handlebar mustache, push the barrel harder against my temple, and fire.

Goo Girl

Thomas Tessier

The snow started falling early on Friday evening. Only flurries that didn't even stick; the wind blew them around in swirls like dust. But it was going to be a long weekend. The storm was expected to pick up after midnight and arrive in full force by noon Saturday, lasting well into Sunday. It was shaping up as a classic Nor'easter, with snow accumulating between two and three feet in the area. White stuff flying through the air. So fitting.

She liked snow, and the timing of a major storm on this particular weekend was ideal. Gretchen turned away from the bathroom window and checked herself again in the mirror. She and Drew had Monday off, with the markets closed for Presidents' Day. He had suggested they get away early and fly down to one of the islands. A couple of days of sun and the beach, return on Monday after the roads had been cleared. But she persuaded him to relax and sit it out at home. They had plenty of food and drink on hand, as well as some movies, their usual video games, and music for entertainment. Gretchen had prepared well for just this weekend.

Skip the travel arrangements and all that running around. It would be their own very special, private party: Friday night, all day Saturday, Saturday night, all day Sunday, Sunday night, and much of Monday. When she put it to him that way, Drew reconsidered and smiled.

He was waiting for her now, in the spare bedroom that he'd converted into a home office. Waiting for the fun to start. Gretchen had decided to start with the office fantasy, one of his favorites; a fact that worried her when she first learned it, but now it didn't matter. She was wearing a tight white blouse, open an extra button at the top, along with a very short black skirt. Her hair was done up high, with a thick braid at the back. She wore a choker around her throat, and of course she put her glasses on. Now she was the secretary of his dreams. She walked briskly down the hall and knocked once on the half-open door. Drew was sitting in his leather armchair, an open business magazine in his hands.

"Excuse me, sir."

"Yes?"

"It's after five. Would you like a drink?"

"Yes, please. And have one yourself, if you'd like."

"Oh, thank you. I'll be right back."

In the kitchen, she carefully poured and stirred his drink. She touched the liquid with the tip of one finger and tasted it. Fine. For herself, she fixed a glass of sparkling water with ice and a slice of lime. When she returned to the office, Gretchen leaned forward to hand him his drink, giving him a good view of her cleavage and the filmy blue see-through bra she was wearing. Blue was his favorite color. Drew's eyes locked right in on the open blouse.

"Here you are, sir. It's that new Latvian vodka."

"Ah, good. I've been wanting to try it." He took a sip. "Mmm, good, and strong. Bring the desk chair over and have a seat."

"Yes, sir."

Gretchen bent over to set her drink on the side table. Then she bent over again and gave him a lingering rear view as she pulled the chair around. She sat down, her legs parted enough so that he would have a clear view of her matching blue thong. He loved looking up a skirt. Gretchen stared at him and even let a smirk form around her mouth, but Drew didn't notice. *I loved him,* she thought.

"I'm afraid there's talk of staff cutbacks," he said gravely.

"Oh no." She placed one hand over her breast as if stricken with concern. Two fingers inside the blouse.

"Of course, I'd like to keep you on . . ."

"I love working for you, sir."

He took another long sip of vodka and smiled. "Fortunately, we may be able to work something out."

"Oh, I'd be so grateful."

"I may be able to promote you out of the secretarial staff and make you my personal assistant."

She gave a slight gasp, and her fingers moved as if to calm her racing heart. "That would be wonderful."

"Of course, it would require a new and greater commitment on your part, you would have to take on additional responsibilities. You'd be required to do everything necessary to help me perform up to the best of my abilities, so I can do my own work as successfully as possible."

"Whatever it takes," she said eagerly. "Whatever you need or want me to do, sir, just tell me, and I'll do it. I won't disappoint you."

"Come here and look at these figures."

She went and stood close beside him, bending forward to peer at some chart he had picked up. While he nattered on about revenues and costs and other nonsense, he stared down her blouse, now just inches from his face. His right hand slid up under her skirt, his fingers caressing her thigh, then her ass, and finally slipping inside her thong. Two fingers, moving, rubbing, pushing inside her.

"Just study this graph for a moment."

"Yes, sir." Gasping slightly, licking her lips.

His other hand came up and opened her blouse more, then

lifted her bra up, freeing her breasts. He squeezed them and tugged her nipples, then rolled the palm of his hand over them.

"There's a lot of stress in my job," he told her. "I have a great deal of responsibility on my shoulders."

"Oh, I know, sir. That's one of the reasons why I admire you so much and enjoy working for you."

He pulled her around to the front of his chair, so that she stood between his open legs. His hands still playing with her.

"And sometimes the pressure and tension become so great . . ."

"When that happens, you need to relax, sir." She dropped to her knees and reached for his zipper. "You just sit back and let me help. This will take a while; it can't be rushed. But you'll feel *much* better. . . ."

And when he came, her mouth was open, her face uplifted, her tongue sticking out. The cumdump he enjoyed so much.

The snow was falling at a steadier and heavier rate by the time they were on their fourth round of drinks. They were on the living-room carpet, in front of the television, playing *Grand Theft Auto*. Not her favorite game, but one of his. Drew had a dress code for video games too. He wore only a pair of flannel pajama bottoms, and Gretchen could only wear bikini briefs or a pair of flimsy boy shorts, some shade of blue.

She could tell that he had a nice buzz working now. It was easy for her; all she had to do was keep serving the drinks and do whatever he felt like doing to pass the time. He was a man of simple wants and needs.

Gretchen had moved in with Drew at his condo seven months after they started going together. She'd been sharing a large apartment on Dwight Street in New Haven with Carolyn and Sue. That wasn't bad, but it was hardly ideal. When their lease came due for renewal, Gretchen was ready to pull out. She was staying overnight at Drew's place more and more often as it was, so the time for such a move seemed perfect to both of them.

Gretchen loved Drew, and he loved her.

She was twenty-four and had never lived with a guy before, so there were some inevitable adjustments. Looking back now, she could see that it was mostly a matter of getting to know him: to know him truly.

Drew was an investment counselor, or a broker. Something like that; Gretchen wasn't exactly sure. He worked at a small but reputable financial firm in New Haven. In the first few months they started going together, Gretchen got to know three guys on Drew's work team: Gary, Rick, and Ron. They were more than co-workers; they were Drew's main friends. Like Drew, they were bright young go-getters, eager to advance themselves and to make a great living. And like Drew, they were vodka lovers. The four of them would get together every couple of weeks to kill a bottle of some new brand they had discovered. They were okay. They clearly looked up to Drew. He was their team leader. The first couple of times Drew hosted vodka night, Gretchen had felt excluded and ended up reading a book or watching TV in bed. But she did adjust; she knew she had to let Drew have some space of his own to enjoy with his buddies. She didn't like or dislike them.

Game over, Drew tossed the controller aside.

"Hey, open your mouth, baby."

Gretchen opened her mouth, and he slid three fingers between her lips. She licked and sucked them. He loved that, loved the way she'd roll the tip of her tongue across his fingertips. Give him that, he could be ready fast—and frequently. He steered her onto her belly and pulled her briefs down. Gretchen wasn't wet, but he seldom made her wet anymore. He didn't seem to notice, or mind. He pushed into her, working back and forth until her body did begin to cooperate and loosen up, seemingly on its own.

It hurt a little, then her mind could kind of lose itself for a while in the rhythmic pounding, and then it was over.

* * *

"Another drink?" Drew asked her as he stood up.

Gretchen scrambled to her feet. "I'll get them."

"That's okay. My turn." He was a little tottery.

"No," Gretchen insisted, placing a hand on his chest and gently pushing him back toward the sofa. "I'm serving you, remember? You wanted to go to the islands, and I promised I'd serve you *all* weekend."

He hesitated for a moment. Then she could see it coming back in his mind. "Oh yeah, cool," he said. "I'll put a movie on for us."

"Good idea."

Gretchen measured and poured his drink carefully. It amazed her that when the time had come, earlier that evening, she didn't hesitate. She'd never imagined that she would be capable of such intense emotional focus and sense of purpose. Nor that it would feel so *right*.

"This is good shit," Drew said as he took the drink.

"Cheers," she replied with a smile.

Gretchen tried to follow the movie, one of those smash-bang action jobs that Drew found so engrossing. The little things you learn about another person: their taste in movies, music, food, clothes, cars. Maybe they tell you something, or maybe you just think they do.

After the first couple of months, the fun started to go out of it for her. He was, somehow, different. Or maybe her expectations were. He was not as affectionate as she would've liked. One time, when they had squabbled about some trivial matter, she tried to end it happily by putting her arms around him and saying "I need a hug." But he firmly stepped away from her embrace and said, "I gave you one a couple of hours ago." And he went into his office and closed the door hard. He was making her learn his way.

Sometimes he would look at her—and she would get this crazy feeling that he was laughing inside. At her. Maybe she *was* crazy.

Still, Gretchen knew she probably would have carried on with things as they were, learning to adjust, accept, and abide. A relationship is not a simple thing to cast aside easily or quickly. No one likes to admit defeat or failure, or to be alone again.

But that day came. She was working from home because she had a bad head cold and a very sore throat. She had to e-mail some urgent documents, but her laptop froze; the hard drive had crashed. She had the documents backed up on a memory stick, so she went into the office to use Drew's computer to send them out. Gretchen saw a corner of a photograph sticking out from a pile of papers on his desk, and she recognized a bit of her hair and the office carpet. The photo had been printed from the computer. It was a picture of her. Eyes closed, mouth open, face uplifted, tongue out, all splattered in white. A few minutes later, she found the e-mail—Drew had sent that photograph to Gary, Rick, and Ron. His team. The vodka buddies.

Gretchen turned her head and looked at Drew. He was completely absorbed in the movie.

"Hey," she said. "You're ready for a refill."

She remembered the exact occasion, because it was the first time he asked her to let him give her a facial. She was a little surprised, because he'd never hinted at it before. But now that they were together, if that was one of his fantasies, Gretchen didn't mind.

The photograph was a different matter. She might even have agreed to let him take it, if he'd asked first. It was obvious how he'd done it. Drew owned one of those little digital cameras the size of a credit card. Didn't make any noise, didn't need a flash. The picture quality was mediocre, but it did take a photograph. He came, he shot the pic while her eyes were closed, and he put the camera behind him on the desk or stuck it in his shirt pocket. It wouldn't have taken but a couple of seconds.

E-mailing it to the guys was the betrayal beyond retrieval.

"Let's go to bed," Drew said.

"It's not late," Gretchen replied. "Have one more."

"Ehhh . . ."

"Come on, have a nightcap with me."

"If I agree?" Drew bargaining as usual.

"Handjob."

"Okay," he said. Then added, "While rimming me."

"Of course," she said, taking his glass.

Gretchen must have slept well, because she woke up the next morning feeling rested and refreshed. Drew was still asleep when she slipped out of bed, his breathing a low rumble. She went to the window and looked outside. The air was full of snow, snow falling thickly and heavily in huge fluffy flakes. It looked so beautiful; it reminded Gretchen of times she had played outside as a child while the snow was falling, gleefully running around and catching flakes on her tongue.

She went into the kitchen and put the kettle on for tea. It was a few minutes before noon. Well, they had been up kind of late.

That decisive day a few weeks ago, she knew immediately that she was going to leave Drew. But her anger was so great that it wouldn't let her just throw some things in her car and drive away. He had more than that coming to him, and for all she knew, he might not even be that upset if she did bolt. No, Gretchen realized that she had to think and plan. The pain she felt *demanded* its own form of articulation, one that would take time.

I know why I'm doing this to you, she thought. *But I still don't know why you did that to me.*

Because that is who you are? Is that all?

Drew stumbled out of the bedroom around two-thirty that afternoon. He felt dizzy, he said. He complained of a stomachache. He couldn't get down one sip of coffee. Gretchen sat him down on the couch, but he was so drowsy he soon stretched out on it. She propped him up with a couple of pillows and tucked a light blanket around him.

"Honey, I don't feel so good."

She smiled. "You have a first-rate hangover, is all."

"Yeah, I guess. Jesus, I'm hurting."

"I'll get you a glass of sparkling water. It might help settle your stomach a little, and you're probably dehydrated anyhow."

"Okay," he said weakly.

She turned the television on for him and placed the remote in his hand. When she returned with the water a minute later, Drew was shaking his head listlessly.

"What's the matter?"

"Picture's kinda blurry and jumpy."

Gretchen laughed gently. "*You're* the one who's blurry and jumpy, is what I'm thinking."

Drew looked toward the window. The units on the other side of the courtyard were completely hidden by the tremendous snowfall in progress. He seemed to want to say something but couldn't find the strength. He put his head back on the pillow and closed his eyes.

"You want to sleep some more?" Gretchen asked.

"No. I'm just resting."

"Okay. If you need me, I'll be in the kitchen tidying up."

She picked up the bottle of Latvian vodka. Wow, Drew had consumed about two-thirds of it. With her encouragement, of course. She put the bottle back in the liquor cabinet, where it belonged. She took Drew's tumbler and washed it thoroughly in warm soapy water. She then rinsed it and set it on a paper towel on the counter, to dry in the air. She took a jar from the collection of spices at the back of the counter. It had contained thyme, but she'd thrown the thyme away last week, and now the only thing inside the jar was about a quarter-inch of clear liquid. Gretchen poured that down the drain, and washed and rinsed the jar. She dried it with another paper towel and put it with the other empty bottles and cans in the recycling bin by the kitchen door. She dropped the plastic cap in the trash basket beneath the sink.

The only time Drew got up over the next eight hours was to go to the bathroom. He reeled and lurched as he moved, and Gretchen had to help him get there and back.

"I'm soooo sick. . . ."

"Maybe you should get some food inside you."

"Noooo . . ."

"Drew, you have to have something."

"A little more water."

"Okay."

She brought him another glass of San Pellegrino.

"I still can't follow the TV," he said. "I, like, move my eyes, and it hurts inside my head."

"You had a lot to drink last night. I was surprised when I looked at the bottle on the counter and saw how much was gone."

"Yeah, but . . . never this bad."

"Just close your eyes and rest. That's the best thing."

He wasn't feeling any better at eleven that night, when Gretchen helped him back into bed. He appeared to fall asleep almost immediately. She stayed with him for a while, sitting on her side of the bed. His body moved restlessly, and he let out a groan every couple of minutes.

Gretchen was tired. She went into the living room and stretched out on the sofa. She pulled the spare blanket around her.

She went over it in her mind yet again. Had she done it correctly? Had she measured accurately? Were her calculations right? Would it work? She'd done her research well, or so she hoped. Something that would soon disappear in the body without leaving a trace. Leaving only permanent damage. It had to be easy to acquire from any number of ordinary retail outlets, with no way to connect her to its purchase.

Yes, there was such a thing. Now it was just a question of exactly how extensive and permanent the damage was.

She wouldn't leave him right away; that would look bad. Gretchen knew she had to stay for a while and take care of him. Besides, she had a lot of things to do and preparations to make before she could leave. Find a new place to live, for starters. But she also knew that it wouldn't be long; a couple of weeks? A month or so? She still had a life ahead of her. It wasn't here, and it wasn't with Drew.

She woke early on Sunday morning. The snow was still falling steadily outside, and it was at least two feet deep against the kitchen storm door. She turned on the TV to get the latest report. The storm was stalled over the area and would continue to dump snow until early afternoon.

Gretchen thought it was beautiful.

Sudden sounds of Drew thrashing around in the bedroom, his voice frantic. She rushed to the door and saw him half-standing, holding on to the bed for support. He'd knocked the clock radio off the nightstand. He had a wild, vacant expression on his face, his eyes darting back and forth.

Methyl alcohol.

"Gretchen! I can't see!"

Good. The damage done.

"I'm right here."

His face turned toward her, but she stepped a couple of yards to the side. "No, I'm here."

"I can't see you. Just—blurry shapes."

It will get worse.

She moved again. "Drew, I'm right here."

His head swiveled, his eyes scanning uselessly.

"You have to get me to the hospital. Right now!"

"Honey, that's impossible. There's more than two feet of snow on the ground, and it's still falling. The roads are closed, and the plows won't be out until late this afternoon. If you're not feeling better tonight or tom—"

"Gretchen!" he screamed.

She stepped toward Drew, to help him back into bed.

"I'M BLIND!"

Gretchen smiled at him as she took his arm.

I hear you. I get the picture.

Nocturnal Invasions

A Cal McDonald Mystery

Steve Niles

I've been called a lot of things in my life, but sexy is not among them. I've heard junkie, bum, crazy person, and fucking lunatic, but never sexy, not even from the few lovers I've had.

I mean, I got a body covered with bumps, bruises, and contusions almost twenty-four–seven. Not the kind of thing you want to cuddle with, ya know.

My name is Cal McDonald. I'm a private detective, and I deal with the weird shit, the macabre, and the bizarre.

I don't have the best luck with women. I had a steady a couple months back, but she bolted. Her name was Sabrina. I'd be lying if I said I didn't miss her.

I was in bed on a Saturday, trying to remember what I did the night before. My head pounded like a hammer, and my stomach gurgled. I'd blacked out. Again.

My knuckles were bruised and bloody. In the caked, dried blood I found a blond hair. My hair is dark. I also found a tooth fragment lodged in a flap of broken skin on my left fist.

So I'd been in a fight. No big deal.

What bugged me was the wet spot on my crotch and the

acute soreness that radiated from down under. If I didn't know better, I'd say I'd been fighting and fucking the night before, and, lucky me, my mind was a blank. All I had was a hair, a tooth fragment, and a sticky wet mess in my pants.

I knew myself well enough to know the injuries and the sex were not related. I don't mix the two, and I don't like people who do. I'd most likely beaten the shit out of a dude and then somehow hooked up with a woman before or after. The two might not even be related.

I hate hangover mysteries, and this one was a fucking ball-breaker. Literally.

As I stood there in the living room, holding open my waistband and staring down the front of my pants, Mo'Lock, my best ghoul and partner, appeared at the door, staring at me.

"What are you doing?" he asked.

I knew I was busted, so I went along. "Checking out my junk," I said back. "What the fuck does it look like?"

Mo'Lock was of the ghoul variety, the living dead, but, luckily for all of us, the kind of walking dead that doesn't need anything from humans.

Except for Mo. I guess he needed me as a friend. We'd been partners a long time. Almost ten years. He'd even dragged his dead-ass from DC to LA when I sort of moved without telling anyone.

I was about to close the top of my pants when I noticed something else. There was blood beneath my boxers as well. I panicked and pulled them open wider. There was a soup of bodily fluids inside. I recognized semen and vaginal fluid, but there was also blood.

And the rest of the tooth was there too, embedded right in the side of my sore-ass nut sack. I reached down and took the fragment out. It was slightly larger than the other piece.

The ghoul stepped over and watched as I placed the second tooth fragment next to the other. They fit and almost made a whole tooth.

I looked at the ghoul. He looked down my pants.

"You have any idea where I was last night?" I asked the dead man, closing my pants.

The ghoul shook his head. "I saw you early in the evening. You were quite inebriated, and you were *not* alone."

Okay, great. This is the info I was looking for. Super.

Mo'Lock held up his hand before I got all excited, "You were walking with a vampire."

Man, I must have been wasted.

"What'd she look like? Any bloodsucker we know?"

"She was unknown to me."

Then it hit me. Vampire. Broken tooth. Sex. Blood. What the fuck had I gotten myself into?

I bolted for the shower like a jackrabbit down its hole. I used the hottest water I could and checked every inch of my body.

I seemed okay. Even the nut-sack wound was minor, and also the only source of the blood.

I checked my neck. There were a couple scratches, but nothing new or too deep. I checked my arms and wrist and ankles. I didn't find any fang marks anywhere. I even had the fucking ghoul come in and look my back over.

"You are covered with scratches," he said somberly.

"Do they look infected?"

"I sense no evil coming from them," the ghoul said. "If these are the wounds made by a Nosferatu, I believe you have escaped the infection."

I stared at the ghoul. "How about a simple 'no'?"

Then I kicked him out of the bathroom.

I washed off and checked my parts for any further damage. Besides the usual and pre-existing wounds, I seemed to have escaped with a scraped sack and a scratched-up back.

Evidently I'd had the best sex of my life, and I didn't have a clue who with, other than the fact that it may have been with an undead woman.

After the shower, I went through my clothing, looking for

clues. I found zero dollars in my wallet, which was par for the course. No numbers or anything I hadn't had the day before.

The whole time I sat on the couch rifling through my stuff, the ghoul stood at the front window and stared out, down to the streets of Koreatown below.

I'd slept most of the day. It was already turning to night again. Good. The last thing my throbbing head needed was sunlight.

I found what I was looking for in the pocket of the jacket I'd worn the night before. Inside the left pocket was a book of matches from a bar. It was called the Fang Club.

Then it all started coming back to me, and I really started feeling sick.

The night before had started innocently enough, with a gram of brick hash and a bottle of pills. I smoked and swallowed and chased it all with a bottle of whiskey.

By nine o'clock I was already trashed.

At nine-thirty the phone rang.

Like a fucking idiot, I answered.

"Is this Cal McDonald?" the female voice on the other end asked.

I made some sort of grunting sound, made myself laugh, and choked an affirmative response along the lines of "Yeah."

Her name was Nichole Harris, and she was calling me because her husband, Chad, had disappeared a few nights before, after he called from a bar called the Fang Club. She thought, you know, maybe something happened to him and wanted to see if I'd look into it.

I gave her my rates. She agreed. I said I'd check out the club.

I figured good ol' Chad had probably met a girl and left his wife. I doubted even vampires were dumb enough to hang out at a place called the Fang Club, let alone hunt at one. I laid my bets on Chad having a chubby for goth girls and ditching the wife.

That was my theory, anyway.

I know I went to the club. It was in North Hollywood. Just a dump of a place with walls painted black and purple and filled with eighty-pound boys and girls made up to look spooky.

The music was perfect for a night of brooding and sneering. I doubt if anybody in the bar had ever dealt with the true undead, or they wouldn't be pretending to be one.

I sat at the bar, asked the bartender about Chad, and pounded back a few. After that, I woke up home with a scratched-up back, a sticky wet mess in my drawers, and a busted sack.

I stared at the matchbook, all black with white fangs and a touch of red on the tips, and tried to piece together the rest, but it just wasn't there.

Mo'Lock finally turned from the window and spoke to me. "Did you check your car?"

"I parked it out front," I said, concerned. "Is it gone?"

The dead man shook his head. "No. It is still there, but I've seen you park better."

I walked to the window and looked down. I'd parked in front of the apartment all right, on the sidewalk right outside the door to the stairs. I must've just drove up and poured out.

I went down and moved the car. It had a couple tickets and a boot on it. The ghoul ripped the boot off with a single yank, breaking the metal like it was plastic, and then I moved the car to a proper parking spot and checked it out.

The ghoul stood by as I inspected the car. In the front was the usual mess, but the backseat was clear. It was usually covered with papers and garbage. Shit.

There was a wet spot right in the center of the seat. It was mostly dried from the daylight but moist enough to still be sticky in the cracks of the seat. I cautiously smelled the sticky on my fingertips. There was no odor whatsoever. Very odd.

Evidently I'd had sex with an odorless vampire.

Mo'Lock was standing off to the side. The sun hadn't fully gone down, and, even though the light didn't hurt him, he preferred the shadows like any self-respecting ghoul would.

"Did you see me come home last night?" I asked him.

"I was inside the office. You came through the door," he rumbled, "and said nothing to me before you passed out on the couch."

"Wait, I thought you said you saw me with someone."

The ghoul hesitated. "That was earlier."

"Oh."

I nodded. Figured.

I had no other option than to retrace my steps of the previous night. After a quick replenishing of drugs and alcohol, I got back in the Nova and peeled for North Hollywood.

By the time I was cruising over the hill, past the Hollywood Bowl, the sun was down. It was late February, and the nights were dry, with a cool breeze coming in from the coast.

It was one of those evenings where the city looked peaceful. You'd never suspect that within the hills and valleys dwelled some of the most heinous evil that walked the earth. And besides the entertainment people, there were also killers and monsters of all kinds.

On the other side of the hill was the Valley, a huge spread as flat as it is crowded. It was a grim place. I lived there before my home was leveled by a creature made of the pieces of murdered weightlifters. I'd only been in the Koreatown office/apartment for a couple months.

The Fang Club was on Magnolia Avenue about a block up from where it crossed with Cahuenga Boulevard.

It was a plain stucco building painted black, with no windows and only a single door inside. That's where the sign was: a poorly painted copy of the graphic on the matchbook.

Outside the door stood a muscle-bound kid with black eyeliner and a spankin' new Misfits T-shirt. He stood with his arms crossed so he could tuck his hands underneath and make his arms look bigger.

I parked the car across the street and smoked a few before heading inside. It was still early. I figured I had time to get my buzz on good and tight before scoping the creepy club.

As I sat there, several groups of people came up. Most of them were dressed in standard goth garb, all black, purple, and red vinyl and leather. The hair styles varied. Most had normal day-hair greased up to look like a widow's peak, and the women had lots of attachments, or whatever they call them.

Most of them looked like kids in their twenties out for a good time, posing and wishing they were dead. Every tenth or so person would arrive solo, and some of these folks looked older.

I saw several women walk by whom I couldn't keep my eyes off of, and I found my attraction to them disturbing. I hunted vampires.

I found it damn annoying that I got heated up seeing women who essentially dressed like vampires, or at least what people think they look like.

Actually it was pretty close. Real vampires and vampires of legend are pretty similar. They like to dress up and play it all dramatic and fancy-pants. I really fuckin' hate vampires.

But, and this is a big-ass but, I had to admit there was a certain allure to the women bloodsuckers. There was something about them that was so sensual. Maybe it was how dangerous they were, that they could make you cum and drain you of your life at the same time.

I'd killed every vampire I'd ever come across, with few exceptions. Men, women, children, it didn't matter. They have to be killed.

I try to never engage, and I certainly never touched any. They are, despite the romantic notions people have formed, disgusting, rotten, dirty, infected creatures that spread disease and misery wherever they go.

But yet, yeah, the women bloodsuckers are kind of hot.

I dunno. Maybe I just like black.

After a couple smokes laced with hippie-nip, I pounded back a fifth and got out of the car. It was past ten. I figured I must have hit the place around the same time the night before.

As I crossed the street, the hulk in the Misfits shirt spotted me and did a double take. Real quick, but I saw it. He either recognized me or hated me on sight. Either one didn't feel too promising as I stepped up to the door.

"You got ID?" he demanded.

Maybe I was wrong on both counts.

Then I froze, reaching for my wallet. I looked like a lot of things. One of them isn't too young to drink. The doorman was fucking with me.

I took out my wallet and showed him my license. He snorted at it, then looked me in the eye.

"You gonna make trouble tonight?"

Okay. Good. He knew me.

I went along. "Yeah, sorry about that," I said. "I guess the cold medicine I took yesterday didn't mix too well with the drinks."

"I guess not."

And that was it. He stepped aside.

A big donut.

I didn't want to push him for info. If I let on that I was so wasted I didn't remember being in the place, he might've thought better than to let me in. I let it dangle. At least I knew for certain I was at the club the night before.

My big mistake was glancing sideways as I entered. I caught a glimpse of the doorman smirking as I passed and as he turned away. I was shit-ass stoned, and maybe it was me being paranoid, but something told me I wasn't.

Inside, I stood in the dark, waiting for my eyes to adjust. It wasn't much inside either. The walls were, you guessed it, black. There were paintings on the wall—cutesy, wide-eyed monsters and shit. I didn't like it. There were tables with candles stacked in a mass, and booths with velvet curtains.

The bar was decent and well-stocked. It was big enough and busy enough to need three bartenders: two women and a guy. All three had too much makeup, like it was the club uniform.

You could tell, outside of this club, they would have no part of the scene. They all looked the same, healthy and athletic in that LA way.

I moved through the crowd and made eye contact with as many people as I could to see if I got a reaction. In every case, male or female, I got the cold, closing-eye turn-away. Every blow-off was a suspect eliminated.

Then I saw a reminder of the reason I was even in the fucking club in the first place—Chad Harris was sitting at a table with a young woman dressed like an undead astronaut. She had so much makeup on, I doubted I'd be able to pick her out of a lineup without it.

I walked straight over to the table and stopped a couple feet short. Harris had eyeliner and a new black Hanes T-shirt on. Even under the getup I could see he was closer to my age than that of the girls.

I took out a small credit card–size camera I carry on me and pointed it at the couple.

"Smile!" I yelled and snapped an adorable shot of them cuddling.

I put the camera away.

"Chad Harris?"

"Y-yeah."

Just wanted to make sure I had earned my rate.

"Go home to your wife. You look like an idiot."

I turned and walked back the way I'd come.

My natural homing mechanism led me straight to the bar. I tried to get in on the far left, closest the entrance, but the crowd was thick and annoying, so I tried the center. It wasn't much better there, so I pushed right where the dude was tending.

As soon as he saw me, his eyes went wide as Don Knotts's. Needing his hand to slap over his mouth in horror, he dropped the drink he was preparing, backed away, and then *bolted* out the back door.

I exploded through the crowd and shoved my way clear to the bar. One guy thought about getting in my way until I looked him in the eyes. He knew he would die or get very injured, and he stepped back, making way for me to drunkenly leap over the bar.

I landed on the slick rubber matting on the floor and was immediately bum-rushed by the other two bartenders, the women. One elbowed me in the face while the other caught me and twisted my arm. In less than two beats, she had me pinned to the wall next to the still-swinging back door.

"You let Jimmy be," she said.

"Lady, I just want to ask him some questions."

She told the other bartender to get back to the bar. She'd handle me.

And she did, by trusting me and letting me go.

"Don't you think you caused Jimmy enough grief for one weekend?" she asked.

She had long black hair, intense eyes, and a build like a boxer.

I took a deep breath and dumped a big pile of total honesty. "Look, Miss—"

"Bekka."

"—Bekka. I'm not entirely sure what the hell I did last night," I said sheepishly. "That's why I'm here."

"To find out?" She smiled.

I could see she was trying to contain laughing in my face. I suddenly felt my face flushing red, and my stomach lurched, thinking of the possibilities of what I'd done.

Now, all of a sudden, finding the vampire I *might* have screwed wasn't so important.

I was about to speak again when the smile dropped off her face, but not because of me. She was reacting to someone or something behind me. My first thought was Jimmy with an axe.

"You mean to tell me you remember nothing?"

The soft, low voice speaking to me at least let me know I wasn't going to get split in half.

I turned, and there stood a woman about my height, with blond hair, green eyes, and the whitest skin I'd ever seen. She looked like she had been carved from marble and covered with silk. Her lips were full and glistening red. That was the only makeup she had on.

I was pretty sure she was a vampire.

She had the expression of a woman who was deciding if she was mad or not. The longer I stood there with my face as red as my eyes, she seemed to lean toward not being mad.

I must have stood there stammering for a full minute before she allowed the smooth lines of her face to glide into a slight smile as she told Bekka to get back to work. She said she'd explain what had happened to me.

"Come with me, Cal," she said and walked to a private area behind the far wall.

It was completely dark.

I followed, glancing back to see Bekka and the other bartender talking and looking at me. For the first time since I'd arrived, I felt a hint of danger and touched the gun jammed in my waistband.

Ahead, the gorgeous blond vampire had stopped at a doorway covered only by a curtain. She held the curtain back and asked me to step inside the dark room.

I went inside, and for a beat she was behind my back. I felt a cold chill all over my body. I knew the feeling. I'd felt it before. It had only happened once or twice, when I'd almost been killed and someone had allowed me to live for whatever reason. I'd turned my back on a vampire. She could have ripped my spine out, but all she did was close the curtain and offer me a seat.

It was a small, private party room, with overstuffed chairs and couches built into the walls. There were tables with black roses in a vase. I flopped down into one of the couches.

"Would you like a drink?"

"Yes. Whiskey. Whatever you have is great."

She smiled and poured me a drink, then slid in next to me.

"Do you even remember my name?"

"No." What was the point in lying?

She smiled. "It's Gwen."

"Hello, Gwen."

"I own this club."

I looked her in the eyes, and she just leaned in and kissed me, real soft like, and my head lit up like a torch.

It was familiar. It was good.

"Now do you remember me?"

I nodded and went in for another kiss. It was soft. It was wet. It was perfect.

Except for one thing.

She was cold.

I pushed her away and moved my hand toward my gun. I had every intention of taking it out and shooting.

She hardly moved. What struck me most about her reaction was that she didn't seem surprised.

"You think I didn't know who you were?" she said.

I stopped. "What?"

"You think I didn't know you were Cal McDonald?" she asked calmly but convincingly. "You think I didn't know what you did for a living?"

I moved my hand away from my gun and swigged the whiskey. I had to process what was happening.

If I got her right, she was basically saying we had indeed had sex the night before and that *she* was the one who took the chance, because I'm the bad guy who kills her kind. She kills my kind too, but that's a whole other can of worms.

She ran her hand on my cheek and smiled gently, like all of a sudden I was the one to worry about. "I do not feed on humans. I have a way to get blood through hospital donors. I told you this last night. I do not kill to survive."

I nodded and felt her hand. Between her touch and the kisses, my blackout began to break apart, and I remembered bits and pieces of the night before. I remember talking, hearing her voice, and touching. Not much after that, but enough to know it was a good thing.

Then I looked up. "Then who bit my nuts?"

She fell off the couch laughing. I saw her fangs as she laughed. It was more than unsettling.

Every fiber of my being said *Blow her brains out, cut her head off! She's a goddamn vampire, you idiot!*

But I had to know.

And she relished telling me.

Evidently I'd already had a night of it before Gwen and I had even met. I'd been at the bar doing shots and yakking it up with Jimmy. The bar had these special shows on Friday nights. They have spooky singers and spooky jugglers. Shit like that.

The night before, they had a suspension act—you know, those freaks who hang by their nipples from hooks. They had this whole big show, and I was trashed as all hell. Jimmy told the others later that I was washing down a fucking pill with every shot.

Long story short, I pulled down my pants, tried to swing on a chain, and bashed my crotch into Jimmy's mouth. This is how I came to meet Gwen. The doorman scraped me off the floor and threw me in the back room where we sat.

After she was done telling me, all I could muster was an "Oh my God" as I held my head.

"And you did try to kill me," she added bluntly.

Keeping my head firmly gripped in my hands, I tilted and looked at her. "Shit, what'd I do?"

She ran her finger along my chin and chest.

"Well, I went back to your place, and we went again in the back of your car."

She paused for a second.

"And you fell asleep on top of me. I was almost pinned when the sun came up."

"Oh God, I am so sorry."

"It's okay. A tall ghoul helped get you off me."

Fuckin' ghoul lied to me! That fucking ghoul was always butting into my life. I guess this time he thought he'd help me by saying nothing. Stupid ghoul—lying is for humans.

Gwen rubbed my back and whispered in my ear. "The point is, sweetie, I had you in here unconscious. I knew who you were and what you do. I could have killed you. I could have handed you over to countless enemies."

She kissed my cheek.

"But I decided the best thing to do with you was fuck."

I looked at her and nodded. I wrapped my big mitt around her slim waist and pulled her close. We kissed, and she started to undress me.

As we sank into the overstuffed couch, I thought about stupid-ass Chad and his wife who owed me some cash. I actually thought about how completely insane my life was, how nobody knew the life I lived. I thought about the pills in my pocket and the drink on the table.

Well, fuck the pills and the booze. I wanted to remember this time.

And I did.

Less Than Perfect

P. D. Cacek

"*It's not you—*"

God, how many times had she heard those words? A hundred? A thousand? She didn't even want to try and guess. The question of how *many* men had said those words was easier to answer: all of them.

Every man she'd ever dated, every last one of them—from the first pathetic fumblings on a stack of gymnastic mats with the captain of the junior varsity football team her senior year in high school, to . . . *Jesus* . . . to Kev326 from Heartlinks.com, her thirty-sixth attempt at an Internet relationship—

"It's not you, Jeannie—"

And maybe it was the way he'd said it—his voice still husky, breathless from lovemaking . . . sweat still glistening across his shoulders and in the hollow of his spine as he dressed, not being able to face her—that made her laugh. Soft and low and bitter as raw tea . . . but it did make him turn around.

But even then he didn't look at her, not really. Kev326's gaze never left her naked breasts.

"Go home."

"No, let me explain first, okay? I couldn't believe it when I first saw you. . . . God, I thought I'd died and gone to heaven. You're perfect, Jeannie . . . absolutely perfect."

And there it was.

They'd had their two weeks where they talked about a nebulous future they might share, laughed and dined and went from making love to fucking, and she'd just convinced herself that what she was feeling was love and not desperation. Two weeks (check). The insubstantial banter (check). Self-delusion (double check). The brand new set of 300-count, periwinkle blue Egyptian-cotton sheets (check, check, check). And parting line (check, please).

"Why?"

He looked surprised at the question, even more surprised when Jeannie pulled the sheet up to cover her breasts. They always looked surprised, and their answers were always variations on the theme she was coming to know by heart.

"Oh God, honey . . . it's going to sound like shit, but . . . you're so beautiful, the kind of woman any man would be thrilled to have—"

"But."

"Okay, but you're too perfect. I've seen the way men look at you when we're together and, yeah, it was a real ego boost. At first. Now I feel like I'm in competition with you every minute. People look at us, and I know they're thinking: 'What's a goddess like her doing with a slob like him?' And I'm not a slob! I take care of myself . . . work out three times a week, eat right, and haven't gotten kicked out of any beds. . . . Sorry. But a man likes to feel that, sometimes, he's the center of attention, you know? Told you it'd come out sounding like shit, but like I said, it's not you—"

"It's me."

"What?"

Jeannie leaned forward and pulled a tissue from the box that rested on one corner of the huge mahogany desk between them, dabbing at her eyes to distract Dr. Drake from the sudden crimson glow in her cheeks. The tissues were soft and smelled of lilacs . . . definitely not her usual Dollar Store brand.

"I said it's . . . Oh, sorry. I thought you said something."

Donald Drake's mother undoubtedly thought he was a handsome man—with intense emerald eyes, a finely chiseled face, and the body of an Adonis. But she was, after all, his mother, and mothers—as Jeannie knew from experience—could be as exceptionally kind as they were unintentionally cruel.

"My little girl's a doll . . . just a beautiful little doll!"

In reality, Dr. Donald Drake—M.D., F.A.C.S., Board Certified, member of the American Board of Plastic Surgery, the American Board of Surgeons, the American Society of Plastic Surgeons, and featured on both NBC and the FOX network—looked more like a prime candidate for his own talents than a god.

Poor Mother Drake.

His green eyes were intensified only by the thickness of his bifocals, and his face, though pleasant enough, appeared to have been chiseled from soapstone instead of marble. He had wrinkles and bags and pouches of skin beneath his jaw that actually jiggled when he spoke. Jeannie dabbed at her eyes again, this time to cover her quick double-check of the name stitched onto the front of his white lab coat.

Yep. Dr. Drake . . . the beloved and chosen of 87.6 percent of the blogs she'd researched.

"Amazing."

"Sorry?"

"Oh." Jeannie waved the tissue in surrender. "Nothing . . . you were saying?"

He smiled, and the loose flesh under his chin and cheeks was pulled tight. It didn't help much.

"I said that it's not often I see such a perfect example of the human form," he said.

Real tears filled her eyes and caught them both off guard.

"Oh God, I'm sorry. Please, Ms. . . . er, Ms. . . ."

While he scrabbled for her file—one sheet, brand new, just filled out—Jeannie took a deep, shuddering breath and held it until the urge to scream had passed.

"Ms. Wallace . . . I'm sorry. I didn't mean to upset you . . . or sound like a candidate for a sexual-harassment case." Dr. Drake's owlish eyes met hers. "It was supposed to be, though poorly phrased, a *professional* compliment."

Jeannie nodded and wound the soft, lilac-scented tissue around her right index finger until she could feel her pulse.

"It's all right, really," she said. "It's . . . it's not you, it's me."

His eyes widened when she started laughing.

"Sorry . . ." It took some time for the giggles to subside into the occasional hiccup, and through it all, he never stopped looking at her. "But . . . it's just . . . I hear that a lot from the men I date. It's never me, you see, it's always them. . . . *They* say I'm too perfect." Jeannie took a long, cleansing breath and felt the pulse in her finger speed up. "So that's why I'm here, Doctor. . . . I want you to fix that."

He leaned back, adding another few inches of doctor-patient separation. "Fix what?"

"This."

Jeannie stood and released the hold on the tissue in order to run her hands across her face, her breasts, the flat plane of her belly and firm thighs. She stayed away from her hair, however—her "Do-It-Yourself" bleach job (*"Your hair's like silk. Perfect."*) that had successfully stripped the natural honey gold to brittle corpse white. It looked . . . *awful* with her natural peaches-and-cream complexion . . . but it was a start.

Her mother, however, thought it was lovely. *"You'll have to tell me if blondes really* do *have more fun."*

She took a deep breath before repeating, "This . . . *body.*"

He shook his head, obviously not getting it.

Jeannie had expected this, so she'd dressed accordingly. A gentle tug on the spaghetti-strap bows at her shoulders, and the simple cotton shift slipped to the floor, puddling around the ankle-straps of her sandals. What remained was the sheerest pair of thong panties she owned. She never wore a bra, in the as-yet-futile hope that the weight of her twin 38D's would eventually break down the muscles that held them intolerably, unyieldingly . . . *perfect.*

Life was just not fair.

Jeannie took another sigh, deeper than the first, and felt her nipples, rose pink, flawless, harden in the office's air-conditioned breeze.

"*Now* do you understand, Dr. Drake?"

The loose skin on the doctor's face twitched, but no soothing words of sympathy or agreement reached Jeannie's ears. It was only when she hooked her thumbs into the thong's straps, in preparation of dropping them as well, that he finally managed a breathless "Stop!"

"I just wanted you to see what I have to deal with, Doctor."

"Believe me," he gasped, "I see . . . but I still have no idea what— Please . . . would you mind getting dressed?"

"You're not going to examine me?"

"Uh—no. This is just a consultation. Please?"

Jeannie nodded but took advantage of the request by turning around and bending from the waist to retrieve her dress so the doctor could see, firsthand, the heart-shaped perfection of her ass. It was one of the things she hated most about her body and had never given her anything but trouble. Even concealed beneath sweatpants or oversized T-shirts, it was the red cape to which every man-bull was drawn. She couldn't walk down the street . . . even a *good* street in the heart of the Financial District, without her ass immediately inciting lip-smacks, kissy sounds, and moans of admiration from even the tightest white collars.

"Oh, yeah, baby . . . gimme some 'a that!"

"Hmm HUMM!"

"Jesus, you're so tight!"

"Oh baby, I could fuck you like this forever."

"I love your ass . . . it's perfect."

"You're perfect."

"It's not you, it's me."

When Jeannie finished tying the straps on her right shoulder, she sat down—prim and proper again, legs crossed, hands folded in her lap, fingers retrieving the tissue she'd left on the chair—and waited for the doctor to stop hyperventilating. She thought his reaction a bit strange . . . considering what he did for a living.

"Now do you understand, Doctor? There's nothing *wrong* with me. My body is . . ."

"Perfect?"

Jeannie closed her eyes, squeezing past the pain. "Yes."

"Then . . . I'm afraid I still don't understand, Ms. Wallace. I'm a plastic surgeon. I help people feel better about their looks by—"

Jeannie opened her eyes. "Exactly!"

"Excuse me?"

Scooting to the edge of her chair, she offered him her brightest smile. "That's why I'm here, Doctor. I want you to make me feel better about my body."

"Uh-huh."

"Can I . . . can I ask you something a bit personal, Dr. Drake?"

The veins on his nose brightened. "I suppose so."

"Do you like the way you look?"

He smiled and, for a moment, looked slightly less troll-like. "Yes, I do. I know too many other surgeons in my profession who think they have to look like models or no potential client will take them seriously. I don't think that's necessary, and my practice has not suffered unduly from the fact that I am *not* Prince Charming. I'm a hell of a good plastic surgeon, Ms. Wallace, and that's all that matters to me."

"And that's why I'm here. You're the best, I've done my homework."

He smiled.

"So help me to look . . . normal."

"Normal?"

"Less . . . perfect. You saw my body. There's not one bump or pucker or scar to make it . . . interesting. I've always been a quick healer. Good genetics, I guess."

"And this is a problem?"

"Yes. Men don't want perfection, Doctor, at least not for long. So I want you to . . . to—"

"To give you a Persian Flaw."

Jeannie felt her brow wrinkle but knew the lines wouldn't last no matter how long she held it. "A what?"

"I don't know if it's a myth or based in fact, but years ago, when the ancient Persians made a carpet, they purposely created a flaw in that carpet . . . with the reasoning that only God—Allah, in this case—could be perfect. I suppose they thought that God doesn't like to share perfection."

"No, He doesn't." Jeannie sat back in her chair, and, for a moment, the only sounds in the office were the whisper of the air conditioner and tick of the wall clock. "So, you'll help me?"

"Help you?"

Jeannie leaned closer, heart pounding so hard she knew it must be making the front of the shift jump.

"Yes, nothing much," she said, "just a little reverse cosmetic surgery. Maybe thin out my lips or make my ears stick out or—oh, maybe break my nose so it curves a little to one side. That would work. And I definitely want my breasts to sag. I've never worn a bra, you see, and . . . Is there something wrong, Dr. Drake?"

There was a definite green tint to the skin beneath his eyes.

"You're joking."

"No."

"Ah."

He kept saying that, "ah," for almost a full minute while he nodded and looked at her chart and looked at her and nodded and nodded again. Jeannie sat back in her consultation chair and waited for him to finish.

"You're serious."

"Oh God, yes!"

"That's crazy."

"You're crazy, do you know that?" That was her mother's response to everything Jeannie ever tried to do to look like everyone

else. "*You're beautiful! Any woman on the planet would KILL to look like you, and all you do is complain. You're crazy.*"

"I'M NOT CRAZY!"

"I—I never said you—"

"I just want what every woman wants . . . to be loved for MYSELF, not for my body."

"But your body is—"

"NOT ME!" Jeannie's fingers bent into claws that raked the shift. The tiny pains reminded her of the time she'd tried to cut off her breasts. She was ten, an early bloomer, and the girls at school made her life hell.

"*Look it's Boobie!*"

"*Bet you think you're better than us, huh?*"

"*Freak!*"

"*Slut!*"

"*Skank!*"

"*Barbie doll! Barbie doll!*"

Her mother, the one person who should have understood, didn't. When she found Jeannie in the garage, naked from the waist up, the training bra sliced in half, the knife point dimpling the flesh of the burgeoning perfection, she did the only thing that could stop her—then and now—she called Jeannie's father.

"*Frank, come here! Your daughter's crazy!*"

Jeannie slowly lowered her hands. "I'm not crazy, Doctor, but this body isn't *me.* I'm more than that."

"Of course you are."

"Then you'll help me?"

"Ah. Ms. Wallace, this is possibly the most unusual request I've ever heard *anyone* make, and that's including the man who wanted me to clip his ears and put implants into both cheeks so he could look more like his bullmastiff."

"Did you?"

"No, Ms. Wallace, I did not. What I did, however, was suggest he see a colleague of mine, Dr. Benjamin Margrove."

Jeannie felt a chill that had nothing to do with the air-conditioning. "He's not a plastic surgeon, is he?"

"No. Dr. Margrove is one of the top psychiatrists in the field."

Jeannie took a deep breath, controlling the urge to scream. "I know how this must sound, but I just want a body that a man can *live* with, not compete against. I want to be *normal.*"

The doctor's eyes softened behind their prison wall of glass. "I think I understand, Ms. Wallace. For the most part, very few people are completely happy with the way they look. Have you considered methods other than cosmetic surgery?"

Jeannie sat up straighter, heart pounding. "Such as?"

"Oh . . . such as, well . . . ah . . ."

He stumbled along. She would no more tell him about some of the other nonsurgical *methods* she'd already tried than she would about her one attempt at self-surgery. That would have sounded crazy, but she had tried. S&M clubs. Bondage freaks. Men more than willing to add a little bare-knuckled graffiti to the canvas of her body. But bite marks heal and bruises fade and even her left nipple, *accidentally* torn during an overenthusiastic acting out of "Barbarian and Slave Girl," had mended without so much as a visible line.

Tattooing and piercing weren't options. Those were recognizable and, in most cases, delicate body art. The last thing *her* body needed was something else to draw attention to itself.

". . . uh, well, there's . . . um. . . ."

Jeannie exhaled and let him off the hook. "Whatever it would be, Doctor, would just make me *different* in another way. I just want you to make my body like everyone else's. A little less than perfect, you know?"

She smiled. He cleared his throat, then leaned forward to scribble something on a prescription form.

"In your case, however, I think this may have more to do with brain chemistry than physicality."

"I'm *not* crazy, Doctor."

"No, no, of course you're not, but I think you may have a perception problem. This is Dr. Margrove's office number—he's right here in the building. If you like, and I'm not saying this because I think you have serious problems, I'll call him and see if he can talk to you. He usually doesn't see anyone on Thursdays, so this won't be an appointment. He'll just listen and maybe suggest a few things. If you think you'd like to see him regularly, that's up to you to decide. You're a very beautiful woman, Ms. Wallace, and I think you'll be much happier in the long run if you can find it in yourself to accept that."

He held the sheet of paper out to her as he stood. Jeannie followed his example but looked at the name and office number—308, six floors down—instead of meeting his eyes.

"And if I still decide I want the surgery, after *talking* to Dr. Margrove?"

"Then we'll discuss your options. Go on now. I'll call him and make sure he isn't taking a nap."

Dr. Margrove wasn't anything like she expected.

He was nice, with an infectious laugh, easy manner, and the most beautiful gray eyes she'd ever seen. Five steps into his office—softly shadowed in the late afternoon light, steps muffled by the thick wall-to-wall carpeting—and Jeannie felt a familiar heat drench the tiny scrap of fabric between her legs.

"I—I usually don't make appointments like this," she stammered, already trembling.

"But this isn't an appointment," he answered, taking her hand in a firm grip that didn't let go until he'd led her to a soft leather chair. "This is just a meeting . . . of a friend of a friend."

And she laughed and he laughed and asked if she'd like a drink. She would. She did. He joined her—*as a friend of a friend*—then listened, quietly and without judgment, as she explained.

And decided to ignore the three-date policy.

Her mother had always wanted her to marry a doctor.

"Well, Don's right about one thing," he said after finishing off his own blended scotch and soda, and Jeannie steadied herself for the dreaded murmurings of *perfection*, "you're beautiful."

A compliment. Okay, she could handle that.

"But my esteemed colleague and poker buddy doesn't realize just how much a burden beauty can be, does he?"

Jeannie's heart skipped a number of beats. *He understood.* It took several swallows of her highball before she could answer.

"No, he doesn't,"

"And given what he does for a living, he should, wouldn't you think?"

She nodded, not trusting her voice.

"Tell me why you want to change your looks."

Jeannie finished her drink and accepted another, stronger by color in taste, before she repeated her tale about the "Too-Perfect Princess and the Many Ungrateful Nights."

She finished her second drink long before she came to *"and she only wants to live happily ever after . . . like everyone else."*

Ben—*because they weren't doctor and patient, just a friend of a friend*—set his glass, still almost full, down on the small coffee table next to their chairs before taking hers. When the glasses sat next to each other, side by side, he took both her hands in his and leaned forward.

Jeannie could smell the mellow whiskey on his breath, the crisp scent of his aftershave.

"Would you like an opinion?"

"Please."

"The only trouble with you, my dear Ms. Wallace, is that you're dating a species of the human male that we, in my professional specialty, categorize as 'Losers.'"

Jeannie hadn't expected that either and, with the help of the two drinks she'd consumed in little under fifteen minutes, laughed so hard she actually snorted.

"See," he said, his laughter much more controlled, "you're not perfect. Perfect women do *not* snort. And as for these

'Losers,' let me just add that there are a number of men who go after drop-dead gorgeous women as simply a status thing. Like test driving an expensive sports car they have no intention of buying. It's an ego boost they think will make them the envy of all their similarly-engaged 'Loser' friends.

"But owning a sports car requires careful and conscientious maintenance. So, after all the friends have seen it, and he's milked as much self-worth as he can out of it, he turns the car back into the dealer and moves on to the next ego-fix."

His hands gently squeezed hers.

"When they say 'It's not you, it's them,' they're not lying. It *is* them. There's nothing wrong with you, Jeannie . . . except your choice in men."

Jeannie sat there and blinked until the threat of tears had passed. He was right. Jesus, she never realized what she'd been doing—picking men who'd already picked her, then following their lead like some gullible lamb to the slaughtering pen. *Shit!* It *was* her fault . . . and it *wasn't* them, it really wasn't.

It was *her.*

His hands tugged. "You okay?"

And she smiled back. "Yeah. Thank you."

"No thanks necessary." He moved forward in his chair until their knees touched. "And let me just apologize for my weaker brethren. You are absolutely the most beautiful woman I've ever met."

The blush came naturally, despite the number of times she'd heard those same words, as did accepting the open-mouthed kiss when he pulled her into his arms. His tongue wasn't the least bit shy of making itself at home . . . and when it finished exploring her teeth and lips, it traced a path to her neck before backtracking to her ear.

The prickly, rippling sensation began at her shoulders—tiny at the start, like the first drops of a mountain stream after a hard winter, gathering speed and strength as it flowed down her body. Her nipples tightened at its passing; her heart pounded.

The stream became an unstoppable, churning cascade that pounded the swelling flesh of her clit.

"Absolutely beautiful," he purred, his breath tickling, his tongue finding new places to taste. "How could you think otherwise?"

Jeannie moaned, head thrown back, exposing her throat in surrender. "Please."

His laughter raised more goosebumps as he stood. The scent of musk filled the air in front of Jeannie's face.

"Ladies first," he said and dropped his pants.

His cock was big, thickly veined, and tasted like saltwater. Undoing the straps, Jeannie shimmied the dress to the floor before leaning forward to take as much of him as she could. She only managed half, but that seemed to be enough. Groaning, he sank his fingers into her hair, snapping off a few brittle white strands, and held her steady while he moved slowly back and forth against the ridge she'd made of her tongue.

"Oh God. . . baby."

Sweet words to counter the taste of pre-cum at the back of her throat.

With one hand Jeannie traced his balls with her nails—carefully, softly, just enough distraction to keep him on the edge without falling over, with the other, she slipped one finger, two, into his ass.

"JESUS! OH GOD! I'm close . . . oh God, I'm close. Wait, wait . . ."

The vacuum in Jeannie's mouth made a popping sound when he jerked out and bent down to fumble with his pants. He had the condom open and out before Jeannie could stand.

She never managed to get her panties off. Kneeling, he grabbed her legs and laid each over a chair arm. The sodden piece of material between them cut into her, heightening the pleasure-pain. All it took was a quick tug, and they literally gave up the ghost.

"Oh God . . . scoot forward . . . that's right. Oh yeah. Oh baby."

He slipped two fingers into her cunt as far as they would go, pulled them out, and shoved them back in. Jeannie bit her bottom lip to keep from crying out in pleasure.

"You like that, don't you? Oh yeah, you *like* that. I know what you like. . . . I know what you need."

His fingers moved faster, in and out and in and out, and he laughed softly when Jeannie's body tightened around them. Her clit was diamond hard.

"Hold on, baby . . . let it rise . . . c'mon . . . just hold on. Are you close? Ready?"

Jeannie gripped his arms and arched her back, grinding her cunt against his hand.

"Now . . . NOW!"

He pulled his fingers out, and her body spasmed—the orgasm imploding on itself one second only to reverse direction an instant later when he drove his cock into her up to the hilt. His shoulder, hidden beneath its crocodile-embroidered polo shirt, muffled Jeannie's scream of ecstasy.

"Relax, baby, I'm just getting started."

Lungs heaving, hips bucking, hands clawing, they finished simultaneously. He got up first, excusing himself as he went into the office's adjoining bathroom to clean up and give her time to dress.

When he returned, face washed, hair slicked back, she was still in the chair, legs spread, naked.

"Uh, shouldn't you be . . ." He pointed to the shift on the floor.

Jeannie's smile trembled for a moment. "You—you taste good. Can I have some more, please?"

He straightened the polo shirt's collar.

"I, um, don't think I'd be able to . . . right now."

Jeannie lowered her legs, pouting just a little because men told her it was cute.

"Okay, we can do that later. I have nothing planned for tonight and—"

"Can't. I have . . . plans for tonight."

"Plans?"

He walked to a desk that was smaller than Dr. Drake's. On it was a framed photo that Jeannie hadn't noticed when she first walked in. The woman in the photo was lovely, not beautiful. She wasn't perfect.

"Oh. Your wife?"

He followed her gaze. "Just a girlfriend."

Just.

"So, how was the test drive, Dr. Margrove?"

"It wasn't like that."

"Of course not." She slipped the dress on over her head and tied the shoulder straps without looking at him. "Could you do me a favor, at least?"

"If I can."

"Will you convince Dr. Drake to perform surgery?"

"No. You don't need surgery, Jeannie . . . you need therapy."

"I'm not cra—" She stopped. It would be *crazy* to try and convince him of that. "Is there a ladies' room on this floor?"

He seemed surprised by the question. "You can use this one."

"I'd rather not, thanks. Is there?"

Standing, he pulled a key attached to a neon-pink rectangle of plastic on which the words "WOMEN—THIRD FLOOR" were inscribed and set it on the edge of the desk closest to her.

"End of the hall, to the right. You can just leave the key there. I'll have Maintenance get it in the morning. And take this."

Jeannie took the business card. There was another doctor's name on it . . . in a building across town.

"I think you might feel better about yourself if you did talk to a therapist, and she's one of the best. Does a lot of work with teenage girls. Eating disorders, self-image issues, that sort of thing. Make an appointment."

She didn't thank him or say good-bye.

Jeannie made her way to the last door on the right in silence.

She'd been in enough offices to know that the windows therein are only for show. Not so with windows in public restrooms. The one in the WOMEN—THIRD FLOOR was small, but after removing a rusted bent nail that acted as the security precaution, opened all the way. The view from the window was of another corporate-owned building, the windows facing her shut and empty . . . possibly more bathrooms. Below, three stories down, was a narrow courtyard that had been converted into a miniature green space. There were a few benches, a trash can or two, a man sitting on one of the concrete benches, smoking, talking on a cell phone.

It was perfect.

Three stories wasn't high. People and animals and even small children survive falls from that height without major damage. And the man on the bench would be able to call an ambulance.

In the last moment, before she pitched forward, Jeannie caught her reflection in the mirror over the sink and smiled. Her body was tense, frightened. She blew it a kiss.

"It's not you. . . . It's *me*."

"Ms. Wallace? Can you hear me? It's Dr. Drake. Ms. Wallace? Listen. You're in the hospital, but you're all right. You have some broken ribs and a slight concussion, but you'll be fine."

Jeannie forced her eyes open and immediately closed them. The room was filled with dazzling white light. It hurt. Her eyes hurt. Her face hurt. Her body ached.

Good.

"H-how . . . am I?"

She felt the bed shift slightly as he leaned forward.

"The doctors on your case can tell you more, but I can say that they expect a complete recovery. Internally."

Without opening her eyes, Jeannie lifted her hand—she could feel a bandage—toward her face. Another hand stopped it and returned it to the thin hospital mattress.

"You've suffered massive trauma to your face, and that's why I'm here. I spoke to Ben Margrove, and he said you seemed a bit troubled when you left him, but I can't help to think that this was nothing more than a horrible accident. Was it?"

Jeannie forced her eyes open. Only one seemed to work.

"My face?"

"I'll do the best I can, but . . . I'm afraid the damage was extensive."

"Will there be . . . scars?"

His owl-eyes darkened. "I'm afraid there may be some."

Jeannie smiled at him through the misty anesthetic haze and felt something tear open on her cheek. "Perfect."

Son of Beast

Graham Masterton

Helen dropped her pink toweling bathrobe onto the floor and was just about to step into the shower when her cell phone played "I Say A Little Prayer."

She said, "Shit." She was tired and aching after sitting in her car all night on the corner of Grear Aly, waiting for a rape suspect who had never appeared. But the tune played over and over, and she knew that the caller wasn't going to leave her alone until she answered. She picked up the cell phone from the top of the laundry basket and said, wearily, "Foxley."

"Did I wake you?" asked Klaus.

"Wake me? I haven't even managed to crawl into bed yet."

"Sorry, but Melville wants you down here ASAP. Hausman's All-Day Diner on East Eighth Street. It looks like Son of Beast has been at it again."

"Oh shit."

"Yeah. My feelings exactly."

She parked her metallic red Pontiac Sunfire on the opposite side of East Eighth Street and crossed the road through the whirling snow. It was bitterly cold, and she wished that she had remembered her gloves. As she approached the diner, she shook down the hood of her dark blue duffel coat so that the two cops in the doorway could see who she was.

Klaus Geiger was already there, talking to the owner. Klaus was big and wide-shouldered, so that he looked like a linebacker for the Bengals rather than a detective. His dirty-blond hair was all mussed up, and there were plum-colored circles under his eyes.

"You look like you haven't slept either," said Helen.

"I didn't. Greta's cutting two new teeth."

"The joys of parenthood, right?"

Klaus turned to the owner and said, "Mr. Hausman, this is Detective Foxley from the Personal Crimes Unit. Mr. Hausman came to open up this morning about a quarter of six and found the back door had been forced."

The owner took off his eyeglasses and rubbed them with a crumpled paper napkin. He was balding, mid-fifties, with skin the color of liverwurst and a large mole on the left side of his chin. "I don't know how anybody could do a thing like that. It's like killing two people both at once. It's terrible."

Without a word, Helen went over to the young woman's body. She was lying on her back with her head between two bar stools. Her black woollen dress had been dragged right up to her armpits, and although she was still wearing a lacy black bra, her panties were missing. Her head had been wrapped around with several layers of cling film, so that her eyes stared out like a koi carp just beneath the surface of a frozen pond.

Like all of the nine previous victims, she was heavily pregnant—seven or eight months. A photographer was taking pictures of her from every angle, while a crime-scene specialist in a white Tyvek suit was kneeling down beside her. He almost looked as if he were praying, but he was using a cotton-bud to take fluid samples.

The intermittent flashing of the camera made the young woman's body appear to jump, as if she were still alive. Helen bent over her. As far as she could tell without unwrapping her head, she was young and quite pretty, with freckles and short brunette hair.

"Do we know who she was?" asked Helen.

"Karen Marie Dozier," Klaus told her. "Age twenty-four. Her library card gives her address as Indian Hills Avenue, St. Bernard."

There was no need to ask if the young woman had been sexually assaulted. There were purple finger bruises all over her thighs, and her swollen vagina was overflowing with blood-streaked semen.

Klaus said, "Same MO as all the others. And the same damn calling card."

He held up a plastic evidence envelope. Inside was a ticket for Son of Beast, the huge wooden roller-coaster at Kings Island amusement park, over two hundred feet high and seven thousand feet long, with passenger cars that traveled at nearly eighty miles an hour. Helen had tried it only once, and she had felt as sick to her stomach as she did this morning.

"That's nine," said Lieutenant Colonel Melville. "Nine pregnant women raped and suffocated in sixteen months. *Nine*."

He paused, and he was breathing so furiously that he was whistling through his left nostril.

"The perpetrator has left us dozens of finger impressions. He's so damn lavish with his DNA that we could clone the bastard, if we had the technology. He always leaves a ticket for the roller-coaster ride. Yet we don't have a motive, we don't have a single credible witness, and we don't have a single constructive lead."

He held up a copy of the *Cincinnati Enquirer* with the banner headline, NINTH MOM-TO-BE MURDER: COPS STILL CLUELESS.

Lieutenant Colonel Melville was short and thickset with prickly white hair and a head that looked as if it were on the point of explosion even when he was calm. Today he was so frustrated and angry that all he could do was twist the newspaper like a chicken's neck.

"This guy is making us look like assholes. Not only that, no pregnant woman can feel safe in this city, and that's an ongoing humiliation for this investigations bureau and for the Cincinnati Police Department as a whole."

"Maybe we could try another decoy," suggested Klaus. He was referring to three efforts they had made during the summer to lure Son of Beast into the open by having a policewoman walk through downtown late in the evening wearing a prosthetic "bump."

Helen shook her head. "It didn't work before, and I don't think it's going to work now. Somehow, Son of Beast has a way of distinguishing a genuinely pregnant woman from a fake."

"So how the hell does he do that?" asked Detective Rylance. "Do you think he's maybe a gynecologist?"

Klaus said, "Maybe he's a gynecologist who was reported by one of his patients for malpractice and wants to take his revenge on pregnant women in general."

"I don't think so," said Helen. "Not even a gynecologist could have told that those decoys weren't really pregnant, not without going right up to them and physically squeezing their stomachs. But if Son of Beast knows for sure which women are pregnant and which ones aren't, maybe he has access to medical records."

"Only two of the victims attended the same maternity clinic," Klaus reminded her. "It wouldn't have been easy for him to access the medical records of seven different clinics—three of which were private, remember, and one of which was in Covington."

"Not easy, agreed. But not impossible."

"Okay, not impossible. But we still don't have a motive."

Helen picked up her Styrofoam cup of latte, but it had gone cold now, and there was wrinkly skin on top of it. "Maybe we should be asking ourselves why he always leaves a Son of Beast ticket behind."

"He's taunting us," said Detective Rylance. "He's saying, here I am, I'm going to take you on the scariest roller-coaster ride you've ever experienced. I'm going to fling you this way and that. You're helpless."

"I'm not sure I agree with you," said Helen. "I think there could be more to it than that."

"Well, look into it, Detective," said Lieutenant Colonel Melville. "And—Geiger—you go back to every one of those maternity clinics and double-check everybody who has access to their records. I want some real brainstorming from all of you. I want fresh angles. I want fresh evidence. I want you to find me some witnesses who actually saw something. I want this son of a bitch hunted down and nailed to the floor by his balls."

Helen went back to her apartment at three-thirty that afternoon, undressed, showered, and threw herself into bed. It was dark outside, and the snow was falling across Walnut Street thicker than ever, muffling the sound of traffic, but she still couldn't sleep. She kept thinking of Karen Dozier staring up at her through all those layers of cling film the way she must have stared up at the man who was raping her.

She thought she heard a child crying out and the slow clanking of a roller-coaster car as it was cranked up to the top of the very first summit. But the child's cry was only the yowling of a cat, and the clanking noise was only the elevator at the other end of the hallway.

She switched on her bedside lamp. It was 7:35 PM. For the first time, in a long time, she missed having Tony lying beside her. They had split up at the end of September, for all kinds of reasons, mostly the antisocial hours she had to work and her reluctance to make love after she had witnessed some particularly vicious sex crime. She had found it almost impossible to feel aroused when she had spent the day comforting a ten-year-old boy whose scrotum had been burned by cigarettes, or a seventeen-year-old girl who had been forcibly sodomized with a wine bottle.

She went into the kitchen and switched on the kettle to make a cup of herbal tea. In the darkness of the window, she saw herself reflected, a slim young woman of thirty-one years and seven months, with scruffy, short-cropped hair and a kind of pale, watery prettiness that always deceived men into thinking that she was helpless and weak. She decided that she needed some new nightwear. The white knee-length Sleep T that she was wearing made her look like a mental patient.

The kettle started to whistle piercingly. At the same time, her phone began to play "I Say A Little Prayer." She took off the kettle, picked up the phone and said, "Foxley."

"I didn't wake you, did I?" said Klaus.

"What's this? Déjà vu all over again? No, you didn't wake me. I'm way too tired to sleep."

"I've just had some old guy walk in from the street, says he can help us with You-Know-Who."

"You have him with you now?" She had picked up on the fact that Klaus had deliberately refrained from saying "Son of Beast." The investigations bureau had never released the information that the Moms-To-Be Murderer had left roller-coaster tickets at every crime scene, nor what they called him.

"Sure. He's still here. He says he needs to speak to you personally."

"*Me?* Why does he need to talk to me?"

"He says you're the only person who can do it."

"I don't understand. The only person who can do *what?*"

"He won't give me any specific details. Look"—he lowered his voice—"he's probably a screwball. But we're really clutching at straws, right, and if he can give us any kind of a lead—"

Helen tugged at her hair. Her reflection in the kitchen window tugged at *her* hair too, although Helen thought that her reflection did it more hesitantly than she did. "Okay," she said. "I'll be crosstown in twenty minutes. Buy your screwball a cup of coffee or something. Keep him talking."

* * *

She drove across to Cincinnati Police headquarters on Ezzard Charles Drive with her windshield wipers flapping to clear the snow. Klaus was on the fourth floor, sitting on the edge of his desk and talking to an elderly man in a very long black overcoat. The man had a shock of wiry gray hair and rimless eyeglasses. His face was criss-crossed with thousands of wrinkles, like very soft leather that has been folded and refolded countless times. An old-fashioned black homburg hat was resting in his lap, and his hands, in black leather gloves, were neatly folded on top of it.

Klaus stood up as Helen came into the office. "This is Detective Foxley, sir. Foxley, this is Mr.—"

"Hochheimer," said the elderly man, rising to his feet and taking off his right glove. "Joachim Hochheimer. I read about the murder of the pregnant woman in the *Post* this evening."

Helen didn't take off her coat. "And you think you can help us in some way?"

"I think it's possible. But as I have already said to your associate here, it will require a considerable sacrifice."

"Okay, then. What kind of considerable sacrifice are we talking about?"

"Do you mind if I sit down again? My hip, well, I'm waiting to have it replaced."

"Sure, go ahead. Klaus—you couldn't buy me a coffee, could you? I think I'm beginning to hallucinate."

"Sure thing."

When Klaus had left the office, the elderly man said, "Young lady—you may find it very difficult to believe what I am going to tell you. There is a risk that you will dismiss me as senile or mad. If that turns out to be your opinion, then what can I do?"

"Mr. Hochheimer, we're investigating a series of very brutal homicides here. We welcome any suggestions, no matter how loony they might seem to be. I'm not saying that *your* suggestions are loony. I don't even know what they are yet. But I'm trying to tell you that we appreciate your coming in, whatever you have to tell us."

Mr. Hochheimer nodded, very gravely. "Of course. I consider it an honor that you are even prepared to listen to me."

"So," said Helen, sitting down next to him. "What's this all about?"

He cleared his throat. "As you know, hundreds of German immigrants flooded into Cincinnati in the middle of the nineteenth century to work on the Ohio River docks and in the pork-packing factories. Among these immigrants was a family originally from Reuthingen, deep in the forests of the Swabian Jura. They were refugees not from poverty but from prejudice and relentless persecution."

"They were Jews?"

"Oh, no, not Jews. They were a different sort of people altogether. Different from you, different from me. Different from the rest of humanity."

"Their bloodline came originally from Leipzig, from the university, which is one of the oldest universities in the world. In the fifteenth century, several physicians at the university were carrying out secret genealogical experiments to see if they could endow human beings with some of the attributes of animals, or fish, or insects.

"For example, they tried to inseminate women with the semen from salmon to see if they could produce a human being who was capable of swimming underwater without having to breathe. They tried similar experiments with dogs, and horses, and even spiders.

"Today we think such experiments are nonsense, but we should remind ourselves that in fourteen hundred and thirty, people were still convinced that a pregnant woman who was frightened by a rabbit would give birth to a child with a harelip, or that an albino baby was the result of its expectant mother drinking too much milk."

"Go on," said Helen.

"Almost all of the experiments failed, naturally. But one experiment—just one—was what you might call a qualified success. A young serving-girl called Mathilde Festa was impregnated with sperm from a horse leech. The idea was that her child, when it was grown, could be trained as a physician and suck infected blood from its patients' wounds itself, without the necessity for leeches."

What a nutjob, thought Helen. *To think I got out of bed and drove all the way across town to listen to this.*

"Forgive me," she said, trying to sound interested. "I thought that leeches were hermaphrodites, like oysters."

"They are, but they still produce semen. Some species of leech have up to eighty testes."

"Eighty? Really? That's a whole lot of balls."

Mr. Hochheimer closed his eyes for a moment, as if he were trying to be very patient with her.

"I'm sorry," said Helen. "I'm kind of frazzled, that's all. I haven't slept in thirty-seven hours. And I'm beginning to wonder what point you're trying to make here."

Mr. Hochheimer opened his eyes again and smiled at her. "I understand your skepticism. I told you that this wouldn't be easy to believe. But the fact is that Mathilde Festa gave birth to what appeared to be a normal-looking baby, except that his skin was slightly *mottled* in appearance. He was also born with four teeth, which were rough and serrated, like those of a leech.

"After his birth, the physicians at Leipzig kept him concealed, because the university authorities and the church would have been outraged if they had discovered the nature of their experiments. But when he was four years old, the boy managed to escape from the walled garden in which he was playing.

"The physicians found him two days later, in the attic of an abandoned house close by, in a deep coma. Beside him was the body of another small boy, so white and so *collapsed* in appearance that they couldn't believe that he was human. Mathilde

Festa's son had bitten this small boy and had sucked out of him every last milliliter of blood and bodily fluid and bone marrow, until the unfortunate child was nothing more than an empty sack of dry skin and desiccated ribs.

"What was even more remarkable, though, was that Mathilde Festa's son had grown to nearly twice his size. He had been only four years old when he escaped from the garden. Now he looked like a boy of eight."

"This is beginning to sound like something by the Brothers Grimm," said Helen.

"A fairy story, yes. I agree. If they had strangled Mathilde Festa's son there and then, as they should have done, that would have been an end to it, and nobody would ever have believed that it really happened."

"But they didn't strangle him?"

"No—at least two of the physicians were determined that their life's work should not be lost. They believed that the death of one small boy was a small price to pay for successfully interbreeding one of God's species with another. They smuggled Mathilde Festa and her boy to Munich, and from Munich they took him to Reuthingen, deep in the forest, where he grew up as a normal child. Or as normal as any child could be, if he were half human and half leech. Mathilde Festa christened him Friedrich."

"I hate to push you, Mr. Hochheimer, but it's getting kind of late, and I'm very tired. How exactly is any of this relevant to the Moms-To-Be Murderer?"

Joachim Hochheimer raised one hand to indicate that Helen should be patient. "When Friedrich was grown to manhood, he took a wife, a very simpleminded farmer's daughter who hadn't been able to find any other man to marry her. They were very happy together, by all accounts, but they were persecuted by other people in Reuthingen because of the strangeness of Friedrich's appearance and also because of his wife's backwardness. Children tossed rocks at their cottage, and whenever they went out people shook their fists at them and spat.

"One day, when she was walking home from the village, a gang of young men attacked Friedrich's wife. She was pregnant at the time with Friedrich's first child, almost full term. The young men dragged her into a barn, and one of them raped her. Or *tried* to rape her."

He hesitated and squeezed his hands together as if he couldn't decide if he ought to continue. His leather gloves made a soft creaking sound.

"Go on," said Helen. "I deal with sex crimes every day, Mr. Hochheimer. I've heard it all before."

"This, young lady, I don't think that you *have* heard before. As the young man forced his way into Friedrich's struggling wife, her waters broke. Her womb opened, and the baby inside her seized her attacker's penis with his teeth.

"The young man was screaming. His friends helped him to pull himself out. But the baby came out too, its teeth still buried in his penis, and even when his friends battered the baby with sticks, it refused to release him. He fainted, and his friends ran away.

"The next morning, Friedrich found his wife lying in the barn, desperately weak but still alive. Close beside her, sleeping, lay a young man, naked, almost fully grown. Beside him, amongst the bales of straw, lay something that was described as looking like a crumpled nightshirt, except that it had a face on it, a face without eyes, and tufts of hair."

Helen sat back. "Well, Mr. Hochheimer, that's quite a story."

"A description of what happened was written in great detail by one of the physicians from Leipzig, and his account is still lodged in the university library. I have seen it for myself."

"You think it's true?"

"I assure you, it is completely true. The descendants of the family of which I spoke are still here in Cincinnati."

"Well, it's a very interesting story, sir. But how can it help us to solve these murders?"

"It said in the *Post* that you have been unable to track down your suspect in spite of a wealth of evidence. It said that you have even tried decoys pretending to be pregnant, but your suspect seems to know that they are not genuine."

"That's correct."

"Supposing a decoy *were* to be genuine."

"That's impossible," said Helen. "We can't possibly ask a pregnant woman to expose herself to a serial killer. What if something went wrong? The police department would be crucified."

"Ah! But what if the pregnant woman were quite capable of defending herself? What if her unborn child were quite capable of protecting her?"

Helen suddenly understood what Joachim Hochheimer was suggesting. It made her feel as if she had scores of cicadas crawling inside her clothes. At that moment, Klaus came back with a cup of coffee in each hand.

"*Foxley?*" He frowned. "Are you okay? You look like shit."

She ignored him. Instead, she said to Joachim Hochheimer, "You're seriously suggesting that some woman gets herself pregnant with one of these—leech babies? And allows the Moms-To-Be Murderer to rape her . . . so that it—?"

She imitated a biting gesture with her fingers.

Joachim Hochheimer shrugged. "There would be no escape for him. Perhaps you think of it as summary justice, but what choice do you have? To allow him to continue his killings? To allow even more innocent young women and their unborn babies to be slaughtered?"

"Jesus," said Helen.

Klaus put down the coffee cups. "You want to explain to me what's going on here? What's a goddamned leech baby when it's at home?"

Again, Helen ignored him. "Why me?" she asked Joachim Hochheimer. "Why did you come to see me?"

"I read an interview with you, the last time a young pregnant woman was murdered. You are young, you are unattached, you have an award for bravery. I don't know. I suppose I just looked at your picture and thought, this could be the one."

"And how were you proposing that I should get pregnant?"

"The Vuldus family have a son who is only two years younger than you. Richard Vuldus."

Helen stared at him. The desk lamp was shining on his eyeglasses so that he looked as if he were blind.

"It's impossible," she said. "Even if I believed you—which I don't—it's totally out of the question."

Joachim Hochheimer stayed where he was for a while, nodding. Then he stood up and said, "At least you know about it now. At least you have the option to try it, if you change your mind. Here—take my card. You can usually reach me at this number during the night."

He put on his homburg hat and left the office. When he had gone, Klaus said, "What the hell was *that* all about?"

"You were right," said Helen. "He *was* a screwball. One hundred and ten percent unadulterated FDA-rated screwball."

She spent the next four and a half days checking every single mention of the roller-coaster Son of Beast since its official opening on May 26, 2000—on the Internet, in newspaper cuttings, in transcripts of TV and radio news reports.

When it had opened, Son of Beast had broken all kinds of records for wood-constructed roller-coasters. The tallest, the fastest, the only woodie with loops. It had cost millions of dollars to construct and used up 1.65 million board feet of timber.

She had almost given up when she came across an article from the *Cincinnati Enquirer* from April 25 two years previously.

"SON OF BEAST KILLED OUR BABY"
MAN LOSES LAWSUIT

A judge yesterday threw out a $3.5 million lawsuit by a Norwood man who claimed that a "violent and hair-raising" ride on the newly opened Son of Beast roller-coaster caused his pregnant girlfriend to miscarry their baby.

After his girlfriend confessed to the court that the roller-coaster ride had not been responsible for her losing the child, Judge David Davis told Henry Clarke, 35, a realtor from Smith Road, Norwood, that he was dismissing the action against Paramount Entertainment.

Jennifer Prescott, 33, admitted that she had booked in advance to have her pregnancy terminated at a private clinic in Covington, KY, and had used their ride on the Kings Island attraction to conceal what she had done from Mr. Clarke.

Mrs. Prescott is estranged from her husband, Robert Prescott, also of Norwood. She told the court that she started an affair with Mr. Clarke in November last year, believing him to be a "kind and considerate person."

But he became increasingly possessive and physically abusive, and she had already decided to leave him before she discovered that she was expecting his baby.

She invented the roller-coaster story because she was terrified of what Mr. Clarke would do to her if he discovered that she had deliberately ended her pregnancy.

Helen printed out a copy of the news story and took it into Lieutenant Colonel Melville's office.

"What do you think?" she asked him.

Lieutenant Colonel Melville read the article, took out his handkerchief, and loudly blew his nose. "Mr. Clarke has a pretty good resumé, doesn't he? A history of domestic violence.

A motive for attacking pregnant women. And a reason for using the name Son of Beast. Let's pick this joker up, shall we, and see what he has to say for himself?"

But there was no trace of Henry Clarke anywhere in Cincinnati or its surrounding suburbs. He had left his job at Friedmann, Kite Realty Inc. only two weeks after he had lost his court action against Paramount. He had left his house in Norwood too, leaving all of his furniture behind. His parents hadn't heard from him, not even a phone call, and he had told none of his friends where he was going.

He had sold his Ford Explorer to a used-car dealership in Bridgetown, to the west of the city center, but he had taken cash for it and not exchanged it for another vehicle.

"I have such a feeling about this guy," said Helen the week before Christmas, when she and Klaus were sitting in the office eating sugared donuts and drinking coffee. "He's vanished, but he hasn't gone."

The sky outside the office window was dark green, and it was snowing again. People with black umbrellas were struggling along the sidewalks like a scene out of a Dickens novel.

Helen went to the window and looked down at them. "That could be him, under any one of those umbrellas."

"Don't let your imagination run away with you," said Klaus. "Do you want this last donut?"

Helen wasn't letting her imagination run away with her. On Christmas morning the body of a young pregnant woman was discovered underneath the Riverfront Stadium. Her head had been wound round with four layers of Saran Wrap, and she had been raped. Her name was Clare Jefferson, and she was twenty-three years old.

Helen stood underneath the gloomy concrete supports of the stadium, her hands in her pockets, watching the crime-scene specialists at work. Klaus came up to her and said, "Happy Christmas. Did you open your presents yet?"

The red flashing lights on top of the squad cars were a lurid parody of Christmas-tree lights. Helen said, "*Ten*. Shit. Isn't he ever going to stop?"

One of the crime-scene specialists came over, holding up a roller-coaster ticket. "Thought you'd want to see this."

She couldn't sleep that night. She took two sleeping-pills and watched TV until 2:30 AM, but her brain wouldn't stop churning over, and her eyes refused to close. She had arranged to see her parents tomorrow in Indian Hills Village, to make up for missing Christmas lunch, but she knew already that she wasn't going to go.

How could she eat turkey and pull crackers when that young girl was lying in the mortuary, with her dead baby still inside her? Son of Beast had raped and suffocated ten women, but altogether he had murdered twenty innocent souls.

She switched on the light and went across to her dressing table. Tucked into the side of the mirror was Joachim Hochheimer's visiting card. She took it out and looked at it for a long time. He was a lunatic, right? If sixteenth-century physicians had managed to cross a woman and a horse leech, surely it would have been common medical knowledge by now. At the very least it would have been mentioned in *Ripley's Believe It or Not*.

And even if it really *had* happened, and Mathilde Festa really *had* managed to give birth to generations of descendants, surely the leech genes would have been bred out of them by now.

And even if they hadn't been bred out of them, and it was still genetically possible for a woman to become pregnant with a creature like that, could she bring herself to do it?

She sat down on the end of her rumpled bed. She thought: *If this is the only way that Son of Beast can be stopped from murdering more women and unborn babies, I'm going to have to find the courage to do it myself. I can't ask anybody else.* Not only that, it was the twenty-sixth day of the month, and she was ovulating. If there was any time to conceive a Vuldus baby, it was now.

She picked up her phone and punched out Joachim Hochheimer's number.

He opened the door for her. The hallway was so gloomy that she could hardly see his face, only the reflection from his eyeglasses.

"Come in. We thought that you might have changed your mind."

"I very nearly did."

Inside, the apartment was overheated and stuffy and smelled of stale potpourri, cinnamon and cloves. It was furnished in a heavy Germanic style, with dusty brocade drapes and huge armchairs and mahogany cabinets filled with Eastern European china—plates and fruit bowls and figurines of fan-dancers. It was on the top floor of a nineteenth-century commercial building overlooking Fountain Square, right in the heart of the city. Helen went to the window and looked out, and she could see the Tyler Davidson Fountain, with the Genius of Water standing on top of it, curtains of ice suspended from her outstretched hands. All around it, dozens of children were sliding on the slippery pavement.

"The Vuldus family rented this apartment from the shipping-insurance company that used to occupy the lower floors," said Joachim Hochheimer. "That was in 1871, and they have lived here ever since."

He came up to her and held out his hand. "May I take your coat?"

"Listen," she said, "I'm really not so sure I want to go through with this."

He nodded. "It is a step into the totally unknown, isn't it, which not many of us ever have the courage to take. If you feel you cannot do it, then of course you must go home and forget that I ever suggested it."

"Is he here?" asked Helen. "Richard Vuldus?"

"Yes, he's in the bedroom. He's waiting for you."

"Maybe you can give him my apologies."

"Of course."

For a long moment, neither of them moved. But then Helen's cell phone played "I Say A Little Prayer For You." She said, "Excuse me, Mr. Hochheimer," and opened it up.

It was Klaus. "Foxley?" he demanded. "Where the hell are you?"

"I had an errand to run. I'm free now. What do you want?"

"We just had a first report from the ME. Clare Jefferson was two hundred seventy-one days' pregnant. About three days away from giving birth."

"Oh God."

"Not only that, Foxley. She was expecting twins."

Helen closed her eyes, but inside her mind she could clearly see Clare Jefferson lying on her back in the dark concrete recess underneath Riverfront Stadium, her head swaddled in plastic wrap, her smock pulled up right over her breasts, and the red emergency lights flashing. Inside her swollen stomach, two dead babies had been cuddling each other.

"Helen? You there?"

"I'm here."

"Are you coming into headquarters?"

She cleared her throat. "Give me a little time, Klaus. Maybe an hour or so."

"Okay. But we really need you here, soon as you can."

Helen closed her cell phone and dropped it back into her coat pocket. Joachim Hochheimer was watching her intently, and he could obviously sense that something had changed.

Helen said quietly, and as calmly as she could, "Maybe you can introduce me to Richard."

* * *

The bedroom was furnished in the same grandiose style as the rest of the apartment, with a huge four-poster bed with a green-and-crimson quilt, impenetrable crimson drapes, and a bow-fronted armoire with elaborate gilded handles. On either side of the bed hung oil paintings of naked nymphs dancing in the woods, their heads thrown back in lust and hilarity.

Richard Vuldus was standing by the window looking down at Fountain Square, wearing a long black cotton robe with very wide sleeves, as if he were a stage magician. He was tall, with long, black curly hair that almost reached his shoulders. Helen saw a diamond sparkle in his left earlobe.

"Richard," said Joachim Hochheimer. "Richard, this is the young lady I was telling you about."

Richard Vuldus turned around. Helen couldn't stop herself from taking a small, sharp intake of breath, almost like a hiccup. He was extraordinarily handsome, but in a strange, unsettling way that Helen had never seen before. His face was long and oval and very pale, and his eyebrows were arched, almost like a woman's. His nose was thin and straight, and his lips were thin but gracefully curved, as if he had just made a deeply lewd suggestion but said it in such a way that no woman could have resisted it.

He came up to Helen with his robes softly billowing. The cotton was deep black but very fine, so that with the bedside lamp behind him, she could see the outline of his muscular body and his half-tumescent penis.

"Joachim!" He smiled, holding out his hand to her. "You didn't warn me that she was beautiful!" His eyes were mesmerizing: his irises were completely black, and they glistened like polished jet. His voice had a slight European accent, so that "beautiful" came out with five syllables, "bee-aye-*oo*-ti-fool."

"I'm Helen," said Helen. Her heart was beating so hard against her ribcage that it actually hurt.

"I know," said Richard Vuldus. "And I know that this cannot be easy for you, in any way. But I assure you that I will do my best to make you feel at ease. Even if what we are doing today is not out of love for each other, it is out of love for innocent people, yes, and unborn babies who do not deserve to die?"

"I—ah—I guess we could put it that way."

"Perhaps you would like a drink?" Joachim Hochheimer asked her. "A glass of champagne?"

"I have to go on duty later. Besides . . . if we're going to do this, I'd rather just get it over with."

"Of course," said Richard Vuldus. He came closer to her, and now she could see what Joachim Hochheimer had meant by *mottled*. There were faint dark gray patches around his temples and across his cheekbones and down the sides of his neck. He had a smell about him too. Not unpleasant—in fact it was quite attractive—but different from any other man she had ever known. Musky but metallic, like overheated iron.

"I'll leave you alone now," said Joachim Hochheimer. "If there's anything you need—if you have any more questions—"

"There is just one thing," said Helen. "What do *you* get out of this? Don't tell me you're just being public-spirited."

Joachim Hochheimer looked surprised. "I thought that was obvious, dear lady. What *we* get out of it is a new member of the Vuldus family—one with new blood. We have been trying for generation after generation to breed ourselves back to purity, and we are not too far away from that now. They cursed us, those physicians, all those centuries ago, by interbreeding us. But the time will eventually come when all of the monstrosity is bred out of us."

Richard Vuldus took hold of her hand. His fingers were very cold, but they were strong too. "You will be doing our family a great service, Helen, and we thank you and admire you for it."

Helen nearly lost her nerve. Not only would she have to make love to this strange young man, she would have to carry his baby, and when she was nearly ready to give birth she would have to risk her own life and her baby's life to trap Son of Beast. Even if she succeeded, she would be faced with a nightmare. She would have to find a way of explaining what had happened to Son of Beast, and a way of making sure that her new child escaped and was safely returned to the Vuldus family.

It was madness. It was all madness. She was just about to turn around and ask for her coat back when Richard Vuldus laid both of his hands on her shoulders, held her firmly, and looked directly into her eyes. His eyes were so black it was like looking into space.

"The day we take no more risks, Helen, that is the day we lie down and die."

She didn't know what to say to him. Behind her, Joachim Hochheimer quietly closed the bedroom door.

"Come," said Richard Vuldus. He led her over to the side of the bed, closer to the bedside lamp. He touched her hair and her cheek. "Do you know what I see in you? I see a woman of such complexity. A woman who needs to show what she can do but has not yet discovered a way to do it. Maybe this will be the way."

He drew her soft blue-gray sweater over her head, so that for a moment she was blinded. When she emerged, he gently teased up her hair with his fingertips.

"You should grow your hair," he told her. "You would look like a dryad with long hair. Free and wild. A child of nature."

"Can we just—?"

"Of course."

He tugged down the zipper at the side of her skirt and unfastened the hook and eye. She stepped out of it, so that she was standing in front of him in nothing but her lacy blue bra and black pantyhose. He kissed her forehead, although she didn't want kisses, in the same way that prostitutes never wanted kisses. This was business, not love. At least she supposed it was business. She began to feel light-headed and disoriented, as if she hadn't eaten for two days.

With his long, chilly fingers, Richard Vuldus released the catch of her bra. Her breasts were small and rounded and high—drum-majorettes' breasts, Tony used to call them. Richard Vuldus touched her nipples, and they crinkled and stiffened.

"You should imagine now that we have been friends for a very long time," he murmured. "Maybe we knew each other at college. We were never lovers but looked at each other from time to time and knew that if things had turned out differently, we might have been. Now, tonight, many years later, we have met again by accident."

He slipped his fingers inside the waistband of her pantyhose and gently tugged them down to her thighs. He cupped the cheeks of her bottom in both hands, and then he let his left hand stray around to her vulva. One long middle finger slipped between her lips, touching her clitoris so lightly that she barely felt it, but it was so cold that she became aware of her own wetness. She shivered—but against all of her instincts, she was aroused.

He lowered her into a sitting position on the bed. Then he knelt down in front of her and drew her pantyhose all the way down and off her feet. As he did so, he took hold of each foot and kissed it in turn, his fingers working their way between her toes, his thumb pressing deep into her insteps. She had gone to a reflexologist once, to relieve her tension, but she had never had her feet massaged like this before. Every time the ball of his thumb rolled around the bottom of her foot, she felt as if he were kneading her perineum, between her vagina and her anus, and the sensation was almost unbearably erotic. She began to feel delirious with pleasure.

He stood up and leaned over her, kissing her forehead. She found herself tilting her head back so that she could kiss his neck, and then his chin, and then his lips.

"There is such darkness in the world," he whispered. "There is darkness so deep that sometimes we have despaired of ever finding our way out of it. But tonight you and I will light a light, no matter how small, and everything will gradually brighten, and we will see again."

"Kiss me," she said, and as he kissed her, she plunged her hands into the soft blackness of his robes and felt his body underneath, his hard muscles, his ribs, his hips.

He straightened up and drew the robes over his head like the great black shadow of a raven flying overhead. The robes fell softly onto the floor, and he was naked in the lamplight. He was wide-shouldered, but his stomach was very flat, and Helen could see the definition of every pectoral and deltoid and bicep as if he were a living diagram of the human body. He was completely hairless—no chest hair, no underarm hair, no pubic hair—and his skin was smooth and faintly luminous, with a pattern of those darker patches down his sides and around his thighs.

His penis was fully erect now, and it was enormous, with a gaping plum-colored glans, already glistening with fluid. Helen reached out and took hold of the shaft and gripped it tight; his distended veins felt like the twisted creepers around a tree trunk.

She lifted her head so that she could kiss his penis, but he gripped her shoulder and pressed her back. "Not that way," he said. "We must conserve everything we can."

She said, "You're incredible. I never met a man like you before. Ever."

He climbed onto the bed next to her. He said nothing but firmly turned her over onto her stomach. Then he knelt behind her and took hold of her hips and lifted her into a crouching position.

"I am the father of your child," he said. "I am nothing more than that."

With that, he parted the cheeks of her bottom with his thumbs and positioned the head of his penis between the lips of her vulva. Helen lowered her head. She felt as if the pattern on the quilt were alive and that its swirls and curlicues were crawling underneath her like green-and-crimson centipedes.

Richard Vuldus slowly pushed his erection inside her, and it felt so large that she couldn't help herself from gasping. He drew himself out again, hesitated for a second, and then pushed himself inside her a second time, so deeply that she could feel his naked testicles against her lips.

God, she had never had sex like this before, ever, with anybody. She almost felt as if she were going mad. The blood pumped through her head so hard that she could hear it, and she started to tremble. Not only was her body completely naked, but her soul too. She felt subjugated, dominated, but lusted-after and needed. She pressed her head down against the pillow and reached behind her with both hands, spreading the cheeks of her bottom even wider so that Richard Vuldus could penetrate her deeper. There was a brutal urgency in Richard Vuldus's love-making, and he forced his penis into her faster and faster. She was so wet that they were both smothered in slippery juice.

Helen could feel an orgasm beginning to rise between her legs, and her thighs started to quiver. She squeezed her eyes shut and gritted her teeth and gripped the quilt tight. All the same, it hit her before she expected it, like a huge black locomotive coming out of the darkness with its headlight glaring and its whistle screaming.

"*Ahhhh!*" she shouted. "*Ohmygod ohymygod aaahhhhhh!*"

As Helen quaked and jumped, Richard Vuldus climaxed too. She actually felt the glans of his penis bulging, and the first spurt of sperm. He pumped again, and again, and again, as if he had been storing up this semen for years and could at last release it, every drop of it, and find relief.

He continued to kneel behind her for a few seconds, his hands grasping her hips, but then he slowly rolled over and lay on his back. Helen rolled over too and lay close beside him.

"You, Richard Vuldus, are simply amazing." She reached out to touch his lips with her fingertip.

He took hold of her wrist and moved her hand away, gently but firmly. "This was not for love, Helen. Not my love for you, nor your love for me. This was for justice, and revenge."

She stared at him, and then she sat up. "You mean to tell me that meant *nothing* to you?"

"It meant everything. More than you can know."

She hesitated for a moment. Then she climbed off the bed and retrieved her clothes from the floor.

"Thank you, Helen," he said softly.

She pulled her sweater over her head. "Don't mention it. I'll let you know if you've succeeded in knocking me up."

When she left the apartment, Joachim Hochheimer took hold of her hand and tried to raise it to his lips, but Helen pulled herself away.

"Thank you, *gnädige Fraulein,*" he said. "We are forever in your debt."

Toward the end of January, she began to feel tired, and her breasts began to feel swollen, but she was still not convinced that Richard Vuldus had succeeded in making her pregnant. He had made love to her only once, after all; and besides that, she was beginning to convince herself that she had dreamed the whole incident. She had gone back to Fountain Square several times during the evening, and she had seen no lights in the Vuldus apartment. She had called Joachim Hochheimer too, but nobody had picked up.

"What's bugging you?" Klaus asked her as they sat in First Watch Café one morning, eating bacado omelets and drinking horseshoe coffee.

"Please?"

"I said, what's bugging you? You haven't heard a word I've been saying."

"I don't know. Sorry. I feel weird."

They had driven only a few blocks down Walnut Street before she tugged at his coat and said, "Stop the car! Stop the car, please!"

She just managed to open the door and lean over the gutter before she was sick—half-chewed bacon and avocado and eggs, in a steaming gravy of hot coffee.

That evening, she took a home pregnancy test, and yes, it was positive. She stood staring at herself in her bathroom mirror. *My God, what have I done? What kind of a baby is growing inside me?*

She went back into the bedroom and sat on the edge of the bed. At that moment, the phone rang.

"Detective Foxley? Helen? This is Joachim Hochheimer speaking."

"Oh, yes?"

"Everything is well, yes?"

"It depends on your point of view, Mr. Hochheimer."

"You are expecting Richard's child, is what I mean."

"Yes, Mr. Hochheimer."

"Thank you, dear lady, from the bottom of my heart."

She put the phone down. Almost immediately, it rang again.

"Foxley? It's Klaus. S.O.B. has done it again."

"Where?"

"The Serpentine Wall, Yeatman's Cove. Do you want to meet me down there?"

"On my way."

She pulled on her sweater and took her duffel coat out of the closet. She was just about to leave the apartment when her stomach tightened and she felt a rising surge of nausea. She hurried into the bathroom, knelt down in front of the toilet, and brought up a fountain of chili and cheddar cheese.

Klaus said, "You're *pregnant?* You're kidding me. By whom? You didn't tell me you had a new boyfriend."

"It's nobody I've ever talked about."

"So what are you going to do? You're not going to *have* the kid, surely? How are you going to be a single mom and a detective at the same time? I mean—I'm assuming that the guy isn't going to marry you. Maybe he is."

"No, he's not going to marry me."

Klaus swirled the remains of his beer around his glass and

shook his head. "You're full of surprises, Foxley. I have to give you that."

"I surprise myself, most of the time."

"Well," said Klaus, "just make sure that you check with me before you choose your maternity clinic."

"Why's that?"

He took a roughly scrawled diagram out of his inside pocket. "I may be wrong, but I've been looking into the records of the various clinics which were attended by Son of Beast's victims. There's nothing in any of them to suggest that Son of Beast could have hacked into any medical records. But today I realized that his eighth victim was a patient at the same clinic as his first victim, and his ninth victim was a patient at the same clinic as his second victim, and so on. It appears to me that he has a list of seven clinics and that he's picking his victims from each clinic in rotation. I could be wrong, but it's beginning to look like a pattern."

Helen took the diagram and frowned at it. "So he wouldn't necessarily need any access to medical records. He simply goes to the next clinic on his list and follows his victim out of the building when she leaves."

"It's beginning to look that way."

"But why should he do that? That means that we can predict which clinic he's going to pick his next victim from, and we can stake it out."

"That's right. And the next one is . . . the Christ Hospital on Auburn."

But when winter melted away, so did Son of Beast. After the killing of a thirty-one-year-old mother-to-be at Yeatman's Cove, there were no more Moms-To-Be murders for seven months, and they began to wonder if he had given up, or left Cincinnati for good.

Eventually, Lieutenant Colonel Melville decided that the stakeout at the Christ Hospital was no longer cost-effective and assigned the surveillance team to other duties.

For Helen, that summer seemed to last forever, one sweltering day after another, week after week, month after month. The city was suffocating, and this year there was a teeming plague of cicadas sawing away noisily day and night and penetrating every crevice of every building, cramming themselves into office ventilation systems and tangling themselves in people's hair. The windshield of Helen's Pontiac was permanently smeared with cicada guts.

Meanwhile, the baby inside her grew and grew. Her sickness passed, but she still felt exhausted, especially when the baby started to wriggle and heave inside her all night. Every Thursday afternoon she went to the Christ Hospital, waited for fifteen minutes in the ladies' room, reading a book, and then left. If Son of Beast were still in the city, watching and waiting for his next opportunity, she wanted to make sure that she gave him a victim with regular patterns of behavior.

She didn't actually attend the maternity clinic. This birth had to be off the books, unregistered. All the same, she bought books on pregnancy and made sure that she took plenty of vitamins and kept her blood pressure down. She developed a desperate craving for five-way chili—spaghetti, chili, cheese, kidney beans, and onions—and she found it a daily struggle to keep her weight down.

It was a lonely time. She kept away from her friends and her family because she wanted as few of them as possible to know that she was expecting a baby. And as the months went by and Son of Beast failed to reappear, it seemed to be increasingly likely that she had suffered this pregnancy for no purpose.

Only Klaus came round regularly to see her, and each time he brought her flowers or a box of candies. In August, when she was eight months' pregnant, he brought her a little blue-and-white knitted suit, with a hood.

"How do you know it's going to be a boy?" she asked him.
"Because I can't imagine you having a girl."

On a thundery afternoon in the first week of September, she drove up to the Christ Hospital as usual and parked her car. It was only four-thirty, but the sky was black, and lightning was flickering over the hills. She was walking toward the hospital entrance when she noticed a man in a gray raincoat standing under the trees. She made a point of not looking at him directly, but when she went through the revolving doors into the hospital lobby, she quickly turned her head, and she could see that he had been watching her.

She went to the ladies' room and sat in one of the cubicles. Baby was being hyperactive today, churning and turning inside her. There was no reason to suppose that the man in the gray raincoat was Son of Beast, but somehow she felt that the time had arrived, that the cogs of her destiny were all beginning to click into place. Baby turned over again, and she began to feel deeply apprehensive.

She waited for twenty minutes. Then she left the ladies' room and walked across the lobby and out of the revolving door. It was raining, hard, so that the asphalt driveway in front of the hospital was dancing with spray. There was no sign of the man in the gray raincoat.

She pulled up her hood and hurried toward the parking lot as fast as she could. Lightning crackled, almost directly overhead, followed by a deafening barrage of thunder. She reached her car and unlocked the door and was just about to climb in when somebody's arm wrapped itself around her neck and lifted her upward and backward, throttling her.

"You're going to do what I tell you!" said a thick, sinus-blocked voice.

"I gah—my baby—*gah*—can't—!"

"You're going to come around to the back of the car and you're going to open the trunk and you're going to climb in. You got that?"

"I can't—breathe—can't—!"

With his right hand, the man reached around and twisted her car keys away from her. "If you don't do what I say, I'm going to cut your belly right open, here and now. Give me your cell."

"Please—I—*gah*—"

"Are you going to do what I tell you? Give me your cell!"

The man was compressing her larynx so hard that Helen could see nothing but scarlet, and stars. She fumbled in her pocket and took out her cell phone and handed it to him.

"You're going to do what I tell you, right? And you're not going to scream, and you're not going to try to run away?"

She nodded.

The man shuffled her round to the back of the car, as if they were a clumsy pair of dancing partners.

"Open the trunk. Go on, open the trunk. Now get in there. Hurry it up, before somebody sees you. And don't try anything stupid."

Awkwardly, she lifted one foot into the trunk. As she did so, however, she twisted around and yanked her gun out from under her coat.

"*Freeze!*" she screamed. But the man was too close to her, and far too quick. He grabbed her wrist with both hands and twisted it around so hard that it ripped her tendons, and the gun clattered onto the ground.

"You're a *cop?*" he shouted at her. "You're a fucking *cop?*"

He pushed her violently into the trunk, next to the spare wheel, and shoved her head down.

"You've been trying to trap me? Is that it? You got yourself pregnant on purpose, just to trap me?"

Helen tried to lift her head, but he jammed it down again. Then he slammed the trunk lid, and she was left in darkness.

She heard him climb into the driver's seat and start the engine. Then he pulled out of the hospital parking lot and made his way toward Auburn Avenue. As he drove, Helen was swung right and left and jostled up and down. She tried to work out which direction he was taking, and how far they had driven, but after a while she gave up.

He seemed to drive her for hours, and for miles. But at last he slowed down, almost to a crawl, and she could hear traffic, and sirens, and people's footsteps. He must have taken her downtown, to the city center.

He turned, and turned again, and then she felt a bump, and the car drove slowly down a steep, winding gradient. An underground parking facility, she guessed.

At last the car stopped, and she heard the man climbing out. The trunk opened, and he was standing there, looking down at her, a fortyish man with gray hair and a heavy gray moustache. He had a broad face which reminded Helen of one of her uncles, but he had piggy little eyes and thick, purplish lips, as if he had been eating too many blueberries.

He had brought her down to what looked like the lower level of an office building. It was gloomy and cold, with dripping concrete walls and a single fluorescent light that kept flickering and buzzing as if it were just about to burn out.

"All right," the man ordered her. "Out."

"You're not going to hurt my baby?"

"What do you care?"

"You can do whatever you like, but please don't hurt my baby."

"Oh, my heart bleeds. When did any woman ever really care about her baby? Now—*out.*"

Helen climbed out of the trunk. The man reached up to pull down the lid, and as he did so, Helen dodged to the left and started to run. Almost immediately, however, he caught up with her, seized her arm and tripped her up. She fell onto her back on the rough concrete floor, her head narrowly missing the rear bumper of a parked Toyota.

She twisted and struggled, but the man clambered astride her and pressed her down against the floor, with his knees on her upper arms. He was very heavy and strong, and even though she had graduated best in her class in unarmed combat, she found it impossible to throw him off.

"Women—" he panted. "You conceive babies, don't you, but you only give birth to them so long as it suits you. You don't give a shit about human life. All that matters to you is your own convenience. In fact—*you*—you're worse. You've used your baby to try to trap me. You don't even care that your baby is going to die when you die. How fucking sick is that?"

"Please—" Helen begged him.

But the man lifted her head and banged it hard against the concrete. Then he banged it again, and again, until she was half-concussed and she could feel the wetness of blood in her hair.

He took a roll of Saran Wrap out of his coat pocket, and he pulled it out and stretched it over her face. She was so stunned that she couldn't stop him. She tried to take a breath, but all she managed to do was suck the cling film tighter.

The man wrapped her head around and around. Helen couldn't move and she couldn't breathe and she could barely see. The man loomed over her as if he were in a fog.

In spite of her training, she panicked. She thrashed her head from side to side and kicked her legs. But the man opened her coat and dragged up her blue corduroy maternity dress, and then he pulled her pantyhose down around her ankles. Her blood was thumping in her ears, and all she could hear was a deep, distorted echo, as if she were lying at the bottom of a swimming pool.

She couldn't see the man unbutton his own coat, but she felt him lever her thighs apart. He pushed his way inside her with three grunting thrusts, until he was buried deep. Then he leaned forward and stared at her through the cling film, his face only an inch away from hers. He looked triumphant.

Suddenly, she felt a warm gush of wetness between her thighs. At the same time, there was turmoil inside her stomach, as if the baby were rolling right over. The man screamed like a girl and pushed against her chest.

"*Aaagghhh*! Christ! Let go of me! Let go of me! *For Christ's sake you witch let go of me!*"

Helen felt an agonizing spasm, and then another, and then another. The man kept on screaming and cursing and trying to pull himself out of her. Helen tore at the Saran Wrap covering her face and managed to rip most of it away. She took a deep swallow of air, but then she started screaming too. The pain in her back was more than she could bear. She felt as if she were being cracked in half.

There was a moment when she and the man were locked together in purgatory, both of them shrieking at each other. But then suddenly the man managed to heave himself backward, and Helen felt her baby slither out of her. The man fell onto his side, crying and whimpering, his heels kicking against the concrete.

Helen sat up. She was so stunned that everything looked jumbled and unfocused, but she could see that the man was fighting to pull something away from him.

"*Get it off me! Get it off me! Get it off me!*"

She held onto the Toyota's bumper and tried to pull herself up. Gradually, however, her vision began to clear, and what she saw made her slowly sit back down, quaking with horror.

Between the man's legs, biting his penis right down to the root, was a black bladderlike creature with glistening skin. It was the same size as a newborn baby, but it wasn't human at all.

The man was slapping it and pulling it, but it was obviously too slippery for him to get any grip, and the thing was stretching and contracting as if it were sucking at him.

"*Christ, get this off me!*" the man screamed, and it was more of a prayer than a cry for help.

In front of Helen's eyes, the black bladderlike creature swelled larger and larger, and as it did so, the man's struggling became weaker and jerkier. After only a few minutes, he gave a epileptic shudder, and his head dropped back, with his neck bulging. But the creature wasn't finished with him yet. It continued its stretching and contracting for almost twenty minutes more, its formless body growing more and more distended, until it was nearly the same size he was. Then it rolled off him with a wallowing sound like a waterbed and lay beside him, unmoving.

Helen felt another twinge of pain, and another, but after a third contraction her afterbirth slithered out. It was black and warty, unlike any afterbirth she had ever seen before. She kicked it away, underneath a car. If there had been anything in her stomach, she would have vomited.

After what seemed like hours, she managed to stand up. She crept over to the man and looked down at him. He looked like a parody of a man made out of pale brown paper, like a broken hornet's nest. Even his eyeballs had been drained of all their fluid, so that they were flat.

She sat down again, resting her back against a pillar. What the hell was she going to do now? She could retrieve her cell from the dead man's body and call Klaus. But how was she going to explain what had happened here?

She looked at the creature. She doubted if it was going to lie there for very much longer, digesting the fluids that it had sucked from its prey. What was she going to do with it if it started moving again?

She heard the sound of a vehicle driving down the ramp. A black panel van came around the corner, its tires squealing, and stopped a few yards away from her, with its headlights full on. The doors opened, and Joachim Hochheimer appeared, closely followed by Richard Vuldus, both wearing long black coats.

"My dear lady," said Joachim Hochheimer, reaching out his hand to help Helen to her feet. "How are you feeling?"

"How did you know that I was here?" she croaked. Her throat was so dry that she could barely speak.

"We have been following you every day, ever since you became pregnant."

"I never saw you."

"Well, let us say that after all of these centuries of persecution, we have learned how not to be noticed."

Richard Vuldus went straight over to the creature and hunkered down beside it, laying his hand on it with pride and awe.

"We have done it, Joachim! At last we have purified the genes."

Helen took Joachim Hochheimer's elbow for support. "What *is* that disgusting thing?" she asked him. "I thought I was carrying a baby all that time . . . not a thing like that. I feel sick to my stomach."

"You shouldn't be revolted, Detective. It is not a baby, no, but a horse leech, *Hirudo medicinalis*. The Vuldus family have been trying for generations to return to their original form, and with your help they have achieved their aim at last. This horse leech will now breed others, with the size and intelligence of humans, but all the qualities of a leech."

"But how is it going to survive? Where is it going to live?"

"Caesar Creek Lake. It covers two thousand eight hundred acres, and there are dozens of inlets where it can conceal itself and flourish. Richard, you must help me lift it into the van before its skin dries out too much."

"And what about *him*?" asked Helen, nodding at the flattened body of Son of Beast.

"Don't worry . . . we will dispose of him for you. He will vanish as if he had never been born."

Joachim Hochheimer helped Helen to climb into her car, while Richard Vuldus retrieved her keys and her cell from Son of Beast's coat. He gave her his wallet too. Helen opened it and found six tickets for the roller-coaster ride, and a Kentucky driver's license in the name of Ronald M. Breen. But there was no doubt that the man in the ID photograph was Henry Clarke, one-time realtor of Smith Road, Norwood.

"You have our deepest gratitude," said Richard Vuldus.

"Sure," said Helen. She started the engine and backed up. Richard Vuldus raised one hand to her in salute, but she didn't wave back. She drove up the ramp, out of the parking lot, and into the afternoon rain.

She drove slowly back home to Walnut Street, with tears streaming down her cheeks.

GIRL WAS "SUCKED DRY" SAYS CORONER

A 17-year-old Waynesville girl whose body was recovered from Caesar Creek Lake early yesterday was said by the Hamilton County Coroner to have been completely drained of all her blood and all bodily fluids.

Dr. Kenneth Deane was at a loss to explain what had happened to her, but said there was evidence that she had been bitten by a "very large aquatic creature with serrated teeth."

Cincinnati Post, March 17.

About the Authors

TREVOR ANDERSON

Anderson is a retired writer of soft-core sex novels. His *Hot Blood* story marks the Californian's triumphant return to the genre he helped to create in the 1960s.

STEVE ARMISON

A veteran emergency-room doctor, Armison has removed a long list of objects from bodily orifices and knows firsthand how dangerous uncontrolled lust can be. Armison says that men should carry implements in addition to condoms for protection, like a wooden stake, for instance. This is Armison's first published fiction.

DAVID BENTON

Benton's work can be seen between the covers of *Vintage Moon* and on the pages of *Red Scream* magazine. He currently resides in Milwaukee, Wisconsin.

P. D. CACEK

Cacek has published over one hundred short stories . . . and still managed to find time to write four novels and a collection. Two more collections are due soon: *Eros Interruptus*, a collection of her erotic stories, including the Bram Stoker winner "Metalica," and *Sympathy for the Dead*, a collection of ghost stories; as well as appearances in *Dark Visions 12, Lords of the*

Razor, The Secret Life of Vampires, Weird Tales, Flesh and Blood, and *The Burtarian*. She is currently working on her latest novel, *Officer of the Dead*, and preparing to move into a haunted house.

CHRISTINE CROOKS

Crooks lives in Southern California, where she writes speculative fiction, romance, and horror. Her racing romance novel, *Thrill of the Chase*, is now available. Her shorter work has appeared in *Sinisteria, Chimeraworld #4,* and *Aoife's Kiss.*

W. D. GAGLIANI

Gagliani has published fiction and nonfiction since 1986. His Bram Stoker Award-nominated novel *Wolf's Trap* appeared in 2006. His erotica has appeared in *Gallery* magazine, the webzine *1000 Delights,* and the anthology *The Black Spiral: Twisted Tales of Terror*, and other stories have been published in anthologies such as *Robert Bloch's Psychos, The Asylum 2, Extremes 3 and 4, Small Bites*, and *Wicked Karnival Halloween Horror*, among others. His book reviews appear in *Cemetery Dance, Hellnotes, Chizine.com, Crimespree, Flesh & Blood,* and others. He lives and writes in Milwaukee, Wisconsin. Visit him at www.williamdgagliani.com.

JEFF GELB

Gelb is trying to reconcile his love of Judaism and the Torah with his passion for writing and editing sexy horror stories. Someday maybe he'll figure out how to do both without suffering major Jewish guilt.

CODY GOODFELLOW

Goodfellow composed soundtracks for pornos in college and has been going downhill ever since. His novels, *Radiant Dawn* and *Ravenous Dusk,* are a two-part epic of modern

Lovecraftian horror. His stories have appeared in the anthologies *Horrors Beyond, Hardboiled Cthulhu, Daikaiju,* and *Wastelands Within,* as well as the magazines *Cemetery Dance, Third Alternative, Book of Dark Wisdom,* and *Red Scream.* He lives in San Diego.

ED GORMAN

Gorman has written books in several genres, but suspense fiction remains his favorite. In novels such as *The Autumn Dead* and *A Cry of Shadows,* Gorman has demonstrated that he is "one of the most original crime writers around" (Kirkus). Gorman has published more than one hundred short stories, with which he has filled out six collections of his work. His novel *The Poker Club* was filmed in 2006.

ROBERTA LANNES

Lannes is a native of Southern California, where she has been teaching high-school English and fine and digital art for thirty-three years. Her first horror story was written and sold in Dennis Etchison's UCLA extension course in Writing Horror Fiction and appeared in his *The Cutting Edge* in 1985. Since then she has been much published in the science fiction, fantasy, and horror genres, including *Alien Sex, Best New Horror, Splatterpunks, Bradbury Chronicles,* and *Dark Delicacies.* Her website is www.lannes-sealey.com.

GARY LOVISI

Lovisi is a Mystery Writers of America Edgar Award-nominated author (2005) who has been writing for as long as he can remember. Lovisi is the founder of Gryphon Books and editor of *Paperback Parade* and *Hardboiled* magazines, and sponsor of an annual book collector show in New York City. To find out more about him, his work, or Gryphon Books, visit his website at www.gryphonbooks.com.

GRAHAM MASTERTON

It has been thirty years since the release of *The Manitou,* Masterton's first feature film (now reissued on DVD), but now *Ritual* was filmed by Italian director Mariano Baino for release in 2006. Since his return from a four-year sojourn in Cork, Ireland, Masterton has been busy with a fourth Manitou novel, *Manitou Blood;* a novel based on the Beltway snipers, *Touchy & Feely;* a fourth Night Warriors novel, *Night Wars;* a vampire novel set in the 1950s, *Descendant;* a Wendigo novel, *Edgewise;* and a collection of new short stories, *Festival of Fear.* Masterton has recently toured Greece and Poland, where his name is engraved on the celebrity plaque in the lobby of the Bristol Hotel, Warsaw, alongside Mick Jagger and Margaret Thatcher.

LISA MORTON

Morton is a Bram Stoker award-winner who has written screenplays (most recently the vampire thriller *Blood Angels*), animation (*Van-Pires*), and two books of nonfiction (*The Cinema of Tsui Hark* and *The Halloween Encyclopedia*). Her short stories have most recently appeared in *Dark Delicacies, Mondo Zombie,* and *Cemetery Dance* magazine. She lives in the San Fernando Valley with actor Richard Grove and can be found online at http://www.lisamorton.com.

STEVE NILES

Niles is one of the writers responsible for bringing horror comics back to prominence and was recently named by *Fangoria* magazine as one of its "13 rising talents who promise to keep us terrified for the next 25 years." In 2002, the success of *30 Days of Night* sparked renewed interest in the horror genre; it is being developed as a major motion picture with *Spider-Man*'s Sam Raimi producing and David Slade directing. In June 2005, Niles and actor Thomas Jane (*The Punisher*) formed the production company Raw Entertainment, which has a first-look deal with Lions

Gate Films. Niles and his *Bigfoot* co-creator, rocker Rob Zombie, have sold the film rights to Paramount Pictures. Niles will be handling script duties. Also in development are adaptations of *Wake The Dead, Hyde, Aleister Arcane,* and *Criminal Macabre.* Niles is currently working for the four top American comic publishers—Marvel, DC, Image, and Dark Horse. Niles resides in Los Angeles with his wife, Nikki, and their three black cats.

DAVID J. SCHOW

Schow is a short-story writer, novelist, screenwriter (teleplays and features), columnist, essayist, editor, photographer, and winner of the World Fantasy and International Horror Guild awards (for short fiction and nonfiction, respectively). Peripherally he has written everything from CD liner notes to book introductions to catalogue copy for monster toys. As expert witness, he appears in many genre-related documentaries, has traveled from New Zealand to Shanghai to Mexico City for same, and recently turned to producing/writing/directing DVD supplements. He lives in a house on a hill in Los Angeles. Website: www.davidjschow.com.

D. LYNN SMITH

Smith has spent the last fifteen years writing and producing such television shows as *Murder, She Wrote; Dr. Quinn, Medicine Woman;* and *Touched By An Angel.* Her short stories have appeared in *After Hours, PanGaia,* and *Dark Delicacies.* She has also published nonfiction articles in the *Dark Shadows Almanac* and *Fangoria.* Smith is currently working on a science fiction novel, *The Shaman's Gene.* Her website is dlynnsmith.com.

THOMAS TESSIER

Tessier is the author of several novels of terror and suspense, including *The Nightwalker, Phantom, Finishing Touches, Secret Strangers,* and *Father Panic's Opera Macabre.* His novel *Fog*

Heart was cited by *Publishers Weekly* as one of the best books of the year, was a Bram Stoker Award Finalist, and received the International Horror Guild Award for Best Novel. His first book of short fiction, *Ghost Music and Other Tales,* received the International Horror Guild Award for Best Collection. Tessier lives in Connecticut and is finishing a new novel and a new collection of short stories.

STEVE VERNON

Vernon's stories have appeared in *The Horror Show, Cemetery Dance, Karl Edward Wagner's Year's Best Horror, Horror Garage, Flesh & Blood, Corpse Blossoms,* and many other magazines and anthologies. His novella "Long Horn, Big Shaggy—A Tale of Wild West Terror and Reanimated Buffalo" can be ordered at any bookstore. His new collection, *Nothing To Lose,* was published in 2006. Vernon's latest, *Four Ride Out,* a four-novella collection of weird western horror starring Brian Keene, Tim Lebbon, Tim Curran, and Vernon, will be out in 2007.

RICHARD WILKEY

Wilkey first published erotic horror in several men's magazines back in the mid-80s. Following that, he focused on personally experiencing some of the acts he'd been writing about. Fortunately, he survived his admittedly bizarre behavioral streak and has returned to the safety of writing about the darker side of sex rather than experiencing it directly. "Taking matters into my own hand, so to speak, should be much safer," Wilkey says with a grin.

CHELSEA QUINN YARBRO

A professional writer for more than thirty-eight years, Yarbro has sold seventy-nine books and more than eighty works of short fiction and essays. She lives in her hometown—Berkeley, California—with two autocratic cats. In 2003, the World Horror Association presented her with a Grand Master award.

DAVID ZELTSERMAN

Zeltserman writes mostly dark crime fiction and has had short stories appear in a number of magazines, including *Ellery Queen* and *Alfred Hitchcock*. His first psychotic dark crime novel, *Fast Lane,* was published in 2004. Two more dark crime novels, *Small Crimes* and *Bad Thoughts,* are due to be published in 2007. Zeltserman is a veteran of *Hot Blood* who lives and writes in Boston and insists that only part of his *Hot Blood* story is autobiographical.